THE

DEATH GRASP,

OR,

A FATHER'S CURSE.

A ROMANCE OF STARTLING INTEREST.

BY THE AUTHOR OF " ELA, THE OUTCAST," " ANGELINA," " HEBREW MAIDEN,"
" MANIAC FATHER," ETC., ETC.

"I am a man
So wearied with disasters, tugged by fortune,
That I would set my life on any chance
To mend it, or be rid on't."—SHAKSPEARE.

LONDON:

PUBLISHED BY E. LLOYD, SALISBURY-SQUARE, FLEET-STREET.

THE
DEATH GRASP;

OR,
A FATHER'S CURSE.
AN ORIGINAL ROMANCE OF STARTLING INTEREST.

No. 1.

CHAPTER I.

THE GAMESTERS. — THE TREACHEROUS FRIEND.

It was on a lovely summer's evening, in the year 1595, that Master Barnard Swinton, proprietor of an English hotel, near Abbeville, in France, had taken his seat at his door, with a small table before him, a bottle of the best wine in his cellar, and a full determination to enjoy himself, as was his custom at every opportunity which presented itself.

Mine host of "Le Auberge de Sirloin," as he had chosen to call his establishment, out of respect to his native country, was a good, portly, rosy-gilled specimen of John Bull epicureanism, and, with a countenance so good-humoured and cheerful, that no one, to look at him, would suppose for an instant that he had ever known what trouble was; but in that idea they would have been most decidedly wrong, as poor Master Swinton was plagued with the greatest trouble a man can endure, viz. a scolding wife.

What motive it was that induced Master Swinton to emigrate from England and to settle in France, we have no exact means of ascertaining, but imagine it was that which stimulates most persons to do the same,—a fancy that they can do better abroad than at home; but this is a matter of no consequence; certain it is that he was there established, and was not only doing what is now technically called "a roaring trade," but it was currently reported he had saved a sufficient sum to retire at any time he might think proper.

Now, as we are saying, Master Swinton had taken his seat outside the house, and having twice or thrice applied himself to the bottle, began to feel in that happy state of contentedness which makes the cares of this life fade before us like "the baseless fabric of a vision."

"Well," soliloquised mine host, smacking his lips after a deep potation, "marry, and there is nothing like a bumper or two, after all, when the fatigues of the day are over, and a man's wife is out of the way. Peace then condescends to make friends with one, and we can wag our tongue without hazarding the loss of one's nose, by that sharpest of all instruments, a woman's passion."

"Barnard Swinton! Barnard Swinton, I say!" at that moment exclaimed a shrill voice of the most unmusical tones, upon hearing which, the individual named, changed countenance remarkably, and replacing the glass he was in the act of raising to his lips on the table, he looked as uncomfortable as any misanthrope need wish to be.

"Here comes my perpetual hurricane," he muttered to himself, "now for an hour's snarling, snapping, storming, and raging; oh, dear! oh, dear!—that woman's temper will certainly drive me crazy. Ever since I left London, and have become the landlord of an hotel in France, her pride and arrogance have led me a worse life than a dog."

He had not time to say more, before Mrs. Swinton rushed from the house in a furious passion, and looking at her unfortunate spouse, as if she were half inclined to inflict summary punishment upon him, she vociferated:—

"Barnard Swinton! Barnard Swinton! thou art one of the most lazy varlets in Christendom. Here thou art, at thine old game, fuddling away all the profits of our hotel, and lounging thy time away, while I, thy poor, delicate, and amiable little wife, am obliged to slave like a horse from morning till night. Barnard Swinton, thou art a brute, a savage, a——"

"Now, my dear," interrupted her husband, meekly and pacifically.

"Barnard Swinton!" screamed the termagant, with increasing wrath, "I will be heard."

"Indeed thou wilt," returned Swinton, "and all over the town if thou bawlest in that manner."

"Barnard," cried Mrs. Swinton, stamping her feet and almost choked with rage, "thou ought to be ashamed of thyself; thou art a nasty——"

"Will that incessant tongue of thine never be worn out?" said her spouse.

"No," replied Mrs. Swinton, with a most provoking sneer, "it has been in constant use upwards of forty years, and it's as good as ever it was yet, and thou shalt know it too. It is a scandalous thing, I mean to say, Mr. Barnard Swinton, here is Le Auberge de Sirloin, as full of customers as it can hold, and all the waiting upon them, cooking for them, and everything else, is left to me, while thou dost nothing else but sit and drink thy wine as if thou wert some great nabob."

"Now, now, my dear Cicely," observed Swinton, mildly and persuasively, "I must say that thou art complaining without a cause. If I do rest myself a bit, and enjoy my glass, after the old English fashion, hast thou not got our son Caleb and the maid Pauline to assist thee?"

"Yes," returned Mrs. Swinton, "and a very pretty pair they are; there's Pauline is so deeply in love with Caleb, that she don't know what she's about half her time, and smashes all the crockery in the house; and as for that stupid fellow, Caleb, his predilection for birds will drive me mad. He's turned every room in our hotel into a bird-cage or a pigeon-house. But this is all thy doings, Mr. Swinton."

"Mine, my love?" said her spouse.

"Yes," replied his wife, "didn't thou bring the boy up to be a Whitechapel bird-catcher and fancier, when we were in London, and now he has nothing in his head but larks and linnets, robbins and bullfinches, tumblers, powters, black baldheads, and all other such nonsense. A very pretty pair of birds he'll make soon, forsooth ; we sha'n't have a feather to fly with ; but here comes our two guests, Monsieur De Buoisson and Monsieur De Floriville, and I declare if M. De Buoisson does not look as if he were dying with melancholy. I am afraid they are two very wild young gentlemen, but then they are so liberal that—but what art thou standing gaping there for, Mr. Swinton ? Wilt thou see to attending to business or not ? Oh, if I were not the most amiable, meek, and patient woman in the world, I——"

She had not time to finish the sentence before the two gentlemen of whom she had been speaking made their appearance, and amidst a profusion of courtesies from Mrs. Swinton, and a simple John Bull nod of the head of her spouse, they walked into the house.

They were both remarkably handsome men, but the figure of Adolphe de Floriville was more noble and commanding than that of his companion, and there was an expression of melancholy stamped upon the features of Eugene, which but very ill accorded with the vivacious countenance of the former.

Eugene de Buoisson and Adolphe de Floriville had been friends and companions from their boyish days ; both were of noble families, and at the death of their relations, came into possession of ample fortunes, which they had, however, greatly impoverished by acts of dissipation and improvidence, and ruin alone stared them in the face, if they did not quickly abandon their wild career ; but it is hard to escape when youth once becomes involved in the vortex of folly. Monsieur de Floriville had formerly been a colonel in the French army, but for some particular reason, which we will not pause to inquire into at present, he had quitted it abruptly. Fontainbleau was the native place of Eugene and Adolphe, where they had estates that nearly joined each other, but for a considerable time past they had been staying at *Le Auberge de Sirloin*, for reasons that will shortly, probably, be explained.

"Come, come, Eugene," said Adolphe, when they had seated themselves in their own room, and the latter had called for wine, " chase away the gloom that sits upon thy brow, and become once more a man. What's the use of indulging in these fits of melancholy and abstraction? Thou wilt find them but sorry companions, methinks."

" Oh, Adolphe," replied Eugene, with a sigh, " how canst thou talk thus ? Am I not a dissipated profligate, who hath already brought disgrace upon my once unsullied name ? Have not the cursed dice brought me to the brink of ruin, and at the very time when fortune had marked out for me a prospect of enviable felicity in my union with the beauteous Laurette Cha——(A frown passed over the features ... at the mention of her name.) ... basely, cruelly abused the con... and the marquiss, her father,

have reposed in me ? And how can I dare again venture into her presence, when I have rendered myself in every way so unworthy of her hand ? Alas ! my mad folly hath ruined me."

"Psha !" ejaculated De Floriville, impatiently, " no more of this ! Why, thou art a very coward, indeed, to quiver thus at the frowns of fate. What if fortune looks cross to-day, a turn of the dice to-night may illumine her brightest smiles ! Come, come, Eugene, I cannot see thee thus : be seated, and over a bottle of wine, listen to the voice of friendship. Wine thou wilt find is an excellent antidote for the spleen, and, by the saints, our host sells no bad medicine. Drink, Eugene, and be thyself again."

" No, no," returned Eugene, " I cannot drink ; wine would but add fuel to my already burning brain ! Adolphe, what a fool I have been to suffer the enjoyment of a few fancied hours of pleasure thus to sink and degrade me in the world. Of my once princely fortune, scarce enough remains to keep me from the level of the meanest hind, and even Laurette and her father, I imagine, begin to suspect me, for now they meet me with looks of coldness that freeze me. Oh, cursed dice ! ye have destroyed all my hopes for ever !"

Had any one taken the least notice of the countenance of Adolphe at this moment, they must have observed the look of exultation and satisfaction that passed over it ; but it hastily disappeared, and turning to his companion, he said—

" Why, can this be the once gay and reckless Eugene de Buoisson ? He who used to marvel that men could be sad, and laughed when people talked of sorrow ? Eugene, art thou mad ?"

" Mad !" repeated Eugene, bitterly, " yes, I am. But why, Adolphe, remind me of my errors ? Why recal to my memory the damned recklessness which has hurried me headlong to disgrace and infamy ? Oh ! I am not, indeed, the Eugene de Buoisson that I once was. I am no longer the happy, guiltless Eugene who once was the pride of adoring parents, striving by deeds of honour and rectitude to adorn the rank of life fortune had placed me in, and gaining the admiration of the old and the young. I am a fallen wretch, despicable to myself, and abhorrent to all around me."

" Really, Eugene," remarked De Floriville, " thou hast become a most egregious coward, a perfect misanthrope. Psha ! be more thyself ; drink—I insist upon it. Why, thou art not beggared yet, and am I not thy friend ? To-morrow night the dice may retrieve thy fortune, and then thou canst, if thou likest, become what the world terms ' a man of honour,' and who will take the trouble to question thy past conduct ? Laurette loves thee ! she will become thine ; bring with her a splendid dowry, and then thou wilt be a man again."

"A man!" reiterated Eugene; "never! No, Adolphe, Laurette can never be mine; her coldness already convinces me that she knows my guilt, and loves me not; and, base as I am, never will I bring disgrace and infamy upon her, by uniting her to my misery."

"Ha! ha! ha!" laughed De Floriville, ironically, "why what a philosopher thou art, Eugene. But trust me all will yet be well. This evening I promised to meet a party at the Count Bellevoir's chateau; thou must accompany me; and hark ye, a turn of the dice may make thee richer than ever thou wert."

"Tempt me not, Adolphe, to my ruin again, for may eternal curses light——"

"Bah!" interrupted De Floriville, "wouldst thou for such a very delicate sense of honour, forsooth, resign fortune, Laurette, everything? Drink! drink!"

"No, no, it will only instil false and transitory pleasure into me, to distract me the more afterwards."

"As I was saying, Eugene," continued Adolphe, without appearing to take any notice of the latter observations of his companion, "the count's party this evening: wilt thou accompany me thither? The play will be strong. There are several of the *innocent* expected there; dost thou understand me? Besides, thy lovely inamorato will attend—the fair Elvira."

"Elvira!" repeated Eugene, "oh, name her not! It was she who, with frail charms and delusive pleasures, sunk me lower in the gulph of iniquity; but the veil is torn from mine eyes; I loathe—I detest her—and will see her no more, unless it be to breathe my curses in her ears and spurn her from me for ever!"

"Eugene," observed De Floriville, in serious accents, "this headstrong folly will destroy thee. It will, unless checked, hurry thee into that very state of despair and wretchedness thou dost but now anticipate. Knowest thou not that the hot, revengeful blood of Italy flows within Elvira's veins, and, if it be once aroused, what may she not do to accomplish her vengeance? Thy name, thy character, thy liberty, nay more, the very life of Laurette, may fall a sacrifice to it."

"The life of Laurette," ejaculated Eugene, shuddering; "horrible though! But yet it is too probable. Wretched fool that I was to place myself in the power of a mercenary and revengeful woman, to be won to destruction by her siren smiles. Adolphe, my friend, teach me how to act; I will be guided by thee alone."

"Nothing is more easy if you will be guided by my advice," said Adolphe, scarcely able to restrain the expression of his exultation at the success of his scheme; "accompany me this evening to Count Bellevoir's; stake boldly and fear not the result. Meet Elvira with your accustomed smiles, and leave the rest to me."

"It shall be so," replied Eugene, after a brief pause; "I feel myself again! Thanks, Adolphe, for thy counsel; I will accompany thee. Once more will I grasp the dice, and redeem my former wealth, or become a beggar! I will meet Elvira, I—I—I—but give me wine! Ah! that has restored me, my mind is ready for anything. I will go and arrange my person for the party, and will then rejoin thee. Laurette, thou shalt be mine, or I will perish!"

"Laurette, thine, never!" exclaimed Adolphe, as Eugene quitted the room. "Ha! ha! ha! so my bird is caught. This night, Eugene, seals thy fate for ever! Fool! he little suspects the snare that I have laid for him. Laurette loves him not, but on me bestows her affections, and if I succeed in prejudicing the mind of her father against him, he may be willing to sanction my suit, although he has hitherto denied me his house, and refused, from some cause which I cannot imagine, to receive me even in the character of a friend. However, the anonymous letter I have sent him may have the desired effect, and I may be able, gradually, to ingratiate myself in his favour; at any rate, I doubt not that if he remain obstinate, I shall be able, in time, to prevail upon Laurette to consent to a private union, and the forgiveness of the marquess will, doubtless, very soon be obtained. This night, if my stratagem fail not, the remnant of Eugene's fortune will be mine. Eugene, I have been the plaything of thy puny virtues too long. Honour! virtue! Pshaw! they are baubles none but fools would grasp at. I will now to Laurette while Eugene prepares himself, and see how works my stratagem."

CHAPTER II.

THE LETTER. — THE MEETING. — THE DISCOVERY.—THE RUINED GAMESTER.

THE Marquess de Chamont was one of the wealthiest *noblesse* France, at the period this tale commences, could boast of, and he united every amiable quality to riches. He contributed with a lavish hand towards the distresses of the poor, and was prompt to become the patron of humble and struggling merit. His wife had been dead for some years, and Laurette was his only child; on her his sole happiness, his every hope, was fixed, and never could parent behave with more unbounded affection than he did towards her.

Laurette de Chamont was just seventeen, and language would be by far too weak to do justice to her personal charms; they were only equalled by the graces of her mind. Wherever she went, she excited love and admiration, and she needed but once to be seen to make an indelible impression upon the heart. Her accomplishments were of the first order, and they were greatly enhanced by the elegances of her mind; and she was pointed at as a bright example to those of her own sex who resided in the neighbourhood of the chateau. Young as she was, Laurette had already received the marked attentions of many young noblemen who had sued for possession of her hand and affections; but, although naturally of an ardent disposition, she had never yet beheld the man whom she could love with the passion due to a husband; and though she declined their offers, she did it with such grace, that it only served to increase their admiration of her.

It was an accident that introduced Eugene de Buoisson and Adolphe de Floriville to the notice of Laurette and her father. The former were journeying not far from the Chateau de Chamont, when the vehicle broke down, and they were both very much hurt. The chateau being the nearest to where the accident took place, they were conveyed there, and the marquess and Laurette received them with their usual kindness and hospitality. The Marquess de Chamont received an extraordinary impression in favour of Eugene the moment he beheld him, but no sooner did he ascertain the name of Adolphe, than a strong emotion shook his frame, he turned ghastly pale, his lips quivered, he uttered a deep groan of agony, and covering his face with his hands, he rushed from the room.

Surprised—thunderstruck at his singular conduct, Laurette in vain sought to elicit from him the cause of this agitation; but he evaded her questions, and commanded her never more to repeat the name of Adolphe in his presence. Alas! little did the marquess know the pain he was inflicting upon the gentle bosom of his daughter by this injunction! from the first moment she beheld Adolphe de Floriville, he firmly held possession of her heart.

The marquess would never see De Floriville, and as soon as he had recovered from the effects of the accident, he desired him peremptorily to quit the chateau, intimating that he must positively dispense with the honour of his future visits; but without assigning any reason for such singular and unaccountable behaviour.

Indignant and surprised as he felt, Adolphe stifled his feelings of resentment, and obeyed the mandates of the marquess, but he quitted the chateau with sentiments of mingled pain and delight; the beauty of Laurette had enraptured his senses: nay, more—he had seized an opportunity of obtaining an interview with her, in which he had made a confession of his love, and obtained an acknowledgment from the beauteous girl of the reciprocal sentiments that had taken possession of her bosom.

Adolphe concealed his sentiments and the return they had met with from Eugene, who had also become fascinated with the charms and virtues of Laurette, and having made the same known to the marquess, he received him in the most favourable manner, and without consulting her feelings, as he had ever

before done, he commanded her to receive him as her future husband.

It may be readily imagined with what emotions of pain Laurette received these injunctions, but, accustomed implicitly to obey the smallest wish of her father, she offered not a word in opposition, not a murmur of regret; and the marquess, therefore, was constrained to believe that she approved of the choice he had made.

Eugene de Buoisson had certainly made a most favourable impression upon Laurette, and had she not have seen Adolphe, she felt convinced she could have loved him; but so well did the latter conceal the real vices of his character, that nothing, she felt convinced, could erase his image from her heart. At first she thought of confiding to Eugene the secret of the mutual passion which she and Adolphe felt for each other, and of appealing to his honour and generosity to abandon his suit; but then, when she recollected the extraordinary prejudice which her father had imbibed against Adolphe, and the utter hopelessness that he would ever give his assent to their vows, she abandoned the idea, and determined to make a sacrifice of her own happiness, rather than act contrary to the will of the marquess, her father. She, therefore, forwarded to Adolphe a letter, in which, giving expression to the paramount place he held and must ever hold in her affections, she implored him to endeavour to forget her, and to submit with fortitude and resignation to the decree of fate, however painful it might be, and by which it seemed to be ordained that they should never be united.

To this letter Adolphe returned an answer, teeming with the most unbounded affection, and wherein, after reiterating the avowal of his unbounded love, he appeared at the most painful sacrifice, to yield to her wishes. But so far from this, he had determined, at all hazards, to frustrate the hopes and wishes of Eugene, and ultimately to accomplish his own designs by obtaining possession of the hand and fortune of Laurette. So well did Adolphe play the hypocrite, that Eugene never suspected him, and imagined he was his best friend, while he was, in fact, plotting everywhere for the destruction of his future peace. It has been seen the villanous part that Adolphe had already acted, and he had succeeded much better than he had even expected; he had played with such advantage on the weakness of Eugene as to place him in the most questionable positions, and the marquess, as he had noticed, did not receive him with the same warmth that he had previously done.

Having advanced his plot thus far, Adolphe determined to carry the rest by a *coup de main*, and it will be seen how far he succeeded.

On the evening that the events which we have described in a previous chapter were being enacted at *Le Auberge de Sirloin*, Laurette was seated in a melancholy mood in her apartment, ruminating on the severity of her fate, when she heard the voice of her father talking in tones of extreme warmth as he ascended the stairs. A deadly chill came over her in an instant, and she foreboded some approaching calamity.

"Oh, my father," she soliloquised, "how my heart sinks when I hear thy footsteps on the stairs; formerly it leaped for joy at the sound of thy voice, and I would rush into thine arms eager to obtain thy approving kiss."

Before she had time to say more, the room door was thrown open violently, and the marquess entered in a state of great emotion, and holding an open letter in his hand. Laurette, surprised at the agitation he evinced, flew towards him, and looking up with the deepest anxiety in his countenance, she ejaculated—

"Something has occurred to disturb thee, my dearest father; oh, pr'ythee tell me what is the cause of the deep emotion you betray."

"Read that letter!" replied the marquess, placing the epistle in her hand; "the villain—the hypocrite—but, no matter, his intentions are frustrated."

Laurette, with eager haste, took the letter, and to her infinite astonishment, read the following words :—

"MY LORD MARQUESS,—As a sincere friend to yourself and your amiable daughter, I warn you against taking into your bosom a viper that will assuredly sting your peace and that of your daughter for ever. Eugene de Buoisson is a villain, and only seeks the hand of Laurette to save himself from utter ruin, which he has brought on himself at the gaming table. If you doubt the truth of this statement, visit the Count Bellevoir's chateau this evening, and you will be satisfied. Go disguised."

"There, Laurette," said the marquess, with breathless impatience, "what thinkest thou of that epistle? Can it be possible that any man can be so base, especially one in whose favour I was so greatly prepossessed?"

Laurette was so surprised that she found herself incapable of answering for awhile; but, notwithstanding the hope which suddenly arose in her bosom, that this would be the means of breaking off the match between her and Eugene, she could not be guilty of the injustice of placing any reliance in the truth of the assertions of a man who chose an anonymous way of making his accusations, and she expressed that opinion to her father.

"But does not the writer inform me where I may have ocular demonstration of the veracity of his accusations?" hastily returned the marquess. "What can be more reasonable or feasible than this? I will be at the place mentioned this evening, and at once satisfy my doubts, and if Eugene has acted with such heartless duplicity, never more shall he cross the threshold of the Chateau de Chamont."

Without waiting to hear any reply, the marquess hastily quitted the room to put his design into execution, and left Laurette in a state of mind it is needless for us to attempt to describe. He had not been gone many minutes, when Fanchette, her waiting-maid, entered in much haste, and ejaculated—

"Oh, ma'amselle, my lord, the marquess, has just popt out of the garden-gate in such a flurry, and——"

"Well?"

"Why," replied Fanchette, "just as he popt out, who should pop in but——"

"Who?" anxiously demanded Laurette.

"Why, ma'amselle," returned Fanchette, "one of the prettiest young men in France, I do believe; with a figure as straight as a dart, an eye like a hawk, and——"

"Pray, do not be so tedious," interrupted Laurette; "who was it?"

"Who should it be but Monsieur de Floriville, the friend of Monsieur de Buoisson?" answered Fanchette; "but, la! he is so much handsomer than Monsieur Eugene, that I declare if it were not that I am betrothed to Gervois, the gardener, I would'nt mind marrying him myself."

"A truce with this nonsense, Fanchette, and tell me the particulars," said her mistress.

"Well, then, you must know, ma'amselle," said the waiting-maid, "that I had no sooner opened the gate and let out my master, than up comes Monsieur Adolphe, and giving me a kiss (excuse my blushes, ma'amselle),—and giving me a kiss, he said I was a very pretty young girl, and told me to inform you, ma'amselle, that he was in the garden, and only required five minutes converse with you."

"Monsieur de Floriville—Adolphe—and at this juncture, too," exclaimed Laurette, with much emotion; "how very wrong to tell him, Fanchette, that I—I—but stay, I will go myself to him."

"So," said Fanchette, as her young lady left the room, "Ma'amselle Laurette has got two strings to her *bow*, and yet she seems not determined with which to tie the *knot*. Well, certainly these great people are very strange characters; they are ashamed to live single; they are ashamed to own their love, and—Well, it's not the case with me, for I'm sure if a fine handsome young fellow like Adolphe de Floriville was to make love to me, I should not long keep him in suspense."

Laurette, with a palpitating heart, hastened to the garden, where she found Adolphe waiting. We will pass hastily over this interview, which was one of the most affectionate they had ever had. Adolphe urged the violence of his passion, with all that force of rhetoric with which he was so amply gifted, and implored her to consent to his wishes, namely, a secret union; and in support of his arguments exhibited the harsh treatment of her father towards him, and the unjust power he was seeking to exercise, by compelling her to grant her hand where she could not also bestow her heart. He also endeavoured to convince her that her father would soon forgive her, when he found that they were irrevocably united; and advanced many other points to endeavour to gain her consent to his wishes, which it will be unnecessary here to mention here.

At first Laurette shrunk from his proposals with a feeling approaching to horror, but the strength of love will always triumph ultimately over every other feeling, and Laurette possessed all the weakness of her sex. His persuasions prevailed over her, and she gave her consent to be secretly united to Adolphe de Floriville the following day, he promising to have all the necessary arrangements ready at a certain hour, when he would meet her a short distance from the chateau.

Delighted at the success of his schemes, De Floriville hastened from the Chateau de Chamont to the Count Bellevoir's, where he had resolved upon the completion of his infamous designs against the unsuspecting Eugene, and thither we must request the reader to follow him.

In a gorgeously decorated *salon*, splendidly lighted by numerous lamps, and which cast their effulgent beams upon the richly fretted roof, were seated at different tables, a number of handsomely attired young men, all engaged in play, while others were lounging about, and to a close observer, would not seem to be so entirely disinterested in the proceedings as they affected to be. The expressions in the countenances of the players were of a varied description; there was the elated look of success - the quivering glance of hope - the fiendish expression of exultation—and the wild, the maddening, the vacant stare of despair. In the midst of this, a party of the loungers before alluded to, amusd themselves by singing with the most uproarious gusto, the following appropriate chorus, which seemed to have been composed for the purpose of being sung at their ruinous meetings :—

" Merrily all, cheerfully all,
    Whether good luck or bad luck befal ;
    With venturous hands the dice we hold,
    For the enticing yellow gold !
    Oh ! what pleasure, what delight !
    E'en if fortune frowns to-night,
    To-morrow she may enter here,
    And in her brightest smiles appear.
            Then, merrily all," &c.

At the centre table, with several others, were seated Adolphe de Floriville and Eugene ; the former watching the issue of the game with a look of exultation, which told too plainly what success was attending his nefarious schemes ; and the latter seeming to play with all the madness of desperation and despair.

"Good again, by Jupiter !" exclaimed one of the gamblers, as a large stake was again won by Adolphe and those who were in the plot with him ; " Monsieur Buoisson, thou art an unluckly dog."

" Some infernal spell is upon me," cried Eugene, frienziedly ; " but, by Heaven ! I will struggle hard ! play on again. Even though beggary be my fate, I will stand the hazard !"

Again did the unhappy Eugene take the fatal dice in his hand, and again was he unsuccessful, and Adolphe, leaving the table for a moment, in a tone of triumph said aside to himself—

" By hell ! the sport goes on famously ; another throw, and Eugene will be a beggar, while all his fortune will be at the disposal of myself and my well-taught myrmidons.— Ah ! he grasps again the fatal dice ! Madness guides his hand ! They are thrown !"

At this moment a triumphant peal of laughter burst from the villains with whom Eugene had been playing, and Adolphe, no longer able to restrain the full expression of his disgusting exultation, exclaimed aloud—

" He's lost !—he's ruined. Ha ! ha ! ha"

Eugene threw down the accursed instruments of his ruin ; clasped his forehead with a groan of agony, and rushed wildly from the table, amid the laughter and sneers of his unprincipled companions.

" 'Tis done !" he cried, " the fiends of hell have completed their accursed work !—I'm ruined !"

His eyes suddenly resting on Adolphe, he advanced hastily towards him, and observed—

" Ah ! Adolphe, my friend."

" Thy friend !" reiterated Adolphe, with a look of contempt ; " idiot, thinkest thou Adolphe de Floriville owns a beggar for his friend ?"

" Gracious Heaven ! Adolphe, do I hear aright ?' gasped forth the unfortunate victim. " No, no,—it cannot be ; some infernal delusion overwhelms my senses, I—"

" Indeed it is no delusion," interrupted Adolphe, with cool indifference ; " I have played the hypocrite long enough to accomplish what I sought, and now I throw off the mask, and tell thee Adolphe de Floriville no longer knows the beggared outcast, Eugene de Buoisson. Adieu, sir ; thou art in no fit mood to suit my palate ; but I offer thee good advice ; if thou wouldst hide thy shame and misery from the world, retire to a monastery ; fasting and penance are well suited to such as thou art."

Having thus delivered himself, Adolphe quitted the place, with a sarcastic laugh, and at that moment the Marquess de Chamont entered at another door, disguised in a large mantle, and his eyes immediately rested upon the distracted Eugene, who, with his hands clasping his forehead, was transfixed to the spot, and seemed the statue of despair and horror.

" So then," said the marquess, " the letter spoke the truth, for yonder the wretched youth stands, wrapt in all the dellrium of conscious guilt. I can scarce contain myself while I gaze on him."

"The secret's out then," cried Eugene, "I have been betrayed—deceived—entrapped —and now I'm made the mock and scorn of my despoilers. Madness! I shall choke! I feel a demon gnawing at my heart! And shall I tamely view the wretches depart with the gold they have plundered me of? No, I will wring it from them!"

With these words the wretched man, thinking it was Adolphe, grasped the marquess with the strength of madness, and with frantic wildness, exclaimed—

"Villain! give me back my gold! Thou shalt not rob me! Thou shalt not leave me to poverty and wretchedness! Give me my gold, I say, or I will have restitution in thine heart's blood!"

"Madman! let go thy sanguinary grasp," ejaculated the marquess, struggling with Eugene; "wouldst thou add murder to thine other crimes? Wouldst thou take the life of the father of Laurette, the Marquess de Chamont?"

Eugene released his hold in an instant, and staggering back a few paces, fixed his gaze with the most ghastly expression of horror and surprise upon the marquess, who had thrown off his disguise.

"Great God!" he cried, "do my eyes deceive me, or am I the wretched victim of some damned spell? The Marquess de Chamont here?"

"Yes," answered the marquess, sternly, "it is the Marquess de Chamont, the father of her thou wouldst basely have brought to shame and misery. I have discovered thy vices, Eugene, and henceforth we are strangers to one another."

"Oh, in mercy, for pity's sake hear me!" cried Eugene, with agonizing emotion.

"Not a word," replied the marquess. "I am fully satisfied of thy guilt, and henceforth despise thee. Venture not into my presence or that of Laurette, or thou mayest repent thy boldness."

Without uttering another word, the marquess fixed upon Eugene one look of stern reproach, and immediately left the place.

"My lord! my lord!" cried Eugene frantically, and looking hastily round him; "but no," he continued, "he's gone, and I am doomed to misery for ever. I shall go mad. The tortures of the damned rack my bosom. Oh, horror! horror!"

He rushed wildly forth, with the air of a maniac, and made his way towards the hotel, whither he soon arrived, and scarcely conscious of what he was doing, entered the house. On the way to his chamber, he encountered Caleb, the son of the host, who started back with amazement when he beheld him, and exclaimed—

"Deary me, Mounseer de Buoisson, how pale you do look, you seem as if—"

"What, fool?" demanded Eugene, fiercely.

"La, mounseer," said the simple lad, starting back, "how you frighten me! I didn't mean to offend you, but you look ill: do take a drop of wine, and that will revive you. Perhaps you have been *misfortunate* to-night, and it's very provoking to—"

"Damnation!" interrupted Eugene, "the very hind mocks me! Am I sunken so low as to meet the pity of an ignorant, lowly boy? Beggar! wretch! But I *am* mad. I know not what I say or do. Pardon me, boy; I am ill—very ill;—show me to my chamber, I would be alone. Show me to my room I repeat; to silence—to solitude—to death!"

He groaned aloud with mental agony, and rushing past Caleb, who stood staring at him with stupified astonishment, entered his chamber, and closed the door after him.

CHAPTER III.

THE MURDER.

"WELL," said Caleb, as Eugene thus abruptly retired, "if that Mounseer de Buoisson is not mad, I'm a fool. Now I shouldn't wonder if he has lost all his money at the gambling-house, and that he's going to blow his brains out, or cut his throat."

He was interrupted in his soliloquy by a loud knocking at the door, and hastening to it, in no very pleasant mood at being kept up so late, he gave admittance to Adolphe.

"Now boy," demanded Aolphe, in harsh and impatient accents, "has Monsieur de Buoisson returned?"

"Indeed he has, mounseer," answered Caleb, "and in such a temper."

"Psha!" cried Adolphe, haughtily, "cease your impertinent loquaciousness, sirrah, and retire; I need not you to show me my way to my chamber, when I am so disposed."

"But hadn't you better, mounseer——"

"Begone, I say!"

"Well," muttered Caleb, as he quitted the room, "they are a very pretty pair of black birds, sure enough."

Adolphe took his seat at the table—his manner was restless, and there was an expression in his countenance which showed the desperate workings of his soul. He leant his head on his hand for a few minutes, and then arising from his chair, paced the room with hasty and uneven steps. At length he returned to the table, and after another second or two spent in rumination, he said—

"Yes, it shall be so;—mine own safety, my union with Laurette; - my fame—credit —honour—all depend upon it. Eugene must die!—Die?—It is an awful word; but there is no alternative!—While he existed it is not probable that he would see me live in luxury on the fruits of his ruin;—nay, more, that he would patiently see me lead to the altar her whom he so ardently loves; and who, I firmly believe, would have returned his passion, had it not been for my guilty machinations. He would betray me—he would denounce me—he—but my dagger's point shall this night, this hour, seal his lips for ever. The key of my chamber will open the lock of his apartment. All is now hushed in sleep—I can easily effect my purpose, and suspicion will not dare to point a finger at me. All the world will think that, driven to despair by his losses, he hath himself struck the fatal blow."

Adolphe paused. He almost trembled to look around him; an indefinite feeling darted through his veins. He walked with noiseless steps to the door of the chamber, and opening it, listened. But he could not hear the least noise: the silence which prevailed seemed like that of death, and the heart of Adolphe shrunk back with horror at the deed he contemplated. He quietly closed the door of his room, and once more resumed his seat.

"Psha!" at length he ejaculated—"this is childish. I have become a weak fool. All is still. No one can hear his dying groans, and——my heart recoils from the sanguinary deed. Guilty as I am, my hands were never yet stained with any other blood than that of the enemies of my country: and shall they now? Bah! what an effeminate idiot have I become! Ah—here is wine!"

With eagerness he seized the bottle, and filling a glass, quaffed the contents with frenzied haste.

"It has revived my wavering courage," he said. "My heart is firm again. I feel competent to the most daring deed. Let me away and do the hellish work, lest my heart again falter. Now for the deed of blood!"

As Adolphe de Floriville thus spoke, he drew forth his dagger with an air of desperation, took up the lamp in his other hand, and after once more listening, to make sure that no one was moving about, he quitted the room, and striding stealthily along the corridor, ever and anon looking back, as his fears brought to his imagination the sound of footsteps pursuing him, he gained the door of Eugene's room. Here he again paused and trembled. He placed his ear to the keyhole, and the thick breathing of his intended victim convinced him that he was asleep. Again a dreadful sensation of terror came over him, and he was half inclined to return immediately to his own chamber, and to abandon his blood thirsty design. He had moved several paces back for that purpose, when the idea of his treachery and deliberate villany being discovered, Eugene being reinstated in the good opinion of the Marquess de Chamont, and receiving the hand of the lovely Laurette, recurred to his memory, and once more nerved him for the hellish deed. He cautiously unlocked the door, and shading the lamp with his mantle, entered the room. Here he was obliged to lay hold of the back of a chair to support himself, and a deadly sickness came over him, which he found it almost impossible to conquer. But nothing occurring to alarm him, by degrees he regained his courage, and even ventured to approach the couch. Here he hesitated, and

concealed the light; but hearing nothing to excite his suspicions, he went by the side of the couch, and passed the light several times across Eugene's eyes, to be certain that he really was not dissimulating.

"Yes, he sleeps," he whispered to himself. "My victim sleeps to wake no more: and yet 'tis hard for one so young—so noble, thus to perish Fool!—what coward feeling is it that thus unnerves me? Does he not stand betwixt me and happines?—wealth—honour—all? Ah! that thought mans me, and my hand is firm again!"

For the second time Adolphe approached the couch, and raised the dagger in the air, when at that moment Eugene moved, and he started tremblingly back, concealing himself behind the bed curtains, in a breathless state of agitation.

Eugene began to talk in his sleep; and as the intended murderer listened to the following words, his mind underwent a variety of the most painful emotions.

"Oh! frown not upon me, sweetest Laurette," said the sleeper. "Forgive me. I admit that I am a wretch, unworthy of thy love, still I can endure anything but thy scorn."

Adolphe trembled, and his heart misgave him.

"He only dreams," murmured he. "What a fool I am thus to linger. I will conquer this childish feeling. By hell he shall not escape me!"

In a moment of desperate determination, Adolphe rushed up to the couch, and once more raising his arm in the air, he cried, in hoarse but determined accents—

"Eugene, thy time is come!—Die!"

With these words the murderer twice buried the fatal weapon in his defenceless rival's bosom, who started up with convulsive emotion, and staggered from the couch, exclaiming, in broken accents—

"Ah! I am murdered! Wretch, who art thou that hast done this fiendish deed?"

Adolphe, horror-struck at the crime he had committed, stood transfixed to the spot, and Eugene, staggering up to him, grasped his arm with the strength of death, and gasped forth—

"Ah! villain—monster—I have thee! Thou shalt not escape me now! I—I——"

The lamp had fallen to the floor, and the light became extinguished; but Eugene retained his hold of his murderer, who struggled violently, but in vain, to release himself. In this manner they reached the casement, in at which the moon was shining brilliantly; and its rays darting upon the countenance of Adolphe, Eugene recognised him.

This was a moment of the most intense horror. Eugene fixed his dying glance with ghastly expression upon the countenance of he whom he had once thought to be his dearest friend, and in a hollow impressive voice, gave utterance to the following words—

"Oh! Adolphe—is it from thine hand I

receive my death? I—I—I did not think thee capable of this! But hear me, murderer—mark the dying words of thy unfortunate victim and tremble! For this deed do I invoke a malediction upon thine head!—Peace shall henceforth be a stranger to thy breast! In the festive scene—in thy waking hours, and in thy fevered slumbers, my spirit shall evermore be with thee! My ghastly cheek—my bleeding form—my filmy eye—shall be thy constant objects; and as dying I clutch thee now, so thus, in life and in death, shall my cold, clammy hands grasp thee!"

As the murdered Eugene thus spoke, in accents that penetrated to the very soul of the appalled and horror-struck Adolphe, he grasped his throat, and fixed an awful look upon him: his eyes suddenly became glazed, but remained unclosed. He gradually relaxed his hold, and then fell heavily to the floor a breathless corpse!

The murderer had accomplished his bloody purpose, and no sooner had he done so than compunction rushed upon his mind. He gazed but a moment on the mangled body of his friend, covered his face with his hands, and, with a groan of the most indescribable horror, rushed back to his own chamber.

CHAPTER IV.

THE PORTRAIT.—THE INJUNCTION.

PERPLEXING were the thoughts that harrassed the bosom of Laurette after the interview with Adolphe, and the promise he had exacted from her. One moment she repented having so readily yielded to his persuasions, and reproached herself with having been easily prejudiced against Eugene de Bouisson, and the next she could have cursed herself for having acted in a manner that her sense of the duty she owed her father forbade. But had not Eugene rendered himself unworthy of her love?—Had not Adolphe, his best friend, the companion of his childhood, his constant, faithful friend, since assured her of his vice—his dissipation—his duplicity? Had he not informed her that, while he pretended to be solely devoted to her, he was basking in the favours of a lacivious wanton?—And could she doubt what Adolphe stated? Oh, no—he, at any rate, could not, would not, deceive her! But then, her father!—had he not forbidden her to think of Aldolphe, to mention even his name in his presence? and yet she had promised clandestinely to become that man's bride! It was the first act of disobedience she ever remembered to have been guilty of towards her father, and she shrunk from it with horror! But yet, so ardent, so powerful was the passion she enterthined for Adolphe, that she could not bear to think of deceiving him, although the greatest misery should be the consequence. Besides, was not her father acting in an arbitrary manner by seeking to compel her

to bestow her hand upon the man she could not love; while he, to whom her whole soul was devoted—to whom she was so powerfully attached, that she would freely have sacrificed her life for him, she was not only forbidden to think upon him, but he had been insultingly ordered never to come near the house, and without any reason being assigned for such harsh and ambiguous conduct? What reason could the marquess have? What charge could he make against one whom he had never before seen, until the accident which had occurred to him and Eugene de Bouisson brought him to the house?—To her, indeed, Aldolphe de Floriville appeared to be all that was good, generous, and noble. She had never known her father to be capricious before; yet, in this instance, she must consider he was so. She awaited with the utmost anxiety to hear the result of her father's visit to the Chateau of the Count Bellevoir, for should the contents of the letter turn out to be correct, the marquess had expressed his determination to abandon all thoughts of Eugene, and to discard him from his friendship for ever. But then, again, should he do so, what difference would it make in her situation, no more than that he would not endeavour to force her to become his wife? He would never sanction the address of De Floriville, and therefore, what had she to hope from him?—Nothing! No! No!—he allowed her no alternative! He would fetter her affections! And, though she felt great repugnance in doing so, she must be guilty of an act of disobedience, or else sacrifice not only her own happiness, but that of Adolphe for ever.

As hour after hour waned away, and her father did not return, she felt more and more uneasy, and she sought in vain to banish from her mind those dismal forbedings that would arise in it, in spite of all her efforts. Ten—eleven—twelve o'clock passed, and yet the marquess did not come back. Something surely must have happened to him, she thought. She was too uneasy to retire to-bed, for she could not sleep while she remained in this state of fear, doubt, and uncertainty. She summoned an attendant, and desired her to dispatch two or three of the male servants in different directions, to see if they could hear anything of him; and then, again, seated herself by the casement and became once more buried in a profound reverie, similar to that we have been describing. A short time longer elapsed, and the men returned, having met with no success in their researches; and now the agony of Laurette was wound up to a pitch bordering upon frenzy. At that moment she fancied she heard his tread upon the stairs, and the next her imagination filled her mind with the most dreadful apprehensions. Surely Eugene, or any of his wild and reckless associates, had not committed any violence upon him. And yet what could she think of his prolonged absence? She paced the chamber in a state of the utmost uneasiness, and in the all-absorbing influence of the racking thoughts that now distracted her brain, Adolphe was for a while forgotten.

To add to her terrors, the moon suddenly became obscured, and the heavens denoted an approaching storm. In a few minutes the rain descended in torrents; the thunder rolled, and the lightning flashed vividly. At that moment the hour of one pealed from the bell of a neighbouring monastery; but still the Marquess de Chamont did not return.

The uneasiness of Laurette increased with every moment that elapsed, for what can be more painful than suspense, especially under such circumstances? Every murmur of the blast, which at intervals whistled through the different long avenues of the chateau, and shook the casements, conveyed with it a feeling of dread presentiment of some approaching horror to her heart; and more than once she started and looked fearfully around her, as she felt almost certain that she heard a low moaning sound. But then again she conquered her emotion in a slight measure, and blamed herself for her weakness. Yet was it not strange that her father, who was a man of the most regular habits, should continue absent at this very unseasonable hour? and when she recollected the place to which he had gone, and upon what errand, she could not, in spite of her efforts to the contrary, help again encouraging those terrors and apprehensions she had before suffered to take possession of her breast. These increased to such an insupportable degree that, unable longer to remain in the place, she hastily threw her mantle over her shoulders, and was about to leave the room, to go she scarcely knew whither, when she heard a loud knock at the door!—Her heart palpitated violently against her side, and her limbs trembled so, that she could with difficulty sustain herself. She endeavoured to go down stairs, but had not the power; and in the meantime she heard the door opened, and the next instant the voice of her father speaking to the servant who had let him in.

"Thank God! he is safe," she gasped forth, and sank into a chair without power or motion. She heard the marquess hasten to his own apartment with heavy steps, and he closed the door with a violent bang after him.

"Something has occurred to disturb him greatly," she reflected; "doubtless, he has discovered that the anonymous writer has spoken the truth."

Unable to think of retiring to her couch until she had satisfied her doubt and suspense, having somewhat conquered the agitation which the excitement of the moment had occasioned her, she resolved to seek an interview with her father, before he sought his pillow; and taking the lamp in her hand, she arose, and descended the stairs with a light step. When she reached the door of the apartment, she paused, for she heard him pacing the room with hasty and uneven steps, and frequently uttered loud and passionate expressions.

"The villain! the shameless hypocrite, thus to attempt to deceive me," she heard him exclaim; "he, too, on whom I had fixed my hopes; whom I thought so good and virtuous, and upon whom I looked with as much affection as if he had been my son. This will bring upon me the scorn and ridicule of all who know me. Fool that I was to be so easily cajoled. What could I expect from one who had chosen the hated Adolphe de Floriville for his friend and companion?"

The heart of Laurette sunk with powerful emotion when she heard her father thus speak of that man to whom she had resigned her heart, to whom she had even given her assent to become clandestinely his wife.

"Powers of mystery!" she reflected, "what can be the cause of this remarkable antipathy to Adolphe? Why should my father be so prejudiced against one whom, until the accident occurred which brought both him and Eugene de Buoisson to the chateau, I imagined he had never before seen?"

The marquess was now silent, and she made a hasty effort to stifle her emotion, then gen ly tapped at the room-door, which was almost immediately opened by her father himself. He looked very much agitated, his countenance was flushed, and his lips quivered. He started back in surprise when he beheld his daughter, and seemed confused.

"Laurette, my child," he observed, his voice assuming all those affectionate accents in which he was ever wont to address her; "how now, not at rest yet, and such an hour? —how is this, my sweetest?"

"Oh, my dear father," replied Laurette, "thou canst not think so unkindly of me as to suppose that I could retire to my couch and thou away from home, and at such an hour. Frightful terrors and forebodings have haunted my imagination, and I was fearful that something had befallen thee."

"Good girl, good girl, God bless thee!" said the old man, kissing her tenderly. "Oh, Laurette, should I lose thee, alas! what would become of me?—But no, no;—Heaven will not be so unkind to me as to deprive my declining years of thy fond care and attention; and I ought to be grateful to it that I have been able to discover the real character of that villain, upon whom I would have bestowed so inestimable a treasure, and which would thus have been the cause of such incalculable misery to us both."

Laurette trembled as her father thus spoke, and was almost tempted at once to acknowledge the deceptive part she was acting towards him, and implore his forgiveness; but, again, the strength of her love for Adolphe rose in vivid characters to her mind, and completely overpowered every other sentiment.

"Thou art agitated, my dear father," she said at length, " I prithee retire to thy chamber; the adventures of the night have disturbed thee, and——"

"Thou sayest true, my Laurette," answered the marquess,—" the contents of the letter have been confirmed by me. I met the hypocrite at the chateau of that unprincipled spendthrift, the Count Bellevoir, raving in all the madness attendant upon ruin! Eugene de Buoisson is now a beggar!"

" Unhappy man !" exclaimed Laurette, fervently.

" Unhappy !—yes; and does he not richly deserve all the unhappiness he may experience ?" said the marquess. " Has it not all been brought upon him by his own depraved and profligate habits? and would he not have deceived both me and thee, my child ?—would he not have obtained possession of thy fortune but to squander it away in the same manner, and have brought the most unmitigated misery upon us ?—Ah! what noise was that ?"

Laurette started and turned very pale, at the same time that her father looked carefully around the room, for she could almost have sworn that she heard a stifled groan, which seemed to proceed from the spot upon which they were at that moment standing.

" Psha! how foolish I am getting; it was nothing more than the wind," he remarked at last. " Laurette," he continued, " I discovered everything as my anonymous correspondent had represented it, and in his society, I beheld one, whom I firmly believe, has been, in the first instance, the accurst tempter who hath lured him to vice:—one whose name never rises to my memory without exciting the utmost disgust and hatred; —Adolphe de Floriville!"

" Adolphe de Floriville !" gasped forth Laurette, her cheeks becoming ghastly pale, and her limbs trembling so violently, that had she not grasped her father's arm, she must have fallen.

The marquess fixed his eyes with sternness and astonishment upon her countenance, and, with a look which seemed as if it would penetrate to her soul, he said—

" Laurette, what means this extraordinary agitation at the mention of that name?"

" Oh, my dear father, why this——"

" Answer me, girl, and without equivocation," interrupted the marquess, in tones of impatience and severity she had never heard him assume before; " why, I repeat, when that detested name is mentioned, dost thou evince such powerful emotion ?—Often have I noticed thee before."

" Nay, my dear father," faltered Laurette, " why speak to me so severely? How have I deserved this ?—and why——"

" Laurette, Laurette, beware," said the marquess, in solemn accents; " beware, I repeat, how thou obeyest the injunctions I did once before impress upon thee; and, as thou valuest my love, as thou wouldst not in-

cur my malediction, encourage not a thought of that man ; mention him not ; breathe not his name in my presence, or ever avoid dwelling upon it but with disgust and abhorrence."

Laurette tried to speak, but the words that would have escaped her were stifled by the power of her feelings, and the manner of her father   Her bosom heaved convulsively, and with difficulty did she prevent herself from sinking to the floor. The marquess watched her for a few moments in silence, and it was evident that the most powerful emotions were struggling in his breast; then, suddenly grasping her arm once more, he led her with gentle violence towards one side of the room, before which a long black curtain was always drawn. To this, with an air of the most impressive solemnity, he directed her attention, and after the lapse of a few seconds, during which interval he was trying as much as possible to stifle his agitation, he said—

" Thou hast often wished to penetrate the mystery, Laurette, which is concealed behind this sable drapery ;—it hides from vulgar gaze that which, next to thee, my child, I value more than mine own life! Before the treasure hidden from view behind that curtain do I pay my daily orisons, and never before retiring to my couch, do I miss kneeling before it, and breathing a blessing upon the memory of that sweet saint it represents. Behold, Laurette, what thou hast lon; been anxious to have revealed to thee ! —gaze and worship with thy father."

As the marquess thus spoke, he slowly drew back the curtain, and the eyes of Laurette rested upon the portrait of a lady of such exquisite beauty, that her whole attention was transfixed in a moment with feelings of the most indescribable transport. The countenance possessed an expression that was truly angelic, and such was the admirable skill with which the artist had performed his task, that you might almost imagine that the bosom of the portrait throbbed with the pulsation of life.

The marquess noticed the emotion, and the tears stood trembling in his eyes; and, although he made several efforts, he was unable for a few seconds to give utterance to a syllable. At length, however, in a voice of the deepest anguish, he ejaculated—

" Laurette, I see thou dost feel agitated and entranced at the sight of this but faint resemblance of one who now looks down upon us from that seat of Heavenly bliss to which her virtues entitle her. Is it not lovely ?—Is it not——"

" It is Heavenly !" exclaimed Laurette, fervently—" I could gaze for ever upon the portrait, and every moment would my admiration increase."

" And who thinkest thou that portrait represents ?"

" Feelings of delight, of irresistible power rush upon my heart," cried Laurette, "feelings such as I never before remember to have experienced.—I cannot mistake them.

—Oh, no, no, no!—my mother!—this—this must be her dear resemblance; what other being than that blessed saint could have inspired my bosom with such strange emotion?"

"Thou sayest right, Laurette," said the venerable marquess, with a burst of anguish which she found it impossible longer to control, "that portrait is the resemblance of that dear but unfortunate woman who bore thee!—Oh, she was too fair for this earth, and the fell destroyer—the arch demon—the accursed villain, who—but let me not think upon it, or I shall go mad! Come nearer, Laurette. Nearer—nearer! Nay, why dost thou tremble? Thy lips quiver, and—kneel, girl, kneel with me."

The marquess knelt before the portrait, and Laurette, as a sensation she could not understand came over her, knelt also, and awaited in a state of fearful suspense, what was to follow.

"Now, Laurette, hear me," said her father, in yet more solemn and impressive tones than he had before spoken—"repeat, I command thee, as thou valuest my love, repeat after me every sentence that I shall utter.—Dost hear me?"

"I do, my father," faltered out Laurette; "but oh, why this violent agitation?—why so solemnly enjoin her who never disobeyed thee yet?"

"Swear then, that eternal hatred shall inhabit thy bosom for the offspring of those who injured that sainted being that portrait represents!" ejaculated the marquess, and his whole frame became terribly convulsed with the intensity of his agitation; "breathe with me a curse upon the hated miscreant's memory, and invoke the heaviest malediction upon the head of his descendant that can attend mankind."

"Oh, my fater, why this violence?—why this——"

"Ah! dost thou hesitate, girl?" cried the marquess, and his eyes rolled with an expression of wildness and wrath upon his trembling and astonished daughter. "Away! thou art a deceiver! Thou lovest me not; thou wouldst bring tears of suffering down these furrowed cheeks, and rend that heart, which has borne up against maddening anguish only for thy sake! Oh, God! and is it for this that I——Laurette, Laurette, thou hast this night almost snapped asunder the only chord which bound me to life! Thou shalt no longer gaze upon those features that seam alone to reproach thee with disobedience to thy fond, thy too indulgent father. Begone!—To thy chamber, I say; I am in no mood to hold further converse with thee."

"Father! father!" exclaimed the distracted damsel, "surely I cannot hear aright!—But, no, no, no;—the events of this night have so perplexed thy mind, that thou knowest not what thou sayest. Thou needest rest; I would retire to my chamber, but cannot—dare not do so, under the weight of thy displeasure. Alas! how deeply dost thou wrong me, my dear father!—What have I done to merit this?—The enemies of my poor mother, must, of course, be mine; but I cannot—I must not utter such frightful language—my heart revolts at the thought. Spare me, father—prithee, spare me—and to-morrow thou mayest be more calm, and I will listen to thee, patiently and willingly, and as far as my duty to Heaven will permit me, obey thy wishes."

The marquess paused a moment, and looking stedfastly in the face of his daughter, seemed to be struggling violently with the powerful emotions that distracted his heart. Then the tears fell fast from his eyes, and seemed to afford him some slight relief. He snatched the trembling form of Laurette to his bosom, and pressing her fervently to his heart, he kissed her cheeks, her lips and forehead, at the same time ejaculating—

"Pardon me, child, I have been too harsh; but, but—oh, how could I doubt her who has ever been so kind—so attentive, so dutiful to her poor father?—It was wrong—very wrong of me to give way to such weakness. My Laurette deceive her father!—Oh, no, no, never!—impossible!—There, good night—good night; and all good angels guard thee!—Leave me, I pray!"

Laurette once more threw herself into the arms of her father, and kissing his venerable cheeks vehemently, in a voice half stifled with sobs, she repeated his prayer, and taking up her lamp, quitted the room, and the marquess closed the door after her. Still she felt far from easy, and remained at the door for a few seconds and listened. She heard the marquess utter his usual prayer, prior to retiring to his couch, and, then, all becoming silent, she concluded he had sought the comfort of his pillow. She began to ascend the stairs to her own chamber, when again a most melancholy presentiment crossed her mind, and she returned, and once more listened at the door of her father's chamber; but all remained as silent as death, and hearing him breathe strongly, she naturally concluded that he had fallen off to sleep, and, therefore, feeling more satisfied, she again began to ascend the stairs. Just before she reached her chamber-door, a strange sensation of horror crept through her veins, and she could almost have sworn that she saw the shadow of a human form flit past the end of the corridor, with the switness of thought. At that moment, the bell of the neighbouring monastery, in solemn tones, tolled forth the hour of two.

Laurette entered her chamber, where her feelings, greatly excited by the unusual events that had that night occurred to her, almost overcame her. The strange and violent conduct of her father; the oath and the bitter curse he had endeavoured to extort from her; the portrait, and the ambiguous words the marquess had made use of, all rushed with irresistible force to her recollection, and she wrung her hands, and clasped her burning temples, with the intensity of her anguish.

"Alas! wretched, sinful Laurette," she cried, "hast thou not become an hypocrite? Art thou not really deceiving the best of fathers?—And shall I, after this painful interview, still remain resolved to yield to the importunities of Adolphe, and become his wife in a secret manner, and without the sanction of my father?—Has he not threatened me with his curse if he should do so?—and could I expect to be happy by adopting such a course?—Besides, has he not forbidden me to think of Adolphe; never to dwell upon his name, unless it is with disgust and abhorrence?—And shall I dare to disobey him?—No, Adolphe; to-morrow we may meet, but it must be for the last time!—My duty to my father compels me to sacrifice my affections in obedience to his will. But to forget Adolphe!—oh, how I shudder at the thought!—Alas! Laurette, unfortunate maiden, too clearly art thou doomed by Fate to endure the most poignant misery. Better would it be for thee wert thou at rest in the silent tomb, with her who brought thee into the world."

A paroxysm of tears choked her further utterance, and covering her face with her handkerchief, she gave free indulgence to her sorrow. At length, completely worn out with suffering, and the heavy cares that oppressed her mind, she threw herself upon her couch, and gradually sunk off to sleep.

CHAPTER V.

THE ASSASSIN.—THE DEATH GRASP.

WE will leave our readers to imagine the feelings of the wretched Adolphe de Floriville after he had committed the hellish deed. In a moment his conscience upbraided him for the crime he had perpetrated; and, on reaching his own room, the torments of the damned rocked his brain. The curse uttered by his murdered friend, in his expiring moments, still seemed to ring in his ears; and whichever way he turned, the ghastly looks he fixed upon his countenance, as he breathed the same, seemed to pursue him. He closed his eyes, but he could not shut out the horror of his thoughts. A thousand times did he bitterly repent the demoniacal deed, and would have given the world, had it been at his command, to have recalled the past. But it was too late to repent now, and unless he used the utmost precaution, suspicion would be sure to attach itself to him, and he would be brought into a disgraceful and ignominious situation. This thought aroused him into action; and endeavouring to compose himself as much as it was, under the dreadful circumstances in his power to do, he tried to collect his thoughts sufficiently to devise some scheme by which

it might be supposed that the unfortunate Eugene de Buoisson had committed an act of self-destruction, and which the circumstance of his being well known to have lost the whole of his property at play, would tend to corroborate.

He now remembered that, in the horror and confusion of the moment, after the bloody deed had been committed, he had forgotten to bring away with him the deadly weapon, and the blade of which being marked with the initials of his name, his detection would be inevitable, unless he contrived to get the dagger in his possession again. He must again enter the chamber where the mangled remains of his victim lay weltering in his blood, and remove the evidence of his guilt, or nothing could save him from the ignominious fate his crime deserved.

But, from the bare thought of this, the murderer shrunk appalled with horror, and an icy chill ran through his veins, and seemed to curdle up his blood. But yet he had no other alternative, either to do so, or make up his mind to meet the fate which would most assuredly be his. All the cowardice of guilt shook his nerves, and he stood in a state of horror and uncertainty, not knowing in what manner to act. Still, the idea of being brought to a painful and tedious trial;—his being sentenced to a violent death, amidst the curses of the populace, acted powerfully upon him, and struggling desperately with his feelings, he cautiously opened his room door and listened. All was dark and silent as the grave beyond, and recollecting the last words of Eugene, and the threat he had given utterance to, he started back and closed the door hastily, almost fancying that he beheld his livid and blood-stained features, and felt the *Death Grasp* upon his throat.

Again he hesitated, and again he reflected upon the horrors of a death upon the scaffold; he became more determined than ever, and taking the lamp, the rays of which he concealed beneath his cloak, he once more emerged from his chamber, and having taken the precaution to remove his boots, he proceeded along on tip-toe, until he had reached the door of the apartment, in which was the corpse of the murdered man. Here he breathed short and thick, and a deadly sickness came over him, which he was unable to shake off. At length, he placed his hand on the door, and then once more hesitated, and trembled in a still more violent manner than he had done before.

"Fool! coward!" he muttered to himself at last, "why do I tremble thus?—I did not tremble to commit the deed, and surely I should not now shrink from doing that which will secrete me from detection!"

He started back in a state of the utmost horror, and every limb shook convulsively as a dismal groan smote his ear, and which appeared to issue from the apartment.

Cold drops of perspiration stood upon the murderer's temples, and he grasped at the banisters to save himself from falling.

"It was but fancy," he said, after a pause of several moments; but his lips were livid, and his countenance altogether bore the paleness of death; "but, ah!" he continued, as a sudden thought crossed his brain, "perhaps he still lives!—The wounds I inflicted upon him may not have proved fatal; and should he only recover for a short time, for a few hours, until he will be discovered by the inmates of the house, he will reveal the truth, and my fate will be certain. I must be satisfied upon this point."

Another groan, more audible than the one he had before heard, interrupted him, and again startled him.

"It is no idle imagination," gasped forth the assassin; "this time, at any rate, I am certain that I heard a groan. My surmises are just—Eugene still lives."

Filled with the most indescribable alarm, when he thought of the consequences that would ensue if Eugene recovered, Adolphe forgot all his other terrors in an instant, and, opening the door, entered the room, closing the former cautiously.

The rays of the lamp, which Adolphe, with a trembling hand, had raised above his head, fell full upon the features of the murdered man, who was stretched upon his back, and lying in a complete stream of blood. His features were distorted, and his eye-lids being open, his eyes seemed to be fixed sternly upon the face of the murderer, with all the filmy ghastliness of death. Adolphe covered his face with his hands, averted his head, and could not help uttering an involuntary groan of horror; but hastily recovering himself, he picked up the dagger with which the dreadful crime had been committed, and taking the one belonging to Eugene from his bosom, he first smeared it in his own blood, and then knelt by his side. He knelt down and placed his ear to the mouth of the murdered man, and listened; but all was still; he was quite dead, and was exactly in the same position as when he left him, immediately after the shocking deed. In what manner, then, could he account for the groans which he had so distinctly heard?—Could it have been delusion?—Oh, no; he was certain that it was no idle chimera of the brain!—And filled with the sentiment of the most unbounded consternation, he once more glanced at the pale features of the murdered man, and covering his face with his hands, rushed out of the room.

With the vain hope of drowning the voice of remorse in sleep, he threw himself hastily on his couch, and covered his face with the bed-clothes. The murderer tossed a considerable time restlessly about, the victim of distracting thought, sometimes listening with a feeling congenial with its terrors, to the violent storm which was now raging without. At length, however, he fell into a disturbed slumber. How long he had slept, he knew not; but the horrible circumstances that aroused him could never be erased from his memory. A hand, cold as the winter's ice, and damp and clammy with the moisture of death, clasped his, with the vehemence of expiring agony! Good God! how can we pourtray the horror which paralysed his whole frame? It curdled the current of his quivering veins. The wretched Adolphe jumped, with a cry of terror, from the couch; cold drops of prespiration bedewed his temples, and stood on his erected hair! His limbs trembled convulsively: he snatched up the lamp, the light of which glimmered faintly on the oaken table by the side of the bed, and gazed around the room, in horrible expectancy. No ghastly phantom met his terrified scrutiny! The storm still raged with unabated violence, and the blue forked lightning ever and anon darted a frightful glare in at the casements of his chamber. He endeavoured to regain his composure, and to convince himself he had yielded to the powerful influence of some terrific dream. He again hurried to the bed, and sought to compose his mind to rest. Gracious Heaven! once more he felt the repulsive grasp of death, with greater vehemence than ever! The death sweat seemed to stagnate his whole blood: his hand sank powerless beneath the icy touch! He again started from the bed, and his eyes rolled wildly in their burning sockets.

"Eugene hath performed his promise," he exclaimed, with a burst of agony—his whole frame tottered with emotion—his head swam round, and he sank into a state of total insensibility.

He was aroused from his happy state of unconsciousness by a loud noise in the house, and quickly regaining his equanimity, knowing the urgency of the case, and the danger he might involve himself in, without the greatest care, he jumped up, not doubting but that the noise was occasioned by the inmates of the *Auberge* having discovered the body of the ill-fated Eugene de Buoisson. Adolphe soon became more collected than, from the dreadful occurrences of the previous night could have been expected, and it was not long before he was convinced that he was right in his conjectures, for he heard the voice of Caleb, in doleful accents, vociferating—"Murder! fire! thieves!" and other similar exclamations.

He left his chamber hastily, and then heard a great confusion in the house, and the different occupants of the various chambers rushed out into the gallery, and hastened to the room, whither the loud and terrified outcries of the simple, but humane-hearted Caleb, directed them. When the blood-stained corpse of that unfortunate man who had fallen by his hands was pointed out to him, the complete surprise and unqualified horror he evinced at the dreadful spectacle, was sufficient to remove all suspicions of his guilt from the minds of the beholders, if they had at first been ever so inclined to attach any to him.

"Poor unfortunate gentleman," said Caleb; "well, depend upon it, the rash act has been committed by himself; and I declare I have not been able to sleep all night, for the terrible ideas that would, every now and then, occur to my mind, especially after the dreadful state of agitation he was in when he returned home last night. I strongly suspect that he had been losing something considerable at the gaming-table, and that it took such an effect upon his mind, it has induced him to make away with himself in a moment of insanity. It is very certain that he could not have had his *natural* feelings about him."

"Alas! poor, ill-fated Eugene," cried Adolphe with well affected emotion, "little did I ever expect that thou, the early friend and companion of my childhood, would come to so awful an end as this. He seemed to be half deranged last night, and in spite of all my persuasions, he would persist in playing for high stakes, until he had lost the whole of his fortune."

"Ill-fated man," cried Bernard Swinton.

"It is very clear that he committed the bloody deed with his own hand," observed two or three of the by-standers. Adolphe turned away his head, to conceal a smile of exultation, which he could not restrain, on finding that everything worked so favourably to his designs.

"To be sure he did," coincided Caleb, "there cannot be any doubt of it, poor gentleman, and so you would all say, if you had seen what I did, and if he had said the same to you that he did to me."

"What did he say?" was the eager interrogatory.

"Oh, I'll tell you," answered Caleb. "When I let Monsieur de Buoisson in, he looked so deadly pale, and so wild-like, that it quite frightened me when I saw him, and I felt positive that something very particular must have happened to him to agitate him in such a violent manner. So I questioned him; when he returned me some very cross answers, and spoke in a very surly manner to me altogether, which all those who knew anything at all of Monsieur de Buoisson, must be aware was a very unusual thing with him. Then he begged my pardon: and said he did not mean to speak so sharply and uncivilly to me; desiring me, at the same time, with a look which I shall never forget the longest day I've got to live—and if that should be for a thousand years—to show him to his room—to silence—to solitude—to death; and with that he hastened away, and I saw no more of him until I came up a short time since, as is my regular custom, to call him."

The statement of Caleb was considered quite sufficient, and the circumstance of Eugene having ruined himself the night before, to show that he had committed suicide; and Adolphe having given the necessary instructions regarding the body,

apparently in a state of the most intense agony, quitted the house.

He had not made up his mind as to whither he should direct his steps. Anywhere to escape the scene of the horrible crime, and to endeavour to fly from the maddening thoughts which guilt never fails to engender. But how futile was the attempt. To think of meeting Laurette that day, with his hands, in a manner of speaking, still reeking with the blood of the murdered victim, he could not for a moment endure the idea of. By the following day he might be more composed; and when she heard of the melancholy death of Eugene, she would not be at all surprised that he should break the assignation they had made, although of such remarkable importance. He wandered into the confines of the deep forest, and remained in a dismal glade until a pitchy darkness enveloped the firmament. The keenness of the wind, which swept in hollow gusts through the umbrageous foliage around, urged him, at length, to think of returning. He reached the *Auberge*, and saw the figure of a man wrapped in a large mantle, standing on the threshold. Rather surprised, Adolphe walked towards him; the stranger removed his mantle; at that moment, the moon which had arisen, poured a flood of silvery light upon his person. Powers of mercy! how he started!—the figure of the murdered Eugene stood before him—pale, ghastly, and inanimate.

It would be impossible to do adequate justice to the terror evinced by the murderer, as he gazed upon the phantom of his victim, from whose breast the purple blood still seemed to flow. His limbs shook as if he were afflicted with the palsy: his teeth chattered, his lips quivered, and his heart appeared to be suddenly changed into a lump of ice. For several minutes his tongue clave to the palate of his mouth, and he was unable to give utterance to a syllable, whilst the spectre fixed his filmy eyes upon his countenance with thrilling horror. It approached him nearer and nearer, and now he smiled upon the guilty Adolphe; but nothing could be half so terrible as that ghastly smile.

"Powers of hell!" cried the murderer, in a hoarse voice. "This is no delusive spell! Avaunt, dread spirit! My eyes become seared as I look on thee! Ah! he extends his hands to grasp my throat! Off, spectre—demon! Off—off! Death is preferable to thy dreadful touch!"

A hollow, sepulchral laugh escaped form the awful form before him, and the next minute Adolphe again felt the terrible death grasp. The icy hand of the spectre was upon his throat, and as he writhed in agony and horror, it thus, in solemn and impressive tones, addressed him—

"Murderer, thy wretched victim has kept his word, and will continue to do so! My ghastly form shall ever be before thee! Morning shall dawn, and thou shalt see me! Noon, evening, and night, may wane slowly away, and still thine eyes may behold my grizzly shade! No matter at what hour, or in whatsoever scene thou mayest be, thine eyes shall constantly encounter my bloodless, cadaverous features! When thou openest them they shall rest on me! Thou mayest close them, but thou shalt not be able to shut out my dreadful form! Thou shalt meet me in the light of day, and in the solemn darkness of night! Thou shalt not be able to fly from me! I will pursue thee everywhere as thine own shadow! There is no escape from me even in death! Tremble —tremble, murderer!"

Again a sepulchral laugh burst from the spectre, and echoed awfully through the place. One intense—one terrible look—he fixed upon the horror-struck Adolphe:—a peal of thunder shook the earth :—he relaxed his hold; and as he gradually vanished into the thin air, the assassin sunk senseless to the ground.

How long he had remained there he was incapable of judging; but from the deadly chill which benumbed his limbs, he was inclined to suppose it had been some time. He arose upon his feet. To what a terrible state of mind was he aroused! He trembled in every limb, and he feared to look around him, lest his eyes should once more encounter the appalling form of the murdered Eugene; and, as every word of the dreadful curse he had heard rushed vividly to his recollection, he groaned aloud with the intensity of mental agony, and covered his face with his hands. At length, however, fully awakened to a sense of the danger of his situation, and the chance he should have stood of being detected, had he been discovered by any of the inhabitants of the house, he made a desperate effort to conquer his fears, and to become more collected, lest he should by this violent agitation betray himself; but this was a task he could not, without the greatest difficulty, accomplish, and that only partially. His limbs shook with terror, and he felt an awful sensation, as if the shade of Eugene were still standing by his side. Then, in a futile effort to convince himself that he had been labouring under a delusion, he laughed aloud, and upbraided himself for a fool. But it was like the wild mockery of a wretched maniac, and sounded more awful than any expressions of terror he might have given utterance to.

How terrible—how hideous is the form of that gaunt demon, Guilt, and how frightful are the tortures he inflicts upon the unhappy victims! How dearly does he make them pay for any transitory and evanescent pleasures with which he may have lured them! Of this truth the miserable Adolphe was a shocking example.

It was evidently very late, and the inmates of the *Auberge* seemed to have retired to their chambers, for Adolphe could not perceive any lights in the different casements. Should he arouse them? Oh, no—his heart revolted at the bare idea with a feeling of inexpres-

sible repugnance. Could he sleep beneath the same roof, beneath which was the corpse of that man he had so inhumanly murdered?

"Sleep! sleep!" cried the wretched man, "and can a monster like me expect to sleep again?—Oh, no; did not the shade of Eugene tell me so? I shall never, never know rest again."

"Never!" repeated an unearthly voice, and, in a moment, Adolphe again beheld the countenance of the spectre fixed upon him.

"Horror! horror! he is there again!" cried Adolphe; "shield me! save me!"

He covered his face with his hands, and, totally regardless in what direction he was going, rushed frantically from the spot. He hurried forward with all the wild precipitation of horror and despair, and did not stop until the solemn tones of a bell vibrated on his ears, and recalled him to a full sense of his situation. It was the hour of one. He looked around him, and found that he had entered again into those deep forest recesses, among which he had been wandering the whole of the day. It was a dismal place, and, as the wind whistled among the foliage, it was sufficient to fill the mind with the most gloomy thoughts. Those that racked the brain of Adolphe were fearful enough: but still, any place was preferable to the house from which he had just hastened. He sought some of the remotest shades, and, at length, completely wearied out, he threw himself upon the earth, and endeavoured to compose himself to sleep. It was long ere he could do this; but, at last he did drop into a feverish slumber, from which he was quickly aroused by a renewal of those horrors, from which he had in vain endeavoured to escape. Once more he felt the cold and clammy pressure of the Death Grasp upon his throat, and, with a cry of indescribable agony, he raised his head, and again his eyes encountered the features of the spectre.

CHAPTER VI.

THE CLANDESTINE MARRIAGE.—THE CURSE. THE TALE OF HORROR.

THE mysterious death of Eugene de Buoisson created an extraordinary sensation in the neighbourhood, and the circumstances seemed so well to corroborate the opinion, that it was universally supposed that the unfortunate young man had, with his own hands, put a period to his existence. The news of the catastrophe soon reached the Chateau de Chamont, and the heart of Laurette was smote with horror; while a feeling of an extraordinary, but indefinite character, involuntary stole over her senses, and which she in vain endeavoured to unravel. The marquess, too, whose nature was really mild and charitable, experienced a great shock when he heard of the untimely fate of that man whom he had at one period honoured with his highest regard.

" Poor unfortunate wretch !" he soliloquised, " most earnestly do I pity him for the madness and weakness that have brought him to this untimely end. Heaven pardon him his offences."

The day after the assassination passed away, and Laurette, who was at the place of assignation at the time appointed, saw nothing of Adolphe. This circumstance, however, did not at all surprise her, in consequence of the dreadful· event which had taken place at the *Auberge*, and which, she reflected, would naturally greatly distract his mind, and render him unfit for anything on that day. More powerfully tormented was the mind of Laurette, not only with the thoughts that the melancholy death of Eugene de Buoisson excited in her breast, but her bosom was distracted with a number of conflicting doubts, fears, and perplexing ideas ; wavering between a sense of the duty she owed her father, and the love she entertained for Adolphe. Now she resolved to see her lover again and tell him they must meet no more ; and anon, she could not even contemplate such an idea without the utmost agony ; and, moreover, she could not help thinking that the marquess was acting in a manner quite arbitrary, and seeking to exert an influence over her affections, which neither reason or obedience to his will could authorise. Then, again, the mystery of her behaviour—the solemnity of his injunction ; the dark insinuations he had thrown out against Adolphe de Floriville, and which, to her, were perfectly inscrutable, all tended still more to involve her in perplexity, suspense, and anxiety. The day passed away, as we have before observed, and Laurette heard nothing of Adolphe. The night was a restless one to her, and when sleep did close her eye-lids, her mind was distracted by frightful visions that flitted before her imagination, and filled her with terrible doubts and apprehensions. The following morning, she had no sooner arisen, than Fanchette entered her chamber with a note in her hand.

She no sooner looked at the superscription than Laurette knew it to be the handwriting of Adolphe, and involuntarily she pressed it to her lips, and in spite of the injunctions of her father, she felt that whatever might happen, let him be in ever such adversity, or even disgrace, nothing could have the power to estrange her affections from him. But to forget him !—The idea was not only preposterous, but her heart convinced her impracticable ; and, indeed, much as she was anxious that she should not swerve from the duty she owed to her father, and in spite of the conflicting ideas that had previously haunted her imagination, she felt assured that she could not cease to remember Adolphe with the most unbounded affection.

She opened the epistle which had been forwarded to her by her lover, and in trembling haste perused the contents. It was couched in the most affectionate and impressive terms, of which, in fact, Adolphe was a complete master ; and after assuring her of the deep horror and anguish he felt at the melancholy fate of his friend Eugene, he, in the most ardent manner, implored her not to forget the vows she had pledged to him, and the promise she had made to become his bride. He urged her to meet him on the following day at their former place of assignation, when he would have all the arrangements made for their union ; and he had not the least doubt, that notwithstanding the strong opposition her father had made to his advances towards her—nay, more, to her friendship, or the prejudice he had most unaccountably imbibed against him, he would soon grant them his forgiveness—and not only that, but would be inclined to receive him with all the affection of a parent.

Time after time did Laurette peruse those lines ; and although she too well remembered the aversion her father had from the first moment he became acquainted with his name evinced towards Adolphe, she, knowing the former's natural kind and liberal disposition, would, when he found that her affections were irrevocably fixed upon Adolphe, pardon them for the step they had taken, and receive the latter as his son-in-law, at length resolved at all hazards to meet him, and to fulfil the promise she had previously made him. Accordingly she returned Adolphe an answer to that effect, and agreed to meet him on the following day. This letter she delivered to Fanchette, who had informed her that the confidential valet of Adolphe, who had brought the billet doux to her, was waiting at a short distance from the chateau.

Having done this, her mind was deeply harassed by doubt, suspense, and agitation ; and at one moment she blamed herself for having done so, imagining that she acted wrong ; and at another she commended herself for the resolution, considering that it was a return no more than was justly due to the fidelity and affection of Adolphe, whom her father most unreasonably and unjustly opposed, without giving her any motive for so doing. Sometimes, indeed, a pang shot through her heart, and she remained in a state of uncertainty as to which manner she should act ; she was doatingly attached to her father, and to do anything which might cause his breast a single pang, her heart recoiled from with horror ; but yet, after weighing maturely every circumstance, she could not perceive any reason why that parent should seek to make her happiness the sacrifice to his caprices.

This was a most wretched day to our heroine, and there were times when she was half inclined to alter the resolution she had formed, to return a positive refusal to comply with his wishes in a clandestine manner, and, confessing to the marquess her love for the former, implore his assent to their addresses. But then the strange and unalterable aversion which her father seemed to have to her lover, and the utter hopelessness of her ever be n able to persuade him to yield to their wishes, made her shrink from such a step, and she ultimately came to the determination to act as her affections prompted her.

From a feeling which she found it impossible to vanquish, she avoided the presence of the marquess as much as possible that day, and under a plea of indisposition, retired at an early hour to her chamber, but not to rest ; no, her mind was too much perplexed with the various ideas that crowded upon it, to suffer her to do that, and she recalled the various actions of A lolphe to her memory, to see if there was anything which could give her cause to justify the prejudice which her father had imbibed towards him ; but in vain. He appeared to her a being every way worthy of the affection she had placed upon him, and she could not for an instant doubt but that in the present instance, which would seal their fates, he would act with that strict honour and integrity that appeared to be the characteristics of his character. Then the solemn and imbiguous behaviour of the marquess in the chamber in which was deposited the portrait of her mother, recurred to her memory, and as she remembered every lineament of that angelic countenance, which was so ably represented on the canvas, her bosom swelled with a feeling that was altogether new to her.

" Spirit of my sainted mother," she piously ejaculated, raising her eyes towards heaven, and clasping her hands fervently, " look down upon thy poor child, and instruct her how to act ; if she be about to take a wrong step, oh, in pity to her, assure her by some token of the same, so that she may avoid the error, and continue in the same path of rectitude and honour it has ever been her study and earnest wish to pursue."

She arose from her knees, and as she did so, a sweet and heavenly strain of music seemed to fill the apartment, which rivetted her soul in rapture, and having gradually died away, all became wrapped in the same silence as had before prevailed.

Laurette glanced around the room, half fearfully, and half anxiously, expecting to see the sainted object of her invocation ; but nothing whatever met her gaze, and after a pause of a short interval, she ejaculated :

" Those sounds seem to betoken that heaven approves of the choice my heart has fixed upon, and I will follow the bent of my inclination : yes, dearest Adolphe, I am thine, irrevocably thine—nor do I think that I shall ever have cause to repent of the choice my heart has made."

As she uttered these words, a deadly chill, which she in vain tried to conquer, fell upon her heart, and she could almost have sworn that a deep groan, as if of some person in excruciating agony, smote her ear. Again she cast her timid glances around the chamber, and as she did so, fancy pictured to her the shadowy form of some dark object, which seemed to flit with the speed of thought past the farther and dark side of the room, and immediately vanished ; and such was the terror this occasioned her, that she found it utterly impossible to repress a scream. But quickly afterwards she chided herself for what she considered to be nothing less than childish weakness, and trimming her lamp, as she did not feel inclined to repose, she took up a book which she had been perusing a day or two previous, and endeavoured to divert her thoughts from the subject which at that time engrossed them, by reading its contents. This, however, she found to be a useless task, and she soon threw it aside, and again her mind wandered to Adolphe, and the promise she had made him ; the solemn injunctions of her father, and the portrait of her mother, which the marquess had shown to her, and which, for what reason she could not conceive, he kept concealed in such a mysterious manner from the sight. That he had met with some early sorrow, she could not for a moment hesitate in coming to a conclusion ; but what was the nature of that sorrow, she was entirely at a loss to conceive. And then again, as this thought crossed her mind, she paused and hesitated at the step she had resolved to take ; would not her opposition to his wises add to that grief, and might she not thus be the means of rendering his declining years truly miserable ?— But, no, no ; that was impossible !—a union with a man of the amiable character which she firmly believed Adolphe to be, could only be productive of every happiness, and assuredly could not occasion him any additional cause of sorrow.

At length wearied with thought, and sleep descending heavily upon her eyelids, she retired to bed, and quickly sunk to rest. She arose at an early hour in the morning, and descended to the breakfast-room. The marquess had not yet left his chamber, and as the morning was fine she walked from the house into the garden at the back of the chateau. The beauteous flowers just opening their silken bosoms, breathed their odoriferous perfume upon the air, and came refreshing to the senses of our heroine. Often here had she met Adolphe, and when her father was from home, they had given utterance to those vows that had gained such ascendency in their bosoms. Perhaps, ere long, she would have bid adieu to this spot for ever, and her father might not suffer her to enter again into his presence. But no— she could not believe that her father could ever come to the resolution to discard that child towards whom he had always evinced an affection approaching to adoration. Never could he view with any other sentiment than that of love, his fond, affectionate Laurette. She viewed the different plants with which the garden abounded with an irresistible feeling of melancholy. They had most of them been reared by the hand of her father, and every one of them recalled to her memory some tender reminiscence connected with him. Perhaps, ere long, she might not be suffered to contemplate them, and the heart of him who had reared them might become withered by care.

It had been arranged between Laurette and Adolphe, that after they had plighted their vows at the hymeneal altar, Laurette should return to the chateau and seize the first favourable opportunity that presented itself to disclose to him the secret, and solicit his forgiveness; but much as she trembled at the idea of being separated from her parent, Laurette almost repented having made such an agreement, doubting much whether she should be competent to the task, and shrinking from the idea of meeting the gaze of her father after having been thus guilty of her first act of disobedience towards him. Never, she felt convinced, could she so act the hypocrite, as not betray herself immediately; and she was in a state of torture and uncertainty in which way to act.

After wandering in the garden for more than an hour, she returned into the house, and there found her father awaiting her presence at the breakfast-table. He arose on her entrance, and embraced her with even more than his usual affection, and then leading her to a seat, he observed in a voice of tenderness—

" Thou hast risen early, my Laurette, and lookest pale; hast thou had a bad night's rest, or art thou ill, my dear child?"

"I have not slept well, dear father," replied our heroine, in a voice of tremulous emotion, " and when I did, dreams——"

" Dreams!" interrupted the marquess, with a faint smile; " oh, they are but the mere idle chimeras created by fancy to tantalize us in our sleeping moments, and deserve not a serious thought; for instance, my Laurette, I myself did dream last night that thou wert disobedient to me—that thou hadst disgraced thy fond father's name, and fled thy paternal roof, to throw thyself into the arms of a villain; thus, then, have I not unquestionable cause to treat dreams with contempt and incredulity; for I know that my fond, my gentle Laurette, could sooner suffer an awful death than deceive her doating old father, or wilfully give him cause for a single pang. But, heavens! my child! why do you turn so ghastly pale? You tremble! What ails thee?"

A deadly sickness came over Laurette as the marquess made use of the observtion we have mentioned, and it was with difficulty she could prevent herself from sinking on the floor. In vain she tried to speak for a few seconds; her tongue clave to the palate of her mouth, and as a sensation of indescribable anguish shot through her brain, she almost resolved at once to acknowledge her sentiments for Adolphe, and confess the plot they had formed; but her fear restrained her.

"What is the matter, my beloved Laurette?" repeated her father, with increased emotion; " why do you not answer me?"

" It is nothing, father," said our heroine,

in an agitated tone; "a sudden faintness came over me; but it will soon pass away. With your permission, I will return to the garden for a few minutes, and, probably, the air will revive me."

" Well—well, my child," said the marquess, affectionately, " e'en be it as thou wilt; but I am fearful that thou art not so well as thou wouldst appear to be; in spite of all my efforts, I cannot divest my mind of the dismal thoughts and presentiments that oppress it; and to add to my disquiet, business again compels me to leave thee to-day, Laurette. I will, however, return as early as I can; and I hope thou wilt be able to welcome me with thy usual buoyant smiles and roseate looks of health."

Laurette's emotion increased to an almost insupportable degree; and as she arose to go to the garden, her feelings so overpowered her, that she sunk back in the chair, and burst into tears.

" What means this, my dear child?" interrogated her father, with an expression of the utmost anxiety; " pray, tell me, Laurette; something more than usual must have occurred to occasion this."

" It is nothing—nothing," answered our heroine, again hastily drying up her tears, and endeavouring to conquer her emotions; " I am very weak and silly; but nay—nay, my dear father, a walk in the garden will restore me!"

With these words, Laurette threw her white arms fondly around the neck of the marquess, and kissed him fervently, then tearing herself away, scarcely venturing to look at him, and once more entered the garden.

She hastened to the alcove in which she was wont to sit for hours together, and from whence she could behold spread before her, many a rich and luxuriant parterre, and whose variegated sweets exhaled a fragrance which stole with rapture to the senses. Here, throwing herself upon a seat, she gave vent to the melancholy feeling that oppressed her heart, and bursting into tears exclaimed—

" Wretch, hypocrite, that I am, thus to act with duplicity towards one of the best, the most affectionate of parents! But it is not too late to retract! Shall I confess all, and implore his sanction to our love? But alas! of what avail would that be, when he has so peremptorily enjoined me never to mention the name of Adolphe even, and evinces such an utter aversion to him? And can I resign Adolphe? Oh, no—no; dearest youth, such is the ascendancy thou dost hold over my heart, that all other sentiments fade before it, and in spite of whatever the consequences may be, though the step I am about to take may bring the most terrible misery upon me, I feel convinced that I can bear it with fortitude, rather than resign De Floriville."

The noise of horses hoofs aroused her, and approaching the entrance of the alcove, from whence she could behold the garden gates, at that moment she saw her father on horseback pass by. He saw her; kissed his hand two or three times to her, in the most fervent and affectionate manner, and then rode on.

The agitation of Laurette when she saw him, became most intense, and again she was half inclined to hasten after him, implore him to return, and acknowledge the thoughts and designs which inhabited her bosom; but again the form of her lover presented itself to her imagination, and turning back, she once more resumed her seat, and gave herself up to the conflicting ideas that perplexed her mind.

Hour after hour passed away in this manner, and at length the time at which she had appointed to meet Adolphe, rapidly approached, and as it did, the emotions of our heroine became somewhat abated, and she longed for the moment to arrive, and the ceremony to be over, that her fate might at once be decided.

At length it wanted but a quarter of an hour to the appointed time, and that would be exhausted in reaching the place of assignation. Laurette had returned into the house, and having hastily thrown her cloak over her shoulders, she implored the protection of the blessed Virgin, and with trembling, but cautious steps, she quitted the chateau, unperceived by any of the domestics.

We will pass hastily over the scene that took place upon the meeting of Adolphe and Laurette. In spite of the horrors by which the former was continually haunted, he had so far recovered himself that he appeared not the least disconcerted, and met our heroine with a passionate embrace, and expression of love and adoration, which almost immediately had the effect of dissipating her anguish, and conquering her scruples. They left the vicinity of the chateau, and bent their way towards the Monastery of Saint L'Clair, where Adolphe had made arrangements with a priest of that order to perform the sacred rites. The holy father was at the place of meeting according to appointment; the ceremony was performed, the ceremony which indissolubly united them one to the other, and Laurette de Chamont became the bride of the murderer of his friend; the gamester—the profligate, Adolphe de Floriville!

It was with the utmost difficulty that Adolphe and his new made bride could tear themselves asunder after the holy rites had been solemnised; but, at length, fearful that her father might return before she did, and be alarmed at her absence, especially after the melancholy condition in which he had left her in the morning, Laurette tore herself reluctantly from his embraces, having fixed upon a spot in which they might daily meet, until she could find a fitting opportunity to make known to the marquess their secret marriage, and implore his forgiveness.

She found on reaching the chateau, that her father had not yet returned, a circumstance for which she was grateful, as it would give her some little time to endeavour

to regain her composure, so that she might meet him without giving him any cause to excite his suspicions. This, however, she found to be no easy task, and it was not without the most powerful and painful struggle with her feelings, that she was enabled in any way to accomplish it. At last, however, she did partially succeed, and shortly afterwards she heard her father's well-known knock at the door. And now, again, a deadly faintness came over her; her limbs trembled, and the courage she had previously acquired almost entirely forsook her. How could she meet that parent whose injunctions she had so recently violated; whose peace of mind she had, perhaps, destroyed for ever? Hearing his voice upon the stairs, however, she made a desperate effort, and with a forced calmness, hastened forth to meet him.

The marquess embraced his beauteous daughter with the most ardent affection; then suddenly withdrawing himself from her arms, he gazed at her intensely for a few seconds in silence, shook his head, and observed—

"Still pale—very pale, my child, and trembling; something, I am convinced, has happened to move thee thus! Come—come, Laurette, thou hast, I believe, never hitherto had a thought which thou wouldst wish to conceal from thy fond father; do not, therefore, now, my child, seek to deceive me."

"Deceive thee, father?" gasped forth Laurette, hanging her head, and the words almost choked her.

"Forgive me, Laurette," said the marquess; "my expression may have been too harsh; but—but what strange, what unaccountable feeling is this which comes over me, and which I find it impossible to conquer? Follow me, Laurette, follow me."

Laurette looked at her father a moment in trembling astonishment; he motioned her solemnly to follow him, and shuddering with doubt and apprehension she obeyed in silence.

The marquess led the way to the chamber in which was the portrait of her mother; and having closed the door, he laid his hand upon the arm of our heroine with an expressive gesture, and thus addressed her:—

"Laurette, thou hast, I believe, ever found thy father kind and indulgent? Studious of thy happiness, and scrupulous of anything which might cause thee the slightest anguish. Hast thou not, my child?"

"Oh, why ask me, my dear father?" ejaculated our heroine, in a tremulous voice, and with increased emotion; "thou hast ever been all that fond parent could be; alas! much more kind than I have deserved."

"Nay, my child, not so," returned the marquess: "thou hast well deserved it all; for never was a child more affectionate and dutiful than my Laurette. She could sooner die than by one act, one thought of disobedience, cause a pang in her poor old father's heart!"

"Father, for the love of the Blessed Virgin!" ejaculated Laurette, grasping at the back of a chair to support her trembling form, and a deadly chill falling upon her heart.

"Still this violent emotion, child," said her father, "what can it mean? Something must have happened; I never saw thee thus agitated before! Laurette – Laurette, do not conceal anything from me; I am certain that the dreadful forebodings that have racked my mind have not been entirely fallacious! Speak me, child; oh, speak to me, and ease the strange, the agonizing doubts that distract me!"

Laurette did endeavour to speak, but her violent agitation completely choked her utterance, and her tongue clave to the palate of her mouth. She had never before attempted to play the hypocrite, and she revolted from, and shuddered at the part she was acting. And now did repentance come too late, and she would willingly have made any sacrifice, could she but have recalled the past. She felt herself, as it were debased in the eyes of her father, and averted her face, unable to encounter the intense scrutiny of his gaze!

The marquess grasped her arm with more vehemence than he had done before, and in a voice rendered harsh by impatience and suspense, he exclaimed—

"Laurette, thou dost not speak; thou tremblest, and thy cheeks are blanched with terror; why dost thou not answer me? This is not like my Laurette."

"Nor is this like my father," said our heroine, in tones of forced composure; "thou didst never before doubt the truth of thy child!"

"I know it! I know it! But some accursed spell seems to have fallen upon me, and in spite of my wishes so to do, I cannot banish the suspicions from my mind, that——"

"Suspicions, father?"

"Ay, child, suspicions," replied the marquess; "strange doubts and apprehensions of I scarcely know what, have taken possession of my senses, and they combat my reason so powerfully, that it is unable to defeat them."

The marquess paused for a few seconds, and gazing earnestly upon the countenance of our heroine, sighed deeply, and seemed buried in profound and painful thought.

At length he drew her towards the place where the portrait of the late marchioness was concealed, and pulling back the sable curtain, he pointed solemnly towards it, and then in deep and impressive tones, ejaculated—

"Laurette, once more I direct thy attention to the resemblance of that sainted being, who bore thee, and who is now an inhabitant of Heaven; of her whose soul was unsullied as purity itself; kneel before it, child, and as thou valuest my love, and would invoke the Heavenly blessing of the spirit of thy mother, give utterance to the words that I shall dictate!"

"Oh, father, dear father, spare me—spare thy poor child, I entreat!" sobbed forth the terrified and conscience-stricken Laurette.

"Kneel, I say!" commanded the marquess, in accents approaching to fierceness.

Laurette sunk upon her knees, and her father, still directing her attention to the portrait, thus spoke, in a voice of increased solemnity—

"Swear by the spirit of her who bore thee, by all thine hopes of mercy here and hereafter, and by that Almighty power which rules over all, that thou hast never, and wilt never, under any circumstances, deceive me; that thou wilt never act without first consulting my will!"

Laurette sobbed aloud, but her feelings were so overpowered that not a syllable could escape her lips.

"Ah, thou dost hesitate, girl: thou refusest to take the oath? I will proceed, and thy silence I will receive as an admission of thy disobedience!"

"Father, father," shrieked our heroine, in frantic accents, and looking up in his face imploringly; "forbear—unless thou wouldst drive me mad!—This is cruel!"

"Swear by all Heaven's host, and as thou hopest to share in its glories," continued the marquess, regardless of her supplications, or the violent agitation she evinced, "swear that you will never marry any man of whom I do not approve, that——"

"Mercy! mercy!"

"Swear to hate, to despise, and avoid Adolphe de Floriville, as thou wouldst a pestilence!"

"This—this is too much," cried Laurette; "father, if thou wouldst not see thy child expire at thy feet, forbear to administer to her these fearful oaths!—I cannot—I dare not take them!"

"Dare not, girl?"

"I dare not!"

"Thou wilt not swear then to hate the son of my bitterest foe, Adolphe de Floriville?"

"Mercy!"

"Nay, thou shalt answer me!—Swear, I repeat, to hate, despise, and avoid Adolphe de Floriville, as thou wouldst a pestilence!"

"I cannot—I cannot!"

"Great God! surely my ears deceive me! Then, thou lovest Adolphe?"

"I do—I do!" answered the wretched girl, covering her face with her hands, and groaning with agony.

"Horror—horror!" gasped forth the marquess, striking his forehead, with an air of frenzy; "but, for my sake, thou wilt forget him, Laurette; thou wilt drive him from thine heart!"

"Oh, never—never!"

"Disobedient girl, do as I command thee, or the curse of——"

"Mercy—mercy!"

"Take the oath!"

"I must not; my duty forbids it!"

"Thy duty commands it: what meanest thou?"

"Father, dear father, would'st have me curse my *husband?*"

"Thine *husband!*" reiterated the marquess, in a hollow voice, and fixing upon Laurette a look, which seemed as if it would penetrate to her soul; "but, no—no; this is only cruel mockery; thou can'st not—thou wilt not repeat that dread assertion."

"Father, 'tis true," replied Laurette, solemnly, and in a voice of forced calmness; "I am now the bride of that Adolphe de Floriville thou hast commanded me to hate."

Had the whole wrath of offended Heaven at that moment have descended upon the head of the marquess, he could not have evinced greater horror than he did on this acknowledgment! An expression of madness took possession of his eyes, which became fixed upon the ghastly countenance of his still kneeling daughter, who, with clasped hands, was gazing up at him with looks of the most intense, the most agonized supplication; his limbs seemed as though they were turned into marble, and he stood statue-like and inanimate, while the complexion of his countenance became like that of a corpse! It was several minutes ere he could give utterance to a word; then, suddenly, in tones that were sufficient to strike horror to the heart of the distracted supplicant at his feet, he said—

"The bride of Adolphe de Floriville—my child—but, no—no, away, wretch! thou art no longer my child; thou hast done that which has divided our hearts for ever! Thou hast destroyed the peace of thy once fond father, and turned all his love to the most deadly loathing. Away to thine husband, and never more dare to enter my presence! From this moment I despise thee! discard thee! hate thee! curse thee!—yes, the heaviest malediction of a broken-hearted father light upon thee and the man to whom thou hast linked thy fate! May every sorrow and misfortune pursue thee!—mayest thou endure penury, misery, and want, without a friend near to pity or to assist thee!—may thy days be those of anguish, thy nights those of horror, as they assuredly will, when thou reflectest that thou hast given thine hand to *the hated son of thy mother's murderer!*"

"Father! father!" shrieked Laurette, clinging to his knees with the madness of despair. But he spurned her fiercely from him, and exclaiming—

"Wretch! wretch!" hastened from the room, and with an ejaculation of horror, Laurette sank insensible upon the floor.

She recovered, but to what feelings of horror! The dreadful curse of her father seemed still to vibrate in her ears, and to freeze her blood to ice. But gracious Heavens! surely the marquess could not have spoken the truth! Adolphe, her husband, the son of her mother's murderer! She looked up at the portrait of her who bore her, and at that moment it seemed to frown reproach upon her. She covered her face with her hands, and with a groan of indescribable agony averted her head.

"But why do I remain here?" she cried, "this is no longer my home; he hath disowned me, cursed me! But surely he will relent!—He will yet pardon his poor Laurette! I will away from hence, and at another time seek the presence and forgiveness of my father."

She was turning away from the spot, when suddenly she beheld a note lying on the table. She looked at it; the superscription was in the well-known hand-writing of her father, and was addressed to "Madame de Floriville." With frenzied haste she unfolded it, and half-blinded with tears, read the following words:—

"Wretched woman, learn the fate to which thou hast linked thyself. The monster who gave life to he who thou hast united, was once, as I believed, my friend—I made him my confident—I admitted him to my house—he was my constant companion. Business took me from my home for some time, and in that period the accursed villain dared to confess his loathsome passion to my angelic wife! I need not describe the return he met with; but his desires were the more inflamed. He watched his opportunity, and succeeded too well in obtaining forcible possession of that which no persuasion could have gained—the honour of my wife! Oh, God! my soul freezes with horror at the recollection! The monster escaped—I returned home to find my happiness blasted for ever, my wife dishonoured, and dying of a broken heart! She survived but to tell me the dreadful tale!"

"Oh, horror! horror!" exclaimed Laurette, unable to proceed further; and once more insensibility came to her relief.

CHAPTER VII.

THE WRETCHED HUT.—THE DISTRESSED MOTHER AND CHILD.

WE will now pass over a period of seven years, at which epoch, on a fine day in autumn, there were seated on benches outside *L'Auberge de Sirloin,* a number of persons, including the host Clauson, (who had purchased the business of its late proprietor, Barnard Swinton,) and Caleb, who had now become installed into the office of a gaoler of one of the *Conciergeries* of the district, an office for which his natural humanity but very ill-fitted him.

On another seat, apart from the rest, and shunned by them, sat a man in miserable, tattered apparel, and whose face exhibited all the effects of care and want; yet his features still showed proofs that they had once been handsome, and in spite of his emaciated form, there was an air of nobility in his demeanour particularly striking.

Sighing deeply, this miserable object

arose, and supporting himself on a staff, as he moved from the spot, he said to himself, in accents of the deepest melancholy—

"Now to my wretched hut, to witness the sufferings of my famishing wife and child ; to hear their cries for food, when I have none to give them, and gaze upon the scene of misery my guilt hath caused. Oh, Eugene, my murdered friend—murdered by these accursed hands,—awfully hath thy predictions been fulfilled ! Chamont, Chamont ! thy malediction hath fallen heavily upon thy daughter and her guilty husband. I—I—am very faint. Oh, for one draught of wine, one morsel to eat, to appease the ravenous fiend within me."

As the unfortunate Aholphe (for he, the once gay and fashionable, it was,) thus spoke, he arose, and walked feebly away.

"So," remarked Clauson, the host, "he's gone at last, and glad enough I am of it. That beggar is the most impudent varlet I ever met with. He walks in here every day, and sits himself down with as much effrontery as if he were the finest nobleman in the land. The rascal has even the impudence to ask me for wine and food, too."

"Ah, Monsieur Clauson," retuned Caleb, "you have no nateral feelings; you're a complete owl. Besides, if your nest is so well feathered now, who knows but that poor man's may have been feathered equally as well ?— you don't know what you may come to yourself."

"I dare say," said Clauson, "if his nest was ever so well feathered, it was his own improvidence that has left him now without a feather to fly with."

"Ah !" ejaculated Caleb, with a sigh, "it was not so when my poor father, honest Barnard Swinton, was landlord of this house ; no stray bird ever came to his cage, but there was always a hearty welcome for him. But you have no nateral feelings, I tell you again."

"Let me tell you, Master Caleb, that your father was an arrant fool for his pains. A fine profitable thing it would be for us hotel-keepers, indeed, to lodge and feed all the dirty, lazy, hungry vagrants that come begging to our doors. I am astonished to hear you, a gaoler, too, talk about natural feelings."

"Monsieur Clauson," replied Caleb, bristling up, "I am a man, with the nateral feelings of a man, and though I am a gaoler, I mean to say that I would hang myself if I thought I could ever forget to feel for an unfortunate fellow-creetur in distress."

"Well, well," returned Clauson, rather abashed, "a truce with this argument, and proceed with the story you were relating."

"Well, then," said Caleb, "you must know, as I was saying, it is just seven years ago since I sat up in this very room, waiting the return of Monsieur Eugene, and Monsieur de Floriville, who had put up here for some time. Well, I waited, and waited, and precious late it was ; but at last I heard a knock, and went to the door, and in rushed Monsieur Eugene, with a look of *destruction:* oh, such a look—I shall never forget it. So I thought he was ill, and asked him very politely in my usual gentlemanly manner, to take a glass of wine, just to cheer the cockles of his heart, as they say in England ; but, lor' bless you, he called me a boy, and saying something about *solemnitude* and death, away he ran and went to bed. Isn't that awful ?"

"Very," answered Clauson ; "but did he die ?"

"Yes," poor gentleman," said Caleb, "he committed *fell-in-the-sea* on himself. He was found in the morning weltering in his blood, with a dagger in his hand ; so that there could not be the least doubt but that he made away with himself. Poor young man ! he couldn't have had his nateral feelings about him at the time."

"But his friend, Monsieur Adolphe, what became of him ?"

"Why, to be sure he was in a sad way about it ; but still, I thought he did not seem to have the nateral feelings about him that he ought, and what was more strange than all, only a few days afterwards, he was married in a *clandecent* manner to Laurette, the daughter of the Marquess Chamont, although she had been betrothed to Eugene de Buoisson previously."

"That was strange."

"Yes, indeed it was, and a sorry match they made of it, a very sorry one for her poor lady-bird ; Adolphe turned out a sad wicked fellow, and gambled all their fortune away ; the marquess turned his back on them, and died soon afterwards broken hearted."

"And what became of Adolphe and his wife afterwards ?"

"Why, they lost home and everything, fled the neighbourhood, and have never been heard of since. But I must go, for it is getting late, and I have other business to attend to. Good-night, Clauson, and, I say, if the poor beggar should call again, see if you cannot muster a few nateral feelings, and relieve him ; you will never be a loaf the less in the cupboard for it, take my word. Good-night."

With these words, honest Caleb departed.

In a wretched hut, almost entirely destitute of furniture, and through the crevices of the wainscot of which the wind issued freely, the once beauteous Laurette, now pale, emaciated, and care-worn, stood watching by the side of a humble pallet, which was stretched in one corner of the miserable apartment, and on which reposed the form of a lovely boy, about six years of age. A stormy evening had succeeded a very fine day, and the thunder rolled awfully above, accompanied by vivid flashes of lightning, and fast descending torrents of rain.

Laurette advanced nearer to the couch of her child, and, leaning over him, in tones of the deepest melancholy, exclaimed—

" He sleeps; the poor little sufferer sleeps, calm and unruffled as the first blush of infancy, while I, his wretched mother, am doomed to watch over him with a frenzied eye and a bursting heart. Alas! how pale, how haggard he looks; how wasted his form, how wan his features. Hunger hath done its work. Wake not, my cherub boy; oh, slumber on, thy mother cannot bear to hear thee cry for food, and she, alas! hath none to give. Hark! how the storm rages, and my husband is still absent. Where can he be? Oh, how my heart sinks within me as I behold the ravages of care and want upon his once handsome brow. I see despair in his eye; it increases to madness and desperation, and I tremble every time he leaves our miserable hovel, lest, on his return, his conscience should be loaded with an additional crime. Oh, Adolphe! to what a state of wretchedness and destitution hath thine improvidence reduced us. My father, heavily, indeed, hath thy curse fallen upon us."

At this moment there was a knock at the door, and Laurette hastened to open it. It was Adolphe, who, exhausted with walking and anxiety, sank into a chair. Laurette approached him affectionately, and in accents of melancholy sweetness, said—

" Oh, Adolphe, I am so glad thou hast returned; but thou art wet, and, alas! I have no fire to dry thy tattered garments."

" I—I—I am cold—perishing—wretched," uttered Adolphe.

" Alas!" ejaculated Laurette, " must we still linger in this misery?"

" Still linger—still suffer—ay, till death put an end to it. Laurette, thy father's curse has been well fulfilled. In vain this day have I wondered the city begging for charity: yes, I, Adolphe de Floriville, asking charity—a morsel of bread for my starving wife and child! The rich mocked my supplications; the poor had not the power to relieve me. Oh, Laurette, starvation is a dreadful death."

" Adolphe," returned Laurette, in a voice of deep emotion, " I care not for myself, but to see thee suffer, and our poor child, it drives me to madness. This morning I offered him the last morsel of food our hut afforded, when a tear trickled down the poor starving boy's cheek, and spurning the bread from him, with a look that I shall never forget, he cried, ' Mamma's hungry; Henri cannot eat, and see poor mamma starve.' "

" No more, no more," groaned Adolphe; " you rack me."

" Nay, Adolphe, be calm, and trust in that Power which, sooner or later, will look down upon us with mercy,"

" Mercy!" repeated de Floriville, with a shudder; " oh, dare a wretch like I am hope for mercy? No, no, 'tis past. A curse, a damning curse, is upon me and mine; a spell from which we cannot escape; the curse of friendship betrayed; of virtue deceived; of blood——"

" Blood!" gasped forth Laurette. " Oh,

Adolphe, thy mind wanders. Be composed, and let us retire to rest. Who knows but the morning may bring us happiness? Thy brother, Françoise, must, ere this, have received thy letter, and I know his generous nature so well, that I am certain he will lose no time in hastening to our relief."

" No, no," answered Adolphe, in despairing tones; " thou wouldst quiet me with futile hopes. Oh, Heaven! and is this scene of misery the work of my hands? Laurette, dost thou not hate me?'

" Hate thee, Adolphe? This is cruel; 'tis——"

" But thou must hate me," interrupted her husband, impatiently, " abhor me; fly my presence—shun the path I tread, for pestilence is in it—the curse of a supernatural being, that withers all in its way. Fly me, Laurette: I am a wretch—a monster—the deceiver of my friend—the murderer——"

" The murderer!" cried Laurette, in a voice of the utmost terror.

" My frenzy will betray me," muttered Adolphe to himself; then turning to Laurette, he added aloud—" The murderer of thy father; am I not, Laurette? Did not my union with thee, and my intemperance, break the good old man's heart? Am I not the worst of murderers? Art thou not doomed to a lingering, painful death, through my crimes? Is not my boy, my Henri, sinking into the grave, the victim of care and hunger? And does not each pallid hue that blanches his once rosy cheek proclaim his father a murderer? I shall go mad; my heart will burst; but this pistol shall terminate all!"

As de Floriville thus spoke, he suddenly took a pistol from his bosom, and presenting it at his head, was about to discharge the contents, when Laurette screamed, and rushing forward, arrested his arm, and the pistol was fired off in the air.

" Horror, wretched man," she cried; " what would thy desperate hand perpetrate?"

The report of the pistol awoke the little Henri, who arose from the couch, and running to his father, looked up affectionately in his face, as he said—

" Oh, papa! I am so glad you have come back, for mamma and I were so hungry, and you have brought us food, haven't you?"

" My poor little innocent," said Laurette, weeping, and kissing Henri passionately. " Oh, Adolphe, look upon our child, and shudder at the act thou wouldst have committed."

" Torture me not, Laurette," groaned Adolphe, " my brain is on fire—I am choking. My poor boy shall have food, even though his wretched parent should die in procuring it for him. Let go thine hand, Laurette; I am desperate."

" Adolphe! for the love of Heaven, what wouldst thou do?"

" Procure my child food. Force from the purses of the rich and mercenary that which they refused to my prayers and entreaties. Nay, thou shalt not hold me from my purpose. Food for my boy!—Off!—off!—Food for my boy!"

Thus crying frantically, he tore himself away from the hold of Laurette, and rushed from the hut.

"Oh, Adolphe — my husband. Stay! No—he is gone. Gracious Powers! what deed of horror may he not perpetrate in his present state of mind? I will follow him. Come, my dear child, thy father needs our presence to save him from destruction."

"Oh, come, then, dear mamma, for I am not cold now," said Henri; "let us go and save papa, for I should die if he were lost, that I should."

"Dear, dear boy," ejaculated Laurette; "yes, we will hasten to save thine unhappy parent, or perish with him."

With these words, Laurette took the hand of the boy, and, leaving the hut, followed Adolphe into the forest, not doubting but that he had pursued that way.

The storm raged with increased violence as Adolphe, with the wild air of a maniac, and almost unconscious of what he was doing, entered the gloomy forest. Suddenly he paused, and looking round him, he exclaimed—

"Yes, it shall be done. I cannot gaze upon the pallid features of my famishing wife and child any longer with indifference, knowing, too, that it is my villany which hath brought them to it. Why should such a wretch as I am wish to live? Am I not an assassin, with the cure of my victim upon me; sleeping or walking haunted by his bleeding form and reproachful eye; hourly feeling his deadly grasp upon me, as when, in the last convulsive pangs of death, he clutched my throat, and breathed upon me his withering malediction? Even now I feel his icy touch; it freezes me. Oh, misery refined! Oh, torment unendurable! Hell itself can have no greater torments than those I feel: but this night shall end them all. I cannot be a greater wretch than I now am: and since I have made them miserable by my former guilt, I will, in spite of everything, hazard my soul's eternal welfare to save them from their present horrors, Hark! I hear footsteps approaching this way. Oh, grant that the traveller may quietly yield to my demands, or another murder will be added to the dark catalogue of my crimes. Hist! he comes!"

As he thus spoke, he hid himself among a cluster of trees, and watched the traveller's approach. In a few seconds he reached the spot. He was a tall man, enveloped in a large mantle, and the darkness rendered his features indistinguishable.

"It is a dreadful night," said the stranger, "and the gloom of this forest is awful. I shall be glad when my journey is ended; however, let me push on my way, for I am anxious to reach the place of my destination, where my presence is so urgent."

The traveller now moved on, when Adolphe, wound up to a pitch of desperation, started from the place of his retreat, and stepping into his path, exclaimed—

"Hold!"

"Who art thou, and why dost thou obstruct my path?" demanded the traveller.

"I am a wretched, desperate man, who seeketh thy gold, and will have it at all hazards," answered Adolphe.

"Villain! midnight robber! let me pass, or——"

He was about to draw his sword from its scabbard, when Adolphe presented his pistol at his head, and gave utterance to the following words in a determined tone—

"Nay, then, headstrong, wretched man, since thou madly refuseth me, die!"

As he spoke he fired at the traveller, who, with a deep groan, fell to the earth. Adolphe rushed to his unfortunate victim, and as he did so, the latter ejaculated, in accents of agony—

"Alas, unfortunate Françoise!—thou—thou art slain. Oh, who will now assist thy poor brother?"

"Horror! horror!" groaned Adolphe, dropping on his knees by the side of the murdered man, and looking more narrowly into his countenance; "did I—could I hear right? Oh, speak, wretched stranger, and let me know the extent of my guilt—didst thou not say thy name was——"

"Françoise de Floriville!" uttered the dying man, in faint voice.

"Françoise de Floriville!" cried Adolphe, in a voice of indescribable agony. "Powers of darkness! I have then completed my bloody work Françoise! Françoise! oh, look up, and with thy dying breath curse thy murderer—I, thy brother—Adolphe de Floriville!"

"My brother!" ejaculated Françoise, looking up into the assassin's face with an expression which could never be forgot. "Oh, God! this is too much! But—but I pardon thee, and may Heaven do so likewise."

These were the last words the unfortunate Françoise spoke; he fixed his eyes stedfastly on the countenance of the assassin, and with a groan, fell backward and expired.

Adolphe gazed upon the corpse of his murdered brother for a few moments in stupified horror; then, in a voice of the most insupportable agony, he said—

"'Tis done—the measure of my crime is full. Hell hath now, indeed, a proper victim! My brother! ha! ha! ha!"

The unhappy, guilty wretch laughed hysterically, and as he did so, the spirit of Eugene arose from the earth before his eyes, and grasping his throat with one hand, with the other pointed to the corpse of the murdered Françoise with a ghastly expression of exultation.

"Dread phantom!" cried Adolphe, struggling in the icy grasp of the spectre, "art thou again here? Hast thou come to exult in the completion of thy curse? Off—off! Oh mercy! Spare me!"

Overcome with the power of his feelings, Adolphe fell from the grasp of the spectre, in a state of insensibility, to the earth : and at that moment Laurette and Henri reached the fatal spot.

"Come, my poor child," said Laurette, "Let us hasten, or thy father will be lost to us for ever."

The little Henri ran on a few paces before his mother, and suddenly his eyes encountered the prostrate form of his father, and the body of the murdered man.

"Oh, see here, dearest mamma," said the child, pointing to the objects he had beheld ; "here is poor father asleep, and a man lying by the side of him all covered with blood !"

"Blood! blood!" exclaimed Laurette, with the utmost terror, and starting wildly forward. "Gracious Heaven! what do I behold? Murder hath been here perpetrated. Adolphe—husband, arouse thee! Rash man, what hast thou done?"

At that moment Adolphe did recover, and starting to his feet, looked wildly around him, and in a voice of the deepest horror, exclaimed—

"Is he gone? I do not feel his cold and clammy grasp! I do not see his filmy eyes; say, has he gone? Ah! Laurette—my wife and my child—have ye then come to be witnesses of my guilt?"

"Oh, for the love of Heaven!" supplicated Laurette, "quiet the horrible apprehensions that distract my mind. Tell me, whose accursed hand hath done this dreadful deed?"

"'Twas mine—'twas mine!" groaned the assassin ; "my hand struck the d—d blow—my hand deprived my brother of life !"

"Thy brother!" screamed Laurette ; "oh, horror! horror!—wretched man, thou art lost—thou art ruined for ever! But hark! some one is coming this way ; thou wilt be discovered. Oh, I cannot bear to see thee dragged to prison! Fly—fly while thou hast yet time."

"And would'st thou save from the retributive hands of justice a monster like me? No, no—leave me to my fate. I merit death, and will not flee from it."

"Oh, Adolphe!" ejaculated Laurette, "think of the boy—of me. Come, come ; nay, I will force thee hence."

Thus speaking, Laurette frantically seized her guilty husband by the arm, and was forcing him away, when several voices smote her ears, and the next moment three or four villagers came up to the spot, one of them carrying a lantern.

"It is too late," groaned Laurette ; "we are lost—we are lost!"

"Lost," said one of the men ; "ay, this forest is a very likely place for persons to lose themselves in, dark as it is ; but—who are you ?"

"Oh, we—we—" faltered out Laurette, in tones of confusion.

"Oh, we—we—" mimicked the man ; "she

seems rather bewildered—let us see who they really are, for this forest does not, at all times, own the most respectable tenants."

Without any more ceremony, the man thrust his lantern into the faces of Adolphe and Laurette, and started back, exclaiming—

"Ah! it is the beggar and his wife ; they have been after no good at this time of night."

"There has been foul play here," cried another of the men ; "see, here is the lifeless body of a man, weltering in his blood !"

"Secure the murderers!" cried the others, in a breath : and Adolphe and Laurette in an instant were seized and dragged away, amid the shrieks and tears of their unfortunate child.

CHAPTER VIII.

THE DUNGEON.—THE WIFE.—THE ESCAPE.

THE day of trial was over ; Laurette had been acquainted of the horrible crime with which she and her husband were charged ; and Adolphe, being found guilty, was condemned to an ignominious death. The wretched culprit was seated at a small table in his gloomy dungeon, on which a lamp was placed, which emitted but a faint ray. His face was deadly pale, and his form bent with care.

"But twelve hours more," he soliloquised, "and my career of crime and bloodshed will be terminated by an ignominious death!—But twelve hours more, and thousands of spectators will gaze upon the just fate of the murderer, Adolphe de Floriville—exult in his tortures, and mock his agony! They will shudder as they repeat the dark catalogue of his crimes. His friend betrayed—beggared—murdered!—an innocent girl deluded—her fortune squandered—her father's heart broken—and herself and her child left unprovided in the wide world, for the finger of scorn and opprobrium to point at!—Ah! who's there?"

"It is only I, Caleb Swinton," said the gaoler, entering the dungeon.

"My gaoler!" said Adolphe, with a look of scorn.

"Ah, Monsieur, you need not be so hard upon me," replied Caleb ; "if I am a gaoler, I am possessed of nateral feelings, and I am sorry for you. I know how sweet liberty is, from the cock-sparrow to the canary, and——"

"Leave me to myself," said Adolphe, sternly, and with impatience.

"Oh, no, Monsieur de Floriville, I shall do no such thing," said Caleb. "I can't help my nateral feelings, and that's all about it. But hear me—I am come to save you."

"To save me! Vain boast! Do not mock me."

"Indeed, it is no vain boast though," remarked Caleb ; "but speak low, for there may be spies at hand, and should we be overheard, my wings would be clipped to a certainty, and that would spoil both our flying. Listen—I have made every arrangement with your wife, and she will be here presently in disguise. She will bring with her a large cloak, in which you can conceal yourselves, and pass out of the prison as one person. I shall have the letting of you both out, and I shall take the liberty of letting myself out afterwards, to avoid the trouble of answering any impertinent questions. I have saved a good round sum of money, to which you are welcome; it will carry you to some foreign country, and establish you in some way of business; and if you will let me follow you in the capacity of your servant, I shall be as happy as the birds on Valentine's Day."

"I thank thee, my good friend, for thy generous wishes," said Adolphe, "but I will not avail myself of them. I am tired of life. My crimes have rendered me unworthy of existence: I court death as the only atonement I can make. As for my wife, thinkest thou I would degrade her noble virtue by re-uniting her to an assassin? Never! Her judges were convinced of her innocence on her trial, and it is a sufficient happiness for me to know that she will not suffer for the dreadful crime which my hand alone perpetrated."

"Ah, Monsieur Adolphe!" said Caleb, "you cannot have your natural feelings about you, or you wouldn't talk in that way. Bless your soul! death is a very dangerous experiment, and there is not one in a million that ever gets over it. Be advised by me—think of your poor wife and your little boy, who—bless his heart!—is so pretty and so innocent, and talks as sensible as a magpie. But I must go, for I dare say your wife is at the gate by this time. Oh, dear! what a lucky fellow I was to be made a gaoler, when I can indulge my natural feelings by assisting a poor fellow-creetur in distress!"

"Poor fellow, thine is a mistaken humanity—a wretch like me deserves not pity," observed Adolphe, as Caleb quitted the dungeon. "Liberty! who talks to me of it, while I am fettered with a gnawing, bloodstained conscience? There is mockery in the word! I will spurn the gift—hell cannot have greater torments than those I endure here. But a few hours since, the spectre of Françoise glared upon me; but a few hours since, the fleshless hand of the murdered Eugene grasped my throat, while his sepulchral voice thundered curses in mine ears. Oh, I cannot suffer this! Fly swift ye hours, in mercy to a wretch whose greatest happiness is in the prospect of death."

Thus speaking, the unfortunate Adolphe groaned aloud with mental anguish, and clasped his burning temples. He was aroused by a gentle voice, and, raising his eyes towards the speaker, he beheld Laurette, disguised in a large cloak, and accompanied by Caleb.

"My husband! my unfortunate Adolphe!" she exclaimed, rushing frantically into Adolphe's arms. He drew himself back with a shudder of horror, and looking upon her with an expression of the utmost affection and remorse, ejaculated—

"Embrace me not thus—there is contamination in my touch;—a heartless wretch like me, must not come in collision with purity and innocence such as thine. Nay—nay, do not cling to me—I cannot bear it."

"Oh, Adolphe," sobbed his unhappy wife, "guilty as thou art, still do I love thee with all the strength of woman's most ardent fondness! Live, live to repent—to make atonement. Live for my sake—for the sake of our poor child."

"Ah, Monsieur Adolphe," interposed Caleb, "do muster up your natural feelings, and comply with the wishes of your poor wife. Your little son is awaiting you in the forest; the coast is quite clear; I hold the keys which open to liberty—then do not hesitate."

"Oh, for mercy's sake," implored the distracted Laurette, sinking on her knees, and clinging wildly to him; "here, on my knees, Adolphe, I implore thee! Oh, I cannot bear to see thee thus! Cast from thee these hated fetters!—think of our boy—he will be fatherless—the object of future infamy and scorn. He will be motherless; for too surely, too fatally do I think that I could not survive thy ignominious death! Do not obstinately refuse my prayers, my tears, my supplications."

"Why wouldst thou have me live, Laurette," demanded her husband, in a hollow tone, "to endure an earthly hell?"

"Oh, no," returned Laurette, fervently, "to repent—to seek forgiveness. I will toil for thee—do everything to make thee happy; only live to be a father to our child."

"Oh, torture, torture most exquisite," groaned De Floriville; "Laurette, thy tears unman me; I——I——"

"But thou wilt consent? Oh, yes, I see thou wilt! Bless thee—bless thee for this!"

"My poor child!—my helpless boy!" ejaculated Adolphe, with the most poignant emotion; "Laurette, I will consent to follow you; for my child—for thee—I will yet live."

"Oh, happiness supreme!" cried the devoted wife: "but come, my husband, do not delay; here, beneath this ample mantle we can both conceal our persons. Hark! methinks I hear footsteps approaching! Oh, Heaven, hasten, or all will be lost!"

"But these fetters?"

"I will instantly release you from them," said Caleb; "I have the means."

Caleb immediately unlocked the fetters, and De Floriville cast them hastily from him.

"There," said the humane gaoler, when he had so done, "now then for the cloak; embrace your wife, Monsieur De Floriville, and I will throw it over you."

Adolphe placed his arm round the waist of Laurette, and Caleb threw the mantle over their persons, so as to make it appear as if there-were only one underneath it.

"There you are," said he, "as snug as two birds in a nest. If this be not carrying two faces under one hat, at any rate, it is concealing two persons under one mantle. Now then, be silent ; walk cautiously and follow me ; I will rejoin ye in the forest."

Adolphe and Laurette moved cautiously towards the door of the dungeon, which having reached, Caleb put his head outside, and said, in a voice loud enough for any persons to hear who might happen to be listening—

"Now, Madame, it is time for you to depart, the prisoner must be left alone. Be cautious, all is safe," he added in an under tone to Adolphe and his wife.

Thus speaking, Caleb preceded them out of the dungeon, and having seen them safely out of the prison, he watched his opportunity, and departed himself, resolved to bid adieu to his office of gaoler, and to France for ever.

They reached the forest in safety, and there found the young Henri waiting on the spot he had been instructed to be ready to receive them.

"I feel faint and exhausted," observed Adolphe to his wife, pausing, and leaning against the trunk of a tree ; "and from the noise which we lately heard proceeding from the city, I feel almost certain that my flight has been discovered. If so, escape is impossible, nor do I wish it, for I have justly forfeited my life to the offended laws of my country, and why should I thus sport with a fate which is inevitable ?"

"Oh, do not hesitate thus, when thou standest on the brink of destruction," supplicated Laurette, in accents of the most intense agony ; "alas! Adolphe, guilty as thou art, and hateful as life may be to thee, my heart sinks with horror at the bare thoughts of thee perishing upon a scaffold! Oh, do not delay—if we can gain the deep recesses of the forest, we can secret ourselves until it may be safe to venture abroad. Come—come, as thou hopest for mercy! See, our poor boy pleads for me ; I know thou canst not resist his prayers."

"Oh, papa," cried the sweet child, looking up imploringly in his face, "do, pray make haste ; for should you delay, the naughty men will again put you in that frightful black hole, and I'm sure I should break my heart if they were to do that—that I should."

"Dear – dear child!" cried Laurette, hugging Henri to her heart, and kissing him repeatedly ; "Adolphe, canst thou turn a deaf ear to this innocent petitioner ?"

"Laurette—Laurette, rack me not or I shall go mad ; oh, I can endure anything but thy love—thy tenderness. Thou knowest me not, or thou must hate, loathe, abandon me. True, thou knowest me for a fratricide —a libertine - a gamester - a swindler! But thou hast yet to know me for the betrayer of my hapless friend, Eugene de Buoisson, who loved thee sincerely, and who alone was made hateful to thee by my accursed artifices. Yes, Laurette, I purchased thy love at the expense of honour, and sealed the compact in the blood of my unfortunate friend, Eugene de Buoisson!"

"Horror! horror!" gasped forth Laurette ; "thou canst not mean what thou sayest ; trouble hath turned thy brain."

"Alas! no ; thou judgest too kindly of me, Laurette ; but thou shalt know the whole of my dark career, that thou mayst hate me, as I merit. Laurette, thou seest in me the murderer of Eugene de Buoisson, as well as my brother ; ah! thou mayst, indeed, start ; it was a cruel deed, and dearly have I suffered for it. Laurette, when the purple stream of life was fast flowing from the gaping wound I had inflicted in the bosom of Eugene, and the mist of death was fast gathering in his eyes, in dying agony he grasped me, and breathed in mine ears a damning, withering curse, that, till death, his awful shade should ever meet my gaze—till death, his clammy grasp should be upon me."

"Oh, no more, no more!—I cannot bear it!"

"Ah! dost thou, then, shrink from the bare recital of horrors that I endure in reality? And yet thou wouldst prolong the life of such a wretch as I am. Oh, could I give utterance to one half the terrors I daily, nightly endure, thou wouldst, thou must view me with horror and detestation. The bare recital would freeze thy heart. The phantom of my murdered victim—butchered by me is cold blood—is constantly present to mine eyes ; I cannot shut him out from my sight—I cannot close mine ears to his dreadful maledictions. His icy grasp is ever on me! Ah! see, he is there! He approaches me! Laurette—Laurette, do not let him come near me! Thou art pure and innocent, unless thou hast received contamination by being connected with a monster like me. See, he mocks me ; he laughs at me! Laurette, interpose between me and that ghastly form! Ah, the grasp of death!"

"Adolphe—husband!" cried Laurette, in frantic accents, "to what a tale of horror have I been listening! Wretched, guilty man ; but yet thou art my husband ; the father of my child ; and shall I then—— Hark! I hear footsteps! They approach this way. Oh, hasten, or we are lost."

"No—no, I will go no farther," replied De Floriville ; "do not seek to persuade me ; abandon me, Laurette, to my fate, for had I not better die by the guns of the soldiers than on a scaffold? Ah! they come ; now to meet my fate boldly. They will not, dare not harm thee, Laurette ; and in that certainty, I can die content."

"Oh, be not rash," supplicated his unhappy wife ; "do not rush madly to destruction! But 'tis too late ; they are here. No, Heaven, I thank thee, it is our friend, Caleb."

It was, indeed, honest Caleb Swinton, who had been running until he was in a breathless state of trepidation.

"Oh dear!" said Caleb; "I am afraid it is all up with us. The whole place is up in *arms*, and if we do not make pretty good use of our *legs*, we shall be netted again as neatly as any poor birds ever were."

"No matter," said Adolphe, calmly. "I am resolved to meet my fate."

"Meet your fate!" reiterated Caleb.— "Pooh—nonsense! Only consider how ridiculous both you and I would look, with about fifty bullets through our unhappy carcases! I fancy that would be the way to touch my nateral feelings, and yours too. Now do let me persuade you. Here is money—a good round sum, too: take it—I have plenty without it. And now, if we can only penetrate further into the forest, we may find plenty of places of concealment; and when our enemies have a little abated in the vigilance of their pursuit, we can make our way to the seacoast, and be off to England as quick as carrier pigeons."

"Thanks, thanks, good Caleb," said Laurette, earnestly: "a thousand thanks for thy kindness to we poor unfortunates!"

"Oh, I want no thanks," answered the former: "my nateral feelings prompt me to endeavour to do a good turn to every one. But pray help me to persuade your husband."

Laurette once more fixed her eyes upon the countenance of her husband, with an expression that penetrated deep to his soul; and after a moment or two of great mental agony, he exclaimed—

"Well, well—do with me as thou wilt, for I feel assured it will not be for long."

"There, now you've got your nateral feelings about you again," said Caleb. "I am so glad of it. But ah! Ah! if I mistake not, I see muskets glittering among the trees yonder! The soldiers who are sent in pursuit are close at hand! Oh dear—oh dear! do make haste! Come this way!"

With these words, the kind-hearted Caleb, assisted by Laurette, urged Adolphe away from the spot, and had scarcely done so a minute, when the soldiers arrived at the place they had just quitted

"I am certain the fugitives have shaped their course this way," observed the officer who led them on. "They are doubtless making for the deep recesses of the forest. We must lose no time, and we may probably overtake them.—Proceed!"

The soldiers obeyed this command, and immediately pursued the same course that Adolphe and the others had taken.

Caleb found it a more difficult task to urge De Floriville on than he had anticipated; and when he heard the soldiers close upon their heels his fears overcame his humanity, and he scampered off as fast as his legs could carry him, not stopping even to take breath, until he found himself in a wild glen, where a cataract roared and gushed with terrific fury. This cataract was crossed by a rustic bridge, formed out of the trunks of trees, and altogether the place had a singularly picturesque and romantic appearance.

"That foolish Adolphe," said Caleb, pausing a minute to recover himself—"that foolish Adolphe will be retaken to a certainty. The soldiers must now be within gun-shot of him; and there he loiters, with as much indifference as if it were famous sport to be shot at. However, self-preservation is the first law of natur, so I'll make the best of my way to England by the first ship I can meet with, and turn bird-fancier again; for, after all, nothing suits my nateral feelings so well as the *hanimal* and *wegetable* world!"

Caleb vanished instanter as he spoke, and directly afterwards Laurette, her wretched husband, and Henri, entered the glen.

"Alas!" sobbed forth Laurette, "nothing now can save us! Even now the footsteps of our pursuers sound in mine ears! Oh! Adolphe, thine obstinacy hath ruined us!"

"I know it all," returned De Floriville, with a groan. "Reproach me as thou wilt; I am a villain unworthy of thy solicitude. Let me not involve thee in the destruction which awaits me. Here, take this money, and escape while there is yet time."

"Oh, no! I cannot—will not!" answered the deeply agonised wife. "If thou art resolved to meet our pursuers, I will be thy companion, and, with our child, perish with thee!"

At this moment the voices of the soldiers where heard close at hand.

"Hark!" ejaculated Adolphe. "They come! My fate is at hand! Laurette—Laurette, away!"

"Never, never! Oh! Adolphe—my husband!" cried the devoted woman, throwing herself into his arms, while the little Henri clasped his father's knees, and looked up in his face with the mast intense anguish.

"Laurette, let go thine hold, I say!" exclaimed Adolphe, struggling violently to escape from the embraces of his wife. "My hour is come, and thus do I escape an ignominious death!"

Thus speaking, the wretched man burst from her hold; and darting wildly up the rocky eminence, down which the cataract rushed, he stood on the narrow bridge, ready to plunge in.

"Adolphe, Adolphe!" screamed Laurette. "Forbear, for the love of Heaven!"

"Hold, woman!" cried the officer? "thou art our prisoner!"

"Mercy! mercy!" cried Laurette, sinking on her knees, while Henri followed her example: "spare my husband!"

"Ah!" exclaimed the officer, as his eyes encountered the form of Adolphe. "Behold! yonder is our prisoner!"

"Oh! pray—pray do not kill my poor papa!" implored Henri.

"Adolphe de Floriville," said the officer, "thou art our prisoner. "Surrender, or we must fire!"

"Yield!" exclaimed Adolphe. "What!

to die upon a scaffold? Never! Rather will I perish here than in the presence of a scoffing multitude!—Fire!"

"Die, then, murderer! Soldiers, present!"

"Oh! no - no - no! Mercy! mercy!— For the wife—the child!" screamed Laurette.

"Soldiers, do your duty!"

The men presented their fire-arms towards Adolphe, who stood with folded arms upon the bridge, and were about to fire, when Laurette, wound up to a pitch of perfect frenzy, seized Henri in her arms, and rushing heroically before them, exclaimed—

"Then let thy murderous hands also slay the wretched wife and offspring thou wouldst bereave!"

The soldiers dropped their arms, thunder-struck and apparently paralysed.

Adolphe gazed calmly on for an instant; then, with a laugh of scorn, he cried—

"Myrmidons of the law, behold—thus do I escape ye!"

He was about to leap from the bridge into the roaring cataract, when, at that moment, a loud peal of thunder shook the air, and there appeared by his side a shadowy form, which stretched forth its hand, and grasped his throat, bending his body over the edge of the cliff. Laurette gazed on this awful sight but an instant; then, shrieking hysterically, she fell into the arms of the officer.

"Save me—save me!" cried the murderer, in an awful voice; "the Death Grasp is on me now!'

The next instant he fell into the terrific cataract; loud peals of thunder again shook the air, and the spectre vanished.

CHAPTER IX.

THE DARK LADY OF THE HALL.—THE MYS-TERIOUS STRANGER.

WE will now pass over another period of seven years, at which epoch there was a comfortable hostelrie situated in a village near London, and known by the sign of "The Traveller's Rest." This same hostelrie was kept by as honest a fellow as England could boast of, and possessing a heart as brimful of humanity as he invariably filled his own tankards. Of this fact, we dare say our readers will not entertain a doubt, when we inform them that the worthy host of whom we are writing, was none other than Master Caleb Swinton, now sobered down into the steady, sedate, married man, with as comely a wife as any need wish to have, and two lovely little *fac similes* of himself and partner, yclept a son and daughter.

Caleb Swinton had been proprietor of "The Traveller's Rest" for about five years, having failed in his bird-fancying business, and during that period he had been a thriving man, and was rapidly accumulating a fortune; his house being the best attended of any for many miles around, affording, as it did, "good accommodation for man and beast." By what means he raised the money to get into his house after his failure, will presently be seen. It was night, a fine night in autumn, and Caleb was seated in his private parlour, in company with his wife, Mabel, and their two little children, and busily engaged in conversation, while ever and anon he paid the most friendly visits to the foaming tankard of ale which stood before him; a beverage for which his house was particularly celebrated; and if anything could be judged from appearances, fine fattening drink it was, for Master Caleb had become as corpulent as one of his own butts, and as red in the face as the cheerful fire which in winter always filled the grate in the parlour of the tavern.

"I tell thee what it is, Caleb," said Mabel (whose only fault was that which the generality of her sex possess, namely, curiosity,) "I tell thee what it is; that is the only point upon which thou and I always disagree."

"And it strikes me, my dear Mabel," replied her husband calmly, and smiling kindly in her face, "it strikes me very forcibly, that we always shall. My poor father, of blessed memory, and my late mother, afforded me a sufficient proof that unless a man and woman keep their proper places, there can be no happiness in the matrimonal state."

"Caleb," returned Mabel, "a man should have no secrets from his wife.".

"If a man does not wish to let all the world know his business, he will never make a confident of his wife, Mabel," retorted her husband. "Now, now, do not be cross; thou art the best little woman in all Christendom, excepting one fault which thou possessest."

"And what is that, pray?"

"Well, thou art so confoundedly inquisitive."

"Well, I must admit that, in respect to that failing, if it be one, Caleb, I am a true woman, every inch of me; but I think thou wilt not do me the injustice to suppose that I cannot keep a secret."

"What! a true woman, and keep a secret? Beshrew me, wife, an' I could make thee prove thy assertions, thou wouldst mnke my fortune, for thou wouldst be accounted one of the wonders of the world!"

"Well, well," laughed Mabel, good-humouredly, "there may be some truth in thine observations; but trust me, if the happiness and interest of any person depended on my secrecy, not a syllable should fall from my lips; no, I would die first. But it's no use your talking; I will tease the life out of you, until you tell me all about this mysterious Dark Lady of the Hall, as she is called; for I am certain you are acquainted with her history, and who she is. Why, when you failed in business, who was it lent you money to purchase this house, and start you in the world again?"

" The Dark Lady of the Hall," was the laconic reply,

" And who is it that has befriended us ever since ?" demanded Mabel.

" The Dark Lady of the Hall."

" Who is it that benevolently relieves the wants of the poor in the neighbourhood, and is as remarkable for her Christian charity, as she is for her mysterious manners ?"

" The Dark Lady of the Hall."

" True, the Dark Lady of the Hall; and now, pray, who is the Dark Lady of the Hall ?"

" Ha !" said her husband, archly, and winking his right eye, " that's the very question, and one that I must decline answering."

" What a provoking man thou art, Caleb," returned Mabel, angrily. " Here am I absolutely dying to become acquainted with every particular, and thou wilt not gratify me, although I faithfully promise thee that not a sentence shall ever again pass my lips. Here is a mysterious lady, whom nobody knows, comes from no one knows where, and with her son, that handsome boy, takes up her residence in the old Hall, which had been deserted for so many years before. She always dresses in black, sees no company, and leads the life of a recluse; at the same time the many munificent acts of benevolence she performs plainly shows that she must be immensely rich, or she never could do it. I am on thorns to be made acquainted with her history; all the world is on thorns to be made acquainted with her history ; thou knowest all about it, and yet thou art so inexorable as to refuse to make thy affectionate, kind, indulgent wife, and all the world, acquainted with it."

" That's where it is, Mabel," returned Caleb. " I do decline letting my affectionate, kind, indulgent wife know anything about it, because I am fearful she would make all the world acquainted with it."

" Caleb, on the word of a woman—on my honour—on my veracity—(what else shall I say ?)—I solemnly promise that I will do no such thing."

" Thou wilt keep it a secret, locked within thy own breast ?"

" Oh, yes, that I will," replied Mabel, vehemently.

" Thou wilt never let drop a sentence ?"

" Never."

" Not a syllable ?"

" Not a syllable !" replied Mabel, eagerly.

" Thou wilt promise me not even to whisper a word to any person, without my permission ?"

" Willingly," said Mabel, impatiently.

" Thou wilt keep thy word ?"

" Faithfully."

" Then—then—why—I'll take a week or so to consider whether it would be prudent for me to trust thee or not."

" What a tantalizing, provoking creature, to be sure," said Mabel, in accents of vexation and disappointment; " how canst thou be so cruel, Caleb ?—Now, now, my dear, good-natured Caleb, I am certain thou canst not be serious ; thou wilt not refuse me, wilt thou, dear ?"

" Mabel, Mabel," said Caleb, laughing, and kissing her affectionately, " thou art, forsooth, one of the most coaxing jades in the universe ; and as I really do not believe that thou wouldst be worse than thy word, I have a very good mind to trust thee."

" Oh, now thou art, indeed, my good-natured Caleb," ejaculated Mabel, joyfully, and her bright black eyes sparkling cheerfully and eagerly upon her husband ; " there, now then, begin."

" Very well, then, to begin," said Caleb, drawing his chair closer to his wife ; " to begin—who dost thou think the Dark Mysterious Lady of the Hall is ?"

" What a silly question to put to me ; that's the very thing I want to know. Don't be so stupid, Caleb."

" Well, then, not to keep thee any longer in suspense, Mabel ; thou hast heard me speak of the Marquess D'Chamont ?"

" Yes."

" And of his daughter, Laurette, who married against his will ; and how they afterwards fell into such dreadful poverty ; and how Monsieur de Floriville, in despair, went out into the Black Forest with the determination to commit a robbery, and murdered his own brother in a mistake ; and how he was afterwards taken up, tried, and condemned for it ; and how I was gaoler at the time ; and how I effected his escape ; and how he ——"

" Yes, yes," interrupted Mabel, impatiently, " thou hast told me all that fifty times over."

" Well, then, in the Dark Lady of the Hall, thou beholdest the very Laurette of whom I have been speaking."

" Bless my soul ! is it possible ?—Poor lady ; and is she really the widow of that bad man, who was shot in the forest ; and whom I have heard thee say, was carried away by a spectre ?"

" She is. Ah, poor dear soul, it arouses all my natural feelings, when I think upon what she has undergone. I made my escape to my native country as thou knowest ; but she, poor lady, was tried for plotting her husband's escape, and being a participator in the murder of the unfortunate Monsieur Françoise de Floriville ; although she was acquitted of the latter charge, she was found guilty of the other, and sentenced to a long term of imprisonment. She remained in confinement for more than a year, when a rich relative interceded in her behalf, and succeeded in obtaining her pardon. She was liberated, and came to England, where she had not been long, when the relation I have just alluded to, died, and left her the whole of his fortune. She took up her residence in the old hall, which she purchased, and has there remained ever since. Thou knowest how we met, and the consequences of the same. So now, Mabel, thou knowest the secret for which thou hast been so long teasing, and I hope thou wilt not forget thy promise; although I don't think I have any occasion to caution thee, after what I have told thee."

"Oh, no, indeed thou hast not, Caleb," returned Mabel. "I wouldn't drop a word, which might be the means of injuring the poor dear lady, if I were to be made Queen of England. Well, I declare, if I haven't often thought that this mysterious lady and Madame de Floriville were one and the same person, although I never hinted my suspicions to thee. But, ay, who is that knocking? Some fresh customer to 'The Traveller's Rest,'' and a very impatient one forsooth."

"What, ho!—host—host! House—house! Art thou all deaf, or dead?" exclaimed a loud and disagreeable voice from the next room.

"Neither one nor the other,' answered Caleb, drily, "and thou seemest determined to give me pretty good proof that thou art not dumb, i'faith. Now, master, what is thy pleasure?"

"As few words from thee as possible and those selected with prudence," was the answer.

THE MARQUESS DE CHAMONT REVEALING THE PORTRAIT OF LAUREATE'S MOTHER.

"Humph!" retorted Caleb, "thou art a queer customer, methinks."

"Think what thou likest, but don't give utterance to thy thoughts," observed the man; "I want refreshment."

"Well?"

"And a bed."

"Thou canst have it."

"And then——"

"What then?"

"Why, take thyself off as soon as possible."

Caleb Swinton eyed the mysterious stranger more narrowly, and he was not much prepossessed in his favour by the scrutiny. He was a tall man, with very dark hair, eyes, and complexion, who looked about fifty years of age, but probably was not so old. He had a huge pair of whiskers and moustachios, and a large slouch hat was pulled far down over his forehead. His apparel was very much worn, and covered with dust, as though he had been travelling a long way, and he looked fatigued and weary.

"I wish this fellow had been at the devil, or somewhere else, instead of coming here," muttered Caleb, to himself, as he left the room; "I don't like his appearance at all; and yet it strikes me that I have seen him somewhere before. He is a foreigner. I shouldn't at all wonder if he is not one of the gaol-birds I have had in my charge when I was over in France. I wish I had told him that all my beds were full.

In no very agreeable temper Caleb procured the supper which the stranger had ordered, and returning to the room, placed it on the table before him.

"What dost thou look so hard at me for?" demanded the man, in a surly tone.

"Because thou hast excited my curiosity," answered Caleb.

"And therefore thou givest a licence to thine impertinence, sirrah," retorted the man.

"Sirrah, in thy teeth!" exclaimed Caleb, indignantly; "the greatest knave is always the first to cry out; and I'll let thee know that Caleb Swinton——"

"Caleb Swinton!" repeated the stranger, starting. "Ah! fool that I must be not to notice it before."

"And who art thou?" demanded Caleb, with surprise; "thou seemest to know me."

"Know thee?" said the man with some confusion; "no—no—I know nothing of thee; how should I? I am a stranger in this place, and—but excuse me if I have spoken more abruptly than did beseem me; I have travelled a long way to-day, and am very tired, which has put me not in one of the best of humours. Do not question me any further, but let me partake of my meal, and then I will retire to bed."

Caleb made no reply to this; but once more fixing a searching glance upon the stranger, and endeavouring to recal to his memory where he had seen him before, but in vain, he quitted the room. In a very short time the mysterious man dispatched his meal, and ringing the bell, requested to be shown to the chamber in which he was to sleep. Caleb ordered his servant to conduct him to it, and with a secret injunction to keep a watchful eye upon him—for he was not at all satisfied with his appearance and maners. He sat up for some time after the stranger had retired to rest, and racked his brain to endeavour to recollect where, and under what circumstances he had met him before; but after various conjectures, equally futile, he gave up the attempt, and came to the conclusion he had at first formed, namely, that the stranger had been a prisoner in France at the time he filled the capacity of gaoler.

Great indeed had been the sorrows and afflictions of Madame de Floriville, and of which, in the colloquy which we have just been describing, honest Caleb Swinton had given but a faint sketch. We have detailed the particulars of the events of that awful night, when the guilty de Floriville, Laurette, and the little Henri, hastening through the forest, were overtaken by the soldiers, and the awful fate with which the murderer had met with. In the midst of all the sufferings she was afterwards doomed to endure; when the most imminent peril threatened her; in the hour of her trial; the horrors of that night were for ever present to her memory, and racked her brain. The last words of her husband, and his death-struggle with the phantom of his ill-fated victim, were con-

tinually haunting her imagination, and torturing her mind And then the horrible confession Adolphe had made to her, never returned to her recollection without causing her blood to run icy cold through her veins.

"Good God!" she soliloquised, "and can I really have been so deceived? Oh, surely I could never have become the wife of such a monster; the murderer of his dearest friend —a fratricide! Oh, horror, horror! Well might the malediction—the terrible curse of my father—fall upon my devoted head; and bitterly hath that curse been fulfilled. But surely the punishment I have already undergone is enough for the error of my youth, and which the strength of passion alone led me into."

Tears burst from her eyes, and she paced her gloomy dungeon for a few minutes in a state of the most poignant anguish. Henri, who was permitted to be with her in prison, saw the sufferings of his mother with the most intense agony; young as he was, his bosom was susceptible of the most powerful sentiments of sympathy and commiseration. He threw himself at the feet of Laurette, embraced her knees, and looking up affectionately in her face, implored her with all the force of innocence and simplicity not to weep—to be calm, and trust in Heaven.

The fond parent pressed the sweet boy to her heart in a delirium of affection, and imprinting a thousand kisses on his lips, exclaimed—

"My sweet child—my darling Henri! yes, for thy sake I will endeavour to be calm— for thy sake I will try to remember my unfortunate husband only as thy father. I will seek to erase all the other dreadful circumstances from my memory. I will arouse all my energies, and endeavour to meet my approaching trial with fortitude. Oh, God! the thought of that strikes a deadly chill to my heart; should injustice prevail, and I be condemned to die, what would become of thee, my child? Thou wouldst be left an orphan—friendless in this cruel world. But I cannot bear to think of that, or I shall go mad. No, no—it can never be; the curse of my father will never pursue me with such severity. Oh, wretched, wretched Laurette, to bring into the world so fond, so guileless a being to suffer all the horrors that misfortune can inflict!"

Again the distracted mother hugged her offspring to her bosom, and wept upon his face, while Henri, horrorstruck at the picture she had drawn, clasped his little hands together, and raised his eyes towards Heaven with a look of the most earnest supplication and intense agony.

The day of trial quickly approached, and gradually Laurette became more calm, and trusting in the mercy of Providence, and conscious of her innocence of any participation in the dreadful crime with which she was charged, she determined to meet the painful event with calm dignity.

The day at length arrived and after a

lengthy trial, it terminated as Caleb Swinton had described it, namely, in Madame de Floriville being acquitted of any participation in the murder of the unfortunate Françoise de Floriville, but found her guilty of conniving at and aiding the culprit in his escape from prison. She was sentenced to be imprisoned for a period of ten years, and her child was ordered to be placed in some asylum until he had arrived at an age fitting to be put to some employment. This latter decision distracted Laurette more than all; she threw herself on her knees before her stern judges, and in frantic accents implored them not to tear her child from her. To suffer him to be with her, and she would endure, without a murmur, any punishment, any indignity they might deem it fit to inflict upon her. But they were deaf to her entreaties—callous to the tears—the supplications—the cries of little Henri, who clung to his unfortunate mother, and was with difficulty forced away from her. They tore them asunder, and bore them from each other's sight; and Madame de Floriville was conveyed to that dreary dungeon she had occupied previous to her trial, where for several days she was in a state bordering upon actual frenzy. This blow was almost more severe than any she had before met; her child torn from her, and herself doomed to so long a period of incarceration—alas! what hope was there that she should ever behold him again? None, none; it was utterly impossible that she could survive amidst such an accumulation of horrors. The idea was almost more than her reason could endure, and she frequently prayed that madness might ensue, so that she might be unconscious of the insupportable misery of her fate.

The dungeon she occupied was a wretched place, whose damp and blackened walls frowned despair upon the unhappy prisoner. The only light it received was from a small chink of aperture in the wall, so that day and night it was almost involved in complete darkness. In one corner was a heap of straw, which served her for a bed, and it did not contain any article of furniture. Her food was the coarsest bread, and a jug of loathsome water, daily. She was not allowed books, or writing materials, so that she had no means of decreasing the tedium of her confinement, or of diverting her thoughts from the melancholy subjects that continually haunted them. It would be vain to attempt any description of the sufferings which the unfortunate Madame de Floriville endured; the reader will be able to conceive them better than any language could pourtray them.

In situations similar to those in which Madame de Floriville was placed, the most simple circumstances, and which at any other time would rather excite disgust than pleasure, often occur to lighten the sufferings of the ill-fated prisoner; and so it was with Madame de Floriville; after she had been in her solitary dungeon about a month, she

was one day stretching her limbs upon her wretched pallet, and wrapt in the most dismal thought, when she was aroused by a slight rustling noise, and looking up, she beheld a mouse at no great distance from her, and greedily eating some crumbs which she had dropped on the ground. At any other time, Laurette would have been startled by the appearance of the same, but now she looked calmly on, with something like a feeling of interest. The mouse looked up at her, but did not offer to move, and did not seem to be the least afraid. Laurette was amused at the sight, and this simple incident served for a short time to divert her thoughts from the painful subjects that had before engrossed them. She threw it a few more crumbs, which, having eaten, he quietly took his departure. Every day, after this, at the same hour, the mouse paid his visit to the dungeon of the unfortunate prisoner, and was treated in the like manner, and it last became so tame that it would feed out of her hand, and when he had satisfied himself, he would not offer to move for some time, but would sit at a respectful distance from her, or play among the straw on which she was seated.

It has been shown that the father of Madame de Floriville carried his resentment to the grave, and the fortune which should have been his daughter's, he bequeathed to a distant relation whom he had but seldom seen. This was the Chevalier Desfoignes, a gentleman who possessed great influence at court; he was astonished when he thus fell into such good fortune, for, as we have before stated, he had never been on terms of intimacy with the marquess, and he could not account for his singular decision. Something, however, occurred a few years afterwards, which partly explained the circumstance to him, and pitying the fate of the unfortunate Laurette, he determined, if he could discover her, to do what he considered to be an act of justice; namely, to restore to her the whole, or the greater portion of that fortune of which the wrath of her father had deprived her. But, although he made every inquiry, he was unable to learn anything of Madame de Floriville or her husband, until the circumstance of the dreadful accusation which had been brought against the latter, and the subsequent events made public. After the trial of our heroine was over, the Chevalier Desfoignes resolved to do all that his influence could effect, to obtain a mitigation of her punishment, he considering that it was unnecessarily severe; and, although he could not but deprecate her disobedience in the first instance to the will of her father, he, at the same time, admired the devoted manner in which she had sacrificed her happiness to alleviate the miseries of her unfortunate but guilty husband. He immediately made his way to the palace of the king, and laying the circumstance before him, begged earnestly that a pardon might be granted to his ill-fated relative, or, at any rate, that her sentence might be commuted. He succeeded; her punishment was mitigated from ten years' confinement to one only, and with this joyful intelligence, the good Chevalier Desfoignes hastened to the prison in which Madame Laurette was incarcerated. He obtained an interview with her without the least difficulty, and the scene which followed may be imagined without the least trouble. Laurette threw herself at the feet of her preserver, and with tears of delirious transport, poured forth her gratitude, and invoked a thousand blessings upon his head. The Chevalier was much affected by the interview, and resolved during the remainder of her confinement, to make every arrangement for her support and future welfare, at its expiration. He also succeeded in obtaining her removal to another part of the prison, where she was more indulged; was supplied with a good mattress; allowed better food, permitted the use of pen and ink; and obtained, as a great favour, two or three books to peruse. But what made the terrors of her confinement appear less irksome to her, was the prospect of having her son, the little Henri, so shortly restored to her; and the time seemed to pass quickly away, now that despair was banished from her mind.

At length the twelvemonth expired, and Madame Laurette was released from confinement, and once more pressed her offspring to her heart. The Chavalier Desfoignes escorted her from the prison, and took her to his own chateau, where he immediately resigned to her nearly the whole of the property which had been bequeathed to him by her father, and consulted with her as to the manner which it would be best, or most advisable for her to proceed in future. Madame Laurette could never enough thank the Chevalier for his generosity, and the interest he took in her welfare, and informed him that she had made up her mind to quit France and seek a retreat in England, where she would be unknown, and was resolved for the future to lead a life of seclusion, being altogether tired of the world.

Madame de Floriville, notwithstanding that bitter care had made sad ravages on her face and form, was still lovely, and the Chevalier Desfoignes was most forcibly struck with her charms; but he was confident there was no chance of his passion being returned, and he, therefore, endeavoured to stifle it, and did not mention a word to our heroine concerning the sentiments with which she had inspired him, but expressed his approbation of the resolution she had come to as regarded her future place of residence, and her manner of living.

Madame Laurette did not remain more than a week in France, after her liberation from confinement, and with her son departed for England, where she fixed her residence at the place which has already been described by Caleb, and having engaged a tutor for her son, she shut herself up in the old hall, determined to pass the remainder of her days in penitence, and in performing acts of benevolence. She assumed another name, but was never called by any other name than that of the Dark Lady of the Hall, and the mystery of her behaviour soon created a deep sensation in the neighbourhood, but no one had been able to elicit who or what she was, until she accidentally encountered Caleb Swinton, but who needed no injunction to keep her secret. Remarkably munificent to the poor, she soon gained the esteem of all who lived near her, and there was not any one who did not sincerely pity her—for they were certain that it must have been some very heavy misfortune indeed which could have induced her to take such a solitary course of life, and scarcely to hold any communion at all with the world.

Madame Laurette had not resided many months at the old hall, when the Chevalier Desfoignes suddenly expired, and he not only left her the remainder of the bequest of the Marquis Chamont, but made Henri the heir to his own wealth.

We will now return to the period of which we treated at the commencement of the present chapter. On the morning after the evening that the conversation took place between Caleb and his wife, Madame Laurette was seated in the library, when Annette, her waiting maid, knocked at the door, and on being admitted, with some surprise in the expression of her countenance, informed her that there was a strange-looking man waiting below, and who wanted to see her.

"A stranger, and want to see me!" exclaimed Madame Laurette, turning pale. "Who can he be? Annette, did he ask for me?"

"Why, madame," replied Annette, "he asked for Madame de Floriville; and when I told him that there was no such a person lived here, he said that the person who called herself Madame le Sauge, and was known by the title of the Dark Lady of the Hall, was the individual he meant."

"Good God!" ejaculated Madam eLaurette, 'who can it be that knows me? Surely Caleb could not——but, no, no, I wrong him by such a supposition. Annette, what kind of a man is he?"

"Why, madame," answered the girl, "he is very tall—very shabby—very dark—and very unceremonious in his manners. I don't like his appearance at all; but he says that he must and will see you; that he has come upon business of the most vital importance to you, and that if you will not condescend to go to him, he is determined to come to you. He does not look like a man who will fail to keep his word."

"I am all amazement," said our heroine; "but yet what should I fear? There is no one in the world, now, with whom I am acquainted, except Caleb Swinton, and certainly no one to whom I have given any cause of enmity. Did he not give you his name?"

"He did not, madame, answered Annette; "but hark! some one is ascending the stairs. It must be he! Oh, dear! what will become of us? What a daring, impudent ruffian."

At that moment there was a loud knock at the door of the apartment, and without waiting for any further ceremony, it was thrown back on its hinges, and the mysterious stranger who had put up at "The Traveller's Rest" the previous night, stalked into the room.

A violent tremor came over Madame de Floriville upon the intrusion of the mysterious stranger, and she was so much astonished and alarmed at the singularity of the circumstance, that she was transfixed to the spot and was unable to give utterance to a syllable. The hat of the intruder was drawn far over his forehead, but she could observe that his eyes were fixed upon her with the most searching and intense expression, while he appeared to be moved by some powerful emotion.

"Leave the room," he said, in a harsh and authoritative tone, turning to Annette. Madame de Floriville started at the tones of his voice, and trembled more violently than she had done before.

"Leave the room, girl, I say," he repeated in louder accents.

"Leave the room! gracious me!" cried Annette; "did ever any one hear such consummate insolence before? Here's a strange man forces his way into the house, walks up to my mistress' apartment without so much as saying with your leave or by your leave, and then takes upon himself to order her waiting-maid out of the room. I never heard of such a thing in all my life; as for going, I'm sure I shall not do any such thing, unless my mistress orders me, which I do not think is very likely, and—"

"Do not exasperate me, girl," exclaimed the stranger, stamping on the floor passionately; "I command you to begone."

"You command me!" repeated Annette, pertly, and tossing up her head.

"I command you!" returned the stranger, pointing towards the door; then turning to Madame de Floriville, he added—"Madame, I have something to communicate which is for your ear alone; order this girl to leave this place, or I shall be under the necessity of using force to make her comply."

"Ah! that voice—those tones!" exclaimed Madame de Floriville; "where have I before heard them, and what means this strange emotion?"

"Thou wilt know ere long," said the man; "wilt thou do as I have requested thee?"

"Something to communicate to me," observed Madame de Floriville, "and seek such a suspicious and abrupt method of gaining an interview with me? What can this mean? Tell me, stranger—who, and what art thou?"

"We must be alone first," said the man.

"I will grant thy request, stranger," replied Madame de Floriville; "but mark me, if thy designs be evil, I have those close at hand who will fly to my protection, and punish thee for any outrage thou mayest attempt. Retire, Annette."

"Wh-wh-what, madame!" ejaculated Annette, with an air of astonishment and incredulity: "leave the room—leave you all alone *by yourself* with this—this black-looking, mysterious man? Oh, you can't mean it, I am sure!"

"Begone, loquacious fool!" cried the stranger; and Annette, frightened at his manner, made her exit rather hastily, but with great reluctance.

The mysterious stranger opened the room door, after she had made her departure, and looked out to see if she were listening, or whether any other person was near; then returned into the apartment, and stood gazing at Madame de Floriville for several seconds, with deep earnestness. Laurette was unable to speak for a short time, but becoming more composed, by a powerful effort, she said, in as calm and firm a voice as possible—

"Now, stranger, thy business with me?"

"Laurette!" exclaimed the man, in accents of the deepest emotion.

Madame de Floriville started, and was compelled to lay hold of the back of a chair to support herself, or she must have fallen.

"Again that voice, which rushes upon my ears, and steals upon my senses, like the vision of former days," she gasped forth; "what can this mean!—my name, too! Stranger, for the love of Heaven, do not keep me in suspense, but tell me who thou art, and for what purpose thou hast sought this interview with me?"

"Heaven and I have little to do with each other," said the man in deep, solemn accents, every tone of which seemed to strike upon the heart of Madame de Floriville; "but no matter; my voice thou sayest is familiar to thee? Methinks in should, indeed, be so. Thou hadst a husband."

"Alas! I had," groaned Madame de Floriville; "but why remind me of that? Didst thou know my unfortunate husband?"

"Did I know him! Did I know the unfortunate Adolphe de Floriville? Ay, even as I know myself. Why art thou not with him?"

"Stranger," cried Laurette, "comest thou hither to torture and to mock me? If thou didst know the wretched Adolphe, thou canst not be ignorant that he hath been dead many years."

"Dost thou cherish his memory?"

"Cherish his memory!—Oh, Heaven, which knoweth my mental sufferings for so many years, can bear witness how fondly I do, although I cannot look back upon his crimes without horror and abhorrence. But why do I thus talk to one who is unknown to me, and who hath come hither for what purpose I cannot imagine!"

"Thou hast nothing to fear from me,

Laurette," observed the man in a tone of familiarity, which astonished Madame de Floriville; "suppose thy husband were still living, wouldst thou receive him with all thy former affection, and become again his faithful partner?"

The agitation of Madame de Floriville increased to an almost insupportable degree; and for a few seconds her utterance was completely choked.

"Mysterious man," she at length cried, "why dost thou rack me with such questions?"

"Nay, I will not be satisfied until I have received a direct answer," said the stranger impatiently.

"Whoever thou art, I know not," observed Laurette, with the greatest emotion; "but thou seemest as if thou couldst command obedience from me, and have gained a most powerful influence over my feelings. Thou hast asked me whether I would, were Adolphe still living, become his partner? I answer, Never!—never!"

"Woman, beware what thou sayest," remarked the stranger, and evincing the most violent agitation:—"didst thou not say that thou didst cherish the memory of thy husband?"

"I did! I did! and the Almighty can judge of my sincerity; but to live again the life of crime and horror I did with that unhappy man, would be worse than suffering the most painful, the most lingering death.—Stranger, my disobedience brought down upon my devoted head a father's curse!—That dreadful curse pursued me during the whole time that I and my wretched, guilty husband were together! We never knew what it was to experience one hour's happiness; my conscience tells me that I *should* forget him, and *that* I will endeavour to do. Stranger," she continued, in a voice of great solemnity, and drawing aside a black curtain, "behold these portraits—one is the resemblance of my sainted mother, and the other traces the features of my poor father—that father whose terrible malediction I provoked. This is my school, and here do I learn lessons of penitence. These blessed resemblances are my monitors. Oh, there are moments when I could almost believe they were imbued with life. There are times, when my thoughts wander to my guilty husband, that I could almost swear their lips moved to breathe reproof, and that they frowned upon me. Oh, God, what——"

"Cover them up—cover them up," interrupted the stranger, averting his head, and evincing strange agitation; "I—I——"

"Ah! why this emotion?" demanded Madame de Floriville, with increased astonishment, and fixing a searching glance upon the man; "stranger, reveal to me the purpose for which thou didst seek this interview, and bring it at once to a conclusion."

"Madame de Floriville," said the stranger, with forced composure; "what if I bring thee news of thine unfortunate husband?"

Laurette sighed and smiled mournfully. "Thou canst not bring news from the silent dead," she replied.

"What if I tell thee thy husband still lives?"

"Lives! lives!" screamed Madame de Floriville, and trembling excessively. "But why should I give way to this dreadful agitation? Stranger, thou art either mad, or comest here to drive *me* to distraction. My husband living! Oh, wild delusion! Did not these eyes behold him plunge headlong into the roaring cataract, in the awful grasp of the spirit of his murdered friend? Oh, horror! horror! as the recollection rushes upon my memory, my blood turns to ice, while my brain burns to madness!"

"Laurette de Floriville," said the stranger, in a voice of deep emotion, "thy wretched husband is still alive. I come to bring thee news of him."

"Adolphe, my husband—my—alive!" gasped forth Madame de Floriville "oh, impossible!—Cruel man, thus to sport with the feelings of a broken-hearted woman."

"I speak the truth," remarked the man, with forced composure. "Adolphe de Floreville did not perish. He arose again upon the water uninjured. He battled with the waves, and reached the opposite shore in safety. Yet did he almost regret the instinctive feeling which had prompted him to struggle to preserve his miserable life, and was half inclined to plunge once more into the deep, and terminate at once an existence that had become a curse to him. But then the fear of the future; the dread of that terrible eternity of torture to which his soul was doomed, arrested his purpose, and he resolved to live. He had a purse well filled, which he had received from honest Caleb Swinton; and his present necessities might, therefore, be provided for. But ere he turned away from the spot, the murderer dared to invoke the protection of Heaven for his wife and boy, and then with many a terrible pang, he quitted the place, and wandered on, heedless whither he was going. By the following day he found himself in a distant part of the country, and out of danger; indeed, it was not at all probable that any one would imagine for a moment but that he had perished in the cataract, and his body been carried far away. I will not seek to describe the horrors of his mind. The pale face of the murdered Eugene constantly before him, and the grasp of death upon his throat. How he could endure it, seems wonderful and incredible; but it appeared as if it were his doom to continue to live, to suffer earthly torments, almost equal to those of the damned. At the first town he arrived at, he purchased a change of clothes to disguise himself; dyed his complexion, and with the aid of a wig, it would have been almost impossible for any one to recognise him, even upon the most minute examination. For days he wandered from place to place, undecided what course to pursue, and anxious to become acquainted with the fate of his wife and son. At length, his cash being almost gone, he determined to go to sea. He got a ship without much difficulty, and all suspicion of his real character was at an end. They had not been many days out at sea, when the ship was attacked and boarded by pirates, who murdered the captain and mate, and took the remainder of the crew and passengers prisoners, and sold them for slaves in Morocco. Here the wretched De Floriville endured the most dreadful hardships; sufferings, which, although he thought at that time were a just punishment for the crimes of which he had been guilty, would make the heart shudder. At length he made his escape, and returned to his native land. Here his distress was terrible even to think upon, and at length, made desperate, he turned robber. For some time he was captain of a gang of robbers that infested the forest of ——, but, at length, the government succeeded in discovering their retreat, and sent a force sufficient to vanquish them. A great number of them were slain and taken prisoners, but Adolphe escaped and made his way to England, where he had ascertained that thou and his son were still living, and——"

"No more—no more," interrupted Madame de Floriville, whose feelings were wound up to a pitch bordering upon madness; "to what a terrible, and improbable story have I been listening. Stranger, for what purpose hast thou invented such a tale?—Once more, I ask, thee, who thou art?"

"Laurette," said the man, "the tale I have told thee is no fabrication; Adolphe de Floriville still lives!"

"Where?—where?"

"Behold!—he stands in thy presence!"

As the mysterious visitor thus spoke, he threw off the huge mantle that had enveloped his person, removed his hat and wig, and Adolphe de Floriville, the murderer, the fratricide—who was supposed to have been dead so many years, stood confirmed in the presence of his wife!

"Great God!" shrieked Madame Laurette, "can the grave yield up the dead? Surely this must be a delusion! And yet those features—those well-known tones! Adolphe—Adolphe!"

"Laurette—my wife!" exclaimed the guilty man, as she screamed and sunk insensible in his arms. At that moment the room door was thrown open, and Annette and Henri appeared; but to describe their astonishment at the scene they beheld would be a task far beyond our power. Adolphe was pressing the senseless form of Laurette to his heart, and imprinting the most passionate kisses upon her lips.

Astonishment chained both Annette and Henri to the spot; and the latter, on beholding his mother enfolded in the arms of a strange man, became alarmed, more especially as she was insensible. He was, therefore, the first to break silence; and advancing with a boldness of demeanour that could not have been expected at his age, he demanded who Adolphe was, the reason of his abrupt intrusion into the hall, and what was the occasion of the condition in which he then beheld his mother. At the sound of the boy's voice Adolphe looked up from the pale countenance of his wife, and fixed upon him an eager glance, in which was fully expressed all those powerful feelings that at the moment rushed tumultuously to his heart. As he gazed upon the form and features of that noble boy, all the fond sentiments of a father filled his bosom, and in a voice half choked with agitation, he ejaculated—

"Henri, dearest, noble boy, I—but let me conquer my feelings until another time;—girl, to thy care I resign thy mistress; look well to her, and she will shortly recover;—our interview for the present hath probably been long enough;—but tell her that I will see her again to-morrow."

Thus saying, Adolphe once more impressed a fervent kiss upon the lips of his wife; resigned her to Annette; grasped the hand of Henri vehemently, and exclaiming, "Farewell," he hastily quitted the apartment, and hurried from the hall.

For a few seconds after he had gone, Henri stood in a complete state of stupefaction, totally unable to understand the meaning of the circumstance; and yet there was something in the voice, the words, the manner of the stranger, that rushed upon his mind with the most painful force, assimilated in the events of other days, and which, although he was only a child at the time they happened, were stamped upon his memory in characters that time could not efface. His features, too, careworn as they were, were still familiar to him, and the poor boy stood in a state of trembling suspense, and watched the slow recovery of his mother with the most intense anxiety.

At length, by the care of Annette, Madame de Floriville was restored to sensibility, and opening her eyes, she looked eagerly around the room, and starting, she cried in a voice of alarm—

"Ah!—not here! not here!—whither has he gone?—Or, was it only a dream?—yes—it could not have been reality;—the dead could never arise again in form so tangible! —And yet, methought—nay, I could have sworn not many minutes since he stood before me;—that he revealed himself to me; and told me the story of his sufferings;— and it was so;—I am positive of it.—Oh, tell me, whither has he gone, and why did he so abruptly depart?"

Annette, who was all on thorns to know who the strange visitor was, delivered to her mistress the message he had charged her with, and was in hopes that she would then divulge the name of the man; but in that she was disappointed.

"Left me—and so soon!" Madame Laurette ejaculated: "and yet I ought to be grateful to him for it. I cannot look or think upon him without horror; and yet the deepest affection contests that sentiment! Ah! see—the portraits of my parents uncovered! Good God! Surely they frown upon me! And now I could almost swear that their lips move as though they would breathe a malediction upon me! Can it—is it only imagination?"

She fixed her eyes steadfastly on the portraits, and her bosom heaved with emotion. Annette stood gazing on in stupid amazement, while her curiosity was excited to an almost insupportable degree. Henri listened to the words of his mother with increased surprise and agitation; and when he beheld the wildness of her manner he became dreadfully alarmed, and in tones of the most vehement supplication he cried—

"Oh, my dear—dear mother, why are you thus violently affected? Tell me, I beseech you, what has occurred to cause this, and who is that mysterious man who has but just left the castle?"

"Ah! my son—art thou here?" ejaculated Madame de Floriville, for the first time noticing the presence of the boy. "Did you, then, see him?"

"I did," replied Henri; "and there is something in his manner, his words, and features, that has created an indescribable feeling in my breast. Methinks I have seen him before, and yet I cannot recal to my mind where."

"My poor boy," cried Madame Laurette, "thou hast, indeed, seen him before; but I must conquer this agitation. Annette, thou canst retire."

"Pardon me, madame," returned the waiting-woman, loitering, and much disappointed at the order of her mistress, just at the very moment her curiosity seemed likely to be about to be gratified, and Madame Laurette about to divulge the real character of the mysterious visitor—"pardon me, but—but—have you quite recovered from your late illness, madame, and the fright you——"

"I can ring, should I require thy services, Annette," interrupted her mistress, impatiently.

Annette curtseyed, and reluctantly obeyed; but she took good care to wait outside the door, with her ear to the key-hole, to listen to whatever conversation might take place between Madame de Floriville and her son, being determined, at all hazards, to have her curiosity gratified.

"Dear Henri," ejaculated Madame Laurette, after Annette had quitted the room, and she had sufficiently recovered herself to speak—"dear Henri, thy mother hath this day met with an adventure which seems too strange to be true. All the early troubles of her life have been brought more vividly upon her recollection, and it seems as if her former miseries were about being renewed with redoubled violence. The man thou sawest——"

"Ah, my dear mother," eagerly interrup-ted Henri, "I implore thee to set my anxiety at rest, and inform me who he is and for what purpose he hath come hither?"

"My poor boy, partner of all my troubles, partaker of all my vicissitudes," sobbed forth Madame Laurette, "thou shalt know; but, ere I reveal the name of that unhappy man, I warn thee thou must cease to remember him in the character of——"

Madame de Floriville hesitated, and gasped for breath, while her frame was greatly agitated.

"Of what, dear mother?" hastily implored Henri.

"Thy father!" solemnly replied Madame de Floriville, and with a deep groan she sank on a chair, and covered her face with her hands.

"My father!" cried Henri, in a state of the most indescribable astonishment and emotion; "what meanest thou, my dearest mother? Oh, surely some powerful grief hath turned thy brain; has not my father been dead many years? Oh, yes; although I was very young at the time, well do I remember that dreadful night when he met his death, and the awful circumstances attending it. Even now I could almost picture to my imagination, as distinctly as if it had happened but yesterday, the fearful scene that took place, when my father was about to plunge in the roaring cataract; when—"

"Oh, cease, cease, my boy!" gasped forth his mother; "thou wilt drive me to madness, by recalling those horrors so powerfully to my memory. I tell thee, that thy unhappy, guilty father did not perish; that he still lives, and that the man thou didst behold here but a few minutes since is he who gave thee being!"

"Good God! is it possible?" cried Henri, clasping his hands. "Oh, yes, it must, it must be true; no other being could have filled my bosom with such emotion; but why did he not embrace his son?—why did he so abruptly hasten away? He will, however, be here again to-morrow, and——"

"Henri," interrupted Madame Laurette, solemnly, "again I warn thee to endeavour to forget thy father, unless it is to pray for forgiveness for the many crimes of which h hath been guilty."

"And will he not then be with us again?" said Henri.

"No, my child," replied his mother, "never, never—Heaven forbids it! Oh, Adolphe, wretched man; to what a terrible alternative hath thy crimes driven me! But it is maddening to reflect upon it! Henri, remember my words, and as thou lovest thy mother, endeavour to obey them. Now, now; prithee leave me my child; I wish to be alone."

"Mother, dear mother," said the affectionate boy, clinging to her, and looking up with supplicating fondness in her face, "I do not like to leave thee while thou art thus agitated."

"Nay, Henri," returned Madame de

Floriville, "I must be obeyed. There—there—get thee gone, my dear boy, and fear not for me; I do but wish to commune with my own thoughts, and to prepare my mind for the second meeting with my unfortunate husband to-morrow. Adieu!"

Madame Laurette kissed her son two or three times with the utmost fervour, and when she had with difficulty torn herself from his embrace, she pointed to the door, by which he slowly made his exit, and when he had gone, his mother turned the key in the lock to prevent further intrusion, and throwing herself upon the sofa, she gave free indulgence to the painful thoughts by which her mind had now become completely occupied.

The events of the last few hours seemed so totally improbable that she could scarcely, at times, convince herself that they had really taken place, or were only the offspring of her imagination; but quickly the conviction became powerfully stamped upon her mind, and then was she distracted with the tormenting, the agonizing thoughts it gave rise to. Even now, after all the dreadful crimes he had perpetrated, she felt that the affection with which Adolphe had inspired her in her youthful days, was unabated; that love which had enabled her

LAURETTE SWOONS ON DISCOVERING IN THE STRANGER HER HUSBAND.

to go through so many hardships and horrors for his sake, still glowed with the same fierce flame that it had ever done in her heart; but her soul revolted from the bare idea of being once more his companion. The dread phantoms of his murdered victims, the pale shade of her father, seemed to rise up against such a resolution, and to threaten her with the vengeance of Heaven, if she again became the partner of the murderer—the fratricide! Besides, was it at all probable that Adolphe, whose life was forfeited to the laws of justice, would again wish to live with her, when, by doing so, he must reveal his real character, and be the means of bringing himself to the scaffold? But how could she act?—what would Adolphe do, or what proposals would he make?—Would he resign her, and forbear to remain near the spot where he must endanger the safety of them both? Alas! she feared that he would be obstinate and determined; and his manner now convinced her that he had become inured to crime, and callous to those better feelings that had at times predominated in his bosom. Oh, that he had never been able to discover her retreat, or that he could now be persuaded to enter into some religious house, where, by penance and repentance, he might make atonement for his crimes. She dreaded, yet impatiently awaited for the arrival of the following day. If it were money he sought, willingly would she resign to him the greater portion of her wealth if he would not interrupt her, but retire to some distant part of the country where she might never behold him again; but she greatly feared that he had some more powerful object in view, and a renewal of all her former misery appeared inevitable.

The whole of that day Madame Laurette passed alone in her apartment, and endeavoured to prepare her mind for the interview with her husband the next day; anxious to be able to meet him with that composure and firmness which was necessary, in order that she might carry out the point she had in view. She succeeded much better than she had anticipated, and when she retired to her couch, her mind was more calm and settled than it had even been for some time previous.

———

CHAPTER X.

THE PARLOUR IN "THE TRAVELLER'S REST." THE DEAD ALIVE.—A TALE OF CRIME.

THE inquisitive and loquacious Annette had listened with the most breathless attention to the discourse we have been describing in the previous chapter, and when she heard her young master approaching the door, she vanished down stairs with silent steps and with all possible expedition.

"Good gracious!" she soliloquised, when she was alone; "here's a pretty tale. Quite a romance, I declare; I never heard anything like it in all my life. First my mistress turns out to be not Madame le Sange, but a Madame de Floriville; then the shabby, surly, mysterious stranger proves to be no stranger at all to her, but the dead come to life again, or something very much like it, and her husband! Dear me, I never could have believed that my mistress could have been a woman of such bad taste, as to marry such a man as that. However, she does not seem to feel very proud of the match, or she would not have said what she did, and be so determined not to live with him again. Besides, this man, from all I could hear, must have been guilty of some very heinous crimes, and—dear me! the very thought of it puts me all in a quandary. I must go, as soon as I can find an opportunity to slip out, and inform Gregory all about the matter. Gregory is very inquisitive, and perhaps this may be a feather in my cap, and induce him to make some return of the passion with which he has inspired me; for do all I can, I can scarcely win a smile from him. Well, I have been a very ill-used and unfortunate girl through life; unable to get a lover; and yet, I'm sure, I'm as pretty a girl as here and there one! Heigho! what can the reason be?'

Here Annette prepared to leave the hall, singing in melancholy strains the following appropriate song :—

"They say that beauty, wit, and grace,
    Are very tempting treasures;
A sparkling eye, a rosy face,
    Are sure of wedlock's pleasures.
But, though I am both young and fair,
    No suitors follow me;
No rich youths for my hand declare——
    What can the reason be?
            Upon my word I cannot guess——
            What can the reason be?

"I paint, perfume, and curl my hair,
    And sure I look quite charming;
'Tis true poor swains oft at me leer,
    But poverty's alarming.
There's not a lass but has a beau,
    Around for miles I see;
While I'm neglected doomed to go——
    What can the reason be?
            Upon my word, &c.

"There's Emmeline, the pert brunette,
    Has beaux for her imploring;
And Mary Anne, the young coquette,
    Has twenty!—mad—adoring!
And widow Thompson's got a swain,
    Though she's just fifty-three,
While here, neglected I remain—
    What can the reason be?
            Upon my word," &c.

By the time that Annette had come to the conclusion of this ballad, she had completed her *toilette*, and having ascertained that she was not likely to be wanted by her mistress for some time, she left the house, and set forward to visit her dear Gregory, anxious to impart to him the important secret with which she had become acquainted.

The Master Gregory on whom the affections of the simple Annette were placed, and to whom allusion has been made, was a certain wide-mouthed, gawky ostler at the Traveller's Rest, who, notwithstanding nature had not been very bountiful to him, inasmuch as he was about as ordinary a man as you would meet with in a day's perambulation, was on the most excellent terms with himself, and not only did he consider that he possessed the elegance and grace of Apollo Belvidere, but, moreover, that his countenance was irresistible, and that the qualities of his mind were of the most brilliant order. Ostlers, generally speaking in the present age, are not the most cultivated or intelligent part of the community, and our readers must recollect that Master Gregory Goldfinch was an ostler in the sixteenth century; and we feel it our duty to state candidly, that Gregory was very far from being a refined ostler of that age; yet, what he wanted in real ability he amply made up for in conceit, a quality of which he possessed a super-abundant stock. Talk about rubbing down a horse—broach a subject to him on the quality of corn, or the art of making up a bed—and there Gregory could show off—oh, he was quite at home there; but take him out of the stable, and Gregory Goldfinch was one of the veriest asses to be found.

Strange, however, as it may appear, this

anything but fascinating biped was a favourite with the fair sex, and considered himself a complete lady-killer. He had a goodly share of nonsensical twaddle at his tongue's end, which same nonsensical twaddle, so long as it contains a decent sprinkling of flattery, is extremely pleasing to the female sex generally, and is listened to with avidity, and hence the success of Gregory Goldfinch.

In the estimation of Annette, Gregory Goldfinch was a very great man, indeed, and she followed up her addresses to him with the most determined perseverance; for, as has been shown, Annette had been very unsuccessful in her amatory affairs, (not from any lack of personal attraction,) and the awful and old-maidish age of thirty was rapidly approaching; she was, therefore, resolved, that whether Gregory loved her or not, she would persecute him with her own vows until she teased him into an assent. Gregory, however, chose to come the grand, the dignified, the indifferent with her, and pretended to treat the attentions of Annette as a very great bore: taking care, notwithstanding, occasionally to drop, as it were inadvertantly, a few sentences of flattery, sufficient to inflame the mind of Annette, as he really had an attachment to the damsel, or, probably, to sundry and divers bright pieces of gold, which he had been given to understand, from the most unquestionable authority, she had saved up, and which was enough to form a very handsome little wedding dowry. Gregory, who had his eye to the gold, also had his eye to the maiden, who possessed charms that even the heart of an obdurate ostler could not withstand.

In two respects the dispositions of Gregory Goldfinch and Annette agreed remarkably well—namely, in inquisitiveness and loquacity, and she could not have hit upon a better idea to win the favour of the ostler than the one she had, and Gregory received the information with all due eagerness and amazement, faithfully promising Annette not to repeat a word of the story to anybody else; but, of course, resolving to tell the same to all his acquaintances with as much expedition as possible.

"Well," said the sagacious Gregory, when Annette had finished her story, "hang me if I didn't always think there was something very mysterious about your mistress, that I did."

This was exactly what everybody else in the neighbourhood had always thought, and not only thought, but knew; therefore, perhaps, Gregory Goldfinch did not deserve quite so much credit for his superior penetration as he seemed to imagine he did.

"Very mysterious—very mysterious, indeed," ejaculated Annette. "But now, Gregory, who would have thought my lady, whom every one believed to be a widow, should have a husband living all the time, and that she should have changed her name? And then to have such a strange, uncouth, black looking man for a husband as this

stranger! I wonder what could have induced Madame to elope from him?"

"Ah, I wonder!" repeated Gregory; "but you may depend upon it, it was some *clandecent* action or other, or why——"

"Oh, no Gregory," interrupted Annette, "I cannot agree with you in that opinion, by any means. I am certain that my mistress is too amiable ever to have acted in the manner you suspect. It is more likely that she has suffered cruelty from her husband, and, to judge from the conversation I overheard, it seems evident that he has been guilty of some very heavy crimes."

"Lor'!" exclaimed the ostler; "now, how I should just like to hear the whole of his history. What did you say his name was, Annette?"

"His name?" answered the talkative waiting-woman. "Why—why, his name is——"

"Babbling idiot!" at that moment exclaimed a loud voice close behind them, which made them both start and tremble with fear, and looking up, they beheld the subject of their conversation in their presence. Annette was ready to sink with terror, while the knees and teeth of the loquacious ostler performed a concert of not the most harmonious description, as he gazed at the stern countenance and commanding figure of Monsieur de Floriville.

"Babbling idiot!" repeated Adolphe, "is it thus thou performest thy duty to thy mistress? Get thee hence immediately, and beware how thou repeatest what thou hast overheard to any other person. Thou mayest repent it if thou dost—mark me."

Annette, who was as frightened as if she had been standing in the presence of some supernatural being, attempted to stammer out an apology, but Adolphe stopped her impatiently.

"There, no more, but begone!" he exclaimed, peremptorily, "and attend to the warning I have given thee. As to thee, sirrah, the sooner thou art off to thy manger the better."

Gregory Goldfinch did not relish his customer at all, and, therefore, he was not slow in obeying him; and, taking the arm of Annette, they both departed instanter, without offering any further observations upon the subject.

While this was going forward in the kitchen of the hostelrie, Caleb Swinton was sitting cosily in the chimney corner of the parlour, indulging himself with a jug of ale, and thinking of the singular conduct of the man who had become his guest on the evening before. There was something in his voice and features that was remarkably familiar to him, and yet he could not recal to his memory where he had before seen him, nor could he account for the deep interest he had excited in his bosom.

"Yes, I would stake my life," soliloquised Caleb, lolling back in his easy arm-chair, "I would stake my life that we have met before, but under what circumstances, I cannot imagine."

"So then, Master Caleb," said Adolphe, who at that moment entered the room, "thou dost think thou and I are old acquaintances?"

"Ay, marry do I," answered Caleb.

"Thou thinkest rightly then," returned Monsieur de Floriville; "we have, indeed, often met before, and under very peculiar circumstances."

"Indeed!" said Caleb, looking narrowly at him; "where have we before encountered each other?"

"In France."

"Ah!"

"Yes. Hast thou no idea now?—canst thou not yet form any conjecture as to who the person is that stands before thee?"

"I cannot," replied Caleb; "but I pray thee, if thou hast no objection, to satisfy my curiosity at once."

"I question much whether thou wilt feel anxious to renew the acquaintance," observed Adolphe, in a careless manner; "although thou wilt not be a little astonished when thou hearest my name. Thou knowest the prison of——."

"Ah!" interrupted Caleb, "my suspicions were right, then; thou art one of those gaol-birds of whom I had the custody when——"

"Thou art not much disposed for flattery, Master Swinton," remarked Adolphe, with an ironical smile; "but, indeed, thou sayest right—I was once in thy charge. Dost know me now?"

"No; and after what thou hast said, I very much doubt whether I ought to have any wish to know thee," answered Caleb.

"I told thee thou wouldst not feel very ready to renew the acquaintance," said Monsieur de Floriville, with a bitter smile. "Nevertheless, I will reveal myself to thee, as I shall most likely require thy assistance. Caleb Swinton, in me thou beholdest one whom thou hast long since supposed to be no more. It is Adolphe de Floriville who now stands before thee!"

"Adolphe de Floriville!" repeated Caleb, jumping from his chair, and gazing at the former with the most indescribable astonishment and terror; "stranger, art thou mad, or dost thou think that I am? Thou Adolphe de Floriville?—Why, it is more than seven years since he perished in the forest at Abbeville, and met with a death of horror, but which his crimes fully merited. Ah, many a sorry hour did his poor wife suffer, and—thou Adolphe de Floriville, the——"

"The murderer," added De Floriville; "I know what thou wouldst say. I do not disown—at least to thee—my title. I have become used to it now, but there was a time when I was not quite so courageous upon that point. I was weak then; I am reckless, callous now. But enough of that; I repeat, Caleb, that in me thou beholdest Adolphe de Floriville, the man of crime.

Look closer into my countenance; this wig may have effected the principal alteration in my appearance. Nay, nay, man, come nearer; thou hast naught to fear; I am no spectre, but real flesh and blood. Look at me."

Caleb Swinton did indeed look at him narrowly, and when he removed the wig, he could no longer entertain a doubt that Monsieur de Floriville actually stood before him.

"Why, by Heaven!" he ejaculated, "it is, it must be he. Monsieur de Floriville, wretched, unfortunate, guilty man, by what singular miracle has thy life been spared?"

"Come, come, Master Swinton," said De Floriville, "as little about guilt, and such cant, as thou pleasest; it does not agree with my palate now. There was a time when I gave way to it, but I am not so childish now. Conscience is a bugbear, made use of by priests and—however, we will drop this subject. Thou wouldst know by what means I escaped. I will tell tell."

De Floriville then repeated to Caleb, with the utmost carelessness, the story he had related to his wife, but added several circumstances which he had not thought proper to impart to her. He made no scruple in acknowledging the full extent of his guilt, and in confessing the utter recklessness he had at last suffered to take possession of his mind; and Caleb, who before deeply pitied him, now felt horrorstruck and disgusted while he listened to him.

"The first year or two after my being rescued from death," continued Adolphe, "I passed miserable enough, for I could not stifle the voice of conscience. My thoughts, too, were fixed upon my wife and child, and when I imagined the sufferings to which they were exposed, I became truly wretched. I was now an alien from them; I must never reveal myself to them, or my life would be sure to be the penalty of the same. Thou mayst be sure that the accident which made me a slave in Morocco did not tend to alleviate my misery. I endured great hardships, but at length I became completely hardened, and that which I before could not even think of without a shudder of horror, I was now enabled to endure with the most perfect indifference. I made my escape from slavery; I returned to France, so altered that I thought it would be impossible to recognise me. I was completely destitute, but my mind was soon made up what to do. That night I stopped a traveller in the forest, and demanded his money; it happened to be the captain of the band of robbers which had for many years infested the neighbourhood, and bid defiance to the law. He quickly made himself known to me, and, perceiving that I was a desperate man, he invited me to their place of rendezvous. An offer was made to me to become one of their band, which I readily accepted. Our lawless expeditions were attended with great success, and we amassed considerable wealth. In a short time I became used to the wild life, and was as daring a villain as any amongst them. In a few months after I had joined the robbers, the captain died from the effects of a wound he had received, and, according to our rules, we cast lots who should succeed him in the command. The chance fell upon me, and I was received in my new character with great enthusiasm, I being a great favourite with the whole of the gang. I had not long been their captain, however, when our retreat was discovered ; we were surprised by a force too powerful for us to resist, and most of the gang were destroyed, I having with much difficulty made my escape with a large sum of money. I now made my way to Italy—re-assumed all the style of a man of fashion, and mixed in similar society to that I had been used to in former days. I assumed the name of Chevalier Arnaud, and my company was much sought after by the gay and thoughtless. I told Madame de Floriville not this, recollect, Caleb, but that I immediately came to England. But it was not so ; although I was several times on the point of doing so, hearing that my wife and child were there.

" I have before told thee that I had again launched forth into my former course of life, and my time was almost entirely occupied in scenes of riot, debauchery, and extravagance. In my gambling transactions I was very successful for a time ; but, at length, fortune turned the scales against me, and two or three heavy losses succeeding one another, brought me almost to ruin. To have to abandon my gay life I could not bear to think upon for a moment, and I determined to adopt some plan by which I might retrieve my fortune. It was long ere I hit upon a scheme, which will, doubtless, excite thy wonder and abhorrence.

" I have informed thee what a favourite I was with the fair sex, who, of course, all believed me to be a single man. But there was one who paid me more particular attention than any of the rest, and who had succeeded in implanting in my breast a considerable sensation. This was the Signora Floretta, a very beautiful female, young, accomplished, gay, and fascinating ; and possessing a still greater attraction in my eyes— namely, a very large fortune. To her I now devoted my whole attention ; declared my passion for her, and had the satisfaction to be received with favour. To be brief, in a few weeks after this, the Signora Floretta became my wife."

" Thy wife! Monsieur de Floriville ?" ejaculated Caleb, with unfeigned astonishment and incredulity ; " thy wife, and Madame de Floriville still living ?"

" Even so, Caleb," returned Adolphe, coolly ; " but what was I to do?—I had beggared myself. I shuddered at the idea of being again reduced to poverty. Floretta had charms, accomplishments, wealth ; Laurette was parted from me, I believed, for

ever, and thou knowest what followed—I have told thee."

" Oh, Monsieur de Floriville," said Caleb.

" Hush!" hastily interrupted the former ; " that name must never be mentioned now ; Monsieur Arnaud in future, if you please."

" Well, then, Monsieur Arnaud," observed Caleb Swinton, " can it be possible, I say, that you can so far have forgotten your natural feelings towards your amiable and unfortunate wife and your only son as to have done as you say ?"

" It is, indeed, possible, Caleb, and likewise true," returned Adolphe, coolly ; " I know you will say it was very wrong, and so it was ; but what had I to do with honour or justice ? If I were to say that I forgot Laurette or my child, I should be telling an untruth—they would often rush to my memory in characters so vivid that I was nearly driven to my former horrible state of mind. At such times, however, I had recourse to society and the exciting draught, and I seldom failed to find them very good antidotes for my melancholy. Besides, were I not, I reflected, in a manner of speaking, dead to the world ?—at least, in my former character —entering into a fresh career ; and it behoved me—at least, so I considered—to do the best I could for myself, and to study no one else. I can see that thou dost not approve of this kind of reasoning, and I do not wonder at it. But enough of this—I and Floretta, I repeat, were united, and I once more became the possessor of great wealth, and was thus enabled to indulge in all my wild and dissipated propensities. Floretta and I lived very happily together for some time, and I am convinced that she loved me with the most ardent affection. She was a beautiful woman, and possessed of intrinsic charms far surpassing those of her person. She deserved a better fate. Several months rolled on in this manner, without anything worthy particular notice taking place. In due course of time my wife presented me with a lovely girl."

Caleb Swinton at this again raised his hands and eyes towards Heaven with an expression of astonishment, and then looked at Adolphe with an air of incredulity.

" Well, Caleb," said De Floriville, with an indifferent and hardened smile, " why dost thou express so much surprise, forsooth ? Is there anything so wonderful in Floretta bearing me a daughter ?"

" Oh dear! oh dear!" said Caleb, " there is nothing wonderful, to be sure, in the matter, but then it seems so unnatural."

" On that point thou and I disagree, Master Swinton," remarked De Floriville, " for I think nothing could be more natural."

" Well," uttered Caleb, " may the difference of opinion—you know the rest ; but for my part, Monsieur Arnaud—if I must call you so—it does seem to me so very unnatural that you should marry another woman, and that that woman should bear you another child, and all the while your own right lawful child are alive. But are the two poor things now living?"

"Thou shalt hear. Previous to the last event taking place of which I have informed thee, I had greatly impoverished the fortune I had had with Floretta, having entered with increased spirit into the ruinous course I had formerly pursued. Floretta, at first, took very little notice of my conduct, hoping that I should quickly see through my folly, and reform; but when she found that my extravagance increased rather than abated, she gently remonstrated with me on the subject, and pointed out the ruinous consequences that must ensue, should I persist in my present folly. I pretended to be deeply impressed by her observation, and promised to attend to her advice. For a few weeks after this all went on very well, but at the end of that time I forgot all the promises I had made to Floretta, and entered with redoubled recklessness into those scenes of improvidence that had first led me to crime, and which were quickly working my ruin. Many a pang, many a tear did it cost Floretta, and often did she affectionately expostulate with me, but it was all to no purpose. I confess that there were times, however, when I could not help being much moved by her words, and the suffering I knew I was inflicting upon one who deserved a fate so different; and I could not help reproaching myself severely for my conduct. At such times I would forswear my vices, and vow to abandon my unprincipled companions; but these promises were soon forgotten, and in the wild and destructive vortex of dissipation I lost all thought, all care of everything but my own evil passions. Only a few more months elapsed, and I again found myself a ruined man, and Floretta, my victim, apparently dying of a broken heart. What did I then? I know thou wilt shudder when I tell thee—that thou wilt call me monster, and feel repugnance and abhorrence in my presence; but it matters not—I am now quite used to the scorn, the hatred, and contempt of mankind. Collecting what small sum of money was remaining out of Floretta's once handsome fortune, and a few articles of jewellery, of which I afterwards disposed, I abandoned her and her child, and made my way through France to this country, being determined to find out my wife."

"Heartless miscreant!" Caleb Swinton could scarcely refrain from exclaiming, as Adolphe made this shameful acknowledgment of his unparalleled villany; and a pang of the most poignant regret darted through the breast of the good-hearted man when he reflected that Adolphe, having found out the retreat of Madame de Floriville, would, in all probability, be the cause of much misery to her, and, perhaps, bring upon her contumely and disgrace. He felt such complete horror and disgust at the wretched and guilty Adolphe, that he shuddered at his presence, and could scarcely look upon him

with any degree of patience. Adolphe read the thoughts that were passing in the mind of Caleb Swinton, but he regarded them not; as we have before stated, he had become completely callous to all sense of shame or feeling, and was fully prepared to encounter reproach and detestation. He paused a few moments in silence, and looked at Caleb earnestly, but with the utmost indifference.

"Oh, dear, monsieur," at length exclaimed Caleb, "and how could you possibly be so cruel to one whom you have stated to have been so kind and affectionate to you?"

"It matters not," answered Adolphe; "I did find the heart to do it, and here I am, thou seest. What was the use of my remaining with Floretta and her offspring in misery? I had no means of relieving them, and I had experienced enough of the horrors of want in my former days."

"And that is the very reason, monsieur," returned Caleb Swinton—"for that very reason I should have thought that what you then suffered would have taught you a lesson that you would never have forgot; and that, when fortune again smiled upon you, you would have known better than formerly how to take care of her favours."

"Psha!" remarked De Floriville, impatiently, "what is the use of talking in that manner to a gamester, a robber, and a murderer? I and feeling have long since parted company, and I dare say we shall never be on very intimate terms again—I have no wish to renew the acquaintance. Besides, Floretta is still young and handsome, and will, no doubt, soon forget me, and meet with another husband or a protector. At any rate she must not expect to see me again; and I dare say that by this time all the love she once bore me is turned to hatred, and if she has a wish to see me, it is only that she might have an opportunity of gratifying that vengeance which is doubtless engendered in her veins."

"But for what purpose have you sought out Madame de Floriville?" asked Caleb.

"For what purpose dost thou suppose a man would seek out a wife from whom he has long been separated?"

"You would not force her to live with you again?" said Caleb.

"That depends upon circumstances," answered the other.

"But you forget, monsieur," returned Caleb, "that the world believe you dead."

"And so much the better; Laurette may, therefore, be less scrupulous in receiving me. It would not be quite so safe or convenient for my real character to be known," answered Adolphe.

"But how could you claim her as your wife without revealing the secret?"

"Very easily," replied De Floriville. "Laurette has never been known here by any other name than that of Madame Le Sange. No person except thyself is acquainted with her real circumstances, unless it be that loquacious minx, Annette, who, I suspect, hath been listening to the conversation which passed between me and Laurette on our meeting; but she must be silenced. Who then is to know but that I am Monsieur Le Sange, or Monsieur Arnaud, the husband from whom she had been parted, but to whom she is again reconciled?"

Caleb Swinton shook his head, but made no reply. His fears for Madame de Floriville increased, and he plainly foresaw that fresh misfortunes of a still more painful nature, if possible, than any she had yet endured, were in store for her; and greatly attached as Caleb was to the unfortunate lady, he could not think of it without the most poignant anguish.

"To summon up my intentions in a very few words," said Adolphe, after a pause, "Laurette has an ample fortune—I have not a *sous*; and as I cannot make up my mind to endure poverty when there are the means to avoid it, why I shall e'en take the liberty of putting in my claim upon it."

The disgust of Caleb at the ruffianly manners and determined tone of De Floriville increased every moment, and he could scarcely believe that he heard aright, but was half inclined to imagine that his senses deceived him. Base and cruel as Adolphe had formerly been, yet there were moments when he was most sensitively alive to gentler feelings and the voice of compunction; but here stood a wretch who seemed completely dead to everything but his own guilty passions, and who appeared absolutely to exult in his iniquity. Adolphe noticed the sentiments with which Caleb contemplated him, but they seemed to make no other impression upon him than to amuse him, and for a few seconds he carelessly lolled in his chair, with one leg swinging over the other, and whistling a portion of a licentious air at that time very popular among the profligate young men of France and other nations.

"But, Monsieur," remarked Caleb, at length, in reply to the observations which De Floriville had just before made, "you will pardon my boldness, but I would take the liberty of reminding you that you cannot put in your claim to the property which has devolved upon your wife without betraying yourself, and——"

"Bah!" interrupted Adolphe, impatiently; "and why cannot I do as I have said? Thinkest thou that Laurette will not have too much respect for herself and my son to divulge the secret? Would not eternal disgrace be the consequence?"

"But surely you would not be so cruel as to——"

"It matters not what I would do," interrupted De Floriville; "time will show that. I must have money—I must live unrestrained, unshackled—I cannot abandon my course of life, and I must and will have the means of supporting me in it, of that I am determined."

"Heaven protect the poor dear lady, then," cried Caleb, fervently, "for without its in-

terference I see nothing but misery and ruin before her."

"There, there, no more of this foolery," said De Floriville, "but get thee hence, and bring a bottle of the best Rhenish thou hast in thy cellar. Good wine is far better than a sermon at any time; besides, as it is so long since we have met before, we must e'en drink together for old acquaintance sake. Thou need'st not hesitate, thou shalt have the money for it. I have yet sufficient left in my purse to pay for a few bottles of wine, and when it is empty, why I know very well how to get it replenished."

How deeply did Caled Swinton regret the unfortunate circumstance which had brought De Floriville to his house, or to England at all. He would almost as soon have had Beelzebub himself for a guest as one whom he had every reason to believe was no great deal better. But he felt more for Madame de Floriville, and earnestly prayed that something might occur—some intervention of Providence - to save her from the suffering with which she was now threatened. As to drinking with De Floriville, he shuddered at the bare idea; but still he was equally fearful of refusing him, not knowing to what lengths he might be tempted to go, and being by no means anxious to excite his anger. He therefore immediately hastened to comply with De Floriville's request, and brought a bottle of wine on the table, hoping that when he had despatched it, as it was getting late, he would retire to his chamber, or, at any rate, that more guests might make their appearance, and thus prevent them from joining in conversation together.

Having, much against his will, drank the contents of a glass which De Floriville handed to him, Caleb Swinton took the earliest opportunity of leaving his presence, and busied himself about in another part of the house. On the entrance of two or three guests, Adolphe hastily arose from his chair, and, quitting the room, made his way to his own chamber, much to the relief of our worthy host, who now felt as if a spell were upon his house—a curse—while such a guilty wretch remained in it.

Early on the following morning, one of the servants of Caleb Swinton came to him with a very pale countenance, and in accents of terror informed him that he was very sorry, but that he was fearful he should have to leave his service.

"For what reason?" demanded Swinton, surprised at the terror evinced by the man.

"For what reason!" responded the servant, "why I verily believe that either that mysterious gentleman who has lodged here for the last two nights is none other than the old gentleman himself, or else this house is haunted, to a certainty."

"What do you mean?" asked Caleb.

"Why, I'll tell you," returned the man. "You know I sleep in the same gallery as the mysterious stranger; and last night, and the night before too, I couldn't get a wink of sleep for the terrible noises that proceeded from the room the stranger sleeps in."

" Noises?" responded Caleb.

"Yes," answered the servant, " such noises as I never heard in my life before, and which could only have proceeded from some ghost, or hobgoblin, or devil, or something of the kind. I am not much of a coward, I flatter myself; but I must confess that I never felt so frightened in the whole course of my life before."

"Nonsense, man," said Caleb, who affected incredulity, although he was far from feeling it; " thou must surely have been mistaken; some dream hath alarmed thee."

"Oh, no," said the man, positively, "it was no dream. I was as wide awake as I am at present. Besides, it's not very likely that I should dream the same thing on two successive nights."

" Well, but what kind of noises were they that thou heard?" demanded Caleb Swinton; " describe them to me."

"Why, that is rather a bit of a puzzler to me," returned the man; "but I am certain they were supernatural. There was such a shrieking and groaning, and like the indistinct muttering of a number of voices; then a tremendous weight seemed to fall upon the floor, as if the roof of the house were falling in. After this all would be silent for a few minutes, when the noises would be renewed with redoubled loudness. I remained in bed some time listening to these sounds, and trembling like an aspen leaf, but at last I could not hear it any longer; so I jumped out of bed, and opening the door, looked out on to the gallery, in the direction of the mysterious stranger's chamber; and you may believe me, master, or believe me not, but as true as you sit there, I saw a blue light burning from under the door of the room in which that man sleeps, and there was such a rattling, and groaning, and clanking, as if of heavy chains, that it was enough to make any one suppose that a number of felons had broken loose from prison, and taken up their residence in the apartment of which I have been speaking. Overcome with terror, I rushed back into my room, and locked and bolted myself in, but the noises were repeated at intervals till daylight, which, I can tell you, I was glad enough to see."

"This is a curious story," said Caleb Swinton, who was much alarmed at what the man had been relating, but did not wish him to observe that he was so; " but I still think that you must have been mistaken, or else that you have been dreaming. However, I will make inquiry into the matter; in the meantime, I desire, William, that thou wilt not say anything about it to the other servants."

"I will do as you request, sir," answered William; "but as to sleeping another night in that room, while the mysterious stranger is so close a neighbour of mine, I positively will not. Why, I should be carried away neck and crop some of these nights by the evil spirits I am quite certain he associates with."

" Well, I don't suppose that you will be annoyed with him many nights, if thou art again," said Caleb: "and although I am certain that he is real flesh and blood, and no ghost or devil, as thou seemest to imagine, I confess, William, that I shall not be sorry when I have got rid of my guest."

"I dare say not, sir," returned William; " but either he or I must go soon, and that's all about it. I would not stay in a house where there was such a suspicious character, to say the least of him, not for all the world."

" Rest assured, William," said his master, "that thou hast nothing to apprehend from him, for I know him, and can, therefore, satisfy thee on that point."

" Oh, if you know him, sir," observed the man, " that's quite another thing; though I must say that I don't envy you your acquaintance—excuse my making so bold, sir."

" Enough—get thee gone to thy business, William," said Caleb, " and remember the warning I have given thee, not to say anything about this affair to thy companions."

William promised obedience, and they separated.

CHAPTER XI.

THE INTERVIEW.—THE PORTRAIT.

VERY little did Madame de Floriville sleep on the night after the meeting with her wretched, guilty husband, the particulars of which we have described in a previous chapter; and when for a short time slumber did descend upon her eyelids, dreams of the most alarming description would haunt and torture her imagination. Now, she beheld Adolphe as she first saw him, ere guilt, as she believed, had contaminated him, and when his numerous accomplishments rendered him an object that few females could have resisted. Then again the scene was changed; her father's countenance frowned upon her, and his lips again pronounced that dreadful malediction, which had haunted her imagination ever since; and his long bony finger pointed solemnly towards the portrait of her mother, and recalled to her memory the dreadful story of that mother's wrongs—those wrongs that had been heaped upon her by the father of her husband. From this scene, fancy quickly hurried her to the miserable hut in the forest, where herself, Adolphe, and their son, had endured all the horrors of want. In rapid succession followed the events which had occurred subsequently;—the confession of Adolphe, the murder of his brother, the apprehension, the gloomy dungeon, the trial, the condemnation, the escape, the forest, the bridge of death, the pursuit, the supposed awful death of her husband, and the phantom of his murdered friend; her own trial, her sentence, the separation from her child, her imprisonment, and the many painful circumstances that had afterwards taken place, all these were recalled to her imagination, with visionary horror, in characters so painful that sleep became a misery to her. Fancy was also most busy to conjure up visions of the future, and most alarming they were. At one time she was struggling in the grasp of her husband, who held a dagger to her breast, and whose eyes flashed with the most ferocious determination; at another, she saw Henri seated in friendly intercourse with her father, and seeming to treat her with scorn and neglect. In an instant the scene was changed, and a chapel, gaily decorated and brilliantly illuminated, now met her gaze. Before the altar knelt Henri (who had now grown into manhood,) and a beauteous girl, whose features sparkled with love and happiness. The priest had just completed the bridal ceremony, when suddenly a peal of thunder shook the sacred building to its foundation, and in an instant there appeared, standing in the centre of the aisle, the dread phantom of her (Madame Laurette's) father. His looks were dreadful, and, as he fixed them upon Henri, he exclaimed, in a voice that re-echoed throughout the building—

"Incestuous wretch! offspring of the accursed! *thou hast married thy sister!*"

The words had no sooner escaped the lips of the spectre, than, with a deep groan, the bride and the bridegroom sank senseless to the earth, the scene and the objects in it

THE DREAM OF MADAME DE FLORIVILLE.

gradually faded from Madame de Floriville's sight, and she awoke. Cold drops of perspiration bedewed her temples, a deadly chill was at her heart, her limbs trembled violently, and she looked fearfully around, almost fearing to see the subject of her dream realised; and, indeed, for a few moments scarcely able to persuade herself that it had not been reality.

The latter part of the vision filled her mind with a variety of the most painful conjectures, and created in her bosom the utmost astonishment and mystery. The singular words of the spectre seemed to ring in her ears, and made a wonderful and powerful impression upon her mind; and for some time after she had awoke, she lay tossing restlessly in bed, and racking her brain to no purpose, to endeavour to solve the awful mystery.

"Offspring of the accursed!" she ejaculated; "alas! alas! how painfully—how fearfully do I feel the truth of these words; bitterly indeed hath thy malediction, my father, been visited upon my head; but oh, in mercy, Heaven, let it not descend to my poor boy; if I have not suffered already enough for my disobedience to my parents' will—if I have not made sufficient atonement for an offence which love, too powerful love, and not actual guilt, led me to commit, oh, let me alone suffer, but spare my innocent—my unoffending child. But what could these words mean? His *sister!*—what sister? he is my only offspring, and—but I will not thus give way to apprehension; it was only a terrific vision, created by the wild and feverish state of my brain. It is not at all marvellous that I should be thus weak."

The sun now sent forth his golden flood of light into the chamber of Madame de Floriville, and with a heavy heart, and the most melancholy apprehensions, she arose. In two hours, according to the appointment, she might expect Adolphe, and as the time approached, her fears increased. She shuddered at the very idea of encountering that man, so stained with crime, and apparently so callous to all feelings of humanity—that man to whom she was unfortunately indissolubly bound by the laws of matrimony. Formerly, with all his guilt, she had clung to him devotedly, and shared with him all his dangers and his miseries; and now, although still the terms of that powerful affection she had felt for him, remained in her heart, disgust and horror also had the most powerful ascendancy. The motives that had brought him to her at that time, also, she could not help thinking, were not those of affection (for all such sentiments as that seemed stifled in his breast), but with a guilty determination to extort from her money, and to make her subservient to his vicious propensities. In the interview which had taken place between them the day before, she had well read his thoughts, and the hardened, reckless, callous villain was visible in all he said, and thus rendered him to her an object of the greatest horror. Besides, there were several reasons why she should tremble at the appearance of Adolphe. Her father's curse, the corruption and disgrace any connection with him would undoubtedly bring upon her and her son, and the surprise and suspicion it would create in the minds of the persons in the neighbourhood, and the subject it would afford for the envenomed tongue of slander. Such a circumstance would ruin the prospects of Henri in the world; and yet how to avoid it she knew not.

During the time that Annette was assisting her mistress at the *toilette*, she took the greatest notice of the deep melancholy which oppressed her, and although she was not surprised at the circumstance, knowing, as she did, the cause, her insufferable curiosity and loquacity, made her feel most uncomfortably anxious to become acquainted with every little particular of the affair, and she tried by every sort of manœuvre to elicit the same from her mistress. But Madame Laurette was in no mood to gratify her weakness, and being, above all things, opposed to inquisitiveness, and never liking to make confidants of her servants, Annette succeeded but very seldom in gaining the most trifling piece of information from her.

"I hope to goodness, madame," said the talkative maid, "I hope to goodness that strange and frightful-looking man will not come here again to-day. I'm sure he put me all in a quandary last night after he left here."

"After he left here, Annette?" asked her mistress, with surprise; "where did you see him?"

"Why—why," faltered Annette, "you know, madame, that—that—that is, I am rather partial to Gregory Goldfinch, at The Traveller's Rest, and the little man is stark-staring mad in love with me; which I dare say, madame, you will say, is not the least wonder, considering my personal appearance, and all that; so I went there to pay him a visit."

"Annette," said Madame de Floriville, seriously; "I hope you did not divulge a word to any one about the visit of that person to me."

"Oh, bless your soul, madame!" observed Annette, "how could you possibly suspect me of such a thing? You know I am not so communicative. I am not like many of my sex, always talking and chatting about that which does not concern them; and as to keeping a secret, there's not a female in the universe, I do believe, that can equal me. In fact, I am certain there is not."

"Annette, I caution you, as you value my pleasure, and regard my peace of mind," remarked Madame Laurette, "never to divulge a sentence to any one upon this subject."

"Of course I will not, madame," returned Annette; "you may trust me."

"I hope so," returned her mistress. "The stranger will probably remain in the neighbourhood and may frequently be a visitor here, but you must take no notice of him, and above all, treat him with becoming respect."

"The first part of your injunctions, I will strictly obey, madame," said Annette; "but as for the latter, I'm afraid it's a task I shall never be able to accomplish."

"But you must do so, or else lose my favour."

"Well, I wouldn't do that for the world, madame; but really I think I shall be very much puzzled to comply with your wishes in that respect. He is such an awful looking man—one who appears as if he had been guilty of some dreadful crime or the other. I'm sure I should not like to meet him after dark. Dear me, surely he cannot be related to you, madame?"

"It matters not," answered Madame Laurette; "you know I never like to gratify impertinent curiosity."

"Impertinent, madame?" said the maid abashed; "dear me, how you have mistaken me. To be impertinent, I'm sure, was the farthest thing from my thoughts; and if no one was more curious than I am, there would not be half the mischief in the world that there is. I was only going to observe——"

"Never mind what you were going to observe, Annette," interrupted her mistress, "do as I have desired you, and never venture to mention the subject to me, unless I speak to you about it."

"Very well, madame; but all that I was going to say was, that he almost frightened me and Gregory into fits last night, when he interrupted us in our little bit of chit-chat."

"I am afraid, Annette, that you were talking about something that did not concern you."

"Oh, no, madame, indeed we were not."

"The stranger will be here again this morning," said Madame de Floriville, sighing, as she prepared to quit her chamber; "and remember my injunctions—they must be obeyed."

Annette curtseyed, and promised to do as her mistress desired; and the latter then quitted the apartment.

"A very pretty way she would be in, certainly, if she were aware that I knew all about it," said Annette, when Madame de Floriville had gone; "but I shall never be satisfied until I have learned all the particulars about my lady's husband—the cause of her separation, and what it is he wants with her now. I must have another listen this morning."

Henri, like his mother, had been troubled with painful dreams, his mind being busily occupied with the singular events of the day. His father still alive and returned! It seemed scarcely possible; and the injunctions of his mother, and his own feelings, told him that it was a circumstance at which they had every reason to grieve instead of rejoice. And now rushed to his memory again the painful recollection of those awful circumstances that have been recorded in the early part of this narrative; and, young as Henri was at the time, they were of that powerful and impressive description, that they were not likely to be easily erased from his recollection. Henri shuddered when he thought of them, and yet he could not dwell upon his father's name without feeling all the strength of that affection which nature inspired.

Eager to meet his mother, and to ascertain the state of her mind, and whether she was at all in a condition to meet his guilty but unfortunate parent, Henri arose at an early hour, and walked into the sitting-room, where he awaited until Madame de Floriville descended from her chamber. He flew to meet her when she entered the room, and throwing her arms about his neck, she embraced him with even more than her usual fervour.

Henri fixed his eyes intently upon his mother, and observing how pale and agitated she looked, he remarked—

"Alas! mother, I see you are not well. Care sits heavily on your brow. I am fearful the surprise you have experienced has been too much for your feelings to support. You will never have strength sufficient to undergo the interview this morning."

"Fear not for me, my son," replied his mother; "I am not more agitated than

might have been expected on the occurrence of such an event as that which has taken place with me; and Heaven, I trust, will support me throughout this meeting with your father. Father, alas! I tremble at the name. It is a title to which he has every claim, but which his crimes have rendered it imperatively necessary you should never more bestow upon him."

"Oh, mother, how hard are the rules that stern necessity impose upon me. In spite of all—and notwithstanding my anxious wish to obey you in every respect, there is an instinctive voice within me which keeps whispering, he is still my father, in spite of his offences, and that I must love him as a son."

"It would be unnatural wert thou not to do so, Henri," said his mother; "yet thou must learn rather to pity him for his vices, and to pray to Heaven to pardon him. Let the misery he has brought upon himself and others by his improvidence and folly, be a warning to thee to shun that path whose termination is destruction, and which leads to misery and disgrace."

"This advice, dearest mother," sighed Henri, "shall not be lost upon me;—but may I not be present at the meeting between you and my father?—may I not be permitted to embrace him, since it must be so, for the last time?"

"No, my child, it may not be," replied Madame Laurette; "if I were to permit thee to be present, it might have an effect that I am very anxious to avoid. Besides, there are many things that will doubtless be said which I would not should reach thine ear. Nay, Henri, banish that look of grief and regret, and endeavour to submit patiently to my will."

"I will do so," returned Henri, "because it is my duty; but indeed it will require the exertion of all my energies to do so with the patience you advise, dear mother. Hark! some one knocks at the door."

"It is doubtless he," said Laurette; "now, Heaven, I pray thine aid! Oh! give me fortitude to act as my duty, stern as it is, prompts me. Away, Henri, away; he must not see you."

"I go, mother," observed Henri, "and may Omnipotence grant you its Almighty aid."

Madame de Floriville and her son once more stole a hasty and fervent embrace, and the latter then hurried from the room. Madame de Floriville made a powerful effort to regain her composure, and she partially succeeded. She did not hear any one approach, and yet the outer door had been opened, and the person, whoever it was, admitted. It was just the time that Adolphe had said he would be there, and surely it must be him. She was about to ring the bell to summon Annette into her presence, when she heard some one ascending the stairs; they stopped at the room-door—the next moment they knocked, and directly afterwards the object of her thoughts stood before her.

"Well, Laurette," said Adolphe, after a pause, during which his eyes had been fixed with a searching expression upon the countenance of his wife, "we are alone, I believe?"

"We are," answered Madame de Floriville, in a firm voice.

"I must be certain of that," observed Adolphe, opening the door, and looking out; "there is no one there; but are there no apartments contiguous to this, where a person might conceal themselves and overhear our conversation?"

"There are," answered his wife, "but they belong to me, and no one can obtain access to them without my permission."

"'Tis well," returned Adolphe, "'tis well, Laurette,—my wife, partner of my misfortunes, sole possessor of my love,—thus, thus in my arms let me enfold thee, and——"

Laurette drew back from him with a shudder of horror, and at that moment, to her fevered imagination, Adolphe's hands seemed stained with human blood, the blood of his murdered victims, and the eyes of her father appeared fixed upon her.

"Ah!" exclaimed Adolphe, with well-assumed emotion, "dost thou view me with abhorrence? Dost thou despise and hate me as something loathsome? Oh, Laurette, Laurette, canst thou really have forgotten our early love; the many vows thou has so often made, and after the devoted manner in which thou didst behave to me in my greatest hour of trial? Surely I dream; this cannot be Laurette de Floriville, the fondly attached wife, ready to make any sacrifice for her husband's sake! Laurette, tell me, dost thou hate me?"

"Hate thee, Adolphe," said our heroine, "hate thee? Oh, would that I could; would that I could forget that thou didst ever exist, then might I lose all remembrance of those dreadful deeds with which thy name is associated. Oh, Adolphe, well mightest thou formerly tell me that I should hate thee, abhor thee, shun the path thou troddest, for a pestilence was in it; bitterly have I felt the truth of this, and severely has my heart since been reproached for the strange infatuation to which it yielded, and, in a manner of speaking, made me a participator in the horrible crimes of which thou wert the perpetrator."

"Laurette," returned Adolphe, apparently not in the least moved by the awful reminiscences of the words his wife must have brought to his memory;—"Laurette, thou must forget the past, and live alone for the future; I am thy husband by all laws, human and divine, and I will live with thee henceforward."

"Never!" cried Laurette, resolutely, "thou art no longer my husband; thy crimes have dissolved the union for ever, and rendered thy life forfeited to the offended laws of the country."

"Laurette," ejaculated Adolphe, eagerly, and fixing a searching glance upon her countenance; "wouldst thou denounce me to the world?"

"Oh, no, no," answered his wife, with the deepest emotion. "Heaven forbid! Adolphe, it is thyself that would do so; for how couldst thou claim me as thy wife, without making known thy real character?

"The world," replied De Floriville, "believe me dead;—thou art known only by the name of Madame le Sange; I, as the Chevalier Arnaud: it matters little under which of those names I claim thee. Laurette, my determination is made up; we part no more."

"Oh, Adolphe, hear me, forbear, I implore," exclaimed Madame De Floriville "do not urge that which could only bring us both to destruction, and sacrifice the prospects of our son. Live for repentance, and my prayers shall daily be offered up to Heaven for thy forgiveness, and that happiness may light upon thee."

"Prayers," sneered Adolphe, ironically; "cant, hollow, sickening cant; I want them not. Laurette, wouldst live in luxury and wealth, and know that thine own husband, he whom thou didst once profess to love to distraction, was in poverty and destitution?"

"Oh, no, Adolphe," returned Madame de Floriville, catching eagerly at his words, but with a feeling of the most powerful disgust as she read the sordid motives which guided his conduct, instead of that affection which he would pretend to;—"if it is money alone thou wouldst have, willingly will I share my fortune with thee; my own wants are but few, and, therefore, I covet not useless riches; my Henri is also provided for : therefore, Apolphe, take my wealth, and live away from me, and endeavour, by the rectitude of thy future conduct, to make some atonement for the past."

"Humph!" ejaculated Adolphe, with a disagreeable smile, "how readily and coolly thou canst advise, Laurette; but I tell thee, although, of course, I shall have all that my necessities may compel me to demand of thee, I must have much more before I shall be satisfied."

"Adolphe," said Madame Laurette, "I perceive too clearly that thou art determined to make me still more wretched than thy numerous crimes and vices have already rendered me. Cruel man, is it not enough that through thee I lost my father's home, my father's love; that I suffered all the horrors of destitution and want; that I was afterwards exposed to an ignominious trial, on a charge which freezes my blood with horror when I think of it, and afterwards was doomed to a long and dreary incarceration; separated from my child, and every other earthly pleasure? Were these not enough, I say, but now thou again seekest to expose me to tenfold greater misery and disgrace. Adolphe, thou couldst never have really loved me, or thou wouldst revolt from the course thou art at present pursuing towards me."

"Laurette," returned Adolphe, "thou hast linked thy fate with mine, and nothing must separate us. Thou reproachest me, and accusest me of never having loved thee; but where could thy love have been when thou couldst thus tear me from thy memory, abandon me, and treat me only with thy scorn and detestation?"

"Thou wrongest me, Adolphe, by Heaven, thou dost!" exclaimed his wife: "how I have loved thee, God knows, and thou thyself must feel convinced, although thou deniest it now; and even yet, with all thy guilt, and my father's curse still vibrating in my ears, that passion holds its power over my heart;—but—but, Adolphe, I can say no more; prudence and justice prompts my conduct; if thou wouldst not drive me to madness, leave me. Here is money—money sufficient to keep thee in affluence all the rest of thy days; in pity away, then, repent, reform, and although we may not meet again, rest assured that the prayers, the blessings of thine unfortunate wife shall ever ascend to Heaven for thee."

"Psha!" cried Adolphe, impatiently; "have I not before told thee, Laurette, how I dislike this mawkish cant, fit alone for bigots and children? No more of it; I tell thee I will not only have gold, but I will again become thy partner."

"Oh, never, never; death would be preferable to that."

"Didst thou not vow at the altar, to love none other but me, and to remain faithful to me till death?"

"I did—I did. I have never loved any but thee, Adolphe; thine own crimes have absolved me from the other portion of those vows."

"A shallow argument, which will not answer thy purpose, Laurette," said Adolphe, 'my resolution is irrevocably formed:—I claim thee mine; and, in a few days, shall come and take up my residence with thee."

"Oh, for pity's sake, for the sake of our son, think of the surmises that will be formed by the censorious and slanderous world."

"And what needest thou care for the opinion of the world? It is a weakness that I have long since conquered, Laurette, and which I hope to cure in thee ere long. Besides, can we not quit this neighbourhood, and go where we are not known, and then——"

"Oh, no, no," cried Madame de Floriville, "we may go where we are unknown; but what can drive the remembrance of thy crimes from my recollection? How, thinkest thou, I could be content to live with a man whose hands are stained with the blood of the murdered?—Never! by Heaven!"

"But it shall be so," observed De Floriville, in a stern voice; "prepare thyself, Laurette, to receive once more thy lawful husband to thine arms. Thou hast offered gold, but am I not master of all thou possessest? Is not thy fortune my fortune?—thine home my home?"

"Adolphe de Floriville," said his wife, in firm and solemn tones; "thou hast hitherto found me quiet, passive, obedient: thou hast taken advantage of those feelings, and now think to force me into a compliance with thy will; but thou hast yet to learn that I can resist any attempt at tyranny or cruelty with a determined spirit. Beware, I caution thee; mind that thou dost not arouse that spirit in the present instance, or thou mayest repent it."

"Astonishment!" exclaimed De Floriville, fixing on his wife a look of incredulity; "Laurette threaten! I can scarce believe the evidence of my senses. Woman, what wouldst thou do?"

"I'll tell thee, Adolphe," answered Laurette, firmly; "sooner than I would live with thee again, I would denounce thee to the world as that Adolphe de Floriville, whose crimes have rendered his name odious, and whose life is forfeited to the outraged laws of his country."

"Ah! sayest thou so?" eagerly ejaculated De Floriville, and his eyes flashed fiercely while he spoke. "Can this be Laurette? Can this be she who was once all gentleness and love, and who would now consign her husband to the scaffold?"

"I would fain avoid so terrible a course, Adolphe," returned Madame de Floriville; "but sooner than be forced again to be thy partner, I would adopt it!"

"But the disgrace, the ignominy, it would bring on thy name and that of thy son!" remarked Adolphe.

"Even that I would encounter; nay, death itself, rather than quietly yield to thy wishes. Oh! could I again endure the horrors I have before suffered with thee, and whenever my thoughts have been directed towards thee? Never—never! Adolphe, thinkest thou that I could again live with the ghastly shade of my father ever in my presence, to hear his fearful curse continually ringing in mine ears? Oh, no! no horror could be so great as that. Adolphe, look on the portrait of that man who gave me being. Canst thou gaze upon it without a shudder?—No, I know thou canst not. Ah, see; the eyes seem fixed upon thee. Gracious powers! one could almost swear that they sparkled with life and expression —that they frowned upon thee. Look—look; dost thou not see, Adolphe? There again.—By Heaven, they move!"

As Madame Laurette thus spoke she laid her hand upon the arm of her husband, and directed his attention towards the portrait. He seemed to shrink from the contemplation of it; his lips quivered, and his face became pale. Strange! could it be delusion? Just as Madame de Floriville described it, so did the eyes of the portrait absolutely appear to move, until they finally became fixed on the countenance of De Floriville, with a stern expression, that was sufficient to penetrate to the guilty soul of the murderer. A violent trembling seized upon his limbs, and unable to repress a groan of horror, he averted his gaze.

"Ah, Adolphe, I see," said Madame Laurette, "thou canst not behold this unmoved. Obey the decrees of Heaven; leave me, and at a distance from me live to repent of the numerous crimes of which thou hast been guilty. Here, take money sufficient for thy wants; nay, even the whole of my fortune, but do not again torture me by thy presence."

Adolphe soon recovered himself, and in accents of base determination said,—

"Fool that I am to give way to this worse than childish weakness. Laurette, thine unnatural request but increases my resolution. Think upon the days of our warmest affection, and say, canst thou wish to cast from thee that man thou didst once pretend to adore? Oh, no, thou must not, thou wilt not. Thou art labouring under some strange delusion, which it shall be my study to banish. I will be all that thou canst wish me to be—the same affectionate Adolphe that I was when first we breathed our mutual vows of love. Thy gentle presence, thy blest society alone can soothe me to peace, and draw my soul to repentance. Thou wilt consent;—thou wilt no longer remain obstinate. Let, then, this kiss, this fond embrace——"

"Hold! unhand me, Adolphe!" cried Laurette, as the former once more threw his arms around her, and endeavoured to press her lips to his.

"Nay," exclaimed the villain, "thou seekest to resist me in vain. Wife!—Laurette! —Mine for ever!"

At that moment a deep sepulchral groan smote their ears, and the portrait, from which the sound seemed to proceed, fell to the floor with a loud crash. Adolphe involuntarily released his hold of his wife, and starting to the other side of the room, became transfixed to the spot with surprise and consternation.

"Didst thou not hear that groan, Adolphe?" demanded Madame de Floriville, in solemn accents. "Oh, beware, beware! The voice of the dead speaks to warn thee."

"Can this be real? or hath madness seized upon me?" cried De Floriville. "Psha! what a very idiot I am; this is all some damned mockery."

"It is no mockery, Adolphe," returned his wife, "but the voice of Heaven speaking through the spirit of my father. Do not rashly bid defiance to its Almighty will."

Adolphe returned no answer, but folded his arms, and traversed the room for a few minutes, apparently buried in deep and painful thought. At length, turning to Laurette, he said,—

"For the present, Laurette, I bid thee farewell, but think not that I shall abandon my design; no, in a few days thou wilt, doubtless, behold me again, and I advise thee, then, to receive me in a manner more consonant with my wishes than thou hast

done this day; but ere I go, I must have money."

"'Tis here," replied Laurette, eagerly, and with violent emotion, unlocking an iron chest which stood in one corner of the apartment, and disclosing the glittering contents to the eyes of her husband, "take what thou likest, and, I beseech thee, begone. Heaven be with thee, and turn thine heart."

Adolphe turned upon her a look of scorn, and, taking forth several bags of gold, concealed them beneath his mantle, and moved towards the door.

"Farewell," he repeated, "till we meet again."

"Farewell! farewell!" ejaculated Madame de Floriville; "but Heaven forbid that we should meet again."

Adolphe made no reply, and immediately quitted the room.

As Adolphe was about to quit the house, he encountered Annette, who endeavoured to avoid him, but he commanded her to stop, in a loud tone, and laying hold of her arm, he looked in the timid girl's face with an expression which excited her utmost terror.

"Thou art a babbling fool, girl," he observed. "I was last night a listener to thy pert loquacity, and have every reason to believe that thou hast, by thy prying, become acquainted with my secret."

"Oh, oh—oh—no, really si—sir, I have not, I—I—I didn't listen at the door when you came here yesterday, indeed I did not;" stammered out the silly girl, trembling, and looking excessively pale.

"No falsehoods, girl," cried De Floriville, with increased sternness; "I am not a man to be trifled with. Tell the truth, though thou hast betrayed thyself; art thou not aware who I am?"

"Lor', sir, how should I know?—I never——"

"No more of this equivocation," interrupted Adolphe; "if thou provokest my anger too much thou mayest repent it. Again I command thee to tell me whether thou dost not know who I am, and the relation in which I stand to thy mistress?"

Annette still hesitated, and knew not what to say, but seeing the wrath of De Floriville increasing, and fearful of what the consequences might be, for to her he seemed to be a man who was capable of doing anything, she ejaculated—

"Oh, pray, sir, let go my arm, and do not look so fiercely at me, and I will confess all."

"Dost thou acknowledge to having listened to the conversation which passed between me and thy mistress yesterday?" he demanded hastily.

"Oh, ye—ye—yes, sir," faltered out the alarmed waiting-maid.

"And thou knowest my name, and who I really am?"

"Ye—ye—yes, sir, that is——"

"There, no nonsense," interrupted De Floriville, "thou knowest my secret?"

"Well, well, I—I do then; God spare me!" answered Annette, with more alarm than before.

"Inquisitive idiot!" cried Adolphe, in fierce accents; "thou deservest to be punished most severely for thy pains. But mark me, at the very peril of thy life, dare not to divulge a syllable of what thou knowest to any one, for I shall be certain to hear of it, and thou wilt find that I am a man who will keep his word, especially in a matter of such vital importance."

"Oh, dear no, sir, I won't say a word to any one, indeed I won't," replied Annette.

"I will not be satisfied with thy bare promise, girl," returned Adolphe; "thou must swear to keep the knowledge thou hast so unfairly acquired an inviolable secret from every one. Follow me!"

As De Floriville thus spoke, he unceremoniously opened the parlour door, and entering the room, motioned Annette, with an air that showed he would not be disobeyed, to follow him. Trembling violently in every limb, and fearful of what De Floriville intended to do, Annette would have screamed for help, but she was afraid, for the ferocious looks of Adolphe were sufficient of themselves to excite the utmost terror in the bosom of a much stouter-hearted person than the simple waiting-woman; and she, therefore, entered the room, and he closed the door after her. He looked round the apartment as if searching for something, and at length his eyes became fixed on a painting of the Virgin Mary, which was suspended from the wall, and to which he directed the attention of Annette.

"Thou art a Catholic, girl, art thou not?" he interrogated.

Annette replied in the affirmative.

"Kneel, then, and repeat after me the oath that I shall administer to thee," said De Floriville; "kneel, I say."

"Oh, sir," ejaculated Annette in a supplicatory tone, "do not ask me to do any such thing; your manner terrifies me, and I never took an oath in my life!"

"Then you must take one now for the first time," remarked De Floriville; "come —come, no longer delay, thou tirest my patience, girl. Listen to what I say, and repeat it after me. On thy knees first."

Annette very reluctantly, and much alarmed, obeyed, and then De Floriville gave utterance to the following words, which she was compelled to repeat after him:—

"Swear never to divulge one word to any individual, of the secret which thou hast become possessed of; and if thou failest to keep this oath, may the curse of Heaven, and every possible earthly misery attend thee!"

"Enough," said Adolphe, when the frightened girl had taken the oath; "remember, and beware!"

"Oh, indeed. I shall never forget," replied Annette, arising from her knees.

"Away then, thou mayest retire about thy business," said De Floriville, "and mark me—I ʼll be sure to know whether thou keepest thin oath or not, for though thou mayest not see e, I have means of obtaining information, whic.. no one can form any conception of. Begone!"

Having thus spoken, De Floriville, much to the relief of Annette, quitted the house.

"Well," soliloquised Annette, as she closed the door after him, "he is one of the greatest monsters I ever came near, that he certainly is; I wouldn't meet that man alone in the dark, no, not for all the world, and that's a fact. What a vexatious thing it is now that I am thus bound down by an oath to keep this secret. Here I thought I had got something to talk about for months to come, and now I am deprived of the pleasure of saying a word about the matter to any one. This is positively unbearable. I don't know however I shall be able to keep my oath. Secrets are the most uneasy tenants that can take up their residence in the bosoms of we females. What if I were to leave my mistress? Oh, no, that would never do, for I should never get such an excellent situation, or so kind a mistress again; and Gregory, my dear little Gregory Goldfinch, would not approve of my taking such a step. Well, I must e'en remain where I am, and try to keep this important secret, which if I succeed in doing, it will certainly be a miracle."

Thus soliloquising, Annette hastened to the performance of her domestic duties in no very composed state of mind.

CHAPTER XII.

THE DESPAIRING WIFE.

WE need not attempt to describe the state of Laurette's feelings after the interview she had had with her guilty husband. During the time he was present, by the most powerful efforts, she had sufficiently conquered her emotion to appear with becoming firmness and determination before him; but when he had departed, the feelings that held their influence over her, found vent, and she gave unrestrained indulgence to the expression of the heavy grief which oppressed her overcharged heart. The behaviour and heartless manner of Adolphe at this second interview quite altered the feelings that had before inhabited her bosom, and completely banished from her mind any other sentiments in regard to him but those of disgust and horror. So far from believing that he entertained any of that ardent passion he had formerly avowed for her, she could not help thinking that he now viewed her with indifference, if not with actual hatred, and it appeared as if he took an unnatural delight in seeing her miserable. He boasted, too, of his having become completely callous to the voice of conscience or humanity, and his manners fully testified that he spoke the truth. He lived for himself alone; and so long as he could gratify his sordid wishes, and indulge in his sinful propensities, he cared not on whom he inflicted suffering. It seemed to be almost impossible that there could be a being in the world so totally lost to every good feeling, and especially a man of the superior acquirements and natural abilities of De Floriville. But that that being should be her husband, the father of her Henri, was too dreadful to dwell upon. She could see, from his cool and determined manner, that she had nothing to hope—that he would continually persecute her, and bring misery, disgrace, and degradation upon her. What cursed mischance had saved him from the fate which she thought had attended him—a fate his crimes fully entitled him to?—What unfortunate circumstance had been the means of discovering to him the place of her retreat? Better had it have been for herself and son, she reflected, had they have died, rather than to have lived to undergo the shame and sorrow which seemed to be in store for them. She dwelt upon every word which Adolphe had given utterance to, and which was indelibly stamped upon her memory; and the more she did so, the greater cause did she see for anguish, and the more wretched hid she become. She trembled at the thoughts of De Floriville coming near the house, for his visits would doubtless be observed by the neighbours, and their suspicions and vague surmises be excited. But in what manner could she escape from him? She saw no means of doing so. Were she to dispose of the hall, and retire to another part of the country, she felt confident that he would never rest until he had found her out, and then his persecutions of her would doubtless be increased tenfold. She saw no chance of being released from him but by death, and that she could not wish should take place until remorse and repentance for the many crimes of which he had been guilty had broke upon his soul. Although she had threatened him that she would denounce him to the world, it was merely to alarm him, and to induce him to relent. Such a course was totally foreign to her nature, and the idea of it only filled her mind with horror.

Henri had no sooner heard his father depart than, impatient to see what effect the interview had taken upon his mother, he hastened to her apartment, where her appearance filled the bosom of the susceptible lad with the most poignant regret

"Henri," she replied to his anxious inquiries, "interrogate me not; for, alas! I have nothing to tell thee but that which will make thee wretched—nothing to disclose to thee but the almost certain misery it seems to be our destiny to undergo. Would to Heaven that thou wert arrived at the years of maturity, my son! Then how gladly would I welcome death, which would release me from the heavy weight of cares that bear me down!"

"Oh! mother—dearest mother!" observed Henri, "talk not thus, I beseech thee. Thou hast already suffered much, and the Almighty surely will not inflict upon thee more than thou hast strength to bear. For myself I care not, for I am young, and able to meet misfortune with fortitude, but——"

"Thou shouldst indeed be, my poor boy," said Madame de Floriville, "for well hast thou been inured to it. Thou wert cradled in adversity, and have never known what happiness is since."

"Oh! yes, I have, dear mother," replied Henri, "when I could see thee smile. Then was Henri one of the happiest children in the universe. Do not, then, I pray, give way entirely to despair. Seek to banish the heavy gloom which now oppresses thee from thy mind, and thou shalt smile again, and, if possible, forget that sorrow ever was."

"Alas! my son, thou art too sanguine—by far too sanguine," sighed his mother. "Before thine unfortunate father made his appearance to me, if not quite happy, I was, at least, content; but now he threatens me with a persecution which will break my heart, and ultimately bring the most terrible disgrace upon myself and thee."

"Impossible!" ejaculated Henri. "My father could not be so unnatural—so cruel."

"Cruel!" reiterated Madame de Floriville. "Alas! the wretched, guilty man is insensible to every feeling of humanity. His words, his conduct, fully evince that. But do not pursue this subject further for the present: I tremble to dwell upon it."

Henri obeyed, although he was anxious to be made acquainted with what had taken place at the interview between his mother and his father. Madame Laurette soon afterwards despatched Annette to "The Traveller's Rest," to tell Caleb Swinton that she wished to speak with him, she having come to the determination of asking the advice of her old and honest friend under the pressing and peculiar circumstances in which she was placed. While the money which she had given her husband—and which was a large sum—lasted, she had no doubt that he would not trouble her; but she felt confident that as soon as it was exhausted he would annoy her again, and then, she imagined, with a determination of obtaining all he demanded. And what could she do? How could she frustrate him, unless it were by making known to the French authorities that he was still in existence? But could she be the means of bringing him to a painful and ignominious death? He—her husband, whom she had once loved to adoration, and for whose sake she had made so many sacrifices? No; her heart revolted with horror at the thought: she could rather encounter ten thousand deaths than she could do it.

It need not be said how truly miserable these conflicting thoughts made the unfortunate Madame de Floriville. Had it not been for the sake of her son, she could have looked upon the grave with a contented eye as the haven of rest where all her sorrows would be at an end. But Henri was so young; and should he be deprived of her affectionate care, what, alas! would become of him? She shuddered with horror as she reflected that he would then, undoubtedly, fall into the guilty power of his father; and with such an example before him, what would become of him? He would be ruined—completely ruined. For her boy's sake, therefore, she resolved to struggle against the overwhelming power of her emotions, which otherwise might bring her to a premature grave.

This was a most arduous task, and it would be some time, at any rate, before she could be expected to accomplish it. But, in the meantime, would she not be exposed to the persecution of De Floriville? Had he not told her, indeed, that in a few days she would see him again? and she had too much reason to fear that he was the man who would keep his word, and that, hardened as he now evidently was in villany, and destitute of those better feelings that had formerly held a place in his bosom, he would not be persuaded from his purpose. In fact, Madame Laurette could see no prospect of being able to escape the misery with which her wretched, guilty

GREGORY AND ANNETTE ALARMED BY THE PRESENCE OF DE FLORIVILLE.

husband threatened her, and she looked forward to the period when he might again visit her with a feeling of irrepressible dread. He had her completely in his power, in fact, for she was well aware, although she had threatened him, he knew her gentle nature to well to imagine for a moment that she would reveal the dreadful secret attached to him, and denounce him to the world as a murderer; and, therefore, he would be certain to take every advantage of this knowledge. But to be forced to live with De Floriville again was too horrible even for contemplation. The terrors of their past life passed in rapid review before her mind's eye; the several dreadful crimes he had committed; the ghastly features of his mur-

dered victims, and her blood seemed to freeze in her veins with horror. To become again the companion of that blood-stained man, would be as bad as to endure all the pangs of purgatory, and no fate appeared half so terrible to her in comparison with it. When she remembered the halcyon days of her youth, ere she became acquainted with Adolphe; when she enjoyed the most unbounded affection of one of the best of parents, and received every attention—every indulgence that her heart could wish for; when she remembered this, we say, and compared it with the sorrows she had afterwards undergone, she marvelled how she had been able to support them, and was astonished at her own strength of mind which had not sunk under such unprecedented troubles. And then again would her father's awful curse rush upon her memory in all its most terrible form, that curse which had so fearfully pursued her, and she became nearly distracted.

While the unfortunate wife was thus tortured, let not the reader imagine that De Floriville, in spite of his bold and reckless demeanour, was entirely callous to thought, or that he was wholly released from the horrors that had before tormented him. No; still did the spirit of the murdered Eugene de Buoisson continue to haunt him; still did he feel his icy and clammy grasp upon his throat, in those very moments when he would raise the cup of revelry and dissipation to his lips. He dreaded the approach of the midnight hour; he feared to be alone, for then were his sufferings tenfold. Hideous fiends seemed to grin upon him, and the sepulchral voices of his murdered brother and Eugene, to thunder curses in his ears. There were times when his sufferings became so intollerable, that he was tempted to end them at once by committing suicide; but some inscrutable power ever appeared to arrest his hand; he seemed doomed to live to be a curse to himself and all who came in contact with him; and when he reflected upon the everlasting punishment which awaited him for his crimes in another world, he shrunk from the very idea of rushing upon it, in spite of his earthly torments, with the greatest terror. And yet the wretched man never thought of repentance; he dreaded the very idea of it, and scoffed at that which was the only chance of his obtaining any alleviation of his earthly miseries, or of forgiveness in another world.

As regarded Laurette, he was by no means decided in his own mind what course he should pursue towards her. All regard for her was lost in that selfish feeling which had of late characterised all his actions, and yet he did not, he could not think upon suffering her to live alone, more especially as it would give her an opportunity of triumphing in the determination she had evidently come to, and which she had, in fact, made no hesitation in acknowledging; nay, more, had she not told him that she could no longer look upon him but with feelings of disgust and horror? Had she not told him that she wished to learn to hate him? And his son, too; would she not bring him up to shudder at the mention of his father's name? Yes, she would; and too tamely to submit to this, would be to allow her a triumph he was resolved she should never have to exult in. The manner in which she had behaved to him, had excited in him a spirit of revenge, and he determined that nothing whatever should prevent him from having it fully gratified. For the present, however, he had come to the resolution of not putting his designs into execution, but to keep a watchful eye over the actions of his wife, and not again to enter

her presence until he had sufficiently matured them. One thing highly gratified him; and that was that he was now again supplied with the means to indulge in his improvident and profligate propensities, and he determined to put no restraint upon them, while the fortune of his wife lasted. Thus had the wretched De Floriville determined on the misery of that woman he had, in the first instance, hurled from happiness, and with whom, but for his own crimes, he might have passed (however humble might have been the station to which they were reduced) such days of felicity.

In about an hour, Annette returned to the hall, accompanied by Caleb Swinton, who, upon being ushered into the presence of Madame de Floriville, found her absorbed in tears. The kind-hearted innkeeper, who deeply sympathised with our heroine, looked at her for a few moments in silence, until Madame Laurette had sufficiently recovered herself to speak, when fixing a melancholy glance of welcome upon Caleb, she said—

"Mr. Swinton, I need not tell you how truly wretched I am, for you are aware what terrible cause I have to be so; my husband——"

"Alas! my dear madame," interrupted Caleb, "I know what you would say, and from my very heart I pity you. Pardon me, madame, if I speak too boldly, but I confess that I cannot look upon that unfortunate but guilty gentleman without a shudder of horror, and I feel a sensation come over me as if I were in the presence of some supernatural being. Much, indeed, do I fear that his sudden and marvellous re-appearance will be the cause of much misery to you, and, therefore, do I sincerely regret that he did not perish at that time it was supposed he had."

Madame De Floriville sighed deeply.

"Mr. Swinton," she observed, "you possess a kind heart, and I can fully enter into my feeling. You are the only person in whom I can confide, for no one but you is acquainted with my melancholy history. I requested your attendance that I might ask your advice under the present painful circumstances."

"My dear madame," returned Caleb, "you do me too much honour;—it is true, Heaven knows, that I heartily feel for you, and would do anything I could to serve you; but, I am afraid that you give me more credit than is due to me, when you think me capable of advising you."

"Mr. Swinton," returned Madame de Floriville, "I am confident that you underrate your own abilities. I owe you a large debt of gratitude for your generous, your noble conduct many years ago, and——"

"Oh, pray do not talk in that manner, Madame de Floriville," interrupted Caleb, "or I really cannot remain here. What did I any more than my duty, and as every person who possessed the common natural feelings of humanity would have done?

Besides, am I not indebted to your benevolence for all that I at present possess in the world? Was I not ruined, and brought to absolute poverty, when——"

"Well, well, no matter, Mr. Swinton," interrupted Madame Laurette, impatiently; —"my husband, I understand, has been staying at your house since his arrival in this neighbourhood?"

"He has, madame," replied Caleb, "and I can assure you, sorely against my will."

"Of course he made himself known to you?"

"He did."

"And did he give you any hint as to what were his intentions as regards me?" eagerly inquired Madame de Floriville.

Caleb Swinton here repeated the conversation which had taken place between himself and Monsieur de Floriville, when the latter revealed himself, to which she listened with the most profound attention.

"Base, cruel man!" she ejaculated, when Caleb had concluded; "it is too evident what his guilty intentions are. Heaven pardon him, and bring him to a sense of his guilt."

"So do I heartily wish also, madame," remarked Caleb; "but, after all, I think that Monsieur de Floriville's principal object is to extort money from you, and while you keep him supplied with that, he will not, I believe, trouble you much in other respects. But then, to be sure, it is a very shocking thing to think that you must be ruined by that wicked man, and——"

"Oh, I care not," ejaculated Madame de Floriville, "I could encounter poverty without a murmur; but to live again with him —Heaven forbid!"

"Live with him!" repeated Caleb, "live with the murderer of——; but I ask pardon, madame; my feelings, perhaps, cause me to make too free; but, whatever may be the consequences, since you have been pleased to ask my advice, I say, madame, firmly resist all his persuasions to that effect."

"Ah, Caleb," sighed Madame de Floriville, "I am not surprised to hear you, who are so well acquainted with the desperate character of De Floriville, talk in that manner. What can I do to oppose him if he be determined?"

Caleb paused for a second or two and reflected; then suddenly turning to Madame de Floriville, he answered, in a tone which fully bespoke his sincerity in her cause—

"Madame de Floriville, as I before said, let whatever be the consequences, you must never yield to the threats of your guilty husband; you must not again unite yourself to one whose conscience is loaded with so much crime. He shall not (you may think me bold), he shall not, I say, compel you to sacrifice your character, peace of mind, and everything else, by living with him. Perhaps I may appear too warm upon the subject, but still it is only the respect

and esteem which I feel for you that prompts it, and, therefore, do I trust that you will excuse it."

"My good Caleb," replied Madame Laurette, "for by such familiar title I must still call you—well do I know the feelings that prompt you to the expression of these sentiments, and believe me, I fully appreciate them; how then, tell me, I beg of you, would you have me act? How am I to resist the determination of my husband?"

"But how can he make the attempt to do that which he threatens?" inquired Caleb. "By claiming you as his wife, he must, at the same time, confess his real character, and thus his villany (for by no milder term can I call it) would recoil upon himself."

"Upon that point I have spoken to him," replied Madame de Floriville, "and he has proposed that we continue one of the fictitious names that each of us have assumed, and also to remove to some other part of the country, where we might not only be unknown, but prevent those circumstances that would undoubtedly arise if we remained where we are now living. What chance, then, have I to escape from the wretchedness with which he has threatened me?"

"By revealing his real character; and since he is obstinately determined to rush upon his own fate, bringing him to that punishment which his crimes deserve," answered Caleb.

"Mr. Swinton," returned Laurette, "the same idea occurred to me, and I even threatened him with it: but in spite of his crimes, and notwithstanding I am certain he feels no affection for me, my heart revolts from the bare idea of it. Base and bloodstained as he is, callous to every feeling of humanity, I feel that he is still my husband —one upon whom I formerly placed my most ardent affections; and think you that I could be the means of consigning him to an ignominious death?—Never! never!"

"I commend your feelings, madame," returned Caleb, "which reflect the greatest credit upon your character; but I cannot, nay, I will not suffer you to be made the victim of that guilty man's barbarity. Unless he will agree to cease to annoy you, and to be content to receive a sufficient sum to live upon with prudence, I myself will denounce him to the authorities of France as the same Adolphe de Floriville whose crimes rendered his life forfeited to the offended laws of his country years ago."

"Oh, forbear, forbear, Mr. Swinton!" exclaimed Madame de Floriville. "By such a step you would destroy my peace of mind for ever. From the bare contemplation of such an act as that my heart revolts with a feeling which language cannot do adequate justice to."

"Heaven forbid, madame, that I should be the cause of inflicting any additional misery to that which you have already undergone, and are now suffering," answered Caleb Swinton. "But when I think of the shame and anguish Monsieur de Floriville has occasioned you, and see plain enough that he is determined to occasion you still more, it certainly quite tires out my patience, and I say many things that I do not mean. But I trust you know me, madame, and can well understand my motives."

"I do, indeed, Mr. Swinton," returned Madame Laurette; "and, believe me, I am grateful for the interest you take in my welfare."

"You do me no more than justice, I assure you, madame," said Caleb; "but what grieves me more than all is, that I am at a loss to advise you in what way to act. Some plan, however must be adopted to prevent your husband from annoying you. You must not have your life rendered doubly wretched by being compelled to live with that man whose conscience is so heavily loaded with crime, and whose bad example may have such a pernicious effect upon the morals of your son."

"The very thought of being obliged to become again the companion of De Floriville, fills my mind with the most inexpressible horror," observed Madame Laurette; "nature and humanity revolt at the association. Alas! what a cruel fate has mine been, to have placed my affections upon one who could never have loved me, and who, from the day that I unfortunately become his wife, brought nothing but the most bitter anguish and disgrace upon me."

"Yes, madame," replied Caleb, "you are, indeed, to be pitied; but I do hope that Providence will not again suffer you to become the victim of his cruelty and guilt. Pray endeavour to compose yourself, and to meet Monsieur de Floriville, whenever he may call upon you again, which I do not think will be for some time, and that firmness and decision of manner which will show him that you are determined to resist his persecution to the utmost; and by so doing, and supplying him with money, he may be induced to desist."

Madame de Floriville shook her head doubtfully.

"I fear that such a result is hopeless, good Caleb," she observed. "Adolphe's inexorable character is well known to me, and I have too much reason to fear that the stronger the opposition on my part, the more obstinate will be become. Could I escape to some distant part without his knowledge, I might avoid the sorrow which I have now too much reason to apprehend."

"I am afraid, madame," returned Caleb, "that he would be almost certain to discover you, wherever you might go, and persist in his resolution, unless you were to return to France, where the idea of his own danger, and the fear of being recognised, would prevent him from following you."

"Ah!" ejaculated Madame de Floriville, "that is a good thought: there, at any rate, I should be secure from his persecution. But then, mingling again in those scenes

where I endured so much misery and shame, would recall the past continually to my mind, in still more painful characters than ever. I had hoped in this seclusion to have been enabled to pass the remainder of my days, in uninterrupted tranquillity, but, alas! how futile was it. What sorrow does one act of indiscretion and disobedience to a parent's will entail upon the unhappy being who has thus erred."

"You reproach yourself too severely, my dear madame," remarked Caleb Swinton; "but I would advise you to think maturely of my suggestion, and in the course of a few days make up your mind. In the meantime I will endeavour to think upon some plan to further your wishes, and to release you from your present situation. It is a pity that you had no means to conceal the fact of your wealth from him; for had he believed you to have been still poor, I do not think he would have troubled you."

Madame de Floriville expressed her acquiescence in this opinion, and they both remained silent for a few minutes. Caleb Swinton, in repeating the conversation he had had with Adolphe, had omitted that portion of it which related to his having again married, for he wished not to wound her feelings, as this additional evidence of the disgusting and abominable villany of her husband would, undoubtedly, have done. After some more conversation to the same effect, Caleb Swinton took his leave of Madame Laurette, deeply sympathising with her in misfortunes, and being determined to do all that he could to frustrate the designs of Monsieur de Floriville, and to rescue her from the fate she had so much reason to fear.

Adolphe did not again make his appearance at "The Traveller's Rest," a circumstance at which Caleb Swinton felt highly gratified, and the servants much relieved; for the one we have mentioned was not the only person who had complained of having heard the strange and alarming noises, proceeding from the direction in which Monsieur de Floriville had slept; they all spoke of it; and, indeed, to such a pitch had they suffered their fears to arrive, that they gave Caleb warning to quit his service; and he was apprehensive that, if the report reached the ears of the public, the frequenters of his hostelrie would become less numerous than they had hitherto been. A week passed away since Adolphe's last visit to his wife, and they had neither heard nor seen anything of him. They had not the least doubt but that, being now supplied with money, he had gone to London, in order that he might mingle in the false pleasures and frivolities of life, and the intense anxiety and dread which Madame de Floriville had laboured under, while she believed him to be near the spot, became abated, and she was enabled to reflect upon the circumstance and the course it would be best for her to adopt, in order that she might escape any future annoyance. Sometimes she would almost come to a determination to follow the suggestion of Caleb Swinton, and make her departure as secretly as possible to her native country, where she might live in the same state of seclusion as she did here, and, probably, unknown and forgotten by all. Then the dread of again beholding those scenes where she had experienced such unprecedented and accumulated sufferings, tempted her to abandon the idea, and to remain where she was and brave the worst, more especially as the time passed rapidly away, and still she neither heard nor saw anything of the guilty cause of her anguish. Caleb had made every inquiry after him, but he could find no person that could give him any information respecting him, or whither he had gone. Weeks and months elapsed in the same manner, and De Floriville did not again trouble his wife by his presence, or even communicating with her by letter; and there were moment when she would think that some accident had befallen him, and that she was released from him for ever; but this hope was too flattering to last long, and she would quickly be aroused to all that state of uncertainty and anxiety to which the circumstances were calculated to give rise.

Six months glided away, at the end of which time Madame Laurette received a letter the hand-writing of which she immediately recognised as that of her husband. Her heart sunk within her when she beheld it, and a cold tremour ran through her veins. With a trembling hand she broke the seal, and read the contents, which were as follows:—

"De Floriville, doubtless much to the disappointment of his wife, still lives, and most likely ere long she will see him again. For the present he requires money, and unless the sum demanded is forwarded to the place mentioned in this letter, immediately, he will take the liberty of calling for it himself."

"Sordid, cruel man!" exclaimed Madame Laurette, when she had perused this laconic epistle, "I see plainly that you will not rest until you have ruined me. No doubt the money I before gave him has been dissipated at the gaming-table, and such frequent acts of extortion, if I do not seek some means to escape from this place, and retire to some spot where he may not find me, will speedily bring me to poverty."

The sum demanded by De Floriville was a very large one, but Madame Laurette readily forwarded it to the place he had directed in the letter, which was in one of the fashionable streets of London, for she was convinced that unless she did so, he would not fail to keep his word, and annoy her by his presence and importunities again; and at the same time she felt certain that, while the money lasted, he would not trouble her, and in the interim, something might occur to place her beyond his power altogether.

When Caleb Swinton was made acquainted with this circumstance, he again urged his former suggestion, and endeavoured to persuade Madame de Floriville to seize the present opportunity to return to her native country, where De Floriville would not think of following her, as he might be certain that, if he should be there recognised, he would be brought to an ignominious death. Madame Laurette admitted the reason of this idea, but yet she dreaded to behold again those places with which she had been so dreadfully connected; and if she should be known, she would, in all probability, meet with the stigma of the ungenerous world. Caleb, however, found very little difficulty in combatting these objections, saying that Madame de Floriville had no occasion to go near those scenes she had in early life been accustomed to, but, on the contrary, she could seek another part of France, where she had not before been, and where there was no probability of her being known.

Madame Laurette could not help acknowledging the justness of Caleb's observations, but to England she had become so attached, that it was some time ere she could think upon leaving it with any degree of patience. She saw no other way, however, of ridding herself of Adolphe, and she, therefore, made up her mind, but very reluctantly, to do as the worthy host advised. Many bitter pangs of regret did it cause her to think she should be compelled to break up her home—that peaceful retreat, in which she had hoped that she would have been suffered to live undisturbed for the rest of her days, and to seek an asylum in that country where had originated all her troubles; and while was anxious for the time to arrive when she should be beyond the power of Adolphe, she could not look forward to it without a mingled feeling of the most poignant regret and dread.

Henri heard of his mother's intentions with no very pleasurable feelings; he had never, young as he was, known what real peace was until they came to England, and, consequently, that had drawn his affections towards it; while, on the other hand, the name of his own country recalled nothing but the most awful and afflicting circumstances to his memory. But reason told him that such a step was absolutely necessary for the sake of his mother, and for his own welfare, and he, therefore, sought to submit to the necessity with patience.

Henri was now sixteen years of age—tall, graceful, and extremely handsome. His features bore a striking resemblance to those of his father when he was young; but all the placid mildness of his mother blended with the expression of his countenance. His eyes were sparkling and intelligent, and his high pale forehead evinced an intellect expansive and brilliant. He displayed abilities far superior to those usually shown by persons of his age; his perception was remarkably quick, and his thirst after knowledge was most untiring. The gentleman whom Madame de Floriville had engaged to direct his studies, was admirably qualified or the task; and in addition to his great abilities and numerous accomplishments, was a most amiable man. The mildness and benevolence of his character had drawn the affections of his young pupil towards him, and he looked upon him as a father. With avidity he attended to his instructions, and nothing could afford him greater pleasure than when he could do anything to elicit his approbation.

Madame Laurette, much as she esteemed the amiable character of Mr. Wakefield, which was the name of the gentleman, had, from a feeling of delicacy, forborne to make him acquainted with the circumstances of her early life; and all that he knew of her history was, that she had suffered many heavy afflictions, and that they had been occasioned by her husband, whom he believed now to be no more. But now when she had made up her mind to leave England, and wished him to accompany her, she resolved to impart to him the particulars of her melancholy story, hoping in him to find an excellent friend and adviser.

This required all her energy to accomplish; and it was with an aching heart she detailed the crimes of which her husband had been guilty, and the sufferings they had undergone, brought on entirely by Adolphe's dissipated and profligate habits. Mr. Wakefield listened to the narrator with the utmost astonishment, horror, and pity; and when she had concluded, he gave utterance in accents that bespoke his sincerity to the feelings of commiseration he experienced for her misfortunes, and his abhorrence for the crimes of which Monsieur de Floriville had been guilty. He perfectly approved of the resolution she had formed, and considered that it was the only alternative she had, under the painful circumstances, without revealing the name of her husband to the world, and consigning him to that punishment from which he had so miraculously escaped, and which his sanguinary crimes merited. He expressed the pleasure he felt in Madame Laurette having made him her confidant, and assured her that his advice and assistance, in any way, should ever be at her service.

Madame de Floriville was now glad to think that she had made Mr. Wakefield acquainted with her history, since in him she could always find a sensible adviser and a sincere friend. Mr. Wakefield had himself been the child of misfortune; and heavy calamity in his youthful days had over-clouded all his prospects for the future, and given his manners and mind a tone of melancholy, that accorded with the disposition of Madame de Floriville.

All the preparatory arrangements for their leaving England were undertaken by Mr. Wakefield, and he settled everything with as much despatch as possible, and entirely to the satisfaction of our heroine. The house and its valuable furniture was disposed of to a great advantage—Madame de Floriville, however, preserving the portraits of her father and mother, and several other articles which she particularly prized, and in a month from the time at which the latter had made Mr. Wakefield acquainted with her history, everything was in readiness for them to leave England. Madame he Floriville parted with her old friend, Caleb Swinton, with much regret, and requested that he would not fail to correspond with her as often as convenient, which Caleb promised to do, and to forward her all the information concerning her husband that he could obtain.

Little more than a week after the departure of Madame Laurette, Henri, and his amiable tutor, Mr. Wakefield, had left England, behold them settled in a handsome villa, in a retired, but romantic spot, no great distance from Fontainbleau, and where our heroine, by the advice of Mr. Wakefield, assumed the name of Madame L'Clair. Soon as she became more confident of her being secure from the persecution of Adolphe, she began to feel more composed; and in the society of Mr. Wakefield, and in watching the rapid progress of her son, she began to feel tolerably composed. But, in spite of all her efforts, she found it impossible to prevent her thoughts from frequently wandering to the events of the past, and to the conduct of her guilty husband; and constantly did she pray to Heaven to bring him to repentance and remorse; but that there was any hope of anything short of death staying him in his wild and wicked career, she thought it was useless to expect.

From all that Mr. Wakefield could ascertain, the dreadful occurrences that had taken place at Abbeville were either unknown or utterly forgotten by any of the inhabitants there; and, therefore, after Madame Laurette had resided there for a few weeks, she acquired confidence, and frequently walked out, finding that the life of seclusion she had hitherto led was likely to make sad inroads upon her constitution. She was usually accompanied by Mr. Wakefield, who passed for a relation, and the delightful scenery in the locality of her residence, afforded her much pleasure, and was exceedingly beneficial to her health.

Mr. Wakefield had an only sister, of whom he had frequently spoken in the highest terms to Madame de Floriville. She had been for some years residing at Lucerne, but soon after her brother and our heroine had settled at their present place of abode, the former received a letter from her, announcing the death of her husband, who had left her without any family, and in very comfortable circumstances, and had a great wish to take up her future residence somewhere near her brother, so that she might have the pleasure of his society. Mr. Wakefield presented this letter to our heroine, who, having perused it, remained for a few moments in a thoughtful mood. She had often listened to Mr. Wakefield's glowing description of his sister's amiable qualities, with a feeling of pleasure and admiration, and judging from the character of the former, that he would give only a faithful portraiture of her, she was already disposed to view her with the utmost regard and esteem. Circumstanced as she was, the society of an amiable female—one in whom she could confide all her thoughts and secrets—was to her a great *desideratum*. The description of Mrs. St. Aubyn just realised her idea of such a female companion; and she, therefore, expressed to Mr. Wakefield a wish that he would write to his sister, and invite her to the villa, where, in all probability, matters might be arranged to the satisfaction of all parties.

Mr. Wakefield gladly availed himself of such a proposition; nothing could be more consonant with his wishes, and he was certain that his sister and Madame de Floriville would be delighted with each other. He, therefore, immediately despatched a letter to that effect, also enclosing a very kind one from our heroine to Mrs. St. Aubyn, who, in a few days, returned an answer, expressive of her sense of the kindness of Madame Laurette, and gladly accepting the invitation, promising to make her departure for France as speedily as she could make the necessary arrangements.

A fortnight only elapsed after this before the arrival of Mrs. St. Aubyn at the villa. The meeting between her and her brother, whom she had not seen for some time before, was of the most affectionate description, and our heroine immediately became prepossessed in Mrs. St. Aubyn's favour—a feeling which that lady evidently reciprocated.

Mrs. St. Aubyn was several years younger than Mr. Wakefield, and was a remarkably handsome woman. Her countenance was fully expressive of those intrinsic virtues which her brother had so warmly eulogised; whilst her manners were most urbane and highly polished, evincing a taste of the first order, and a mind expansive and cultivated. Hers was the heart that could deeply sympathise with the sufferings and misfortunes of her fellow-creatures, and which was ever ready to sacrifice its own peace to alleviate distresses of others.

The day of her arrival at the villa was one of the happiest that Madame de Floriville had passed for many years; and before they separated for the night, it was finally settled that Mrs. St. Aubyn should take up her residence in the villa, and mutual vows of the most ardent friendship were exchanged between them. Had they been the acquaintance of many years, instead only that of a day, they could not have evinced a warmer feeling towards one another; and Mr. Wakefield, who argued from it the best possible results to Madame de Floriville, saw the arrangement with the most unbounded satisfaction.

The next morning, the new friends met at an early hour, and after they had partaken of their repast, they retired to the well-cultivated garden, which was attached to the villa, and having seated themselves in a plasantly-constructed alcove, Madame de Floriville proceeded to relate the melancholy and unprecedented events of her life, to which Mrs. St. Aubyn listened with feelings of horror, pity, and astonishment. Such uncommon adversities undergone by one individual she had never before heard of, and, accustomed as she was, to view all Nature with the most merciful eye, had the account come from any other persons than our heroine and Mr. Wakefield, she could not have believed there was such a monster in existence as De Floriville. A thousand times did she thank the lucky chance which had introduced her to one who had so much need of the advice and consolation of a sympathising friend. She expressed her entire approbation of the plan which Madame de Floriville had adopted, and considered she was perfectly safe from the annoyance of her husband while she remained in France. She was greatly surprised at the uncommon fortitude and self-devotion which our heroine had evinced, and could not but admire as well as wonder at the courage which could have supported her through so many severe and dreadful trials—trials, the bare recital of which was enough to make the human mind shudder.

The deep sympathy which Mrs. St. Aubyn evinced, and the affectionate manner in which she expressed herself, went deep to the heart of Madame Laurette; and already she began to feel the same sentiment of regard towards the former as if she had been her sister. No one shared more largely in the pleasure of the acquaintance formed between his sister and our heroine, than did Mr. Wakefield; and he began to form the most sanguine hopes that, in time, by the assiduity of the former, Madame de Floriville would be restored to comparative happiness. Nothing, too, could exceed Henri's delight, when he perceived the change which had taken place in his mother, and which he attributed to the cause—the beneficial effects of the counsel and sympathy of Mrs. St. Aubyn—towards whom he felt the most unbounded esteem, and blessed the fortunate circumstance which had brought them together. Notwithstanding the injunctions of his mother, however, and the crimes of which he knew him to be guilty, there were times when he could not help his thoughts wandering towards his father, and feeling an anxiety to know whether he was still alive, or what had been his fate, and willingly would he have made any sacrifice could he, by so doing, have washed out the guilt with which his conscience was loaded, or seen him brought to a sense of compunction; but that, alas! he felt was hopeless.

Caleb Swinton kept his word faithfully, in regard to corresponding with Madame de Floriville, but he had heard nothing more whatever of her husband, and could not form the least conjecture as to where he was, in fact, whether he was still in existence. He was highly delighted when he heard of the alteration there was in the spirits of our heroine, and trusted that she would yet live to be entirely restored to peace.

In this manner a year passed away, and nothing occurred to disturb the tranquillity of Madame de Floriville and her friends; but we will leave them and return to England.

It was on the aniversary of his daughter's birth-day, that Caleb Swinton gave, what he was pleased to call " a bit of a jollification" at at The Traveller's Rest, and it was very late before the guests, who had been specially invited on that auspicious occasion, thought of separating. They had, however, gradually departed; the house was closed, and Caleb and his wife were just about to retire to their chamber, when there was a loud knocking at the door of the tavern, and Caleb, putting his head out of the casement, in no very agreeable temper at being disturbed at that hour, demanded who was there.

" An old friend," was the reply, in a voice which it struck Caleb Swinton he had heard before.

" An old friend—humph!" replied Caleb; " then methinks an old friend might have called to see me at an earlier hour."

" Early!" repeated the man; " I don't know what you may call it, Master Swinton, but I should say you cannot have it much earlier than one o'clock in the morning."

" Who are you?" demanded Caleb; " what's your name? where do you come from? and what do you want here?"

" These are rather too many questions to answer standing here; the whole of it is, I want to seek your hospitality; as regards the other interrogations you have put to me, why, e'en come down stairs and satisfy yourself. I am no drunken night roisterer or thief."

" I have only your bare word for that, and it would not be wise at all times to judge a man by his own flattery. However, I will trust you, so wait there a minute, and I will come down to you."

With these words Caleb drew his head in again, and taking up the lamp, and a pistol which he always had hanging loaded in his chamber for safety, he descended the stairs, and opened the street-door, which he had no sooner done, than the man walked unceremoniously into the parlour; but the instant that the light fell upon his countenance, the honest inn-keeper started back with an exclamation of amazement and terror, while the stranger (as he first appeared to be) burst forth into a loud peal of laughter.

" I told you, Master Swinton," said he, " that you and I were old friends. How are you?"

" Monsieur de Floriville!" ejaculated Swinton, looking with a trembling sensation upon that guilty man, who was elegantly attired, but whose countenance was swollen and disfigured with the effects of dissipation;

" is it possible—and you have come here again?"

" What! do you think it's my fetch, then?' asked De Floriville. " Give me your hand, and you will then find that I am sound flesh and blood."

" For what purpose have you come hither?" inquired Caleb.

" Oh, I am too tired to answer those questions to-night," returned Adolphe; " so just be so good as to light me to my chamber, and you and I will have a little conversation in the morning. I see you would rather be without my company; however, I can't help that—I shan't trouble you long, probably."

" I hope to Heaven not," muttered Caleb Swinton to himself, as he took up the lamp, and led the way to a vacant room, where Monsieur de Floriville hastily bade him good night, and seemed impatient for him to begone. Caleb complied with his wishes, and in a state of much anxiety and uneasiness he returned to his own chamber, where he informed his wife who had thus unfortunately thought proper to visit them again. Mrs. Swinton was as much alarmed as her husband, for the very idea of having such a guilty wretch as she knew De Floriville to be, sleeping beneath the same roof with them, excited her utmost alarm; besides, she well remembered the strange and frightful noises which had been heard by their servants and herself during the time he was staying at the house before, and she dreaded a repetition of them, which she firmly believed would not only frighten her and the servants out of their senses, but completely ruin her and her husband by driving all the customers away from " The Traveller's Rest."

In truth there seemed to be very good reason for these apprehensions, for when De Floriville had been there before, his suspicious and forbidding appearance had excited much talk in the neighbourhood, for notwithstanding the injunctions of Caleb Swinton, his servants had not neglected to make every one to whom they spoke, acquainted with the strange and supernatural noises they had heard, and which had so much alarmed them, and various were the conjectures and speculations they formed upon the subject, most of them agreeing, however, that he was a devil incarnate at least. But Caleb had still greater reason to fear the re-appearance of Adolphe than this; he apprehended that he would conclude that Caleb knew what had become of Madame de Floriville, and that, in refusing to satisfy him whither she had gone, he would subject himself to a species of annoyance he saw no means of ridding himself of without adopting a course, which, for the sake of Madame de Floriville, he could not think of.

After Caleb had returned to bed, he and his wife continued awake for some time conversing upon this subject, and they both heartily prayed that the result might not turn out so bad as they feared it would be; but Swinton was determined, let what might be the consequences, that nothing should ever induce him to betray the confidence which Madame de Floriville had reposed in him, although, at the same time, he could not help thinking that Adolphe would not be imprudent enough to pursue her to the very spot where he was likely to be recognised and brought to punishment for the crimes he had formerly perpetrated, and from making atonement for which he had been so miraculously saved; still he might adopt some means of troubling her, and in destroying that tranquillity which, in the society of Mrs. St. Aubyn and her brother, she was now beginning to experience. Another circumstance drove sleep from their pillow, and

created the greatest terrors in their minds; this was a renewal of those fearful noises that had before created such a sensation, and which seemed to be increased ten-fold. First they heard a noise like that of several persons pacing the room in which De Floriville slept with heavy footsteps. To this, succeeded a sound like that of the falling of ruins, and then an appalling shriek ran through the house, and a death-like silence followed, which remained uninterrupted for some time. It was a great relief to both Caleb and his wife when the morning dawned, and they arose from their couch, the former immediately going down stairs, anxious to obtain an interview at once with his unwel-

MADAME LAURETTE DIRECTS HER HUSBAND'S ATTENTION TO THE PICTURE.

come guest, and, if possible, get rid of him without any of the trouble he was so apprehensive of being subjected to.

Hearing a confused muttering of several voices, which seemed to proceed from the kitchen, Caleb made his way thither, in order that he might ascertain what was the cause of it; and he there beheld all the members of his establishment, from the boots to the chambermaid, assembled, and with countenances expressive of much astonishment and terror, conversing upon the noises which they had all heard as well as Caleb and his wife on the night before. They immediately appealed to their master, and gave it as their decided opinion, that the house was

haunted by an evil spirit, an idea which Caleb found it no easy matter to combat. However, he rallied them into peace as well as he was able, but with very little success, especially when they learned that the mysterious guest who had two or three years before been there was again an inmate of the inn, and they, one and all, determined, if he was suffered to remain, they would quit his service, a resolution which they made no hesitation in candidly apprizing their master of. Caleb, as we have shown, was prepared for this, and he, therefore, answered them accordingly, assuring them that the cause of their alarm, but which he asserted was complete folly, would, in all probability, not remain there many hours. This somewhat appeased them, and Caleb then made his way to the parlour, where he found De Floriville already waiting for him.

"Well, Master Swinton," observed he, on the entrance of the latter, "we will now, if you please, proceed at once to business. Be seated."

Caleb Swinton obeyed, but it must be confessed that he felt far from comfortable in the company of such a man as De Floriville, whose crimes had made him so odious, that they had imparted to his character some-'hing superhuman.

"I can perceive by your manner," continued he, "that you think me by far more free than welcome; but I am not quite certain whether I shall not tax your hospitality for some days. Why do you look so fearfully at me, man?"

"Pardon me, Monsieur de Floriville," returned Caleb Swinton; "but can you wonder, that when I look upon you, and remember the dreadful crimes you have committed, I cannot help feeling the utmost horror, more especially when I reflect upon the terrible curse which pursues you wherever you go? —Last night those awful sounds——"

"Ah!" hastily interrupted De Floriville, and his countenance changed, and a look of agony usurped the place of the previous air of recklessness he had assumed; "did you hear those sounds? They are, indeed, terrible, such as would make a heart of adamant quail; but who can form any idea of the tortures I——Psha!—this is madness! Your nervousness, Master Swinton, I verily believe is contagious."

"Oh, sir," returned Caleb, "it is in vain you may try to treat with indifference the terrible retribution of Heaven; it will ever pursue the guilty, who can only expect relief by sincerely repenting of the crimes they have committed, and endeavouring to make all the atonement in their power."

"Repentance!" cried De Floriville, with a look of scorn; "no, no, that is not for me;—it would avail me nothing. But we will say no more upon this subject. I suppose you wish to know what has brought me here again? Simply, then, it was to seek an interview with my wife, and since I find that she has quitted her former residence, to inquire of you, (for I have no doubt you are acquainted with it,) the place of her present retreat."

"Monsieur de Floriville," replied Caleb Swinton, firmly, "were I to deny that I am aware whither the unfortunate Lady de Floriville is gone, I should tell an untruth; but I have given my faithful promise not to divulge it, and I think you are sufficiently acquainted with my character to know that I will keep my word; be content with the misery you have already caused her, and seek not to add to the heavy weight of guilt which presses already upon your soul.— Madame de Floriville is lost to you for ever!"

"Liar!" exclaimed De Floriville, passionately, and rising hastily from his chair; "I will discover her, though I perish in the attempt."

"Most assuredly, sir," observed Caleb, "her discovery by you would be the signal for your own destruction."

"Ah! what mean you?" quickly and fiercely demanded Adolphe; "do you mean to insinuate that she would betray me?"

"You would betray yourself," answered Caleb. "But, come, this is a useless waste of time, Monsieur de Floriville; the whole of it is, your wife is no longer an inhabitant of this country; more than that you will never learn from me, I am determined."

The most violent rage was evidently struggling in the breast of De Floriville, for he knitted his brows, and, folding his arms, traversed the room for some minutes in such a state of excitement, that he seemed unable to give utterance to a word. Caleb Swinton watched him with the utmost indifference, he having completely made up his mind, and feeling bold when he knew that he was acting in a just cause.

"You may repent this, Swinton," at last Floriville exclaimed; "you know my nature well, and are aware that I am not the sort of man to be foiled so easily, and without retaliating in some way or the other. I ask no more than what is sanctioned by reason and justice; I demand the retreat of my wife."

"Which you will never know from me," peremptorily added Caleb; "pardon me, Monsieur de Floriville, if you compel me to speak too bold; but your crimes, and the manner in which you still comport yourself, have rendered you odious to her, and her own happiness, and the welfare of your son, depend upon her being separated from you. Has she not offered you the means to live in independence away from her?"

"Fool!" cried De Floriville, biting his lips with rage, "is not all she possesses by right mine? But I have deserved all this, for being idiot enough to leave her again. But by hell, she shall not escape me! I will find her out, though in the effort I lose my life!"

"Be not rash, Monsieur," said Caleb, "or you will have reason to repent when it is too late, believe me. If it is more gold you want, I will endeavour to procure it for you, and forward it to any place you may appoint; but why will you persist in that wild and reckless course which must ultimately bring you to ruin?"

"I want none of your moralising," said De Floriville; "once more, and for the last time, I ask you whether or not you will tell me whither Madame de Floriville is gone?"

"I have already told you repeatedly my determination," was Caleb's reply.

"Enough," remarked De Floriville, the most ungovernable rage flashing from his eyes; "then, mark me;—as sure as I now stand in your presence, ere a week has elapsed, you shall have reason to curse your obstinacy. Beware!"

Scowling fearfully upon Caleb Swinton, Adolphe threw his cloak around him, and abruptly quitted the house. The worthy host felt far from easy at the villain's threats, for he knew full well that he would not miss any opportunity which might present itself of fulfilling them; but having acted only as his conscience approved, he quickly became more composed and trusted that Providence would render any scheme of vengeance which De Floriville might have in contemplation abortive. He was very glad to think he had so quickly got rid of him, and Mrs. Swinton was no less astonished and pleased when she heard of it. Her husband did not relate all the particulars of the interview between himself and De Floriville to her; but that portion of it which he did, was sufficient to excite her apprehension, which Caleb found considerable difficulty in quieting.

Several days elapsed, and Caleb Swinton having heard nothing more of De Floriville, and from all the inquiries he made, believing that he had quitted the neighbourhood, he began to forget the threats which the latter had held out to him, and to imagine that Adolphe had quitted that part of the country, to prosecute his search after his wife. It was not long, however, ere he was undeceived in the most awful manner. It was little more than a week after the interview which Caleb had had with De Floriville, that he was awakened, at a late hour of the night, after every one had retired to rest, by a smell of fire, and jumping out of bed, and rushing to the room door, he was horror-struck to behold the house enveloped in flames from top to bottom. With frenzied haste he aroused his wife, and as the raging element was increasing in fury, they had not a moment to lose. They again both rushed to the door, but a fierce torrent of flames drove them back. To escape by the staircase was impossible, for it was all on fire, and all egrees seemed to be entirely cut off.

"Good God! our children, our poor children," shrieked Mrs. Swinton, wringing her hands, and forgetting her own perilous situation, in her anxiety for her offspring; "oh, what will become of them? Horror! horror! They will perish in the flames, for we cannot fly to save them!"

Caleb made no reply, although his agony was as intense as that of his wife. The fire had, by this time, reached the chamber in which they were, and already the flooring-boards began to crackle beneath them. There was little time for reflection, and Caleb saw that unless he made a desperate and immediate effort, himself and his wife must perish in the flames. He rushed to the window, and perceived a number of persons collected around the burning house, and exerting themselves to extinguish the fire, and save the property. He called to them loudly for help, but such was the noise which prevailed, that it was not until the lapse of several moments that he could make them hear, and the fire was now raging fiercely in the room. Immediately on beholding the awful and dangerous situation of Caleb Swinton and his wife, a ladder was procured, by which they descended in safety.

"My children! my children! where are they?" screamed the frantic mother.

"They are saved!" answered one of the servants, "I rescued them from the room below, in which they slept, and conveyed them to the cottage of a neighbour."

"Heaven be praised!" ejaculated Mrs. Swinton, and overcome by the power of her emotions, she immediately fainted.

The house of Caleb Swinton was soon reduced to a heap of smoking ruins, and the property saved was very little. A neighbour gladly received him and his family; no person in the vicinity could be more respected than he was; for in deeds of philanthropy he had ever been foremost, and, in many instances, had afforded that relief which saved many a deserving object from a state of destitution. Caleb Swinton at first imagined that the awful calamity had occurred through accident; but it was not long before his suspicions were aroused against the villain, De Floriville, who had been seen in the locality by several persons, only a short time prior to the fire taking place; and if he entertained any doubt upon the subject, he was quickly convinced of the correctness of it, by receiving a note in the hand-writing of De Floriville, in which he not only admitted the perpetration of the deed, but expressed his exultation at the same, and vowed to be still further avenged, unless Caleb agreed to acknowledge whither his unfortunate wife had gone.

It was a terrible loss to poor Caleb, but he quickly became resigned to it, and felt an innate gratification in knowing that he had acted as his conscience dictated, and had not betrayed the confidence reposed in him by Madame de Floriville, whom he so highly esteemed, and whom he had on so many occasions, run such risks to serve. The threats of Adolphe, however, were the cause of much pain and alarm to him, for he had too much reason to know his implacable disposition, and that he would not fail to seize the first opportunity to put his promises into execution; and, consequently, that it would be necessary for him to retire from the neighbourhood, which would be a most important loss to him, as he would have to re-establish himself in business, independent of the property he had already lost by the conflagration. However, he had no other alternative, without he could form the resolution to bring the incendiary to justice, which, knowing the anguish it would cause Madame de Floriville, he could not for a moment think of doing. With a heavy heart, therefore, was Caleb Swinton compelled to quit that neighbourhood in which he had been for so many years established, and to seek out another place to settle in. He fortunately met with a promising spot, and in a part of the country where he thought it was improbable De Floriville would discover him; and having made Madame de Floriville acquainted with the whole circumstances, he received from her a full indemnification for the loss he had sustained, and a fervent acknowledgment of the sincerity he had evinced in her cause, which plainly showed the strength of his friendship towards her, and strengthened the esteem she had always entertained towards him—an esteem which had been engendered in the first instance by the natural humanity and urbanity of his character; simple and humble, as he originally was, to use his own expressions, he possessed those "nateral feelings" which would have been an ornament to many persons in a different sphere of life, and of much greater pretensions.

Madame de Floriville felt greatly shocked and disgusted at the brutal conduct of her husband, and such was the revolting nature of his character, so callous had he become to all those feelings which entitled him to any esteem in the world, that she could not think of him without abhorrence, and sincerely wished that something would occur to remove him from that world upon which he was such a blot, without his being brought to that ignominious end which his crimes deserved; and which, from the course of life he led, appeared to be inevitable. To contribute any further to his improvidence, she considered would be unjust to herself and her son, and she resolved by all possible means to avoid it, a determination which received the warmest commendation of the amiable Mr. Wakefield and his sister. She was pleased that Caleb Swinton had removed from the neighbourhood in which he had resided until the time of the fire; and from the circumstance of his having assumed another name, she was in hopes that Adolphe would not be enabled to discover him, and thus prevent any annoyance to the former, and destroy every clue to the place of her retreat.

The remembrance of the last event gradually became banished from Madame de Floriville's mind; and, as month after month elapsed, and she heard nothing more of him, she became, in the society of Mrs. St. Aubyn and her brother, more tranquil than she had been for many years before. Henri, too, daily improved in intrinsic qualities and personal appearance, and was a source of the greatest consolation and happiness to his mother under the numerous troubles it had fallen to her lot to endure. One circumstance, however, caused her considerable uneasiness, which was, that it would become necessary for him to travel for the completion of his education, and acquiring that knowledge from personal observation which he could not obtain without. The bare idea of a separation from her son and Mr. Wakefield (who would, of course, accompany him), was sufficient to occasion her exceeding grief; nor could

Henri even comtemplate it with any degree of patience. He was willing to make any sacrifice of his own interest rather than to have to adopt such a course, and it was at last settled to the satisfaction of all parties, Madame de Floriville having latterly so far improved in point of health, as to enable her to undertake to accompany him on his continental tour. This, however, was attended by many causes of regret, and some apprehension; the first of which was excited by the necessity which compelled her to quit that place where she had become settled, and to which she was attached; and the latter, by the chance, if her husband were still living, that he might encounter her in the course of her travels, and become the same source of annoyance and terror to her that he had formerly been, and from which she was protected while in the country where the principal portion of his heavy crimes had been perpetrated. To these necessities, notwithstanding, Madame de Floriville at length became reconciled, and set about making the requisite arrangements for the journey, Italy being the first place fixed upon for their temporary residence.

Nearly another year had now elapsed since the incendiarism committed upon Caleb Swinton by De Floriville, and nothing whatever had been heard of him; so that Madame Laurette and her friends again became more composed, and their apprehensions were considerably quieted, thinking it not at all improbable that his career of guilt had been abruptly terminated by the effects of dissipation, or that, having failed to discover any clue to the place of her retreat, he had given-up his researches after her in despair. To Caleb Swinton Madame de Floriville confided her plans, and requested him, as before, to communicate to her, as early as possible, any intelligence he might be enabled to obtain of him.

Everything being soon arranged for the tour, our travellers commenced their journey, and it was not without the deepest regret and sorrow that they quitted that place which had become so much endeared to them. We will pass hastily over the journey, which was unaccompanied by any incident of sufficient importance to be particularly noticed, and bring them at once to Italy, where they settled themselves in a delightful villa, situated on the margin of a lake, and surrounded by the most romantic and picturesque scenery, affording every enjoyment to the admirers of the beauties of nature. Italy! beautiful Italy! land of sunny skies — and perpetual summer, insensible indeed must be the heart which could not rebound beneath the genial influence of thy clime. It soon had a visible effect upon the spirits and health of them all. Madame de Floriville scarcely ever mentioned the name of her husband, and it seemed as if she had almost succeeded in driving him from her thoughts, while Henri, in seeing the alteration and improvement in his mother, found the principal portion of his own happiness, and became almost a stranger to care.

Madame de Floriville had here, as well as in France, thought it prudent to go under an assumed name, more especially as it would be indispensably necessary that Henri should go into society, and, consequently, that she herself should not live quite in that state of seclusion that she had hitherto done. It was not long ere they had cultivated the friendship of a select few, by whom their society was much courted, and who were likely to advance the interests of Henri.

Henri being of a temperament warm, ardent, and enthusiastic, it will not be a matter of astonishment that the dark-eyed maidens of Italy should excite his admiration ; and in return, his handsome features, noble figure, and gallant address, made him an universal favourite among them. Love, however, was a stranger to his heart, susceptible as it was, until a circumstance took place, which we are now about to relate.

Riding was an exercise in which Henri frequently indulged, and when disengaged from his studes, he would enjoy the delightful scenery with which this charming country abounds. It happened one afternoon, he had proceeded rather farther than was his usual custom, tempted by the fineness of the weather and the beauty of the prospect before him, when suddenly recollecting the time, he was in the act of returning home, when the piercing screams of a female smote his ears, and seemed to proceed from no great distance from where he at that time was. Ever ready to lend his aid to those who needed it, especially a female ; bold and determined, and reckless of danger, Henri turned his horse's head, and hastened in the direction to which he was guided by the cries for help, when his eyes encountered the form of a female struggling in the grasp of a man who bore the garb and appearance of a gentleman. This was enough for the spirited young man, and he galloped up to the rescue ; the man seeing him approach, became more desperate, and raising the female in his arms, was about to carry her forcibly off, when the latter called loudly on him to hold, and the next moment he was alongside of them, and found that the lady was of the most exquisite beauty, while the man bore the countenance of a determined libertine and debauchee.

" Oh, help ! help ! save me, stranger, I implore you, from this unmanly ruffian !" cried the beauteous maiden in accents sufficient to penetrate and excite the compassion of the most insensible bosom.

" Villain !" exclaimed Henri, immediately dismounting from his horse and rushing upon the man—" what means this outrage ? Releasing the damsel, or I will cleave thee to the earth !"

" Insolent boy !" cried the other furiously, and drawing his sword as he spoke ; " forbear to interfere with that which concerns

thee not. Stand off ! or thou shalt quickly have good reason to repent thy daring !"

The maiden by a powerful effort disengaged herself from the ruffian's hold, and flew to the protection of Henri, who had unsheathed his sword, and prepared to defend her with his life. The man rushed impetuously upon him, but Henri met him with that cool intrepidity which plainly showed that the combat would be quickly decided in his favour ; and, in a very few minutes, he severely wounded his antagonist in the shoulder, who dropped his weapon, and uttering the most vile imprecations against his conqueror, fled precipitately from the spot.

Overcome by her terrors, and the excitement she had undergone, the maiden had fainted, and Henri hastily bore her to the margin of a lake which was close by, where he bathed her temples, and used every means in his power to restore her to sensibility. While performing this task, he gazed with the most unbounded astonishment and admiration upon the uncommon beauty of the damsel he had been so fortunate as to rescue. Never had he seen anything half so lovely. She was evidently very young, probably not more than fifteen years of age, but her person was tall and majestic, and symmetry and grace itself. Her eyes were black, and enchantingly brilliant ; her features regular, and redolent of gentleness and intelligence ; her lips were temptingly red and pouting ; and her teeth were, to make no exaggerated use of a common simile, as white as the purest pearl.

It would be impossible to do adequate justice in description to the feelings that took possession of the soul of Henri, as he held this beauteous object in his arms, and endeavoured to restore her to animation ; surprise and admiration held predominant sway in his bosom.

It was some minutes ere the lovely girl gave any signs of returning sensibility ; but at length the exertions of Henri were amply rewarded ; she heaved a gentle sigh, and opening her eyes, fixed them upon his countenance, with an expresssion which made his heart beat tumultously in his bosom, and caused a sensation of the most powerful and exquisite description to rush through his veins. Gently disengaging herself from his hold, while deep blushes mantled in her cheeks, she appeared astonished and bewildered, as she gave utterance to these words—

" Where am I ? Where is that base man who would so cruelly have torn me from my friends ?"

" Beauteous lady," replied Henri, " be not alarmed, I beg of you ; I have been fortunate enough to rescue you from the power of the ruffian of whom you speak, and am ready to conduct you to your friends immediately. Under my protection you have not the least occasion to fear ; but I think it would be advisable to quit this spot as speedily as possible, lest the villain should return with assistance, which I shall not be able to withstand."

"Oh, signor!" returned the damsel in tones of swertness enough to thrill the soul with rapture, "how can I sufficiently express to you my thanks for the service you have rendered me? I had been taking a walk a short distance from the villa of my mother, Signora Venoni, when I was met by the Duke Monterino, who has several times annoyed me with his hateful passion, and but for your timely aid, I should doubtless ere long have been a prisoner in his Casino, the bare idea of which fills my bosom with the most indescribable horror; again, signor, must I confess my gratitude to you; a sentiment in which I know the signora, my mother, will cordially join."

While the maiden spoke, Henri became completely enchanted. He dwelt upon every syllable she gave utterance to, with the most unbounded admiration, and when she ceased, he begged that she would not think herself under any obligation to him; that he felt too happy in having so luckily been made the instrument of saving her from the attemps of so powerful and fearful an enemy, and then once more urged the propriety of no longer remaining where they were, and requested to be made acquainted where Signora Venoni's villa was situated. The maiden was about to reply to his questions, when they suddenly beheld several persons hurriedly approaching, the sight of whom at first excited some apprehension in the bosom of Henri, he thinking it probable that they were the creatures of the Duke Monterino; but his fears were quickly banished when the damsel informed him that they were the domestics of her mother, who had doubtless been sent in search of her. Henri having briefly informed them of what had taken place, gave his horse to one of the men, and taking the arm of the blushing and trembling girl, with her assent, escorted her towards home.

On the way to the villa, Henri engaged his beauteous charge in conversation, and the intelligent yet simple answers she returned completely charmed him. Often as her dark but brilliant eye caught his, a crimson blush would suffuse her cheeks, and added to that exquisite beauty which had captivated Henri at first sight. He could not help mentally blessing the chance which had rendered him the means of preserving her from the violence of the Duke Monterino, and which introduced him to so lovely a being.

They soon arrived at the villa, which was a very beautiful one, and romantically situated; and they were met at the entrance by Signora Venoni herself, who evinced no little astonishment when she beheld her beauteous daughter leaning on the arm of a stranger, and looked to Marceline for an explanation. This the latter gave her in a few words, and Signora Venoni was then most unbounded in her expressions of gratitude for the preservation of her child, and warmly invited Henri to enter the villa. This he very gladly accepted, and was delighted with the easy grace and affable manners of the signora.

Signora Venoni was yet a young woman, and possessed of considerable beauty, her features very much resembling those of her daughter, yet they were imbued with a certain expression of sorrow which gave them an additional but melancholy interest.

The Signora was evidently a most accomplished woman, and appeared to have been used to the fashionable world, although she was now in a manner secluded from it. On inquiring to whom she was indebted for the inestimable service Henri had rendered her, he gave her the assumed name himself and his mother had adopted, and once more declared the happiness he felt at having been made the instrument, in the hands of Providence, of saving the beauteous Marceline from the ruffian violence of the Duke of Monterino.

"The duke," observed Signora Venoni, "is a base man, and it was, therefore, knowing that, on offering his addresses, both myself and Marceline peremptorily rejected him, and I respectfully, but decidedly intimated to him that the honour of his future visits to the Villa di Venoni could be dispensed with. He left the house in a terrible rage, vowing vengeance; but, hearing no more of him, we concluded that he had abandoned his designs, and would not again trouble us. The outrage he has, however, committed this evening, proves that we were mistaken, and that we have still reason to dread him; but, by being wary and watchful, we may probably be enabled to frustrate any designs he may have against us."

"I trust you will, signora," replied Henri; "and I am sure, at any time, whatever humble services I can render you, to prevent his putting his villanous schemes into effect, you may command with pleasure."

Signora Venoni again thanked him, and Marceline expressed her gratitude by a look which penetrated to his soul, and shot through his frame with overwhelming influence. Marceline talked little, but what she did say was so sensible, that it made an indelible impression upon the memory of the listener, and drew forth the warmest admiration.

Henri was extremely sorry when it became necessary for him to depart, and he requested to be allowed the honour of calling again to inquire after the signora and her daughter's health, to which the former assented, and the latter, if a person might judge from her looks, was far from being displeased to think she had done so.

On his way home, Henri did nothing else but think of the adventure and the numerous charms of Marceline, and his heart felt a sensation which was entirely new to him.

On his arrival at home, he furnished his mother with every particular, and expatiated so warmly upon the urbane manners of Signora Venoni, and the beauty and accomplishments of Marceline, that Mr. Wakefield could not forbear smiling and observing, that it really would appear to many persons who were experienced in these matters, that this was an instance of love at first sight. Henri felt confused, and could not make a suitable reply, and Madame de Floriville, having warmly eulogized her son for his conduct, observed, that, from the glowing description which he had given of the signora and her daughter, she felt deeply interested in them, more especially as he had informed her of the melancholy which shadowed the features of the former, showing that she had been no stranger to sorrow, and thus rendering her an object of the deepest sympathy with herself; and that she should be most happy to obtain an introduction to her. This Henri promised to contrive, if possible, on his next visit to the Villa di Venoni, and there the subject would have dropped, had not Henri been unable to restrain the fervent and eloquent expression of his admiration of the numerous charms of the all-captivating Marceline.

On retiring for the night, Henri gave free indulgence to the thoughts that crowded upon his mind, and recalled to his recollection every sentence she uttered, so replete with modesty, sound sense, and virtue. Fair forms and lovely countenances he had often gazed on before, but never had he seen anything so transcendantly lovely as Marceline. He longed for the arrival of the next day, when he had resolved to visit the Villa di Venoni again; and the hours that intervened seemed of more than ten-fold length and tediousness. His dreams that night were those of happiness; bright visions of love and beauty flitted before his busy imagination, and he awoke in the morning with a sensation of pleasure glowing in his breast, which he had never before experienced.

After partaking of the morning's repast, he bent his footsteps with eager haste to the Villa di Venoni, where he was received with the most cordial expressions of welcome by by Signora Venoni and Marceline, the latter of whom, Henri could not help thinking, looked more beauteous than ever.

The manner in which Signora Venoni behaved to him convinced him how much she was prepossessed in his favour, and the account he gave of his mother seemed deeply to interest her, and she expressed a wish to be introduced to her. This delighted Henri, for he hoped it would form the commencement of an intercourse, which would not only be productive of happiness to his mother, but of perfect felicity to himself; and before he left the villa, it was arranged that Madame de Floriville should accompany her son to the Signora Venoni's the following day.

Henri took his departure from the Villa di Venoni with an increased feeling of reluctance to that which he had felt on the previous day. The exquisite beauty and captivating gentleness and simplicity of Marceline, had stamped themselves indelibly on his heart, and convinced him that he felt for her a much more powerful sentiment than mere admiration and esteem.

One circumstance had particularly struck him, which was, that he several times noticed the eyes of Signora Venoni fixed upon him with a look of the most intense earnestness; and when she saw that he observed her, she hastily averted her gaze, and sighed deeply, as if some painful retrospection had crossed her memory. He thought upon this several times, and the oftener he did so, the deeper became the interest he felt for her.

Madame de Floriville, having been made acquainted by her son of the wish of Signora Venoni was very much gratified, and the following day, accompanied by Mrs. St. Aubyn, and Henri, she repaired to the villa. The introduction evidently afforded the utmost delight to all parties, and Madame de Floriville admitted that the beauty and accomplishments of the youthful Marceline, by far exceeded even the most glowing description which Henri had given of them.

The day passed away most happily, and before the new-formed acquaintances separated, they were upon the same cordial terms as if they had been friends for years.

Madame de Floriville was very much pleased at having become acquainted with Signora Venoni and her daughter, and from that day henceforward they were seldom apart, exchanging visits with one another. The pleasure which Henri and Marceline experienced in each other's company, and which neither of their parents sought to check, needs no description; it was very soon quite evident they both felt the same happiness, and that all their thoughts, their ideas, their tastes, corresponded.

One thing surprised them all, and that was, that since the night when Henri de Floriville rescued Marceline from his violence, they had not heard anything of the Duke Monterino, and they were, therefore, in hopes that he had quitted the country.

Although it was evident that Signora Venoni had seen much trouble, and the friendship which had arisen between her and Madame de Floriville, the former was very reserved, and our heroine had been unable to elicit much of her former history, neither had she, consequently, been very communicative on her own part. One day, Madame de Floriville, however, took occasion, in the course of a conversation which ensued between them, to inquire how long it was since her husband's death. The question seemed to agonise the signora, and our heroine, when she witnessed the emotion it caused her, regretted having put it to her.

"My husband!" she at length said; "alas! I know not whether he lives or not. But I o not mention his name—he is a villian, whom would to heaven I could erase from my memory for ever!"

Madame de Floriville sighed when she thought of her own situation, so similar to that which Signora Venoni, in so few words, had described her's to be; but finding that the emotions of the signora increased, she changed the topic of conversation, and there the subject dropped—Madame de Floriville never at any future period venturing to advert to it, although her curiosity was greatly excited.

Several months elasped, and the attentions of Henri and Marceline to each other increased in such a manner that it could no longer be concealed from their parents and friends that a mutual passion had sprung up between them, and of which Signora Venoni nor Madame de Floriville could disapprove, although they considered them yet too young to think of uniting themselves in the indissoluble bonds of matrimony.

Henri and Marceline had made no secret of their sentiments towards each other, and they looked forward to the consent of their parents to their nuptials, with the most sanguine hopes, and formed to themselves ideal scenes of bliss that were, alas! never fated to be realised.

Sigora Venoni had a miniature suspended from her neck, which she seemed always most anxious to conceal from observation; but one day, when she and our heroine were scated at the villa of the former, engaged in deep conversation, it accidentally escaped from her bosom, and became revealed to Madame de Floriville. No sooner had she fixed her eyes upon it, than uttering a loud scream, she was so overpowered by the violence of her feelings that she sunk back in her chair, and immediately fainted. In the miniature, in the lineaments upon which she gazed, she recognised the well-known features of her husband, the guilty Adolphe de Floriville!

The astonishment of Signora Venoni and her daughter at this singular behaviour, exceeded all bounds, and they were considerably alarmed. Assistance, however, having been procured, Madame de Floriville, after the application of such restoratives as were found necessary, quickly recovered, and to the eager inquiries of Signora Venoni and the fair Marceline, as to the occasion of her sudden illness, our heroine's mind was so bewildered that she could not give any direct answer, neither for a minute or two had she any recollection of what had taken place.

Henri was as much surprised as the others, but it was not at the feelings of his mother, for his eye had encountered the miniature, and traced instantly the remarkable likeness it bore to his unfortunate and guilty father, and he was at a loss to imagine how the same had come into the possession of her, and how it was that she thus treasured it up with such affectionate care. But he dared not ask for that mystery to be solved which at present caused him so much anxiety, constrained as he was to keep his real name a secret from every one.

Signora Venoni and Marceline, having, as we have before stated, succeeded in restoring Madame de Floriville to sensibility, again repeated their inquiries as to the cause of her sudden illness, and, at length, as recollection suddenly flashed upon her brain, Madame de Floriville, looking eagerly towards Signora Venoni, exclaimed, in accents of despair—

"Ah! that portrait! the likeness of——"

"Who?" demanded Signora Venoni, in a voice of extreme agitation.

"Of one who——" but suddenly checking herself; "after all, it can only be fancy, and—pardon me, signora—I am very silly to suffer myself to give way to this weakness. But, tell me, I implore you, whom does that likeness represent?"

Signora Venoni sighed deeply, and did not at first answer; but at length she said—

"It is the likeness of one whom, would to Heaven, I had never seen; how many years of bitter sorrow and anguish would it have saved me! But pray do not question me farther; I cannot—dare not answer you!—The subject tortures me!"

"It is strange," observed Madame de Floriville; "but yet it cannot be!—So singular a coincidence, too; but can another have met with misfortunes equal to mine?"

"Alas! bitter, indeed, must have been your sorrows, madame, if they can surpass those I have undergone," returned Signora Venoni; "probably, ere long, I shall reveal to you more minutely the particulars of my melancholy life, and you will then, I am convinced, be satisfied that I have indeed had my share of affliction."

The signora now changed the subject, and seemed anxious not to return to it again; and a strange feeling came over our heroine, which she found it impossible to shake off, and which she was equally at a loss to understand. The circumstance had very much disconcerted her, and she found that it had made an impression upon her mind which she felt convinced she could not easily banish. That the miniature which Signora Venoni wore round her neck, was an exact likeness of De Floriville, she was positive, and also that, whoever the said miniature represented, was closely connected with the signora, she was also positive within her own mind, and the more she endeavoured to fathom it, the more she became involved in a maze of fruitless conjecture. She felt a presentiment of she knew not what, and could not help thinking that something was about to take place to interrupt that tranquillity and comparative happiness she had lately enjoyed. She, however, determined to wait with all the patience she could muster, until Signora Venoni might think proper to fulfil the promise she had given her, namely, to make her more intimately acquainted with her history, which would solve all the present doubts.

She stated the circumstance to Mr. Wakefield and Mrs. St. Aubyn, who were very much astonished, but expressed their firm belief that Madame de Floriville must have been mistaken; but when added to her testimony they had that of Henri, they were convinced that it was not a delusion, and were puzzled to make it out.

The day after this event, Signora Venoni complained of being very poorly, and it was easy to be seen that her illness was to be attributed to the former cause, any reference to the miniature exciting in her bosom the most violent agitation, which she seemed to struggle hard, but in vain, to repress.

Madame de Floriville observing this, avoided speaking upon the subject, and indulged in secret the various ideas and conflicting thoughts to which the circumstance had given rise.

Henri, however, was determined to elicit, by some means or the other, those particulars with which it strongly occurred to him that his mother and himself were in some way connected, and which had excited his interest and curiosity to such a powerful degree.

A few days after the occurrence which we have been relating, Henri and Marceline were seated alone in the gardens of the Villa di Venoni, when the former took the opportunity of referring to it.

"And do you not know, dearest Marceline," said Henri—"do you not know who that likeness is intended for?"

"I do not, Henri," answered his lover; "unless it is that of my father; but my

CALEB SWINTON SAVES HIS CHILDREN FROM THE BURNING INN.

mother has always evinced such violent agitation when I have put the question to her, and laid such strict injunctions on my not repeating it, that I have never ventured to do so since."

"Your father?" asked Henri; "but have you no remembrance of him, my love?"

"None whatever," returned the latter; "I was quite an infant when, as I have since ascertained, he cruelly deserted me and my mother, and I believe he has never been heard of since."

"'Tis strange," said Henri, thoughtfully; "and yet that striking resemblance—I cannot drive it from my recollection."

"Whom did it strike you that it resembled?" eagerly asked Marceline.

"One whose name I am forbidden to speak;—my father!" replied Henri.

"Your father!" repeated Marceline; "oh, it could only have been imagination; or else one of those freaks of nature which we so often see. And why are you forbidden to speak the name of the author of your being, Henri?"

"For fearful reasons which I must not divulge," answered Henri.

"Does he still live?"

"I know not."

"Wonderful! that there should be such

a similarity in the circumstances of my mother and Madame Le Sange," remarked Marceline. "Did your father also abandon his wife and child?"

"He did not," returned Henri, "but events of a most extraordinary nature, and which I must not reveal, brought about a separation which we imagined would have been for ever. If, however, you would not harrow up my feelings with horror, dear Marceline, you will not question me farther upon this subject; in a few days, perhaps, the Signora Venoni and my mother may be induced to confide more particularly in each other, and then everything will be explained, although I tremble at the idea of such a step, doubtful of the result which may be consequent upon such a revelation. Tell me, Marceline, if you are acquainted with the fact, was your father an Italian?"

"He was not," answered Marceline; "he was a native of France!"

"Ah!" ejaculated Henri, with the most unfeigned astonishment, "this is still more remarkable. But his name—it was not Venoni, I suspect?"

"No," returned Marceline, "that name has only been assumed by my mother, for reasons best known to herself, and which I have never taken the liberty to inquire into; and you will probably be not a little surprised when I assure you, that with my real name I am entirely unacquainted."

"Is it possible?"

"It is true. But let us change the subject; for I confess that my thoughts never for an instant revert to it, without my feeling the most acute anguish."

"I will comply with your wishes, dear Marceline," returned Henri, "although I cannot but candidly own that the curiosity I feel to be made acquainted with every particular is almost intolerable. In spite of all my efforts to shake off such a feeling, the recent event has filled my mind with strange forebodings, and I am far from being so happy as I was previously; I feel as if something were about to happen to prevent the consummation of that felicity we have both long looked forward to with the most anxious and sanguine hopes."

"Fie, Henri," returned Marceline, "this is a weakness I did not think you capable of evincing. But come, let us hasten into the villa; my mother will feel surprised that we should so long absent ourselves, more especially as she is alone."

Henri took the arm of the beauteous girl without making any reply, and led her into the apartment. Signora Venoni was impatiently awaiting their return, and was, on their entrance, just about to hasten to the garden to ascertain the cause of their protracted absence.

Nothing particular occurred that day, to render it worthy of being recorded in these pages, and they conversed upon different topics, Henri, at the previous request of Marceline, never venturing so much as to hint at the circumstance which had occasioned them so much excitement. It was rather late when Henri departed from the Villa di Venoni, and he, therefore, hurried on towards home at a quicker pace than he was accustomed to do, fearful that Madame de Floriville, who had not felt disposed to leave home on that day, would feel uneasy. Suddenly, emerging round the corner of a street, he was startled by beholding the shadows of three men upon an opposite wall, and looking up, he saw three persons, who were enveloped in large mantles, just turning round the angle of a building, apparently, as if for concealment and the purpose of watching somebody. Henri's suspicions being aroused, he placed his hand upon the hilt of his sword, and kept a strict eye upon the spot where the men were endeavouring to conceal themselves. They did not appear to take any notice of his action, so he passed on; but he had not proceeded many paces, when a voice exclaimed—

"Ah! by hell it is him! On, on, fellows, and wash your weapons in his heart's blood!"

Henri had only just time to draw his sword, and place his back against the wall, when he found himself fiercely attacked by the Duke Monterino, and two bravos, the former uttering the most fearful maledictions all the time.

For a short time Henri was enabled to defend himself against the unequal and cowardly attack of the ruffians; but he was at length overpowered and disarmed, and fell, apparently lifeless, to the earth, bleeding from the severe wounds which he had received in the body. The Duke Monterino and his two murderous creatures, hearing footsteps approaching, and imagining that the young man was dead, hurried from the spot, and were in a moment out of sight.

CHAPTER XIII.

THE BRIGAND'S CAVERN.

How long Henri had remained in a state of insensibility it was impossible for him to judge; but he awoke to a sense of the most acute pain proceeding from the severity of the wounds he had received from the murderous attack of the Duke Monterino, and the bravos he had hired to assist him; and, looking round, the scene was so different which encountered his eyes to that which he had ever witnessed before, that he was completely bewildered, and for a moment or two all that had recently occurred to him was forgotten.

"He recovers," said a voice near him; and, looking up, he beheld that it proceeded from a man standing by the side of the rude couch on which he was reclining, and who appeared to have been ministering to his wounds.

He was habited in the garb of a monk, and appeared to be about fifty years of age, with features strongly marked, but bearing not the least signs of that mild and benevolent character which his dress would imply. This caused Henri to take a more minute, though hasty, survey of the place in which he was.

It was a lofty cavern, apparently hewn or formed by nature out of a rock, lighted by a large lamp, suspended by a chain from the roof, and the rays of which were unable to penetrate to its full extent. From the observations, however, which Henri was enabled to make, it seemed to be fitted up with all the comfort which could be imparted to such a place, although the articles with which it was furnished were of the rudest make, and evidently the work of unskilful artisans.

The person to whom the apparent monk had addressed himself, was a tall man, of handsome countenance, about the middle age, and whose dress left Henri no reason to doubt for a moment his real character;—he was a brigand.

" Where am I, and what has brought me hither?" demanded the young man, endeavouring to raise himself, but weakness not permitting him to do so.

" Compose thyself," said the monk, if such he were; " thou art in safe hands, and no harm is intended thee: but thou must remain still, or the remedies I have applied to thy wounds will be of no avail."

Then beckoning to the brigand, they both quitted the cavern together, leaving Henri alone, and in the utmost state of astonishment and alarm.

When they were gone, he quickly recalled his scattered thoughts together, and the whole of the circumstances that had occurred to him rushed upon his recollection. He remembered the rencontre he had had with the Duke Monterino and the two ruffians, and having no knowledge of their flight, he could come to no other conclusion than that the brigands held him in their power by the instructions of the former. This idea was, of course, attended with the utmost uneasiness, more on account of his mother and his friends, for whose distress at his disappearance, and probable ignorance of what had befallen him, he felt most acutely, and was for some time in such a state of excitement as to be unable to reflect with any degree of reason or patience.

His wounds were very severe, but they had been very skilfully attended to; and although the pain proceeding from them was very severe, he was led to suppose that they were not dangerous. The idea of the anguish his mother, and Marceline especially, were doubtless enduring, tortured him more than all, and greatly irritated the agony of his own bodily sufferings.

In this state, for more than an hour, he remained without interruption, when, suddenly, the rays emitted by the lamp revealed to him the dark shadow of an approaching form, and the next moment a female form stood by the side of his couch of such exquisite beauty, that he had seldom seen anything to equal it.

It was a young girl apparently not more than sixteen, a lovely brunette, whose handsome Roman cast of features were modelled in the most perfect mould, and whose eyes, so brilliant, beamed forth an expression that completely revitted and entranced the soul. She was attired in an elegant dress of the brigand costume, and which set off the delightful symmetry of her figure to great advantage; and her whole appearance was such as must have excited the deepest interest and admiration in the bosom of the most insensible beholder.

Henri was quite thunderstruck, and was unable to speak; whilst the fair visitor stood gazing at him for a few moments in silence, seeming to enjoy his surprise, and fixing upon him glances of admiration and affection sufficient to entrance the senses. At length Henri was enabled to speak, and in tones that betrayed his feelings, ejaculated—

" Beauteous damsel, who art thou, and for what purpose dost thou visit me?"

The female smiled sweetly, and while crimson blushes suffused her cheeks, she thus replied—

" Henri le Sange, thou art no stranger to me: thou mayst think me bold, but long time have I sought this opportunity—long hath my soul panted to unburthen itself to thee,—that long wished-for moment hath arrived at last,—and—"

She was interrupted by an exclamation of the most unbounded astonishment and confusion from Henri, who, gazing upon her with a feeling indescribable, said—

" Fair maiden, surely my ears deceive me! Such words, and from one whom I never remember to have seen before!"

" Ah signor!" said the lovely stranger, " I am better acquainted with thee than thou dost imagine. This is a large city, and foreigners may meet more observers and admirers than their inordinate partiality for one object may lead them to suppose. I repeat that thou and Zitella, the brigand girl, have often met before ; but absorbed in thy love for the daughter of Signor Venoni, as she calls herself—the fair Marceline—thou couldst not perceive the eye of admiration which secretly watched all thine actions, and dwelt upon thy various merits with that intensity of feeling which left the heart no affections but such as acknowledged the power of thine image. I know that thou mayest deem this confession bold—imprudent—but why should I wish to conceal those sentiments I have in vain tried to conquer? Alas! the certainty of being despised cannot be worse than to be compelled to cherish a secret passion without being enabled to disburthen the mind to the object that hath inspired it."

The beauteous Zitella paused, and the crimson blushes that mantled in her cheeks, and the ardent expression of her eyes, rendered her still more lovely, and spoke more than volumes could have done.

Henri's very soul was transfixed in astonishment, attention, and admiration ; he was totally incapable of returning any answer for a few moments, and was so confused that he could not collect his thoughts so as to return a suitable reply.

"Lovely damsel," at length he said, "thy words have so surprised me that I can scarcely believe that I am awake. Surely I must have misunderstood thee, or I am labouring under an illusion."

"It is no illusion, Henri le Sange," returned the brigand girl ; "Zitella loves thee —loves thee to adoration. Nay, turn not away thine head—if thou canst not love me, do not despise me. Accidentally we met, and no sooner did my eyes behold thee than my heart acknowledged thine influence. I tried to stifle the hopeless passion in my breast, but tried in vain. Love is a guest, signor, who, when once admitted to the heart, is not easily ejected. I felt my love daily and hourly increase ; thine image was ever present to my imagination ; my thoughts were perpetually fixed upon thee. I sought every opportunity to behold thee, and followed thy footsteps whenever I had a chance. Ah, Signor ! Marceline Venoni may love thee, but she cannot half so warmly, so ardently as the brigand girl."

As Zitella thus spoke, she fixed her eyes upon Henri with a look which revealed the feelings of her bosom, and penetrated to his heart. The remarkable circumstance quite bewildered him, and he knew not what to say.

"Who art thou, fair damsel?" he at last said, "and what brings thee in such a situation?"

"I am the daughter of Allesandrio Robelli, the brigand chief," the girl replied ; "the name I bear is Zitella, as I have before told thee. This cavern is among the mountains, and—"

"Allesandrio Robelli," interrupted Henri ; "is it possible? That name so terrible !"

"Nay," observed Zitella, "the world doth my father an injustice. To his enemies alone he is terrible ; but Allesandrio Robelli delights not in deeds of blood."

"But tell me, how came I here?" asked Henri.

"Returning from one of their predatory excursions to this retreat," replied Zitella, "my father and some of his comrades saw thee stretched upon the earth, wounded and bleeding, and out of pity bore thee hither. But hark ! there is my father's signal—I must away—he hath returned. Farewell, Henri, we shall meet again ; and, if thy thoughts are not entirely occupied with the image of the fortunate Marceline, think with pity, if thou canst not with love, upon the brigand girl."

She fixed upon him a look as she spoke which pierced his heart, and then, with a deep sigh, hastened from the cavern, leaving Henri in a state of mind of which the reader may easily form a conception.

The confession of Zitella had completely confused and astonished him, and in spite of all his efforts to the contrary, her uncommon beauty had made a most powerful impression upon him. The situation he was placed in, and the anguish his mother and Marceline were doubtless enduring, soon, however, superseded every other thought, and his uneasiness was almost past endurance. The name of Allesandrio Robelli had gained a terrible notoriety, notwithstanding what Zitella had said to the contrary, and cruel deeds were laid to his charge. Rewards were offered for his apprehension in vain, and he had hitherto eluded all the stratagems that had been formed to apprehend him, and bade defiance to the law. But yet, Henri reflected, he could have no motive for wishing to detain him, neither could he imagine that he would, if Zitella had spoken the truth, he being represented by her as merely acting from motives of humanity.

He was aroused from these reflections by the entrance of the apparent monk who had before attended him, and who, advancing towards the couch, inquired how Henri felt, and whether the pain of his wounds had in any degree abated.

"Who art thou?" demanded the young man.

"Doth not my garb inform thee, son?" replied the man.

"A monk !" exclaimed Henri, in accents of astonishment—"a monk, and the friend and associate of brigands !"

"Even so, my son," answered the monk ; "Allesandrio Robelli and I are old friends, and, therefore, do I perform such offices for him as those which I am doing for thee."

"But shall I not be suffered to leave this cavern as soon as my strength will permit me?" demanded Henri ; "and, in the meantime, will not my friends be made acquainted with my situation?"

"Those questions I cannot answer thee," said the monk. "Allesandrio, however, is very careful respecting those who may have entered his retreat, and it is not probable that he would make thy friends acquainted with thy situation, when, by so doing, he would risk his own safety."

"Why was I brought hither?" demanded Henri.

"Thinkest thou that Allesandrio Robelli is so lost to every feeling of humanity as to leave a wounded man to perish in the streets?" said the monk.

"And where is his humanity, monk, if, after saving me from death, he refuseth me my liberty?" interrogated Henri.

"I do not say that he will refuse thee, son," returned the monk ; "but those are questions I cannot solve. All that I have to do with thee is to see to thy wounds, and thou shalt have no reason to complain of my want of attention."

"Methinks it would better become thee,

father, if thou art sincere in the holy religion thou dost profess, instead of associating with the perpetrators of crime, to exert thyself to bring them to punishment, and to aid those who fall into their power to escape," said Henri, fixing upon the monk a penetrating look. He seemed abashed at his words, and could not make any immediate reply; and at length, after muttering out some incoherent expressions, he abruptly quitted the place, leaving Henri to reflect upon the painful situation in which fate had so unfortunately placed him.

His feelings were so much excited, that it greatly irritated the anguish of his wounds, and his pain was, consequently, most acute. Good reason had he to curse the villany of the Duke Monterino, which had thrown him into such a dilemma, and left Marceline without any one to protect her from his evil designs. This thought tormented him more than all, for he had not the least doubt that Monterino would take advantage of so favourable an opportunity to get Marceline in his power, and ere that, she had been seized by him and conveyed to a place of security. His mother, too, how great must be her sufferings at the uncertainty of his fate! She must be in a state of distraction, and he trembled when he thought of the dreadful consequences that would, in all probability, follow.

The monk visited him several times in the course of the day, and attended to his wounds, but he carefully avoided entering into any farther conversation. One of the brigands brought him his provisions, and invariably left the cavern without speaking a word. Miserably did the day pass away, and as night approached, the gloom of the place increased the melancholy of Henri, and the tumult of his thoughts became unendurable.

Amidst all his other reflections, Henri could not help dwelling upon the words of Zitella with astonishment; nor could he avoid thinking of her beauty without admiration. Notwithstanding the apparent boldness she had evinced by confessing her passion for him, and under such peculiar circumstances, there was a certain simplicity and modesty in her demeanour, which was particularly fascinating, and which had made a deep impression upon Henri's mind, and there was something so romantic in the whole adventure, that he could with difficulty persuade himself it was reality.

We will now pass over a week, during which time the only persons who visited the invalid was the monk and the brigand we have before alluded to. Notwithstanding the excitement of his mind had been very great at first, it had, by degrees, abated, and trusting that the idea of his detention might prove erroneous, he became more composed. In consequence of this, his wounds mended apace, and in a few days more, he was so far recovered as to be enabled to leave his couch. He then requested an interview with Allesandrio, in order that he might thank him

for the attention he had received, and to request that he might be permitted to return to his friends. In a few minutes after he had sent this message by the man who brought him his provisions, the brigand chief entered the cavern.

Henri was forcibly struck by his appearance, and his looks seemed to give the lie to the reports that had been circulated about of his cruelty, and in him he recognised the same man whom he had beheld in the cavern with the monk when he was first restored to his senses.

Allesandrio Robelli, the brigand chief, was a man apparently about forty years of age, and his countenance was remarkably handsome. His features were perfectly regular, and his fine black eyes, so keen and penetrating, sparkled with intelligence. He was very tall, and his strong robust figure was perfect in every point. He wore a most elegant dress of crimson velvet, and profusely decorated with lace and jewellery; and a high-crowned hat surmounted his head, in which was a plume of feathers of the finest white. Altogether his appearance was most commanding and interesting, and Henri could not but acknowledge the forcible impression it had made upon him.

He advanced hastily towards the young man, and greeted him with a very polite bow, at the same time congratulating him on the rapidity with which he was approaching convalescence; and his manner of address was polished in the extreme, and was sufficient to convince any one that his origin had been noble.

"Thou didst wish to see me, Henri le Sange," said Allesandrio; "what would'st thou with me?"

"I would thank thee for the kindness I have experienced from thee, which, from such a source I had no right to expect," replied Henri, "and request thee to allow me to return to my friends, who, doubtless, are in a state of distraction at my disappearance."

"For the service I have been fortunate enough to have it in my power to render thee, I need no thanks," returned Allesandrio; "but as regards thy request, I regret that I have it not in my power to comply with it."

"How?" demanded Henri, hastily.

"There is a rule among the gang, of which I am the chief," replied Allesandrio, "and to which we are all bound by oath strictly to adhere, never to suffer those persons who may fall into our power to quit this cavern again, unless they consent to become one of the gang."

"Ah!" exclaimed Henri, his indignation rising as he spoke, "am I then to be detained against my will?"

"Such a fact, I am sorry to say, is imperative," answered Allesandrio.

"It was an accident which placed me in thy power," said Henri, "thou hast saved my life, and thou, surely, wilt not do away with the debt of gratitude I owe thee for thy humanity, by a deed of cruelty like this ?"

" I have told thee I have no power to act otherwise."

" What good can my detention do thee or the gang ?" demanded Henri.

" At any rate, it will secure thee from betraying us," was the answer ; " this cavern is unknown to all but ourselves, and here we have been enabled to bid defiance to our enemies, and to elude every attempt which has been made to discover us."

" This precaution with me," said Henri, is unnecessary. I am ready to take any oath which you may think proper to administer to me."

" Thy friends have already been apprised that thou art safe," said Allesandrio ; " the rest, as I have before told thee, thou must make up thy mind to comply with. I have not the power to assist thee."

" Oh, pause, Allesandrio," urged Henri, " pause and reflect upon what thou would'st do, and of the consequences that will, in all probability, follow. It cannot be long ere it will be discovered in whose power I am, such steps are certain to be taken by my friends to ensure my restoration, and bring destruction upon thee and thy gang."

A smile of scorn was visible in the features of the brigand chief, when Henri gave utterance to these expressions, and he said—

" They would find that, as they have hitherto done, rather a difficult task. Allesandrio Robelli bids defiance to his enemies, and will never be taken alive. Henri le Sange, thou must make up thy mind either to join us, and take the oaths that bind us to each other, or remain a prisoner in this cavern. Think not, however, that it is my intention to visit thee with arbitrary severity ; —no ; here thou shall have every indulgence that this place can afford. I am no enemy of thine ; on the contrary, I would be one of thy warmest friends, and——"

" Hold ! Allesandrio," interrupted Henri ; " Henri le Sange can never be the friend of a robber and a brigand."

" Well, well, e'en be it as thou wilt," said Allesandrio, " but, perhaps thou may'st yet be glad to alter thy opinion. I have told thee the rule, and thou hast no alternative but to abide by it."

" If it be money that thou requirest," observed Henri, " thou shalt have it, and, I repeat, that I will give thee every security thou may'st demand, to keep all that has transpired, and the place of thy retreat, an inviolable secret."

" I have told thee I have not the power to comply with thy wishes," again returned Allesandrio, " and, as I suppose that is all that thou did'st require to see me for, I will bid thee for the present, adieu. I shall see thee again shortly, when I hope to find thee a little more resigned, and in a condition to enter upon a subject it is my intention to broach to thee."

Before Henri could say another word in reply, the brigand chief bo ed to him politely and quitted the place.

We will not seek to describe the feelings of Henri after the brigand chief had left him, for any attempt to do so must be a signal failure ; but at length, being unable to bear his feelings with any degree of patience, he tossed himself on his couch, and gave vent to them in expressions of the utmost resentment.

The loud shouts of the brigands (who were carousing) from the inner cavern frequently assailed his ears, but nothing could divert his attention from the anguish of his own thoughts, and his agitation arose to such a pitch, that he was in a high fever, and totally incapable of rising from his couch again, the monk being called in to attend him.

We will now return to his mother and his friends, and recount the circumstances that had taken place since he had been in the brigand's cavern.

It would require far greater power of eloquence than we are possessed of, to depicture correctly the state of distraction into which Madame Laurette was thrown, upon the mysterious disappearance of her son. She was more than usually depressed on the day in the evening of which the circumstance took place of which we have been describing, and which threw Henri into the power of Allesandrio Robelli, the brigand chief ; and when the time which he generally absented himself had elapsed, and night had set in, she became so uneasy, that, in spite of the remonstrances of Mrs. St. Aubyn, (whose brother, at her request, had hastened to the Villa di Venoni to make inquiries after him,) had the greatest difficulty in the world to prevent her from leaving the house and going herself in search of him. This terror, as may be well imagined, was not a little increased, when Mr. Wakefield returned, and informed them that Henri had quitted the villa some hours before, and they had every reason to believe that he went direct towards home. A strange foreboding that something had happened to him, at the same time came over Marceline and her mother and they felt very uneasy at his absence, entreating Mr. Wakefield to make every inquiry after him, and to furnish them with the particulars of the result as early as possible. This Mr. Wakefield did, and the information he was enabled to obtain increased the agony which Madame Laurette, Marceline, and her mother had previously experienced. A large pool of blood was discovered on the spot where the combat had taken place between Henri and his assailants, and a portion of his dress, which he had torn away in the affray, fully proved that he was one of the persons who had been engaged in the combat ; and the circumstance of his disappearance gave them too much reason to believe that he had fallen a victim to some villains whose design had been robbery and murder.

The horror of Madame de Floriville and the others was indescribable, and the utmost excitement prevailed in the neighbourhood where Henri was known; but no person had witnessed the event, and could not form the least conjecture to whom they should attribute it. The marks of blood were traced to within a short distance of the mountains in which the brigand's cavern was situated, but there all clue was lost; and it was, therefore, concluded that the unfortunate young man had been attacked by some of the daring gang of Allesandrio Robelli, and murdered, and thus all prospect of his restoration was banished from their minds.

Madame de Floriville was in a complete state of frenzy, and Mr. Wakefield and his sister, who saw but little occasion to form any other opinion than the one she entertained, were at a loss for argument to console her.

No circumstance could have been the occasion of more powerfully evincing the strength of the affection which Marceline entained for Henri, than the one which we are writing. For several hours she was in a complete state of insensibility, and when she did regain her reason, her mind had evidently received a shock, from which it did not seem at all probable that she was likely soon to recover. In vain did Signora Venoni endeavour to console her; the circumstance was too awful to admit of any alleviation of her anguish. Her first, her only love, it appeared, was thus lost to her for ever, and the morning of her hopes, her spring of happiness, was at once overclouded in a manner which nothing could ever dissipate. That Henri had fallen a victim to some of the desperate brigands that infested the adjacent mountains, she entertained not the slightest doubt; but what had become of his body, she could not form the least idea, as it did not appear probable that the assassins would have taken upon themselves the trouble of conveying it from the spot where the crime had been perpetrated. In vain were all the inquiries that were made, and the distraction of all who were interested in the awful circumstances became almost insupportable.

All the arguments that Mr. Wakefield and his sister could make use of to quiet the intense agony of Madame de Floriville were ineffectual, and such was the impression it made upon her mind, that she was confined to her bed, and for several days was in a state of delirium, from which it was apprehended she would never recover. The fate of the unhappy lady was the most adverse and lamentable they had ever heard of; and certainly it did appear that the curse of her father, invoked upon her head so many years before, pursued her with the most undue severity.

"Oh, God!" she exclaimed, when reason had in some degree resumed its sway over her mind, "surely my fate is too severe. Have not the years of bitter suffering I have endured been sufficient to atone for that act of imprudence to which I was urged only by the power of a misplaced affection? My son—my poor murdered Henri, why was I permitted to live to endure such a trial as this? Almighty Father, since it has been Thy will to deprive me in this dreadful manner of the only tie which held me to life, in mercy put an end to my earthly sufferings, by taking me to Thyself."

She wrung her hands, and went off into a paroxysm of grief too violent for description, and defied all the efforts of Mr. Wakefield and his sister to soothe her. What consolation had they to offer her? The untimely fate of Henri appeared too evident to admit of their offering her the least reasonable room for hope. As for Marceline, the dreadful event cast a blight over her young hopes, which nothing could remedy; melancholy was the change which it had worked in her prospects. The gay—the volatile girl had, in a few short hours, fallen into a state of premature old age, and she was seized with a fit of despair, from which nothing could arouse her; in fact, it seemed as if her senses were likely to fall a sacrifice to the heavy shock which her feelings had sustained. Murder was of such common occurrence in that country, and at the period of which we are writing especially, that it was thought no more of than the most ordinary circumstance, and but little or no inquiries were ever made into it, and thus the perpetrators of the most heinous crimes were too often suffered to escape with impunity. Mr. Wakefield was, however, most indefatigable in endeavouring to elicit all the information he could upon the subject, and he was not without hopes that Henri had not perished, although what had become of him, he had no means of forming even the remotest idea.

It had been so long since they had heard anything of the Duke Monterino, that he never for a moment entered their thoughts, or they would, in all probability, have come to the right conclusion.

It was about a week after the mysterious disappearance of Henri, that Madame de Floriville, entering her dressing-room one morning, found a letter on the table directed to her, in a strange hand, and which no one in the place could give her any account of, or in what manner it came there. In the greatest haste and trepidation, she broke the seal, and read the following lines:—

"Madame le Sange may rest her mind contented; her son is not dead. He was found badly wounded by the persons in whose care he now is, but is rapidly recovering. How soon he will see his friends again depends entirely on himself."

This was all that the letter contained, and although it satisfied Madame de Floriville and her friends that Henri was not murdered, it involved them in the same state of mystery as to what had become of him, and in whose power he was, that they had before been in. They racked their brains in vain to form even the slightest idea, and their anguish was very little abated by the circumstance.

Madame Laurette could not ascertain from any of her servants how the letter had been placed where she found it, or from whom it had come, and the mystery was so great that they all became quite lost in perplexity, fear, and doubt, and knew not in what manner to act. The note had stated that the restoration of Henri to his friends depended entirely upon himself, but how it could do so, was to them all perfectly inscrutable. By whom, too, if the letter spoke the truth, had the attempt upon the young man's life been made?—They could not call to their recollection one individual to whom he could have given cause for enmity, the Duke Monterino, as we have before stated, never once entering their thoughts, and the statement in the letter appeared far from probable, as they felt convinced that, if his restoration to them depended upon himself, he would take the earliest opportunity to return. Thus they were left in the maze of perplexity, and without being able to come to any decision as to the best means of extricating themselves.

Another week passed away, and still they could not gain any further intelligence of Henri, and the liberal rewards that had been offered to any one who could furnish them with any information, had all failed to have the desired effect. The misery of poor Marceline had now settled into absolute despair, and it was melancholy to see the rapid inroads which intense grief and anxiety were making upon her constitution, and which defied all the efforts of her mother to obliterate or alleviate. As for Madame de Floriville, she was at times in a state bordering upon distraction, and it was remarkable that she should be able to retain her senses under such a heavy affliction.

Marceline was one day seated in a small arbour in the garden of the villa, wrapped in deep and melancholy meditation, when she was suddenly aroused by hearing her name pronounced in a voice which was familiar to her ears, and looking up, her astonishment and terror may be imagined; when she beheld the hated Duke Monterino standing before her.

"Proud, yet too fascinating girl," he exclaimed, his countenance glowing with admiration and sensual desire, "once more I come to offer you the homage of a heart of which you are the sole mistress. I have sought, but in vain, in absence to drive your beauteous image from my mind; but in spite of the scorn with which you have treated me, I found that to be a task which was far beyond my power to accomplish. Marceline, believe me, I love you to distraction; I am willing to make any sacrifice for your sake; deign, then, to banish the scornful coldness with which you have hitherto treated me from your breast, and hear me, while on my knee I solemnly vow to love no one but you, and to devote all my thoughts, all my attention to the promotion of your happiness."

While the detested nobleman was thus speaking, he had forcibly taken the hand of the blushing and offended maiden, and, in spite of her efforts to release it from his hold, he pressed it to his lips, and breathed upon it the most warm and impassioned kisses.

"Forbear, my lord," she exclaimed, rising indignantly, and fixing upon him a look sufficient to abash the most insensible being; "by what right do you intrude upon me, unbidden, in this manner?—Begone; I have already assured you of my hatred towards you; and the outrage you committed when last we met, was every way calculated to increase that dislike. Leave me, my lord, or I will, by my cries, summon those to my aid you may not be prepared to meet."

"Lovely girl, this obstinacy is ridiculous," ejaculated the duke. "My passion is so violent, that I find it impossible to stifle it. There can be no danger too great for me to encounter for the sake of gratifying it, and——"

"Help—help!" screamed Marceline, terrified at the increasing boldness of Monterino, who still retained his hold of her hand, and urged his hated suit with the most alarming determination.

"Nay, then," exclaimed the duke, "since it is so, I must use violence to secure that which I am determined shall be in my power —namely, the possession of your person. Ah—your cries are vain. I have those at hand who will quickly assist me in my designs. What ho, there!"

Immediately on his giving utterance to these words, three fierce-looking ruffians rushed to the spot, and throwing a mantle over her head, so as nearly to suffocate her, and entirely prevent her from raising any outcry, they bore her hastily away from the garden out at the gate—where, overcome by her terrors, she became insensible.

"Quick—quick—away with her!" cried the duke. "We have not a moment to lose! Bear her with all the speed you can to the carriage! She is mine—she is mine!"

The fellows obeyed the mandates of Monterino implicitly, and the insensible maiden was quickly conveyed to a short distance from the villa, where a vehicle was in waiting, and in which having placed her, the duke seated himself by her side, and the carriage was driven precipitately from the spot.

It would be impossible properly to pourtray the feelings of exultation which Monterino experienced when he had thus succeeded in getting Marceline in his power: it was so great that he could scarcely contain himself. He hung over her insensible form, and gazed upon her uncommon beauty with the most inexpressible feelings of delight, and again and again he polluted her ruby lips with his kisses. He for some time had this design in contemplation; and, having at length succeeded in removing Henri, the principal obstacle to the gratification of his wishes was done away with, and thus his triumph was rendered the more certain. He had been in the neighbourhood, *incog*, for several days past, anxiously watching for an opportunity of accomplishing his design ; and on the day on which it has been shown he wasso fatally successful, he had seen Signora Venoni quit the villa ; and when she did so— having accidentally left the garden gate open —he was enabled to gain admittance into the place, and to take Marceline by surprise in the manner we have described. It was his intention to convey her to a casino he had in a remote part of the country, which he but seldom inhabited, and whree he thought she was less likely to be discovered, and he had taken care to have everything in preparation for her reception.

It was some time before Marceline was restored to sensibility ; and when she again did become conscious, she was so terrified at finding the situation she was placed in, that she almost suffered a relapse, and a deadly chill fell upon her heart, which completely blighted every other feeling than that of the most intense despair.

"Beauteous Marceline, you must pardon me for an act to which I have been alone urged by your scornful treatment, and the power of the love I entertain for you," said the duke, looking into her face in the most

HENRI RESCUES MARCELINE FROM THE DUKE MONTERINO.

persuasive manner. "Be not alarmed—no danger shall attend you ; and every indulgence—every happiness that the most ardent attachment can bestow shall be at your command."

"Villain !" cried Marceline, darting upon him a look of the deepest resentment, "release me. Why am I detained ? Whither are you conveying me ? Restore me to my mother, or you shall have cause dearly to rue this daring outrage."

"Be calm, sweet Marceline," said the duke. "Again I tell you that I mean no harm, and that I will act only as honour dictates."

"Honour !" repeated Marceline, in a tone of the most ineffable contempt. "Pollute not the sacred sentiment by naming it. Did you profess honour, could you act in the base manner you are doing ? Release me, I say, or my cries shall raise assistance, and bring you to disgrace and punishment."

The marquis only smiled scornfully at these threats, for he well knew how futile they were, as they were travelling by a most unfrequented way, and where it was not likely that his unfortunate victim could obtain any aid.

"Marceline," he observed, after a pause, during which he had been contemplating the charms of the poor girl with looks that excited her utmost disgust, "it may, perhaps, be as well to apprize you, that your scorn will have no other effect upon me than exciting me to that mode of conduct I would otherwise avoid. I courted you, in the first instance, with all the humble and modest attention of the most devoted lover ; I made proposals of the most honourable description ; I offered you my hand to make you the partaker of my rank and fortune ; to place you in a situation of the most enviable description ; these proposals you and your mother thought proper to reject with scorn, and I will add, insult ; you rejected them, and driven to desperation by your conduct, and the power of that passion your beauty had engendered in my bosom, I was urged to endeavour to gain forcible possession of you. In that attempt I was foiled by the beardless boy on whom you have, I know, since bestowed those affections you refused to me ; but in this I have been more successful, and think not that I will easily lose the advantage I have gained. For the act of violence I have committed, you may blame yourself only ; but, mark me, I still mean, as I before stated, to act in the most honourable manner towards you ; —I would make you my wife, but if you obstinately refuse willingly to become the Duchess Monterino, I candidly confess that I may be induced to force you to gratify the passion you have created in my breast, without conferring on you the honour of my hand."

"Shameless, unfeeling man !" cried the indignant Marceline, the crimson blushes of insulted modesty suffusing her cheeks ; — "but it is useless talking to one who is like insensible to honour, virtue, or humanity !"

"I can act with forbearance, lovely girl," said Monterino, "I will prove to you, by heeding not, for the present at any rate, any acrimonious words you may apply to me, and I trust that I shall, ere long, bring you to think and act very differently."

"Duke," exclaimed Marceline, with becoming dignity, although her gentle bosom was swelling with agony and fear, "I warn you to forbear, and to restore me to my friends. Whither are you taking me ? and what are your intentions ?"

"My intentions I have already told you," replied the duke, "and as regards your other question, I am taking you to a place of security, where your compliance with my wishes will be your only chance of restoration to liberty and your friends."

"Alas ! alas !" sighed Marceline ; "can such cruelty exist, and that in the bosom of one who pretends to honour and nobility ? But think not that your conduct will go undiscovered or unpunished. Think not that your rank and power will protect you ; no, dearly will you have cause to rue this disgraceful conduct towards one whose ears you have dared to insult with protestations of love."

"Again I tell you, Marceline," observed the duke, "that such threats are completely useless, and that I am far beyond the reach of their power. My plot is so well arranged, that nothing can frustrate it, and ere many weeks have elapsed, you will assuredly be the wife of Duke Monterino."

"Never !" cried Marceline, energetically, "sooner would I die ! No fate can be half so terrible as an union with one so entirely destitute of every claim upon respect or esteem, much more love."

The duke, in spite of his affected indifference, felt the words of Marceline most keenly ; he bit his lips, and he had the greatest difficulty in concealing his chagrin ; he returned no immediate answer to her words, and Marceline, as the carriage rolled on its way, covered her face with her handkerchief, and wept bitterly, for the danger of her situation, and the little room that there appeared to be at present for hope, distracted her mind, and the idea of the dreadful anguish her mother would endure, occasioned her more pain than all. From a being so callous as Monterino, accustomed as he was to mingle in scenes of the greatest profligacy, and to give unbridled indulgence to his licentious passions, she was convinced it would be utterly useless to expect pity, or that he would, by any means, be induced to abandon his wicked designs ; and before her friends might discover that she had fallen into his hands, or whither he had borne her, he might by force have put his diabolical threats into execution, and she would be then lost for ever. As these ideas rushed to the mind of the poor girl, her agitation became so great, that she could not forbear groaning aloud. Monterino pretended to be moved by her emotion, and gently taking her hand, he said, in accents of tenderness he was seldom in the habit of expressing himself, but which he knew so well how to assume on occasions to suit his base purposes—

"Beauteous Marceline, believe me, I cannot bear to see you thus affected ; and although the manner in which you repulsed my suit, unable as I was to banish my ardent love I feel for you from my heart, has forced me to act in the manner I have done, still would I prove to you, by my conduct, that your happiness is dear to me."

"Oh, weak, base hypocrisy," returned Marceline, "can you with shameless front make use of such assertions ? Is this the way to prove your words, by tearing me from my home, my mother, and threatening me with dishonour ?"

"I would make you my bride !"

"If you would entitle yourself to my forgiveness—if you would not make me believe you the most inhuman of your sex, restore me to my home."

"Consent to be mine, and the rising of to-morrow's sun shall see the holy rites performed, and you shall be restored to the arms of the signora, your mother."

"Never ! never will I be forced into a compliance with that from which my very soul revolts," replied Marceline, resuming her firmness.

" Then you know the consequences," said Monterino; " I have told you my determination, and nothing can induce me to alter it. After infinite trouble, I have got you in my power, and I swear that my wife you shall either be by your own consent, or force shall make you my mistress."

Marceline sobbed convulsively, and the violence of her feelings rendered her entirely incapable of returning any reply to the heartless speech of her cruel and unprincipled enemy.

At that moment, the vehicle suddenly stopped, and the duke having put his head out of the window, inquired the reason.

" I beg your pardon, my lord," said the man who was driving it, and who alighted on his master's interrogation being peremptorily repeated, " I beg your pardon, but owing to the darkness of the night, and the intricacies of the forest, I have mistaken the way, and know not where we are."

" Curses light on your stupidity, Guiseppe," cried Monterino, passionately; "this must have been sheer carelessness, so often as you have travelled this way."

" Indeed, my lord," answered Guiseppe, you accuse me wrongfully, I——"

" Fool!" interrupted the duke; " the forest of Montelbano must be known to you every inch;—you shall have cause to repent this. To be benighted in this place, and under such circumstances, curses — ten thousand curses, I say again, descend upon you for your stupidity."

Dismal as was the situation in which they were now placed, it caused a latent hope to spring up in the bosom of Marceline. They might be seen by persons who would be prevailed upon to endeavour to rescue her, or those who had, probably, been sent in pursuit of her, might be led to the spot before they could resume their journey. She looked from the carriage window, and the dreary prospect she beheld filled her mind with terror.

The light of the moon, if there was any, was entirely obscured by the thickly interwoven foliage of the tall trees that seemed to intersect them on every side, and amidst the branches of which, the wind whistled mournfully. It was a fit spot for the perpetration of any deed of horror, and seemed to be the only likely haunt for men of crime, for those who preyed upon the purses of their fellow-creatures, and who would not shrink from the perpetration of any deed to ensure the accomplishment of their wishes. Marceline shuddered, and Monterino gave utterance to the most dreadful imprecations and maledictions on the heads of the creatures in his employ.

" Cannot any of the fellows direct you in the way to extricate ourselves from this difficulty?" he demanded, in fierce tones, of Guiseppe.

The ruffians answered in the negative,

and again the duke stamped and swore with rage.

" There seems to be an avenue of trees to the right," he said at last, after having walked a short distance from the vehicle, " but I know not how far it extends. We will, however, try that way, for here it is useless to remain."

" It is so confoundedly dark," said Guiseppe, " that I am fearful I shall never be able to guide the horses, and we have no lights, or the means of procuring them."

" Do as I command you," ordered the duke, again entering the carriage. Guiseppe obeyed, muttering and grumbling to himself, and the vehicle was again driven on at a slow pace, much to the annoyance of Monterino, who was too much enraged to enter into any further conversation with Marceline who gave herself up entirely to her own melancholy meditations, and the terrors which the situation she was placed in had created. After they had proceeded in this manner for about ten minutes, the vehicle again stopped.

" What's the matter now?" demanded Monterino, as Guiseppe approached the door of the carriage.

" I see a light glimmering at a distance, my lord, which seems to proceed from some habitation," replied the man.

" And have you any idea, now, what part of the forest we are in?" interrogated the duke.

" I have, my lord," said Guiseppe; " it strikes me that we are near the castle of Rivoldino, from which, most likely, the light I observe proceeds."

" Ah !" ejaculated Monterino, "should that idea prove correct, it will be fortunate; the Count Rivoldino is my friend, but he has been absent some time from the castle. It is left in the care of old Marco, his son, and two or three other domestics, and there we should be able to put up for the night. Proceed as fast as you can in the direction of the light, Guiseppe."

Guiseppe bowed and obeyed, and again the vehicle proceeded, with very little more speed than it had done before, on its dreary way.

Marceline saw little to hope, if the surmises of Guiseppe proved to be correct; for should old Marco and the other servants of the castle even have the power to assist her, it was not at all likely that they would venture to incur the anger of the duke, by interesting themselves in her behalf.

After the lapse of about another quarter of an hour, the carriage again stopped, and Marceline, as well as the darkness would permit, beheld the walls of the lofty tower of an ancient castle, which, from a word which Monterino gave utterance to, proved to be the one of which himself and Guiseppe had been speaking.

One of the men alighted, approached the ponderous gate, and pulled a bell violently. It was not, however, until the ringing had been repeated, and the patience of Monterino was quite exhausted, that it appeared to make any impression upon the ears of the inhabitants of the castle; but at length a heavy footstep was heard pacing the court-yard, and directly afterwards a feeble voice demanded who was there?

The duke, who had alighted from the vehicle, and advanced to the gates, answered for himself.

"It is I, good Marco, the Duke Monterino," said he; "I have been benighted in the forest, and must request your hospitality for the night."

Marco uttered something in reply, and then the gates were immediately opened, and revealed the bent figure of an old man, of a venerable, but not over agreeable countenance, with a lighted lamp in his hand. On seeing the duke, Marco drew back a few paces, and then bowed obsequiously to him. Monterino drew him aside, and after engaging him a few minutes in earnest conversation, Marceline saw him put a purse in his hand, whereupon the old man bowed a great deal lower than before. The duke made a sign to Guiseppe, the vehicle entered the court-yard, and was driven up to the porch, the door of which was standing open, and Monterino handed Marceline from the carriage. She looked earnestly and imploringly in the face of old Marco, who eyed her with much curiosity, but evidently with no other feeling, and then, without speaking, she suffered herself to be led by the duke, and preceded by the old man, to a spacious and elegant apartment.

"Remember what I have told you, Marco," said the duke, as the old man was about to retire from the room.

"Your lordship knows well that you can trust me," answered Marco; "I will not fail to caution Jaquelina and Spaladro."

"Enough," said Monterino; and Marco quitted the apartment, leaving the duke and Marceline alone.

Marceline had sunk on a seat immediately on her entering the apartment; and after observing the conduct of Marco, and hearing his observations, had given herself up entirely to despair; and Monterino, after gazing at her in silence for a minute or two, now advanced, and took one by her side. She shrunk from him with a feeling of terror and abhorrence.

"Marceline," said Monterino, "you have, doubtless, perceived that it would be useless for you to make any appeal to these persons. Here we shall remain to-night, but you must be in readiness by daylight to resume our journey.

Marceline made no reply, but averted her face with a deep sigh; and shortly afterwards an old woman, who, doubtless, was the Jacquelina whom Marco and his wife had mentioned, accompanied by a young man, bearing refreshments, entered the room. They both eyed Marceline with the same curiosity as Marco had done, and then proceeded to place the provisions on the table.

"Your lordship will please to pardon the humble nature of the repast," said Jacquelina; "but, of course, now my lord, the count, is away from the castle, we do not provide so sumptuously, and——"

The duke waved his hand haughtily and impatiently, to put a stop to the old woman's loquacity, and then motioned her and Spaladro, her son, to quit the room.

When they had gone, the duke turned to Marceline, and requested her to join him in the repast; but she declined doing so, her heart being too full to suffer her to eat, and requested that Monterino would permit her to retire for the night.

The duke eyed her for a minute or so with an expression of admiration, and then said—

"I comply with your request, Marceline, and rest assured that in this place you will be as safe as if you were in the Villa di Venoni. In the morning, as I before said, by the first appearance of Sol in the eastern horizon, I shall expect you to be prepared to resume our journey."

At the mention of the Villa di Venoni, Marceline could not resist a tear; and Monterino, having summoned Jacquelina, bade her good-night, and ordered the old woman to show her to a comfortable apartment, at the same time repeating the caution he had previously made use of to her.

"There, young lady," said Jacquelina; "you will find this a very comfortable room, and the bed is well aired; and now I wish you good-night."

With these words, the old woman bustled out of the room, which Marceline heard fastened upon her.

Left to herself, Marceline for some time reflected upon her situation, and gave way to the anguish of her feelings; but at length she became more composed, and a hope sprung up in her bosom that something would transpire to release her from the power of the duke, and to frustrate his diabolical intentions.

A cheerful fire blazed in the grate, and the room, which was furnished in the most costly style, had a comfortable appearance, and was calculated to calm the feelings of the unfortunate girl; and, after breathing a prayer for the safety of her mother and the restoration of Henri, she seated herself by the side of the fire, and taking up a book, which she found lying on the dressing table, being disinclined for sleep, she glanced over its contents. It consisted of ancient legends and tales, whose deep interest were sufficient to rivet the attention; but one more attractive than the rest most forcibly struck her, and her thoughts became abstracted from her own sorrows in the romantic incidents which it related. She stirred the fire into a cheerful blaze, and commenced reading the romantic story, which will be found in the succeeding chapter.

————

CHAPTER XIV.

THE CASTLE OF ALTENBURG.

"Come, come, Florian—you must not give way to despair. Providence will not forsake us thus, depend on it. Cheer up—cheer up; and if we can only gain the next village, probably the charity of some kind persons will relieve us. Besides, you know that I am a mortal enemy to melancholy, and I will never be contented until I have succeeded in making you a convert to my temperament."

"I know, dear Julio, that I am a terrible melancholy boy, and would that I had the spirit to battle with misfortune as you can. But surely ours is no common lot."

"Well, that is true, Florian; but what is the use of grieving? That won't mend it, you know. For my own part, I have declared war against sorrow and despair; and something strikes me that I shall ultimately come off victorious. Come, come, my dear brother—I am stronger than you. Lean on me for support, and let us push on our way."

"Alas! Julio, I am so tired that I fear I shall not be able to proceed many yards. Besides, it is so late—so long pest midnight, that we stand not the least chance of gaining a shelter: the inhabitants of the village have, doubtless, long been locked in the arms of sleep. Let us rather lie down here till daylight: an hour or two's sleep would so refresh me."

"But I should prefer having it in bed, Florian. The night dew is not by any means a remedy for the rheumatics, and— But eh! By the light of the moon, I behold a castle peeping from among the trees."

"What a dismal-looking place! It chills my heart to gaze at it even."

"On the contrary, it gladdens mine, Florian. We must not always judge by appearances; and if the castle has an ugly lock, its inhabitants may not be insensible to humanity. At any rate, I will make an appeal to them."

"But recollect the unseasonable hour, Julio."

"And recollect, dear Florian, how pleasant a warm bed would be. I will, at least, make the trial, and they can but refuse us, you know."

"Well, Julio, I will yield to you; but I am fearful we shall not meet with any success. Oh, dear—oh, dear, how fatigued I am, and so hungry."

"Hungry! I am ravenous, Florian; so come along; lean on me, and may good fortune smile upon us."

This conversation took place between two lads of handsome and noble appearance, but humbly attired, and evidently worn out with fatigue and suffering, and the scene in which it took place was one of the most gloomy description. It was just on the borders of an extensive forest, across which they had been travelling for several hours past, in the hope of being able to reach some village, where they might obtain food and shelter for the night, from the kindness and hospitality of some of the inhabitants. They had not taken food for several hours, and were entirely destitute. They were orphans, and knew not whither to direct their footsteps, from to seek protection or relief. Julio was the elder, and was possessed of animal spirits, that enabled him to smile at misfortunes, beneath which stronger constitutions would, probably, have sunk; but Florian was of a more delicate nature, and unable to resist the shafts of care.

Leaning on the arm of his brother for support, Florian suffered himself to be led towards the castle, which was an extensive and gothic edifice, blackened by time, and half covered with moss and ivy. They looked up at the different casements, but saw not the least signs of any person being up. There was no light to be seen in any portion of the building; and Florian, sighing, again endeavoured to persuade his brother to abandon all thoughts of seeking a shelter in the castle, when it appeared to him that there was such little chance of their meeting with any success. Julio was, however, of a different opinion, and, seizing the bell at the ponderous gates, he pulled it boldly, and awaited the result with an assumption of impatience he did not really feel, but which he affected, merely to encourage his brother. Several minutes elapsed, and no answer was returned, and Julio again pulled the bell more violently than before. It was not, however, until he had repeated the same three or four times that they received any sign of the castle being inhabited, when, looking up, Julio and his brother discovered a light glimmering in the narrow casement, just above the porch, which almost immediately disappeared, and presently afterwards a disagreeable voice demanded who was there, and what they wanted? Julio answered; and the return was a surly growl from the individual who had put the question. The bolts, however, were withdrawn, and the doors swinging on their hinges, revealed to them the figure of an old grey-headed porter, who, holding the lamp he carried in his hand above his head, eyed the boy with a stern and forbidding aspect; and then, in a surly tone, he said—

"Why, you impudent young varlet, what do ye mean by disturbing people at this hour of the night? Any one would suppose that it had been some nobleman or the other by the boldness with which you pulled the bell."

"We are poor distressed orphans, sir," said Julio, "who have no home, no friends; we have travelled far, and have not tasted food for many hours; for the love of——"

"Speak louder," cried the old porter, in the same harsh tones; "I am deaf, and cannot hear what you say."

"We are orphans, sir," repeated Julio, speaking in the porter's ear, "tired and hungry; for the love of Heaven, then, grant us shelter and food——"

"Food! shelter!" interrupted the porter, with a repulsive look. "Get ye gone, ye scapegrace knaves, or I may be inclined to treat you with a flogging. Away with you—you shall not come in here."

Before Julio or his brother could remonstrate farther, the surly old porter banged to the doors, and bolting and locking them as they had been before, left the poor boys to their own reflections, and with no other prospect than that of passing the night in the forest.

*   *   *   *   *

Sol had not long mounted his golden chariot in the heavens, when a small hamlet in Provence might be seen in an unusual state of gaiety and bustle, and it was very evident that something particular was about to take place. It was the morning of an annual festival, which was celebrated in the village; and to add to the joy of the occasion, the son of old Ricardo, the father of the hamlet, was to be united to the pretty Lucille, the daughter of the aged Clotilde, the wealthy neighbour of Ricardo.

Ricardo was looked up to with particular veneration by the villagers, for he had been the confidential domestic of the late Count Altenburgh, and his benevolent character entitled him to all the respect that was shown him. Having far more than enough for his own wants, and to provide for his son, his principal delight was in relieving such of his poor neighbours who needed it, and honest poverty never apppealed to him in vain. It was a complete holiday, and every one seemed determined to enjoy it to the utmost, and to do honour to the nuptials of Jerome and Lucille.

Ricardo was himself all joyous expectation, and he had arisen long before any of his neighbours, to make preparations for the festivities of the day. Having left his cottage, he met old Clotilde just leaving hers, and dressed in her best for the occasion. Some persons might have objected to the youthful fashion of her attire; but if there was any particular werkness which the good woman possessed, it was that of a weak memory, which made her forget that she was so old as she really was by some fifteen or twenty years, and hence the somewhat inappropriate style of dressing to which we have alluded.

Ricardo and Clotilde greeted each other with that cordiality which showed the strength and sincerity of their friendship, and expressed their anxiety for the hour to arrive which would still further strengthen that friendship, by the union of their children.

"Oh, Ricardo," said the old woman, "this, I anticipate, will be one of the most joyous days I have ever experienced, notwithstanding the pleasure which never fails to crown the day of our village festival."

"And yet, dame," answered Ricardo, with a deep sigh, "that day never comes round but it casts a gloom upon my spirits, which I in vain endeavour to shake off, for it reminds me of the death of my late noble master, who founded this hamlet, and to it annexed a charity for orphans."

"But it is not known positively that the count is dead," said Clotilde.

"True, dame, it is not," returned Ricardo; "but when we come to recollect how long it is since he has been absent, we have every reason to form that conclusion. Never was there a kinder-hearted nobleman than Count Altenburgh."

"Yes, well do I remember him—he was one of the most amiable men that ever lived; but the baroness——"

"Oh, name her not," interrupted Ricardo; "although she is the count's niece, I cannot think of her without a feeling of dislike I find it utterly impossible to conquer."

"And why should you be so prejudiced against the baroness?" asked Clotilde.

"I have frequently hinted to you why," he answered; "but I will now more explicitly give you my reasons. The Count Altenburgh, you know, married the Lady Imogine; two boys were the fruits of their union; these children and the marriage crushed the hopes of the baroness of inheritance. Three years afterwards the count sailed on important business to Sicily, and has never been heard of since. A very short time after a fire broke out in the castle; it was said to be by accident, although it broke forth in two distant apartments at the same time, and in that wing of the castle, and under the very room where Lady Imogine and the two children slept; they perished in the devouring element. The baroness contrived to escape, but by what means Heaven and herself only knows, and she is now in the possession of these wide domains."

"This is a very mysterious and suspicious affair," said Clotilde; "but surely she could not have been guilty of so dreadful a deed? I would much rather suspect that black-looking steward of hers, Geraldo, who seems to be the depository of all her secrets."

"Psha!" ejaculated Ricardo, "what motive could he have in perpetrating such a crime? although I do firmly believe that there is no deed, however base and cruel, which he would shrink from committing. But I have not told you all, Clotilde. I have heard it whispered, and I strongly believe it to be true, that the boys were saved and conveyed to some place of security by Huberto, the count's faithful domestic."

"Oh, no, I cannot think that; for if they had been rescued, and were still living, they would now be old enough to come forward and claim their rights," said Clotilde.

"It is, however, very evident that the

baroness has her suspicions that they are not dead," returned Ricardo, " or else she would not make such strict searches after them. What can be a greater proof of her guilt than the orders she has issued to have all the children who may come into the village, that may appear to be of the same age as the orphans, seized and conveyed into her presence? But let up drop this subject; it tortures my heart to dwell upon it. Having arranged the settlement with the notary, the lads and lasses of the village may assemble as soon as they think proper; and here they come, a merry party they are, too. Dame, bring out the bride to the door, whilst I stand with the bridegroom at mine, to receive them, as is customary on the feast day."

This was immediately done, and the party of village lads and lasses, gaily attired for the festival, tripped it merrily across the rustic bridge, and dancing around the bride and bridegroom, and their parents, to rustic music, they presented nosegays to the beauteous Lucille. Ricardo then produced a written document, which he proceeded to read to them, according to annual custom, and which stated the heads of the bounty annexed to the anniversary, as settled twenty years before, by the founder of the festival, Count Altenburg. The substance of it was as follows:—That if, on the day of the feast, any orphan, or two orphans, not exceeding the age of sixteen, should arrive as strangers in Altenburg, they should, if found worthy, be adopted and provided for; and, in case of the future absence or death of the Count Altenburg, the funds should be vested in the hands of Ricardo, who was to decide whether the strange orphans be worthy of the provison.

"And now," said Ricardo, when he had come to the conclusion of the document, "you have heard the charter, and, therefore, to church with ye, and after that, for mirth, feasting, and dancing."

The bride and bridegroom, with delighted looks, took each other's hands, and the lads and lasses again dancing to the rustic strains of music, were proceeding to do as Ricardo had commanded, when Julio and Florian appeared upon the bridge, and gazed upon the happy party with looks of envy and admiration. Ricardo and the others observed them, and were struck by their appearance.

"Ah!" exclaimed the old man, "two strange lads, and handsome youngsters, too. One of them seems much affected, while the other looks as gay as the merriest amongst us. Stop a minute, my friends; I must speak to these lads."

Julio and Florian had now descended from the bridge, the latter weeping bitterly.

"Oh, Julio," observed Florian, sobbing, "what a wretched prospect we have before us—othing but despair."

"There, there," said the volatile Julio, "what's the use of being down-hearted about the matter? Suppose we are unfortu-

nate now, we may have better luck another time. See, here are some good-natured looking soul's already; they'll give us a little refreshment, I'll warrant;—won't you, kind gentlefolks?"

Ricardo, whose interest was immediately excited in their favour, inquired who they were. Florian was too much affected to reply, but Julio repeated the same words that he had done in answer to the questions put to them by the surly old deaf porter at the castle of Altenburg, and also informed him of the reception they had met with there.

"And whither come you from, my lads?" inquired Ricardo.

"Oh, sir, a very great distance from here,' answered Julio; " from Borne, in Switzerland; and we have been travelling on foot above a month."

"And your father?" interrogated Ricardo.

"We have no remembrance of him," said Julio; " he died when we were both so young; mother was then reduced by misfortune, and travelled to Switzerland, where she settled in an humble cottage, but——"

"And was she kind to you?" asked Ricardo.

"Kind!" replied Julio, energetically; "oh, sir, she was all affection; never, never can her loss be replaced."

"Is, then, your mother dead?"

"Alas! sir," said Julio, deeply affected, "she is."

"And have you, then, no other relations living?" inquired Ricardo.

"Not one," was the reply; "no relations—no friends."

"Poor lads, poor lads," said Ricardo, compassionately; " but whither are you now going?"

"We are going to Marseilles, sir, but we stepped out of the road, because we heard that there was to be a grand feast at Altenburg, and a wedding."

"How old are you, my lads?" inquired Ricardo.

"Julio is just a year older than I," said Florian.

"And I am just turned fifteen, sir," said Julio.

"Ah, indeed?" exclaimed Ricardo, "this is fortunate." Then turning to the persons assembled, he said—

"I need not inform you, neighbours, after the charter which I have read, that I have full power in this business, but as it is my wish to do that which is satisfactory to every one of you, I will be guided by your decision. These two poor lads, who have come in the nick of time, seem just to answer the first article of the Count Altenburg's intentions; shall I fix on them to be the objects of the bounty? Neighbours, the word."

An unanimous assent was the reply; and Ricardo, then turning to Julio and Florian, who had listened amazed to his words, observed—

"Then, my poor lads, here your journey is at an end."

"How, sir?" demanded Julio and Florian, in a breath.

"Briefly this; that you may set your hearts as well as your limbs at rest," answered Ricardo; "from this moment you are adopted here; taken care of for life, and to be placed in honest employment, fitting your station, by the bounty of the lord of the hamlet, the noble Count Altenburg."

"What, we! we!" delightedly exclaimed the orphan brothers, and tears of joy rushed to their eyes, as they folded each other in a warm embrace.

When they had recovered from the first burst of transport occasioned by this unexpected announcement, they threw themselves at the feet of Ricardo, and clasping his knees, looked up in his face with an expression of the most unbounded gratitude.

"Oh, sir," exclaimed Florian, while tears of gratitude flowed down his cheeks; "this kindness is overwhelming; how shall we ever be able to express our full sense of gratitude for your goodness?"

"Oh, no, we shall never, indeed, be able to do so," said Julio; "but," he added, after a pause, "you are not joking, are you?"

Ricardo raised them, and he spoke in a voice of sincerity.

"Joking, my poor lads? No, I am not used to sporting with the feelings of any person after that fashion," said Ricardo. "But your gratitude is not due to me; rather bless the name of the noble founder of the charity. But come, this point's settled; and look ye, yonder's my cottage; enter there at once, and put down your bundle, and as you appear to be tired and hungry, avail yourselves with welcome of the fare it contains. You will find a brown loaf and half a bottle of wine on the table; regale yourselves; and we will rejoin you presently."

"Thanks, thanks, dear, kind sir," said Julio; "in truth we are very hungry, so we shall not lose any time in despatching the fare you are so generous as to offer us, depend upon it."

With these words, Julio and his brother entered the cottage of Ricardo, and quickly commenced their repast, which they ate with that relish long fasting had given to their appetites; while Ricardo, Clotilde, and the other members of the wedding-party, hied away to the church.

Having finished their meal, Julio and Florian left the cottage, and went forth to meet the wedding-party on its return. They met Ricardo and Clotilde a short distance from the cottage, who had preceded the bride and the bridegroom and their friends, to prepare for their reception, and to see how the two poor lads were faring.

"Here you are, then, my lads," said Ricardo, a smile of kindness beaming in his benevolent countenance; "and I hope you have stowed all safe."

"Oh, yes, sir," replied Julio, "we have stowed all safe, thanks to your hospitality; —our bundle in a cupboard; the brown bread and wine in our stomachs."

"But," said Florian, "there is one thing we forgot to tell you, and you have been so kind to us, that we ought not to conceal anything from you."

"True, brother," observed Julio; "but what have we got to tell? I do not remember anything."

"The little box, Julio, that poor mother gave us on her death-bed," returned Florian.

"And what may the said box contain, my boys?" inquired Ricardo.

"Of that we are as ignorant as yourself, sir," answered Julio; "but show the box, Florian. Mother confided it to the care of Florian, sir; for, though he's the youngest, yet mother always said he was the steady one."

Florian took a small casket from his bosom, which was curiously wrought and sealed, and presented it to Ricardo, who took it with some suprise, the more so when he saw inscribed upon it the following words:—

"To Florian and Julio,—Never open this till Florian has attained his eighteenth year."

"This is very mysterious!" said Ricardo, examining the casket more minutely; "and you say that you know nothing of the contents of this, my lads?"

"Nothing whatever, sir," replied Florian; "it is four years to come before I shall be eighteen, and neither of us would open the box for all the world before the time our dear mother has mentioned."

"And did she say anything when she gave it you?" asked Ricardo.

"When she gave it to us," said Florian, the tears rushing to his eyes, and appearing altogether deeply affected; "oh, we would rather not talk of that."

"I can fully appreciate and sympathize with your feelings, my poor boy," observed Ricardo, "but I must request you to answer the question; it may be of consequence."

"True, it may be," coincided Julio, "and, therefore, I will give you the information you require, sir. Well, then, 'My dear children,' she said—we were at her bedside —she was dying—oh!"

"Come, come—cheer up, my good lad," said Ricardo, compassionately.

"'Take this box,' she said," continued Julio; "'be sure to keep it safely; the happiness of your lives depends upon it, and——'"

"Hush! Julio," interposed Florian, "there is somebody coming."

At this moment Geraldo, the steward of the baroness, entered, and Ricardo hastily thrust the casket in his bosom.

"I thought we could not be long without being interrupted," remarked Ricardo; "it is the impertinent and hateful steward of the baroness."

"Who is the gentleman, sir?" interrogated Julio.

"Mr. Geraldo, the steward from the castle,

who comes, no doubt, with a message from his mistress," answered Ricardo.

"Oh, hang that castle!" said Julio, aside; "I can't fancy anybody that belongs to it."

Geraldo now advanced, and glanced at the boys narrowly, although he evidently did not wish Ricardo or Clotilde to observe the closeness of his scrutiny.

"Good-day, honest Ricardo," he observed, with an assumption of politeness; "Clotilde, my ancient dame, I am happy to see you. I met the procession on the way to the church, and saw you returning; do not let my presence interrupt you."

Ricardo and Clotilde paid their respects sullenly.

"Your presence, sir, is an honour we did not expect," replied the former.

"The sight of so many joyous faces, Master Ricardo, cheers my heart, I assure you," added Geraldo.

"Then I wonder, sir, you don't cheer your heart a little oftener," remarked Ricardo, sarcastically. "I know there is some mischief a-foot," said Ricardo, aside; "I can always tell it by his being so devilish civil."

"These are two pretty boys," said the steward; "whose are they, pray?"

"They are mine," replied Ricardo.

"Yours!"

"Yes, and mine, too, sir," said Clotilde, hastily.

THE PORTER REPULSING JULIO AND FLORIAN FROM THE CASTLE OF ALTENBURG.

"And yours!" reiterated Geraldo, with a look of astonishment; "why, Ricardo—Clotilde, would you bring scandal on yourselves?"

"Scandal, sir?" re-echoed Clotilde; "I defy any one to bring scandal on me; they belong to all the hamlet."

"In fact," added Ricardo, "they are orphans, newly arrived on the feast-day, and adopted by me, with the consent of all the neighbours."

"Oh, according to the Count Altenburg's charter," said Geraldo.

"True," replied Ricardo: "and according to that charter, they are under my care and protection."

"Certain I am, my friends," remarked the steward, "they cannot be under better. How old are you, my lads?"

"Oh, Julio," said Florian, timidly, "do you speak; I am so frightened."

"Frightened!" responded Julio; "pho!" and advancing boldly to Geraldo, he added, "I am fifteen, sir—my brother was fourteen st Monday."

"Fine little fellows for your years," said Geraldo. "Ricardo, why haven't you introduced them at the castle?"

"Oh, thank, you, sir," answered Julio, pertly, "we have had enough of the castle already."

"Are these the same boys that I have been

told the porter drove away from the gate last night?" inquired Geraldo.

"Yes, sir, we are the same," replied Florian, "and very cruelly he used us, too."

"Well, well—he, perhaps, did not mean anything by it," said Geraldo, "and, therefore, you must forget it; I have reprimanded him for it, and you must, therefore, forgive his arrogance. I trust you will more readily do so, when I inform you that he is deaf. Ricardo, the baroness must see them, and to show you, boys, that you have nothing to fear, I will conduct you to her myself."

Ricardo could not help plainly evincing his displeasure at this proposition; Geraldo noticed it, but said nothing in allusion to it, having good reason to believe that he was no favourite with the old man.

"You'll be delighted to go, won't you, my lads?" interrogated Geraldo.

"No, thank you, sir," said Florian dejectedly.

"Egad!" cried Julio, "somehow or the other, I should like to talk to a baroness; I don't think I ever saw one in the whole course of my life."

"Well, then, attend me; no time must be lost," said Geraldo, hastily.

"I must disguise my fears," said Ricardo, aside. He then added aloud; "I am ready to attend you with them directly".

"Psha!" exclaimed Geraldo; "you forget that your company will be required by the wedding party. As soon as her ladyship has seen them, I'll bring them to you in the olive field. Come, my lads, bid good-by for a short time to your protector."

"Good-by, sir," said Julio to Ricardo; "we shan't be gone long."

"Good-by, kind, worthy sir," said Florian, with fervour; and then suddenly seeming to recollect himself, he remarked—"but I had like to have forgot—the little box, sir, if you please."

"Hush! not a word about it," replied Ricardo, aside, cautiously to Florian.

Geraldo had, however, heard what the latter had said, and turning hastily to Ricardo, he inquired—

"A box, say you—a box! Where is it?"

"A pretty casket—a mere toy that—I'm going to lock it up directly," answered Ricardo, confused.

"Oh, no, no—I won't give you that trouble, my good sir," returned Florian, eagerly.

Geraldo fixed a searching look upon the boys, and observing the eagerness of their manner, his suspicions were excited, and he was anxious to know what the box contained.

"What are the contents of the box you speak of?" demanded Geraldo.

"They tell me that it merely contains some trifles belonging to their deceased mother," replied Ricardo.

"Trifling to you, no doubt," observed the steward; "to them, however, a treasure. Why detain it? Their anxiety to keep it in their own possession is very natural."

"Besides," said Florian, "mother bade us never to part with it."

Ricardo reluctantly pulled the casket from his bosom, and placing it in Florian's hand, said—

"There, then, boy; and mind you take very great care of it."

"I can tell you, my dear sir," remarked Julio, with a smile, "you have no occasion to be afraid of the steady one. And now, sir, we are ready to accompany you."

"No doubt we shall all be at the olive field as soon as you," said Geraldo, speaking to Ricardo.

Ricardo and Clotilde now embraced the boys affectionately, and they then, attended by the steward, made their way towards the Castle of Altenburg. On their way thither, Geraldo endeavoured to amuse them with a glowing description of the beauties of the castle, and it was very evident that he took a peculiar interest in the boys, an interest which was unaccountable, considering they were strangers to him.

On entering the courtyard, they saw the old deaf porter, Gaspard, by whom they had been so roughly treated the night before, but he seemed not at first to notice them.

"So, this is the castle, is it?" said Julio, looking around him; "well, it is mighty grand and dismal, to be sure."

"Shall we not soon return, sir?" inquired Florian.

"Ay, ay, presently," replied Geraldo, impatiently; "I am going to inquire of the baroness when it will be her pleasure to receive you. Gaspard!"

The old porter seemed not to hear him, but walked nearer to the boys. Geraldo again called to him in a louder tone than before; but still he appeared not to hear him, and took not the least notice whatever. Julio now approached him, and bawling as loud as he could in his ear, he said—

"Sir, there's Mr. Geraldo talking to you, can't you hear?"

Gaspard now turned towards Geraldo, who looked sternly at him, and made signs to him to withdraw. Gaspard fixed a peculiar look upon the boys, and bowing, obeyed.

"Stay where you are, my lads," said the steward, as he retired; "I will soon return."

"Why, Julio," said Florian, when Geraldo had gone; "the old man looked quite good-natured at us just now."

"Yes, he did, indeed; and his behaviour altogether was so different, that I could not help noticing it," said Julio.

"And how cross Mr. Geraldo is to him," remarked Florian.

"Yes," said Julio, "he is, indeed; but I suppose that's merely to show his consequence as the great lady's great man. Oh, I find that it's easy to be a great man. 'Tis only to stamp your foot—be pompous, and pretend to more consequence than you have a right to."

"Dear me, I am all in a twitter, Julio, till we see this great lady," observed Florian. "What shall we say to her?"

"I must confess, Florian," replied his brother, "that puzzles me a little bit. But don't you remember that Blaize, the carrier, who used to travel to Geneva, told us that all your great folks there talk so flourishingly—they have always the honour to see each other, and hang me, Florian, if I don't try something after that fashion. But here she comes, I declare."

At this moment the baroness entered, and fixing her eyes piercingly upon the countenance of the two boys, she started, and evinced considerable emotion. There was something very forbidding and repulsive in her appearance and demeanour. Her eyes, which were very dark, were particularly penetrating, and looked as though they could peruse the thoughts of those they fixed themselves upon in a moment.

"Ah!" she muttered to herself, "those lineaments; do, then, Altenburg's sons still live; or has my conscience conjured up a likeness?"

She struggled with the feelings these thoughts created for a few moments; and then, in a voice of forced calmness and affected kindness, she greeted them, and bade them welcome to the castle. Julio took upon himself the office of spokesman, which he did in rather an awkward and confused manner — a circumstance which might have been expected, considering that the society he had hitherto mingled amongst had been most humble.

"Your head gentleman, Mr. Geraldo," said he, "told us you would be flattered by a visit from us; and so we flattered ourselves that we shouldn't do you the honour to refuse you: and—so here we are, madam."

"They talk like cottage boys," said the baroness, aside, "yet with intelligence that proves a noble origin; and their air—how graceful—how commanding: their countenances seem to say, 'Disperse our dawn of ignorance, that we may shine in kingly courts two stars of chivalry.' Geraldo informs me," she added, aloud, "that you are adopted in Altenburg by virtue of the established charter?"

"Yes, madam," said the boys, bowing very low.

"Were the noble Count Altenburg here," resumed the baroness—"alas! I fear he lives not, and hourly do I mourn his loss—I think that his unerring judgment would discover in your appearance, my young friends, something above those peasants for whom his bounty was designed."

"Oh, madam," said Julio, "you are too kind—too condescending."

"It is a great pleasure," returned the baroness—"it is a great pleasure for me to act as I suppose he would were he present: I must, therefore, supersede the worthy Ricardo's charge, and take you under my own protection."

"Oh, dear lady," Julio and Florian exclaimed in a breath, "indeed we don't deserve it."

"Nay," remarked the baroness, "I am confident my hopes in you will be fulfilled; you must receive through me, my amiable young friends, an education suited to the qualities which I perceive partial nature has gifted you. You shall lay aside your coarse apparel, and to-morrow appear in habits proper for the condition in which I mean to place you."

"Oh, thank you, thank you, dear madam," said Julio; "from this moment you and I are two gentlemen, Florian."

Overwhelmed with joy, they rushed into each other's arms, and embraced fervently, when the casket escaped from Florian's bosom, and fell to the ground. At that moment Geraldo re-appeared, and his eyes immediately beholding the casket, he whispered hastily to the baroness—

"Quick! secure the casket; 'tis that I told you of."

The baroness stooped eagerly and picked it up.

*   *   *   *

By the time Marceline had arrived at this part of the narrative it was broad daylight, and so interested had she been by the romantic nature of the story, that she had taken no notice of the rapid flight of time. She was, however, aroused by hearing the sound of an approaching footstep on the stairs, and shortly afterwards the room door was opened, and Jacquelina entered.

"Why, I declare," exclaimed the old woman, looking at the couch, "you have not been to-bed all night, although you must have been very tired after your journey: well—well—it surprises me how you young people can do without sleep. Ah! I see you have been reading, and so I do not wonder so much, for that is a very curious and interesting book. It belongs to me; but I have read it through a dozen times, and so has Marco; and, therefore, if you like it, accept it; it may serve to amuse you in a dull moment."

Marceline thanked the old woman, and gladly accepted the gift, for she was anxious to know the termination of the Castle of Altenburg, and the fate of the two orphan brothers.

"It is only just five o'clock," said Jacquelina, "but the vehicle is all ready, and the duke is anxious to resume the journey as quickly as possible. Will you attend me, if you please?"

Marceline arose, and having put the book in her bosom, with a heavy heart she accompanied Jacquelina down stairs, and entered the room in which the detested Monterino was awaiting her arrival. He greeted her with an assumption of kindness, but Marceline made him no reply, and turned from him with a feeling of disgust she found it impossible to suppress.

Jacquelina had spread a repast upon the

table, but Marceline could not eat, and Monterino having slightly partaken of it, he arose, and proceeded to conduct Marceline from the room to the court-yard, where the carriage was waiting. Monterino handed her in, and then followed himself. The same fellows that had attended them the other part of the journey, resumed their places on the outside of the vehicle, and it was driven hastily away.

As the vehicle proceeded speedily on its way, the Duke Monterino endeavoured to engage Marceline in conversation, but she refused to answer him; and at length, apparently tired of his efforts, he ceased his importunities, and the poor girl was left to the indulgence of her own thoughts. Terrible, indeed, were they, and need no description from our pen; but seeing all prospect of relief, at present, was at an end, she mentally breathed a prayer to Heaven for her mother and for Henri, and settled into a melancholy calm.

The country through which they were travelling was extremely picturesque and romantic, and illumed as it was with the first golden beams of the rising sun, glittering beneath that clear and azure sky, for which Italy is famed above all other nations, it might be deemed truly magnificent. Rich pastures spread their fertile beauties to a great extent on each side of the road they were pursuing, while in the distance a long chain of beautifully undulating hills marked their dark lines on the horizon. Marceline insensibly became abstracted for a short time from her own sorrows in the contemplation of nature's wondrous works, and she viewed everything around her with the feeling of an enthusiast. The first odoriferous breath of morn came sweet and refreshing to her senses; and as they proceeded, she felt gradually more composed, and placed a further reliance in the mercy and protection of Providence.

Sweetly and merrily did the birds carol forth their morning song, and all around was happiness. Alas! how different were the feelings of Marceline; but she stifled them all in her power, and looked forward with anxiety to the termination of their journey. Often she beheld a solitary peasant, whistling carelessly as he plodded on his way to his daily toil, and she was tempted several times to call to him and supplicate his assistance; but the uselessness of such a course was quickly made apparent to her, and the dark looks of the duke, who watched narrowly her every action, made her soon abandon it again in despair.

About noon she understood from an observation which was made by Monterino, that they were near the place of their destination; and shortly afterwards, looking from the window of the vehicle, she beheld upon the summit of a lofty hill a noble-looking casino, which she was quickly informed belonged to the duke. Under any other circumstances,

Marceline could not have helped being delighted with it, for nothing could be more enchanting or romantically beautiful than its situation; but now she gazed upon it with an emotion of terror: it was to be her prison—probably the scene of every misery which her most powerful apprehensions could imagine, and she wept tears of bitter anguish as they rapidly approached it. A road was cut out of the hill, which the vehicle slowly ascended; and, at length, it stopped before the grand entrance of the casino. The approach of the carriage had been noticed asceding the hill, and the large folding-doors were thrown open, and several servants, in handsome livery, were waiting to receive them. Monterino descended from the vehicle, and having assisted Marceline to alight, they entered the hall, and the doors were closed upon the liberty of the hapless maiden.

CHAPTER XV.

THE ATTEMPTED ESCAPE.—THE RECOGNITION.

HENRI continued very bad the whole of that night, the distracting thoughts that tormented his brain provoking his illness; but by the skilful treatment of the monk, and the attention which was paid him, by the morning he was so far recovered as to be able to leave his pallet. The situation he was placed in—the confession of the beauteous brigand girl, and the statement of Allesandrio Robelli, were so extraordinary and romantic, that he could scarcely credit their reality; but when he looked around him, the certainty of their truth was too evident. In spite of the nature of the situation he was placed in, and the danger he had good reason to apprehend from it, the beauty of Zitella, and the acknowledgment she had made to him of the passion with which he had inspired her, had made an indelible impression upon his mind. Had he never have beheld Marceline, no female could sooner have enchained his affections; and in spite of the life she was placed in, there was a certain refinement in her manners and language, and a simplicity and modesty of demeanour attached to her, which could not fail to rivet the attention and admiration of all who beheld her.

The words of Allesandrio, her father, also filled his mind with strange conjectures; he seemed to take an unusual interest in him, and had informed him that, apart from his compelling him to become a member of the band, he had a subject of the utmost importance to broach to him, when he was in a more fit state to converse upon it, and he racked his brain in vain to imagine what that subject could be. Marceline and his mother, however, quickly superseded all these reflections, and he was immersed in the most agonizing meditation, when one of the brigands entered, and informed him that the chief requested an audience of him, if he felt himself in a fit condition to comply with his request.

"I am ready to attend you," said Henri; and the man having bowed with all the obsequiousness of one of the most polite cutthroats, motioned to the former to follow him.

The brigand passed under a low arch-way, after having unlocked a door at one end of that section of the subterranean retreat in which Henri was confined, and they entered a low passage, which was very dark, but the brigand carried a lamp, by the faint light emitted from which, Henri was enabled to grope his way along, and to keep close to the heels of his conductor.

The passage was of considerable extent, and the foul air which frequently rushed along the place with pestiferous and almost overwhelming force, threatened several times to extinguish the light. At length they emerged from it, and entered a wide cavern, which was apparently used for a magazine, being piled around with barrels of powder, guns, swords, &c. A lamp was suspended from the roof, in which a light was constantly burning, and the place altogether had a singularly wild and strange appearance. From this cavern three openings branched off in different directions, but the brigand took the centre one, which was a paved passage, and loftier than the other they had traversed; and having got to the end of it, they stopped before a door. And now the attention of Henri was suddenly arrested by the sound of a female voice, singing in tones of such exquisite sweetness, that they were sufficient to enrapture the most insensible individual. The brigand noticed the pleasure with which Henri listened to the melodious notes, and he did not offer to interrupt him. The air was simply beautiful; and with very little difficulty, Henri was enabled to overhear the following words of the song:—

"Sparkling eyes! sparkling eyes!
    Tell the feelings of the heart;
The eye can speak, but words are weak,
    Youthful passion to impart;
Ruby lips! ruby lips!
    Ne'er so well can rapture move,
As entrancing—bliss enhancing,
    When they breathe the vows of love!
                Lira la! Lira la!

"Ruby lips! ruby lips!
    Panting with the maiden kiss;
Joy inviting, how delighting,
    Offering ev'ry earthly bliss.
Ruby lips! ruby lips!
    Stoic coldness e'er reprove;
Ev'ry pleasure, beyond measure,
    Love is Heaven, and Heaven is love!
                Lira la! Lira la!"

The voice ceased; but the entrancing sounds still seemed to vibrate in the ears of Henri, and he remained fixed to the spot for a minute or two, wrapt in astonishment and admiration.

"Who is it," he at length said, "breathing notes of such extatic melody?"

"It is the daughter of our chief, the fair Zitella," answered the brigand.

"Ah The same beauteous girl whom I beheld a few days since?" he inquired. "How exquisitely beautiful!"

"Ay," returned the man: "Zitella is the very soul of the band. She it is who, with her songs of love and notes of cheerfulness, lightens the hearts of our men, after the cares and dangers attendant on our course of life."

"What a pity it is that one so fair, so accomplished, should be placed in such a degrading situation," said Henri.

"Come, signor," returned the man; "our captain awaits your presence."

Piolo—so was the brigand called—gave three loud knocks with his fist on the door, and it was immediately opened; and Henri found himself in a handsomely fitted-up apartment, furnished and decorated with as much taste as one of the rooms in a nobleman's casino, and brilliantly lighted up by several lamps. As he entered, Henri just caught a glimpse of the graceful figure of Zitella, as she retreated by another door; and Allesandrio, having made a sign with his hand, the man who conducted him to the place retired, and left him alone with the brigand chief.

Allesandrio Robelli was seated at the head of a table in the centre of the apartment; and on the entrance of Henri he arose, greeted him graciously, and invited him, with the courtesy of the most polished gentleman, to be seated by his side. Henri obeyed. The brigand then inquired after his health; and having expressed his anxiety for his speedy and entire restoration to convalescence, a pause succeeded, during which Allesandrio appeared to be eyeing the youth with looks of the greatest admiration and interest.

"Henri le Sange," at length said the brigand, "I have already told you the rules of this band, and the consequences that must unavoidably follow your being brought amongst us; but, as I have apprized your friends of your safety, and I have no power to grant you your liberty, I trust you will learn to submit to it, and by taking the necessary oaths of allegiance and fidelity, become one of our bold band."

"Become a lawless brigand! Disgrace myself for ever, and break the hearts of all those so dear to me!" cried Henri, indignantly. "Never!"

"Stop, stop, young man," said Allesandrio, coolly: "not so hasty. You know the alternative, and must submit to one or the other."

"Sooner would I perish!" firmly returned Henri.

"I still feel inclined to think you will change your mind," observed the brigand chief, "and will, therefore, give you further time to reflect upon it. For the present, we will drop this subject: there is another upon which we must now have some conversation, and for which purpose I sent for you. I have a daughter—young, beautiful, and accomplished—born to fill a far different station and who can boast of a birth as noble as the proudest of Italy."

" I have seen her," returned Henri, the remembrance of the brigand girl imparting a feeling of pleasure and admiration to his bosom. " She is, indeed, lovely !"

" Ah !" exclaimed Allesandrio, eagerly, " you, then, admire her ?"

" That man must be very insensible to female beauty who could not," answered Henri, with that candour so characteristic of his nature. " I admire and pity her."

" Pity her ! Why so ?"

" Because she is made the associate of guilt, when she is every way formed to adorn the paths of virtue and rectitude."

" Hark you, young man," said the brigand—" whatever may be the situation in which fate hath placed my Zitella, she is as pure and uncontaminated as virtue's self; and those who would presume to question that assertion must answer for their scepticism dearly to Allesandrio Robelli. Henri le Sange, for months past that fair girl, on whom you have been pleased to express your admiration, hath been suffering all the pangs of first love—all the ceaseless cares attendant on what she deems a hopeless passion. Chance threw the object that hath inspired it in her way, and from that moment her heart was no longer in her possession. She made no secret of her love to me, and vainly did I endeavour to drive him from her thoughts, more especially as the object she loved knew her not, knew not the sentiments he had inspired, and was betrothed to another. Oh ! who shall attempt to control the ardent feelings of first—of youthful passion ? It rages with the fury of the devouring element, defying all efforts to quench it. Daily, hourly did the love of my Zitella for this one object increase : he constantly haunted her thoughts by day—was the vision of her slumbers by night. The roses on her cheeks began to fade, her eyes to lose their lustre, and her demeanour, which was once all gaiety, all hilarity, became thoughtful, pensive, and melancholy. Need I describe to you a fond father's feelings on seeing his only one, who was a portion of his own existence, rapidly pining away, and threatening to sink into a premature grave ? No, I could not. Each pang she felt was the most excruciating agony to me. I made a vow, a solemn vow, to get the object of my daughter's passion in my power, and to leave no means untried to win his love for her whose heart was all his own. In vain I watched the opportunity of putting my plans into execution, until accident brought about that event I so anxiously looked for. What more need I say, Henri le Sange ? Dost thou not guess who is that being to whom I have alluded ?"

" I do—I know it, Allesandrio Robelli," replied Henri, who had listened to the brigand's eloquent harangue with a feeling of the deepest interest. " Well do I know what thou meanest, since the fair girl hath

already confessed to me her hopeless passion."

" Hopeless !" ejaculated Allesandrio.— " Nay, say not so, Henri. Surely thou canst not resist so sweet, so beauteous a pleader ?"

" I love another."

" But she cannot love thee with the strength—the ardour of my poor child. Is she not beautiful ?"

" Most lovely."

" And virtuous ?"

" Or vice never was concealed beneath so fair a countenance."

" Ah, thou dost but do her justice," said the brigand chief. " Purity itself could not be more spotless than she is."

" But she is a brigand's daughter."

" And thou wilt become a brigand also, and——"

" I a brigand !" exclaimed Henri, energetically : " I herd with those who live by rapine and murder ? Never, by Heaven ! Sooner would I suffer the most dreadful death that cruelty could invent."

Allesandrio Robelli remained silent; and, folding his arms across his breast, stood gazing earnestly, and with looks of the greatest admiration, at Henri.

Suddenly the soft strains of plaintive music again vibrated on Henri's ears, and then a melodious voice, which immediately transfixed his soul in rapture, breathed its sweetness around.

" Hark !" ejaculated Allesandrio, marking with delight the looks of admiration that beamed in the countenance of the young man : " can anything be more exquisitely beautiful ?"

It was, indeed, beautiful; for it was Zitella, singing the song which had before so enchanted Henri ; and again he listened with the most indescribable delight to the second stanza :—

" Ruby lips ! ruby lips !
    Panting with the maiden's kiss ;
Joy inviting, how delighting,
    Off'ring every earthly bliss.
Ruby lips ! ruby lips !
    Stoic coldness e'er reprove ;
Ev'ry pleasure, without measure,
    Love is heaven, and heaven is love !
        'Lira la ! lira la !'"

No sooner was the song finished than the music changed to the most lively and exhilarating tones : a curtain at the back of the apartment, in which Henri and the brigand chief were, was withdrawn, and the young man beheld, as if it had been conjured up by a magician's wand, a magnificent saloon, brilliantly lighted up, and in which were sporting, in all the graceful and fantastic mazes of the dance, the beauteous Zitella and several other brigand girls, dressed in the same elegant and picturesque costume as their mistress, and vieing with each other in loveliness of countenance and perfection of symmetry and grace.

The eyes of Henri followed them through

their various entrancing movements with a feeling of the most exquisite transport; and the gorgeousness of the scene before him, possessing almost eastern splendour, charmed and bewildered his senses. But, beautiful as were her companions, their charms were trifling compared with those of Zitella; and, as the young man watched her graceful figure, and every now and then caught her sparkling eyes rivetted upon him with that intense expression of admiration which showed how powerfully he had taken possession of her heart, he could not help feeling for her a sentiment which no other female had excited in his bosom, save Marceline. Allesandrio watched him narrowly; and as he noticed the excitement which moved his features, and how plainly was expressed the admiration which his daughter had already inspired in his breast, his satisfaction was apparent.

Again the music changed to a slow and plaintive air, and Zitella and her lovely companions accompanied it with a variety of entrancing figures, twirling around Henri, and beaming upon him smiles that would have made a stoic's heart melt with love. Then, suddenly, it once more swelled into a lively movement, and the dance continued with an untiring vigour, until the senses of Henri began to reel, and he sank into a chair, overpowered with the variety and strength of his emotions. Immediately the music ceased, Allesandrio waved his hand, and all the dancers, with the exception of Zitella, tripped lightly out of the saloon, while the latter, rushing forward with the lightness of a sylph, knelt at the feet of Henri, looking up into his face with a glance of such an intense, such an indescribable and passionate description, that he felt as though he were enchanted. Some irresistible spell appeared to take possession of his senses; and, raising the enchanting maiden from the floor, he suffered her to sink, weeping and in transport, upon his bosom.

Allesandrio was a delighted spectator of this scene, and the brigand thought the conquest complete; but a moment dispelled the illusion, and recalled Henri to a knowledge of what he was doing, and the danger into which he was falling.

"'Tis done—'tis done!" exclaimed the former, suffering the bright phantom of hope to take too firm a hold of his mind. "Woman's beauty, virtue, and innocence, have triumphed! Henri le Sange loves the daughter of the brigand chief, Allesandrio Robelli!"

"Oh, heavenly assurance!—oh, blissful sounds!" ejaculated the silvery-toned voice of Zitella, as she still entwined her snow-white arms around the neck of Henri, and fixed upon him a look so chaste, yet so languishing, that even insensibility itself must have felt its influence: "and Henri will confirm it? Yes, yes—Zitella's heart tells her that he will: its responsive throbbings assure her that he loves her!"

The words of the beauteous girl aroused Henri to consciousness; and gently disengaging himself from her embraces, he exclaimed—

"Love!—love! Oh, no—no! Deceive not yourself, fair damsel. Henri le Sange can never love any other than Marceline di Venoni!"

"She shall never be yours!" cried Allesandrio, unable to control his feelings at the disappointment and chagrin which this occasioned to the hopes he had too hastily and too sanguinely formed. "She shall never be yours. I swear——"

"Oh, hold, hold, my father!" interrupted Zitella, with a look of supplication; then, turning her soul-entrancing eyes upon the countenance of Henri, with an emotion too powerful for utterance, she added, in accents the most impressive and melancholy—

"'Tis past—the spell is broken—the illusion is gone! The bright hopes that darted for a moment upon my mind like a flood of heavenly glory are dispelled, and Zitella is aroused to the full sense of despair. He for whom she would make any sacrifice—nay, even life itself—he, the first, the only one who has or ever can hold dominion over her heart's fondest affections, has declared he cannot love her, and her doom is sealed. Yet, Henri, must Zitella ever love you with a strength—a fervour no tongue can speak—no language give utterance to. No time—no change shall ever alter her sentiments towards you. Her heart may break; but, in life or in death, still must the image of Henri le Sange ever remain fixed in the inmost recesses of Zitella's soul. Nor will she hate the gentle Marceline because she loves you, too—because she is the syren that holds possession of your heart; but——"

"But you must not—shall not," interrupted Allesandrio, forgetting in the power of his emotions the prudence and coolness that usually marked his character. "Allesandrio Robelli, in whose veins flows the blood of princes, although now the despised and hunted of mankind, will not suffer his only child to be made a sacrifice to——"

"Father—father!" implored Zitella.

"Away, girl, away! Leave me for the present, sweetest; I—I—there, there, my own loved Zitella—retire, retire, and I will be more calm."

As the brigand-chief thus spoke, he drew his daughter to his bosom with the utmost parental affection, parted the glossy tresses from her marble forehead, and imprinted upon it a kiss of ardent love. The poor maiden returned his caresses with the same effervescence of feeling; then, fixing upon Henri a look which beamed a language too powerful for utterance, tears rushed to her eyes, across which she passed her tiny hand—her bosom heaved, she sobbed hysterically, and, turning hastily away, rushed from the place with the greatest precipitation.

Allesandrio Robelli stood gazing at the door by which his daughter had quitted the saloon for a short time in silence, and then turning to Henri, after a moment or two, during which time his mind evidently underwent a variety of emotions, he said, in tones more cool than he had before given utterance to—

"You would make a desert of that which is now lovely and blooming! You would lay waste, with the ruthless power of the blast, that which is now so fresh, so charming! Think you for this Allesandrio Robelli will seek no revenge? Think you that he will tamely submit to seeing the hopes of his child crushed—her happiness blighted—and demand not some reparation?"

"Allesandrio Robelli," returned Henri, firmly, yet desperately, "you arrogate to yourself the credit of being a man of sense and reason, and yet your observations would induce most persons to believe that you have very little claim to either. However, I shall not judge of you so harshly, and, therefore, I ask you whether you would have me bestow my hand upon your daughter when I cannot give her possession of my heart?"

"But you admire her?"

"I have before candidly told you I do," said Henri; "she is most lovely, and, I doubt not, virtuous; and—nay, I will admit that she has made a powerful impression upon me; and had she been aught but the daughter of a man who had spread terror all over the country, and had I never beheld Marceline di Venoni, no one could sooner have gained a place in my heart's warmest affections. But Marceline——"

"You will never see her more," cried the brigand; "unless you consent to become the husband of Zitella, beyond these caverns you shall never more depart."

"Hear me, Allesandrio," said Henri, with eagerness.

"Nay, I am in no mood to argue with you now," answered Robelli; "but be assured that my resolution is fixed. The happiness, the very life of my child rests in your hands, and unless you yield to my wishes, you need not to expect any mercy from me."

Henri was again going to speak, but Robelli waved his hand impatiently, and rung a small silver bell, which was placed on the table before him. The same man who had conducted Henri to the place then made his appearance, and, by the order of the chief, re-conducted him to the apartment or cavern in which he had been before confined, and immediately left him.

The strange tumult of thoughts that now crowded upon the mind of Henri, may readily be imagined by the reader; and he paced the cavern with hasty steps, frequently giving vent to his feelings in the most vehement and passionate exclamations. The impassioned fondness which the beauteous Zitella evinced towards him had excited a very great interest in his bosom, and he could not help thinking of her with a feeling more powerful even than admiration. The determination which Allesandrio had expressed, filled him with the most serious apprehension; for he had not the least doubt but that he would keep his word; and so secret was the retreat of the brigands that he had no chance of being rescued from their power. Here, then, he must remain for the future; his only chance of seeing his mother or Marceline again being by uniting himself to the daughter of the brigand-chief. Good God! he thought, and what must be the sufferings of Marceline and his mother, in this dreadful time of suspense and anxiety! Perhaps grief had already done its work of destruction, and they were no more! The idea was too horrible to dwell upon, and Henri endeavoured to banish it, but in vain. It still pursued him, with increasing violence; and for two hours he continued to traverse the limited confines of the cavern, and to give free indulgence to the expression of his agony.

At length, as near as he could judge, it was evening, and he had just become more calm, and was beginning to indulge in a hope that something would occur to rescue him from his present situation, when he heard the key turning in the lock, and, starting to his feet, by the feeble rays of the lamp, which scarcely permitted him to penetrate into the deep obscurity, he beheld a form advancing towards him, which, on approaching nearer, he discovered to be Zitella. A deep melancholy shaded her lovely countenance, but her eyes beamed upon him the same warm glances of unutterable affection which they had ever done, and penetrated to his heart in an instant.

She advanced towards Henri with a slow and cautious step, and when within a few paces from him, she paused, as if fearful of approaching nearer. Henri acted upon a sudden impulse, and hastening to her, he gently took her hand, and involuntarily raised it to his lips with an air of the utmost respect. Zitella started at the unexpected action, and, raising her eyes towards him with a glance of the most inexpressible delight, a tide of rapture ran through her soul which she had never before experienced; but it was only transient—a moment, and it subsided, and gave place to a feeling of the deepest melancholy; and, in accents of resigned sadness, she said—

"Henri, you have said that you cannot love the brigand girl! You have declared that the more fortunate Marceline di Venoni must ever hold possession of your heart. I will show you the strength of Zitella's love for you. I come to give you liberty!"

"Liberty!"

"Ay, Henri le Sange," said Zitella; "the brigand-girl, to whom your presence is as the light of Heaven,—who feels to live only in your sight—is ready to make any self-sacrifice to save you a moment's unhappiness!

all—all—will she cheerfully brave to restore you to peace—to love—to freedom !"

"' Sweet, gentle,—noble-hearted girl," cried Henri, again pressing Zitella's fair hand to his lips ; " and shall I then suffer you to run such fearful risks for my sake, without the power of making you any return ?"

" You have the power, Henri," said Zitella, energetically, and a tear glistened in her eye ; " nay, do not mistake me ! you have told me that Marceline must be the sole mistress of your heart, and—no matter—all the return I ask is, that sometimes in your prayers you will not forget the poor brigand girl—that you will not hate or despise her who—"

Her voice faltered, and she could not proceed, and Henri, who was deeply affected, knew not scarcely how to answer for a few seconds ; at length, in a voice of the deepest feeling, he exclaimed—

" Kind maiden, Henri will never forget you !—in his prayers you shall constantly be remembered, and next to Marceline, he will love you above all others of your sex !"

The eyes of Zitella brightened in a moment, and dashing away the crystal drops that had gathered upon her cheeks, she said in tones of ecstacy—

ZITELLA VISITS HENRI TO GIVE HIM LIBERTY.

" Delightful words, that come like music from the heavenly choir upon my ravished senses ! Henri, one soft embrace, the last that we may probably have, and then to the task I have imposed upon myself, while my father and the rest of the brigands are absent from the caverns."

Henri enfolded the fair girl in his arms, and pressed a fervent kiss upon her lips ; he felt her tears bedew her cheeks ; and the most powerful emotion throbbed her bosom. It lasted, however, but a short time ; she quickly conquered her feelings, and withdrawing herself from his embrace, she passed her hand across her brow two or three times, as if she were endeavouring to collect her thoughts, and then, in silence, motioned Henri to follow her.

Henri quickly obeyed, and passing from the cavern, they traversed their way along several subterranean passages of great length, until they arrived at an outer cavern, and crossing it, Zitella was proceeding to ascend a flight of steps, when a hasty footstep was heard behind them, and a loud voice at the same moment exclaimed—

" Ah ! what do I hear ? There is treachery afloat !"

Henri and Zitella turned round in consternation at the words, and the light emitted by the rays of the lamp fell full upon the person and countenance of a brigand ; the eyes of the man and those of Henri met in an instant, and an exclamation of the most indescribable astonishment followed ; in the features of the brigand, Henri recognised those of his father—Adolphe de Floriville !

CHAPTER XVI.

THE CASINO.—THE CASTLE OF ALTERBURG CONCLUDED.

THE Duke Monterino led Marceline to a most elegant apartment, and everything which she beheld would, under different circumstances, have excited her warmest admiration, for whichever way she turned her eyes, they encountered something which displayed magnificence and taste. But now she looked at all with indifference, and a feeling of anguish, as a scene got up to dazzle her senses, and to lure her to ruin ; and when the doors of the casino were closed upon her, and she found herself left entirely to the mercy of the hated Monterino, her heart sunk with despair, and her tears, which she had restrained for some time, now burst forth uncontrolled.

The duke led her to a seat, and taking one by her side, he looked in her face with an assumption of the utmost tenderness, and gently taking her hand, said—

"Why do you weep, lovely Marceline, when you have it in your power to enjoy every bliss that this world can bestow ? Dry those tears that fill my soul with anguish—lend a willing ear to my vows—consent to become my bride, the bride of the lord of the noble house of Monterino, and your mother and friends shall be immediately restored to your arms."

"Never !—never !" cried Marceline, with a look of disgust, which she found it impossible to conceal ; "I will trust to the protection of Heaven, who will frustrate your wicked designs, Monterino ; but sooner would I encounter any fate than that of becoming the wife of a man whose conduct proves him to be alike destitute of feeling or honour."

"For the present, Marceline," said the duke, with difficulty stifling his wrath ; "for the present I can bear with your reproaches, making, as I do, every allowance for your excited feelings. But ere long, I am confident, you will be convinced how greatly you have wronged me by the opinions you have expressed. Again I tell you, Marceline, that it is love, unconquerable love, which has alone prompted me to this step, and had you not treated my addresses in the first instance with scorn and insult, I never should have had occasion to have acted as I have done. But do I not now offer you fairly ?—do I not offer to lay a coronet at your feet, and to make you the wife of one to whom the most noble and wealthy damsels of Italy have not presumed to aspire ?"

Marceline covered her face with her hand-

kerchief whilst the duke was speaking, and to whom she scarcely paid any attention, and sighed forth the name of Henri.

"Ah !" cried Monterino, starting from his seat as though an adder had stung him, and scowling dreadfully ; "that detested name ! Still, then, are your thoughts fixed upon that boy who dared to rival me in your affections ! But no matter—he is past the power to——"

"Monterino !" interrupted Marceline, in a state of the utmost agony, "if you have one spark of pity in your breast for her whom you pretend to love, oh, tell me—for you, I am convinced, are the author of all the harm that hath befallen him,—tell me, doth Henri le Sange still live ?"

The duke bit his lips, and frowned dreadfully ; then a savage smile of exultation passed over his features as he exclaimed—

"You will see him no more !"

"Monster ! monster !" groaned Marceline, her bosom heaving violently, with the power of her emotions, "you have murdered him !"

Convulsive sobs choked her utterance, and Monterino, who was unable for the moment to return her any answer, and who felt afraid to approach her, awed as he was by the vehemence of her grief, traversed the apartment, and seemed to be at a loss in what manner to act, and to regret that he had not returned Marceline some more evasive answer to her interrogatory. But in a short time Marceline again looked up, and dashing the tears away from her cheeks, she said, with an air of confidence—

"But no—I will not give way to despair !—my Henri still lives ! Providence would not suffer him to perish by hands like yours. He lives—he lives ! and will yet be restored to the arms of his much-wronged Marceline."

"Never !" cried Monterino, fiercely ; "Henri le Sange restored to Marceline di Venoni—permitted once more to breathe his vows in her ears, and to receive her tender asseverations in return ? Never ! Sooner would I stretch you a corpse at my feet than such an occurrence should take place."

Marceline raised her hands and eyes towards Heaven in horror and despair, and a deep groan escaped her heart. The tone in which Monterino spoke, and the fury of his looks, as he gave expression to the last determination, were sufficient to excite fear in a much more stronger nerved person than Marceline ; and averting her face from him in disgust, she remained silent. The duke looked at her for a moment or two, and then hastily quitted the apartment.

Relieved by his departure, and hoping that he would not again annoy her for some time by his presence, Marceline dried up her tears, and endeavoured to calm her anguish ; she walked towards the casement, and looked forth upon the prospect which it commanded. Lovely, indeed, it was, glittering in the full meridian beams of the sun. The foot of the lofty hill, on which the casino stood, was washed by a clear, pellucid stream, which flowed almost as far as the eye could stretch in a serpentine direction. Over its silvery surface several boats glided, whilst here and there a fisherman's smack caught her eye. To the right and left the scenery was most diversified and beautiful ; and here and there, from amidst the foliage, peeped forth the lofty turrets of a castle, or the humble dwellings that formed a straggling village. Oh, how Marceline envied the lot of the inhabitants of those lowly habitations !

She was aroused from the contemplation of the objects that had interested her, and the thoughts by which her mind was becoming engrossed, by hearing a gentle voice from behind her call—

"Signora ! Signora !"

She turned, and was agreeably surprised on beholding that the speaker was an extremely pretty and interesting looking female, about her own age, who curtseyed very politely to her, and then said—

"Signora, if you please, I am deputed by the duke to conduct you to those apartments which he has appropriated to your future use, and also to inform you that he will not be able to visit you again to-day as he has some appointment of importance. Will you please to attend me, signora ?"

"And who are you, my good girl ?" inquired Marceline.

"I am Marie, ma'amselle," replied the girl, speaking with a strong French accent, "and appointed your *soubrette* while you remain at the casino, if you please."

"Ah, you are French !" exclaimed Marceline, with a smile of pleasure.

"Yes, ma'amselle," replied Marie, "I am, indeed, French. Dear France !"

"Sorry am I to see a young girl like you the servant of the Duke Monterino," said Marceline, looking upon Marie with the deepest interest.

"Ah, ma'amselle, or signora—you will pardon my forgetfulness," returned Marie, "I have been brought up in the family of the duke, and my father and mother are now living in his service ; to others he may be a bad man, but to us he has been most kind. When my poor father was afflicted with blindness, and was unable to provide for myself or my mother, the duke, who was then residing in France, generously took us under his care, and we have remained in his establishment ever since."

"It pleases me to hear of one generous action performed by Monterino," observed Marceline ; "but, alas! Marie, I fear that the case of you and your parents is but a solitary one. Too great reasons have I to believe him cruel, wicked, and unprincipled."

"Well, signora," said Marie, speaking in a low tone of voice, "to be sure I have heard that the duke is very wild and dissipated, but then, you know, I have no business to speak of him in any other way than I have found him, and—But will you be pleased to attend me, ma'amselle ?"

Marceline bowed her head assentively, and Marie led the way from the apartment ; she conducted her up several flights of stairs, and at last entered a very handsome suite of rooms, furnished in the most costly style, and exhibiting everything that luxury or comfort could require.

"These are the apartments allotted to your use, signora," said Marie ; "are they not elegant ? Oh, you will not find another casino in all Italy that can surpass this for taste and beauty. I have the duke's orders that you shall be allowed to walk with me also, occasionally, on the terrace at the top of the building, which is a delightful place, and where any person might sit and enjoy themselves for hours in gazing upon the beautiful scenery for miles around."

Marceline sighed mournfully, and took a seat.

"Alas! Marie," she exclaimed, "that which under any other circumstances would fill my soul with rapture, hath now no charms for me. Am I not a prisoner ? Torn from my home, my friends, and placed in the power of a man whom I cannot look upon without a feeling of the utmost repugnance ?"

"But, signora," said Marie, "surely if the duke offers you marriage, which I have been given to understand he has done, you——"

"Marie," interrupted Marceline, "would you bestow your hand upon a man whom you could only view with sentiments of the utmost abhorrence ?"

"Why, to be sure, signora," answered Marie, "I can't exactly say that I should like to do that ; but, then, to become a duchess !"

"Oh, what is rank—what is title—when not accompanied by happiness ?" cried Marceline.

"Why, to be sure, that is very true, signora, I dare say," returned Marie ; "but I have never been put to the test yet, and, therefore, I cannot tell how I might be inclined to act under the circumstances. But, if you please, signora, I will get you some refreshment, for I am sure you must be hungry after your journey."

Marceline, notwithstanding her mind was so distressed, did feel inclined for eating, and she, therefore, raised no objection to Marie's proposition, who immediately left her for the purpose of doing as she had said.

Marceline was not long left alone to her reflections, for Marie quickly returned with the provisions, which she placed before the former, who partook of them more heartily than she had herself thought she would have done. When she had done, and Marie had taken the things away, she invited the good-tempered girl to take a seat by her side, and then briefly detailed to her the particulars of the duke's conduct towards her, and the villanous means he had adopted to get her in his power. Marie listened to her with the deepest interest, and when she had concluded, she expressed in warm terms her disapprobation of the behaviour of her master, and her regret at the situation in which Marceline was placed, assuring her, at the same time, that she would do all that was in her humble power to alleviate her sorrows, and to render her situation less painful to her. This assurance Marceline kindly acknowledged, and a latent hope crossed her mind that Marie and her parents might be prevailed upon, at some future period, to aid in her escape.

"Dear me!" said Marie, "it certainly was very cruel of the duke to force you away from home, signora, in such a clandestine manner. How truly wretched and anxious your mother and friends must be to know what has become of you."

"Alas! they must, indeed!" said Marceline; "and it is that thought which distracts me more than all. Think you, Marie, that I could ever love a man, or look upon him with the common feelings of esteem even, who could behave towards me in this manner?"

"Why, no, signora," answered Marie, "I should not think you could. But then, you great folks have such different ways of courting to what we in humble life have, that it is difficult for me to form any decided opinion upon the subject. It is the fashion, I have heard, signora, without meaning offence to you, for some ladies never to yield their consent to be married to the gentleman with whom they are, at the same time, stark starting mad in love, until he runs away with them."

Marceline could scarcely repress a smile at this idea of Marie's.

"But then," signora,' resumed Marie, "the worst part of your story is that about the disappearance of the young gentleman whom you say you love. But do you really think that the duke knows anything about that?"

"He has acknowledged to being the base author of it," answered Marceline, "and has even hinted that he has sacrificed the life of Henri to his resentment and jealousy."

"Oh, dear me! how shocking!" ejaculated Marie. "I could not have believed that the duke was half such a bad man; and in spite of his kindness to me and my parents, I shall never be able to look upon him with half the respect which I have hitherto done. But still I cannot believe that he can be so inhuman as to shed innocent blood; and depend upon it, signora, you will find that your lover still lives, and I hope, after what you have told me, that it will not be long ere you will be restored to one another!"

"Thanks! thanks! my good girl, for your kind wishes," said Marceline, looking with an eye of pleasure upon Marie, "and Heaven grant that they may be realised, and the wicked designs of the Duke Monterino frustrated. But surely, Marie, you would not like to see one of your own sex fall a victim to the cruelty of a villain?"

"Alas! signora! in what way could I assist you to avoid such a fate?" interrogated Marie.

"By aiding me to escape from hence," eagerly replied Marceline.

"Oh, Signora, you ask me that which is far beyond my power to perform," said Marie, "and even if I had the means, and were to do it, what would become of myself and my parents? I should bring down upon us the vengeance of the duke, and ruin would follow."

"Oh, no," observed Marceline, "that should not be; from my friends you shall find not only protection, but every attention that gratitude could dictate."

"Oh, signora," returned Marie, "I tremble at what you have suggested: indeed, much as I pity you, and that I really do from my heart, I cannot assist you in that manner; or most happy should I feel in doing so."

"I am obliged to you for your sympathy, Marie," said Marceline, "and will not for the present urge you farther. Notwithstanding what you have said, however, I yet trust that you will find the means to aid me in restoring myself to liberty, and to the arms of my friends."

Marie shook her head; and a silence of some seconds ensued.

"And have you any idea what time the duke will return, Marie?" at length inquired Marceline.

"I have not, signora," replied the girl, "but it is not at all unlikely that he may be absent from the casino all the night; particularly if he falls into the company of some of his profligate companions."

Marceline expressed her pleasure at this.

"And are you to sleep in the same chamber with me, Marie?" she asked, anxiously.

"Yes, signora, if you please," replied Marie, "the duke ordered me to do so."

"For that I thank him!" exclaimed Marceline, whose mind was relieved of a great weight of apprehension by that assurance.

"And now, signora," observed Marie, rising, "you will please to excuse me for a short time, as I have something particular to do for my parents; but I will return to you again as soon as possible. You will find some books in the adjoining room, with which you can, most likely, amuse yourself until my return, which will be in a couple of hours at the longest."

With these words, Marie tripped lightly out of the apartment, and left Marceline to herself.

After Marie had quitted the room, Marceline sat for a few minutes buried in profound meditation on her situation; but at length recollecting what the girl had said to her about the books, and in order that she might abstract her thoughts from the melancholy subject which occupied them, she took forth the volume old Jacquelina had given her, and read the following conclusion of the tale which had before so deeply interested her:—

The baroness could scarcely conceal her satisfaction as she secured the casket, and Florian, turning to his brother, said, in a pettish tone—

"How silly it was of you, Julio; see what

you have done. I am sorry that you should
have stooped for it, madam."

And as the boy spoke, he extended his
hand to receive the casket, but it was not
the intention of the baroness to give it up.

"That hand so prettily held forth must
not be drawn back empty; here, here is
money for you both," she said, with a gra
cious smile, and at the same time placing a
purse in Florian's hand. "Geraldo will accompany you to-morrow to the adjacent
town, where you will buy whatever trinkets
you may fancy."

"A purse of money!" said the delighted
Julio, "oh, my good madam."

"Thank you, good madam," observed
Florian, "but the box is—"

At that moment, Geraldo, to draw the attention of the boys from the casket, crossed
over to them, and said—

"Should you not like to see the castle gardens? They are so beautiful."

"Are they?" ejaculated Julio. "Oh, I
should like it of all things."

"But the box, you know, Julio," said
Florian, who felt very uneasy at the treasure
which he so much prized being detained for
a moment from him. "We must have the
box, you know."

"Pooh!" returned Julio; "do you think
such a grand lady as that wants to cheat us?
We shall be back directly."

"Why, to be sure we shall," said his
brother, more satisfied; "and so, kind sir, if
you please, we are ready to attend you."

"You can go by yourselves, my lads,"
said Geraldo, pointing towards the right;
"that is your way—you cannot miss it."

"Oh, thank you, sir," said Julio. "Come
along, Florian; for I do long to see the gardens, which, no doubt, are very grand."

Thus speaking, Julio took the hand of his
brother, and they both hurried away towards
the gardens. Geraldo and the baroness
looked after them until they were out of
sight, when the former turned eagerly
towards the baroness, little suspecting that
they were watched, or that any one had
been a spectator of this scene; but there
was one who had observed everything with
the deepest interest, and that was old Gaspard, the supposed deaf porter; and he now
concealed himself in a place nearer to where
Geraldo and the baroness were standing, and
where they might not observe him, and appeared to listen attentively to all that passed
between the guilty pair.

"The casket," said Geraldo, "quiets or
confirms our present fears."

"The superscription says, 'Never open
this box till Florian has attained his
eighteenth year.'"

"Let me inspect it, madam," said Geraldo, eagerly.

"What can this mean?" said Gaspard to
himself; and he stretched his head forward,
as if to catch the lowest murmur.

"May we not be observed?" said the

baroness, looking fearfully around the court
yard.

"No, madam," replied her myrmidon.
"I have permitted the domestics to attend
the festival: no soul remains within the
castle but your own guard, who are all
upon the posts, excepting Gaspard, and he
is deaf and superannuated."

The baroness gave the casket into his
hands, and he untwisted the binding, and
broke the seal.

"Be expeditious, then," ejaculated the
baroness, "lest we should be surprised."

Geraldo took two portraits from the box;
but he no sooner gazed upon them than his
countenance underwent a great change.

"Confusion!" he exclaimed. "The portraits of the Count Altenburg and Imogene,
his wife! These brats, then, must be theirs!"

Gaspard evinced the greatest emotion at
this moment; and clasping his hands, he
raised his eyes towards Heaven, and gave
utterance to an exclamation of surprise and
agitation. Geraldo and the baroness were
startled by the sound; and turning round,
they observed Gaspard, who stifled his feelings as well as he could, and pretended to be
walking backwards and forwards across the
yard, without taking any notice or under-
standing what was passing between the
baroness and the villain Geraldo.

Geraldo waved his hand menacingly
towards him, and then, in a fierce and commanding tone, said—

"Fellow, begone!"

Gaspard immediately retired, but concealed himself within hearing, and listened
attentively to the conversation that was
passing between the baroness and her creature. It was very evident that his deaf-
ness was assumed, for the lowest murmur
seemed to catch his ear, and his countenance betrayed the anguish of his mind as
they proceeded.

"May not that man be dangerous?" said
the baroness, after Geraldo had ordered
Gaspard to be gone: "he is continually
pressing upon our footsteps."

"Oh," replied Geraldo, who was busy in
searching the casket, "it is merely the old
fool's zeal. Ah, here is a letter."

Gaspard now again ventured forward,
and listened attentively.

"The letter was written, as the date in-
structs, twelve years ago, and signed Bap-
tiste. Our suspicions were too true. That
grey adherent to the count did save the victims, and secretly conveyed them from us,
when we hoped that they had perished."

"Read—read," said the baroness, impatiently, and in a state of the greatest agitation. Geraldo obeyed, and read as follows:

"DEREST SISTER,—I write this letter on
my death-bed, by a proved friend, who will
recount to you a story of wretchedness and
horror. I send to you, my dear lord, the
Count of Altenburg's two sons, whom their
intentional murderers think are dead, and
whom, thank Heaven, I have saved. Ro-

delph and Sigismund are their names; but, for caution's sake, let them be called Julio and Florian. Disclose not to them their high parentage till riper years have given them prudence and caution to assert their birth-rights."

"That they shall never do!" exclaimed the baroness, in a terrified tone.

"Madam," said Geraldo, "dismiss your fears. I have not yet finished the letter."

Geraldo read the remainder of the epistle, which briefly concluded in the following words :—

"Poor as you are, shelter them as your own, and should you, my sister, die while they are boys, then may the Almighty Providence watch over them!"

"They shall not escape," cried Geraldo. "Now, their certain death must be our only sure pledge of safety."

"Death!" repeated the baroness, turning very pale. "Is there no other way? Oh, my heart sickens at means which we have tried too much already."

"Madam — madam!" returned Geraldo, hastily, "would you abide always in fear? The breath of these two boys is like the glave of justice hanging above our heads, suspended by a hair. While they exist, you yourself, each moment, are in danger of dying—dying infamously."

"They are so interesting! Could you use violence?" demanded the baroness.

"You shall not, while this arm hath power for their defence," muttered Gaspard to himself.

"Beware!" continued the baroness, after a brief pause. "They are now the adopted of the village, and their sudden disappearance would create suspicions that——"

"Hush all those alarms," interrupted Geraldo. "No suddenness—no violence, noble lady—a subtle and slow poison—I have it in my apartment."

"Horrible villain!" ejaculated the old porter.

"See, the boys approach this way, madam," added Geraldo.

"I scarce dare look upon them," faltered out the baroness.

At that moment, Julio and his brother made their re-appearance, and were evidently highly gratified by what they had seen.

"Well," exclaimed Julio, "of all the fine gardens that ever I saw, that is the finest: there's fountains, statues, and grottos. What's that stout marble man, with a broad sword in his hand, sir, at the end of the great walk?"

"That's a gladiator," answered Geraldo; "but after your ramble, I suppose, you will be glad of some refreshment?"

"Yes, if you please, sir," said Julio.

"But you know, brother," observed Florian, "that we promised Mr. Ricardo we should be back soon, and we must keep our word."

"Yes, yes," said Geraldo, "a slight

repast first; and shouldn't you like it in that pretty arbour? Here, Gaspard!"

The old porter came forward, and Geraldo motioned him to bring refreshments into the arbour. Gaspard hastened to obey him, but there was an expression in his countenance, as he turned away, which plainly showed that he had determined to thwart the monstrous designs of the villain, even at the hazard of his own life. The two boys walked into the arbour, and took their seats at the table.

"This is a nice place, Florian, isn't it?" said Julio; "I like it mightily."

"Yes, and so do I," answered Florian; "and, to say the truth, I am very hungry."

"Most opportunely," said Geraldo to himself, as he turned to go away.

"Stay, Geraldo," said the baroness, catching hold of his arm; "whither are you going?"

"Only to bring them something, madam, as a slight addition to their meal."

"Oh, spare them!" supplicated the baroness, in a low and fearful voice.

"Nay, it must be so!" he said; and disengaging himself, he hurried away.

The extraordinary emotion betrayed by the baroness caught the observation of Julio, and speaking to his brother, he said—

"Only see, Florian, how she looks." He then added, addressing himself to the baroness, "are you not well, madam?"

"Yes, yes, boys," replied the baroness, trying to collect herself.

"I am very glad of that, madam," said Julio; "to be sure, you can have nothing to make you uneasy, because you are so rich."

"Do riches always ease the mind?" said the baroness.

"Yes," answered Julio; "rich folks must always be happy, for they can make everybody else so."

"And if we were rich, madam," said Florian, "we would try to be as good as you, and do no harm to anybody."

The baroness averted her face to conceal the power of her emotions, and whispered to herself—

"Their artless observations torture me."

"Oh, here comes Mr. Gaspard," exclaimed Florian, evidently impatient for the refreshments.

"Then you and I, brother," said Julio, "must assist him."

The deaf porter now entered with a small tray of refreshments, and a basket with two partitions, in one of which was a bottle of wine. This they placed on the ground, and Gaspard having looked at them anxiously for a moment or two, retired to the back.

Julio and his brother now quickly arranged the table for their meal, and seating themselves, proceeded to eat without any farther ceremony; but the moment they had begun, Geraldo returned, bringing with him the fatal means of death—the bottle which contained the poison.

"This," he said, whispering aside to the

baroness—"this will lull our fears to rest, ane render their sleep eternal."

"What, Mr. Geraldo," said Julio, "have you brought us more wine? Only see, here's a whole bottle already."

"I knew not that," said the wretch, with well-affected surprise; "but this is very choice; come, then, there's fellowship in exchange; you, my young friends, shall drink of mine, and I of yours."

"Monster!" cried Gaspard, aside, and he watched Geraldo narrowly.

"Thank you, sir," said Julio, in answer to the proposition of Geraldo. "It shall be just as you please."

Geraldo placed the fatal bottle he had brought with him in the empty partition next the boys, and Gaspard never removed his eyes from him.

"So," said Geraldo to himself, "that nearest them is their portion. Now, then, boys," he added, aloud, "eat away, and when you are thirsty, we will drink a health to the worthy baroness."

"We must eat a little more before we drink, sir," said Julio.

During this time, Gaspard never removed his eyes from the actions of Geraldo; but his distress was much aggravated by the villain remaining near the basket.

"I cannot bear to look upon them," said the baroness, averting her face; "no—it must not—it shall not be!"

Geraldo noticed the conduct of the baroness, who was about to make her way to the table at which the two boys were seated, when Geraldo rushed up to her, and taking her hand, said to her apart—

"Stay, stay! I entreat you, madam."

While Geraldo crossed over to the baroness, Gaspard seized the opportunity for which he had been so anxiously watching, and approaching the basket, turned it.

"Madam," continued Geraldo, aside to the baroness, "we are partners in our fears, we must be partners, too, in the action that removes them."

"I cannot—my heart revolts!" she said, breaking from him; "let me go hence!" And as she thus spoke, the guilty woman rushed away in a state of agitation which needs no description.

"What, is the baroness gone, Mr. Geraldo?" said Julio, looking up.

"She will soon return," answered Geraldo: "in the meantime we will drink her health."

"If you please, sir," said Florian, timidly.

"Ay, with all my heart," said Julio. "I should like to drink something nice, now."

"Come, then, we are to exchange, you know; the one nearest the arbour is your bottle, and this is mine," observed Geraldo, and he filled their glasses and his own too.

"What bumpers!" exclaimed Florian; "dear sir, we shall be fuddled."

"Never mind that, brother," returned Julio, with a smile; "it's good stuff, I'll be bound."

"Yes, yes," said Geraldo; "in my opinion, it's all that can be wished for. Health and happiness to the baroness!"

Geraldo and the two boys raised their glasses to their lips, and instantly quaffed off the contents, and Gaspard, who had been watching the success of his scheme with the most painful anxiety, raised his hands and eyes towards Heaven, and mentally ejaculated—

"Merciless Providence! thus may each remorseless villain meet his doom!"

"That draught secures us," said the wretch, Geraldo, aside, "and ensures their fate."

"There, we have had quite enough," said Julio, rising.

"And now, if you please, sir," added Florian, "we will go back to keep our promise with Mr. Ricardo."

"Oh, there is no hurry, none in the least," said Geraldo.

"No hurry!" repeated Julio, with astonishment. "Why, you told him you would bring us back almost directly."

"Oh," said Geraldo, carelessly, "I might have said so; but the baroness has changed her mind; 'tis her order that you pass the night in her castle."

"Phoh! phoh!" ejaculated Julio, "the baroness has been very kind to us, to be sure; but then a promise is a pomise, all the world over, and go we must and will; so now that's flat. Come, brother."

"Stir not, at your peril," exclaimed Geraldo.

"Peril!" repeated Julio, pertly; "hoity, toity! and who are you, pray? If your mistress was here, she wouldn't use us so, Mr. Bantam."

"No, good lady, that she wouldn't," observed Florian, "but don't be so furious, Julio; you frighten me so."

"You are always frightened," returned Julio; "I tell you, we will go; we have a right, and pray who's to hinder us? We shall walk by ourselves, for we don't want your company, Mr. Bantam. Come along, Florian."

"How, urchins," cried Geraldo, stopping them; "are you mutinous? This," he added, aside, "will give a colour to the peasants for their detenticn, and 'twere best they languished here. You would go, then?" he said to Julio.

"Would!" repeated the high-spirited lad; "we will, and by ourselves, too."

"Whither you go now, you must be accompanied," said Geraldo. "What, ho! the castle-guard!"

"Oh, dear Julio," said Florian; "I am frightned out of my wits!"

"I don't care that for him," said Julio, snapping his fingers; "I will acquaint the baroness."

He had no sooner spoken these words than the castle guard entered, and Geraldo ordered them to seize the lads, and place them separately in close confinement; one in the square tower, and the other in the dungeon beneath the terrace. In vain Florian implored, and

Julio struggled; they were both seized, and Geraldo sternly motioned Gaspard to open the doors of their prison, into which they were thrust. Geraldo then commanded all the castle guard, but one, to retire.

"Remain you here," he said aloud, and addressing himself to the guard, "conceal yourself from their sight, but should they converse, and utter ought you think should be communicated, bring me word forthwith; be vigilant."

He retired as he spoke, and the guard concealed himself as he had been commanded. A minute afterwards, Julio appeared at the dungeon window, and Florian at the gate of his dungeon.

"Florian, brother Florian," cried Julio, "don't you hear me?"

"Yes, Julio," replied Florian, "but I do not see you; oh, we shall never see each other again."

"Isn't that Geraldo a great rascal?" said Julio.

"A sad, wicked man, indeed," replied Florian. "Old Gaspard, that we thought a savage, wouldn't have used us so."

"That he wouldn't, I'm sure," coincided Julio; "it was only out of kindness that he frightened us away before from this devil of a castle."

"Did you see how sorry he was when we were locked up?" asked his brother.

"He'd have prevented it if he could," replied Julio, "and I hope he will yet be able to get us out."

"So, then," said the guard, "Gaspard is their friend; I must immediately make Geraldo acquainted with this."

Thus speaking, he retired, and had not done so a second, when Gaspard, who had evidently been watching him, came cautiously from behind the arbour, and crossed over to the dungeon of Julio.

Florian heard him approach, and thinking it was the guard, he retired from the gate. Gaspard looked cautiously round him for a moment, to ascertain whether or not he was watched, and then going to the gate he unlocked it with a key which, with several others, was suspended from his girdle, and brought forth the astonished lad from his dungeon. Florian was about to express his unbounded thanks to Gaspard, when the latter put his finger on his lips, and by a significant look, enjoined him to silence. He then led him to the other dungeon door, which he also opened, and the two brothers rushed into each other's arms, and embraced fervently.

"Dear, dear Gaspard!" exclaimed Julio.

"Dear, good old man!" responded Florian.

Gaspard made no immediate answer, but standing behind them, he threw his arms over their necks as they embraced, and his very gesture evinced the powerful emotion that agitated his bosom. At length he withdrew himself from them, and looking fearfully around, exclaimed in an agitated tone—

"Quick! fly! you have not a moment to lose!"

The two brothers looked at him with the greatest astonishment.

"Why," said Julio, "he hears as clearly now as——"

"Hush!" interrupted Gaspard, in a hurried manner, "all will soon be explained; take these pistols, they are charged, and here, here is the key."

"Of what?" inquired Julio.

"Of the castle gate yonder," replied Gaspard; "you know the way already."

Gaspard endeavoured to detach the key from his girdle, but his efforts were in vain, and while he was thus engaged, footsteps were heard approaching.

"Confusion!" said Gaspard, "some one comes this way—we are lost!—quick! quick! conceal yourselves again in your dungeons."

"But the key?" said Julio, in alarm.

"I will return and give it you," answered Gaspard; "see—they come. Do not delay, or I shall not have the power to serve you."

Julio and his brother hastily did as Gaspard told them, and they had but just returned to their dungeons, when Geraldo and the guard entered. The former looked very hard in the countenance of Gaspard, and then demanded of him—

"Why do you loiter here? Give me your keys." Gaspard obeyed, and Geraldo examined them narrowly.

"So they are all here!" he muttered to himself. "Guard, henceforward let the care of these be yours. Away from the spot," he added sternly, and addressing himself to Gaspard; "to-morrow you shall hear from me. Send hither a sentinel, and be speedy in obedience."

Gaspard and the guard both departed, according to the mandate of Geraldo, who, when they had gone, stood for a second or two in deep rumination, and then said—

"Spite of this man's story, I scarcely think that Gaspard can feel interested for these boys. However, suspicion is excited, and it is proper that he should be taken care of."

The sentinel having made his appearance, Geraldo gave him instructions to the effect that, if the prisoners should attempt to escape, he was to give the alarm by firing his carbine. And further told him to look out from time to time, upon the rampart wall, and to be sure to keep a strict eye upon the breach.

Julio and his brother listened to every word that passed with the most breathless attention, and in a state of the utmost agitation.

"There is a breach, then," said Julio, exultingly; "and by that means we may be able to escape without much difficulty."

"Hush, brother, for the sake of Heaven!" cried Florian; "what's to be done?"

"Why, we must run away," answered Julio.

"But the sentinel has a carbine," observed Florian, timidly.

"We must get it from him," said Julio;

"be firm, and keep close to me. Take one of these pistols."

It was with a trembling hand that Florian complied with this request, and then they stole softly out of their dungeon, and as they did so, saw Gaspard approaching cautiously, and unperceived by the sentinel. Before the man was aware of his danger, Gaspard attacked him, felled him to the earth, wrested the carbine from him, and pointing it at his breast, assured him that the preservation of his life entirely depended on his silence.

"Now save yourselves," hastily ejaculated Gaspard; "hasten to Ricardo; there we shall meet again."

"Heaven bless you, good old man," cried Julio and his brother, emphatically; but he hurried them away. With very little difficulty they scaled the wall; and then, terror adding speed to their heels, they proceeded as fast as they were able in the direction of Ricardo's cottage. When they had reached the wood, which was near the castle of Altenburg, they were compelled to stop and rest themselves.

"What a scamper! I'm quite out of breath," said Julio; "at last we are at liberty again."

"Yes, thank Heaven, and the good old man," remarked Florian; "but at every step I fear we may be retaken."

"If we are stopped, we must fight," said

THE ABDUCTION OF MARCELINE BY THE DUKE MONTERINO.

Julio, "and we have arms. Ah! who goes there?"

The brothers both started, and felt very much alarmed as the shadow of a man's figure met their sight, which their imagination immediately construed into one of their pursuers.

"Who's there?" repeated Julio, affecting a deal more courage than he really felt; "speak! or you're as dead as a door nail."

The man now came forward, and his good-tempered countenance instantly re-assured them.

"Why, youngsters, would you fire upon a stranger?" he asked.

"We are strangers, too," answered Julio; "just come from Switzerland. Are you a friend or foe?"

"I am a friend to the innocent," said the man; "and you are too young, I think, to practise wickedness."

"We have seen so much wickedness in the castle there, from which we have just escaped, that we fancy everybody an enemy," said Florian.

"Escaped!—and from the castle!" ejaculated the man, with much curiosity depicted in his countenance.

"We shouldn't have got out, sir, but for a good old man; he's the porter."

"Ah!" exclaimed the stranger aside; "full well do I know whom they mean."

"The steward first coaxed us in, sir," said Julio, "like a wheedling rascal, as he certainly is."

"Then they made much of us, and treated us," said Florian; "and——"

"Then locked us up in separate dungeons," rejoined Julio.

"And there we must have stayed and died," observed Florian, "if Mr. Gaspard had not helped us to get away; I'm sure he has behaved to us like a father."

"A father!" repeated the man, aside. "How came you in this country?"

Julio, who was prepossessed in favour of the man, without any hesitation informed him.

"Ah!" he cried; "and did Mr. Ricardo act in the kind manner you have mentioned towards you?—He is a worthy fellow."

"Then you know Mr. Ricardo, sir?" said Julio.

"Yes, I—no—that is, I——" replied the man, with some confusion; "I have heard he bears an excellent character. I'll conduct you in safety."

"I hardly know what to make of him," said Julio, aside to his brother. "Look ye, sir," he added, speaking to the man, "first you know Mr. Ricardo, and then you don't know him; then you are a stranger; and then you know every inch of the road; so hang me if I trust to you."

"You have nothing to apprehend from me, I can assure you," said the man, eyeing Julio and his brother with a look of the deepest interest. "Prithee repose your confidence in me, and you will not repent it."

"Well, sir," said Julio, after a moment's deliberation; "after all, I will not doubt you; and, as we cannot do better, it being just night, we'll follow you. Come, brother," he added, speaking aside to Florian, "I am armed, and if our conductor turns out an impostor, he shall have the contents of this pistol for his deceit."

They then placed themselves under the guidance of the stranger, and in a short time he conducted them to the hamlet where Ricardo was awaiting their return with some impatience, the length of their absence having created his alarm and astonishment. Immediately on seeing him, they rushed into his arms, exclaiming in accents of terror—

"Oh, Mr. Ricardo!—Oh, dear!"

"What has alarmed you so, boys?" asked Ricardo; "pistols! What has been the matter?"

"That steward is the greatest scoundrel, that Geraldo,"—said Julio.

"Geraldo!" reiterated Ricardo; "I always thought so; and, to-morow, when I see this steward——"

At this moment the voice of Geraldo was heard without, saying—

"This way; follow me quickly; they must be here."

"Oh, pray, dear Mr. Ricardo, do protect us!" said Florian, very much alarmed.

"Never fear, returned Ricardo; "let him touch you at his peril. I'll teach him what honour is."

He had scarcely spoken, when Geraldo entered with a body of the castle guard. Julio and his brother clung to Ricardo, and looked to him and his friend for protection.

"It pains me, honest friends," said the villain Geraldo, "to cast a gloom on your festivity; but, by the baroness's order, I now appear to claim two culprits who have grossly wronged her."

"Sir," said Ricardo, "I do not think you will find any culprits here; however, if we have any criminals among us, the baroness will vouchsafe to let us know their crime?"

"Those vagrant lads," answered Geraldo, "whom the ardour of your benevolence has too rashly patronised;—'tis shocking to see so much depravity in youth."

"Sir," retorted Ricardo, with pointed contempt; "on the domains of so good a master as the late noble count, it is shocking to find depravity anywhere."

Geraldo bit his lips, and looked rather bewildered and disconcerted as he replied—

"Certainly; but you will find on them a purse."

"This moment as they came back," said Clotilde, "they told us the baroness had given them money; didn't they, neighbours?"

"They did," observed Ricardo, "and the charge rests only on this presumptive proof, let it never be said in any civilised country that the dispensations of the affluent to orphan poverty are so rare as to throw a suspicion of theft on the receivers."

"There's the purse, sir," said Florian, giving it to Geraldo; "he knows very well that her honour, the great lady at the castle, gave it to us with her own hands, for he saw her; we have never opened it yet."

"Think you," said Geraldo, speaking to Ricardo, "think you the baroness would lavish so large a sum on boys to whom, this morning, a few doits appeared a treasure? 'Tis not possible."

"Possible or not," returned Florian, "we will go with you now. Our characters for honesty are dearer than life; 'twas all our dear mother had to leave us."

"Ay," observed Julio, "and for her sake we'll preserve it. Come, we are ready."

"Brave boys!" cried Ricardo;—"every word they utter,—their every look convinces me of their honesty. This time, however, I insist upon going with them."

As Ricardo thus spoke, he took the hands of Julio and Florian, and they were about to follow Geraldo, when, suddenly, martial music was heard, and the next moment, the stranger whom the boys had met in the forest entered, accompanied by a number of soldiers. Everybody looked surprised, but particularly Geraldo, who could not conceal the fear he felt.

"Whose soldiers are these?" he asked,

addressing himself to the man, whose name it appears was Gregoire.

"The king's," answered the latter, "to whom you must submit."

"Are you their leader?" demanded Geraldo, trembling.

"Ay, good Mr. Geraldo," answered Gregoire; "deign to remember me; cast your eyes upon a humble follower of the Count Altenburg; one who has been somewhat more faithful to him than you have proved."

Geraldo started, and turned very pale, as he recognised the speaker; but he quickly recovered himself, and in a tone of indifference said—

"The noble baroness now inherits my ever faithful service. The master whom I was once proud to serve, is———"

"Here, wretch!" exclaimed a well known voice, and immediately afterwards Gaspard rushed in; and throwing aside his former dress and his wig, appeared in a splendid military uniform. Geraldo started aghast at this unexpected sight, and was unable to give utterance to a syllable, whilst the Count Altenburg, for that much-injured nobleman it was, fixed his eyes sternly upon the villain's countenance, and thus continued—

"Miscreant! the disguise which I now throw aside, informs thee I know all thy infamy; come—come, my children to my arms!—embrace your father."

He snatched Julio and his brother to his heart as he spoke, and embraced them with frantic delight, whilst the two brothers were so taken by surprise, that they were totally unable to speak.

"Ah!" cried Geraldo, aside, and biting his lips. "Exposed! then I must brave it well."

He then added aloud to the count:— "Embrace them, count, you will not long enjoy that blessing; a subtle poison is running through———"

"*Thy* veins, not theirs!" cried the count; "thank Heaven, I have preserved my sons. Your accomplice—I blush to call my relative —she is secured."

Turning to the guards, he said:—"Convey him to confinement; he who composed the hellish drug, best knows how long he has to linger, or what his torments may be."

Geraldo was seized immediately, and, with a countenance which bespoke his extreme horror at his approaching fate, and breathing curses upon the head of the count, was borne away. At the same moment loud acclamations rent the air, to welcome the return of that nobleman, and his happy restoration to his children, just at the moment when they were threatened with destruction.

The sequel of this story is soon told; Geraldo died a few hours afterwards, enduring the most excruciating suffering, from the effects of the poison. The baroness was suffered to retire to a convent, where the rest of her days were passed in penitence; while the Count Altenburg and his two sons were restored to those rights from which they had long been so unjustly withheld, and lived for many years to be a blessing to all around them.

By the time Marceline had arrived at the conclusion of this interesting tale, the afternoon had far advanced, and soon afterwards Marie re-entered the room. Marceline was glad when she returned, for she was much prepossessed in her favour, and in conversation with her she might gain, at least, a transient oblivion of her own misfortunes.

———

CHAPTER XVII.

THE ATTACK ON THE CASINO.

"I am afraid, signora," said Marie, on her entrance, "that you must have thought me a long while gone, for, in a strange place, and particularly under the circumstances you are placed in, the time must appear very tedious."

"I have abstracted my thoughts for a short time, or, at least, during your absence, my good girl, by reading a very interesting narrative," remarked Marceline, "but I am extremely glad you have returned, for the kindness of your behaviour to me already convinces me that I shall find a great relief in your society."

"Oh, signora," returned the girl, "I am sure you do me too much honour by the compliment you have been pleased to pay me, and you may rest assured that I will do everything in my power to deserve it, and I regret that I have not the means to contribute further to the relief of the sorrow under which you must suffer."

"I need not tell you, Marie," said Marceline, "how grateful I feel to you for your sympathy. Alas! how much do I need it. But the duke, has he yet returned?"

"He has not, signora," answered Marie, "and, as I before told you, it is not at all unlikely that he may remain away from the casino the whole of the night."

"The duke, you say, has acted with kindness towards you and your parents," observed our heroine; "but in spite of that, have you not reason to suppose that he is a bad man?"

"Why, signora," answered the girl, "after the manner in which he has acted towards you, I should be inclined to think so; but then, you know, he may have been prompted to it in a great measure by the violence of his love for you, and your persisting in rejecting his suit."

Marceline shook her head and sighed.

"Ah, no, Marie," she said, "had he really have loved me, he could not have been guilty of an action which he knew must inflict such bitter misery on me and my dear friends. It would have been more honourable to him to have endeavoured to conquer a passion which he knew could meet with no return. Besides the brutal crime of which he has acknowledged himself guilty, in having probably deprived my lover of life, would be sufficient to stamp him a villain of the blackest dye."

" If he has, indeed, perpetrated a deed of that description," remarked Marie, " I cannot offer anything in extenuation of his conduct."

" And think you it is at all probable that he would accuse himself of a crime of which he is not guilty ?" demanded Marceline.

Marie returned no answer, but her looks implied her coincidence in the opinion of Marceline.

" And have you never heard the character of the duke spoken of in disrespectful terms, Marie ?" said Marceline.

" Oh, yes, signora," replied Marie, " there have been strange reports circulated about him ; but then, you know, the world is very ungenerous, and it behoves us not to believe all that we hear prejudicial to another person's character, especially an individual placed in the distinguished situation of the duke, springing as they may from motives of envy or jealousy."

" That is very true, my good girl," said Marceline ; " but when persons are proved to have acted in the base manner which Monterino has done towards me, we have more reason to give such reports credence. And what are the rumours to which you have alluded ?"

Marie hesitated.

" I do not like to repeat them, signora," she answered, at length ; " but I do not think that you would mention to any one that I told you of them."

" I should be very sorry to say anything which would be likely to cause you trouble, Marie," said Marceline, whose curiosity was excited by what the girl had said.

" I can trust you, signora," remarked Marie. " It is reported, then, that the duke came to his title and estates by no very honourable means."

" Indeed ! How was that ?"

" The Duke Alberto Monterino was the former duke, signora."

" The father of the present duke, I suppose ?"

" No, signora ; his brother. He was many years the senior of the present duke, and after the death of their parents, he was appointed the guardian of the latter until he came of age."

" And how is it said that Alberto discharged that trust ?"

" With the strictest honour and affection. He was a nobleman who bore a most excellent character."

" And did the present duke evince an equal affection towards his brother ?"

" No, signora ; it is said that he ever showed a morose and jealous feeling against him."

" Was the Duke Alberto married ?"

" He was ; and to as beautiful and noble a lady as any in Italy."

" And did they then die ?"

" No, signora," answered Marie : " soon after the present duke arrived at age, he left Italy for England, and during his absence, the unfortunate Duke Alberto was accused of a crime against the state, and fearing the consequences, although most people felt certain of his innocence, with the duchess his wife he took flight. Almost immediately afterwards the present duke returned to Italy, and being in favour of the government, the title and estates of the unfortunate brother were bestowed upon him. There were many who did not hesitate to hint an opinion that he was the primary cause of the false accusation being brought against his brother, for the purpose of obtaining that title and princely fortune of which he envied him, but which the good Duke Alberto was so willing to share with him."

" It is a sorrowful story, Marie," observed Marceline, " and the suspicions entertained against the present duke, appear to me very probable. Had the Duke Alberto any children ?'

" No, signora ; but at the time they absconded, the duchess was supposed to be near her accouchement."

" Poor lady !"

" Yes, signora ; she was indeed greatly to be pitied, and I have often wept when I have thought of her and her husband's misfortunes."

" And has not anything been heard of them since ?"

" No, signora, nothing whatever ; but they, doubtless, left Italy."

" If Monterino has been guilty of this unnatural crime," said Marceline, " he is indeed a villain, and after the manner he has behaved to me, I should believe him capable of almost any atrocity."

" For the sake of human nature," said Marie, " I hope that the duke is wrongly suspected. But hark !—what is the meaning of that noise below ?"

The sounds that reached the ears of Marceline at the same time that they did those of Marie, was the heavy closing of several doors, which was followed by a confusion of voices, and intermingled with loud bursts of riotous laughter.

" Probably it is some of the domestics indulging in a little joviality in the absence of the duke," observed Marie ; " and yet I never heard them so noisy before. You look pale, signora ; do not be alarmed."

Marceline did, indeed, turn very pale, and an involuntary apprehension caused her to tremble.

" I will go below and ascertain the cause of this disturbance," added Marie. " I will not be gone a minute, signora."

Marie quitted the room as she spoke, and Marceline waited in trembling suspense and anxiety until her return. She listened attentively at the door, and her ears were frequently saluted with the same sounds of rude laughter and uproarious merriment. The fears of Marceline increased, and Marie having left the door open, she walked on to the landing, and then ventured to descend two or three of the stairs, and to listen more attively; but the sounds were so confused that she was unable to distinguish anything more than the voices evidently of several men, talking and laughing together. Shortly afterwards she heard a light footstep ascending the stairs, and the next moment Marie made her appearance with a lamp in her hand, and seeing Marceline, beckoned her to re-enter the apartment. Marceline obeyed, and Marie, having followed her in, closed the door, locking it on the inside. Marceline eagerly inquired the cause of the confusion below.

"The duke has unfortunately returned with two or three of his dissipated friends, and they are all evidently very much inebriated," replied the girl.

"Oh, dear!" exclaimed Marceline, with much alarm depicted on her countenance, "This intelligence fills me with terror. Should he have the boldness to approach me while in that state, what will become of me?"

"Let us retire to the bed-chamber, signora," said Marie; "for although I do not think the duke would do as you fear, should he thus commit himself under the influence of wine, not being able to see the light, he might imagine we had retired to rest, and desist from endeavouring to have an interview with you."

Marceline, in a state of increased alarm, which Marie could not pacify, obeyed, and entering the inner apartment, they closed and secured the door after them. They seated themselves by the side of the couch, and gazed at each other with looks of apprehension, but without speaking. A short pause ensued, and then the loud revelry of the duke and his companions again reached their ears.

"I cannot venture to go to bed while this scene of riot and debauchery is going forward below," said Marceline; "in such a state of excitement, have I not good reason to fear that the duke may be led into any excesses?"

"We will remain up for awhile longer," returned Marie; "probably the duke and his friends will shortly be overpowered by the effects of their intemperance, and will retire to their chambers."

"Alas!" ejaculated Marceline, "what a terrible prospect is there before me, placed as I am in the power of such a man."

"Endeavour to keep up your spirits, signora, I entreat of you," said Marie, "and circumstances may not turn out so bad as you apprehend. At any rate, you must muster up all your fortitude and self-possession to enable you to resist the worst."

"Oh, what resistance can I offer to such a determined villain as the detested Monterino?" returned Marceline.

An hour of the most painful suspense passed away, and then the noise of the persons below ceased, and not a sound disturbed the quiet of the casino.

"Overpowered by the deep potations they have taken," observed Marie, "they have, probably, fallen asleep; and if so, all cause for your fears is at an end." ——

"Would that I could think so, Marie," replied Marceline; "but I find it utterly impossible for me to divest myself of my terrors. Alas! my poor mother, how terrible would be your agony did you but know the critical situation in which your daughter is placed."

Marie was about to make a reply, when a bustling sound met their ears from below, and they both listened with the most breathless attention. The persons below seemed evidently upon the move, and presently afterwards they heard the door of the room in which the duke and his friends had been seated opened and closed again, and then the noise of several persons staggering along. The outer door was the next instant opened and closed again, with a loud bang.

"Thank Heaven, they have departed," cried Marie, "and you are safe, signora."

Marceline clasped her hands together, and raised her eyes in thankfulness towards Heaven.

Again there was a pause of some time, and then Marceline and her companion became more composed; and thinking that all danger was at an end, the latter proposed that they should retire to rest; but she had scarcely done so, when they were startled by sounds of a more alarming description than those they had before heard, when they both started to their feet, and looked upon each other in a state of the utmost amazement and consternation.

The sounds they now heard were like those which would be occasioned by the battering in of doors, and the screams of women were intermingled with the clashing of swords and the loud shouts of men.

Marceline clung to her companion, and they were both so horrified that they stared at each other aghast, with pallid countenances, and were unable to give utterance to a syllable.

"Gracious Heaven!" at last exclaimed Marie, "they have surely returned, and have got quarrelling with one another."

"What will become of us?" gasped forth Marceline; "we are lost!—we are lost!"

The noise now increased, and at last the uproar became completely deafening. Suddenly there were loud cries of "Fire! fire!" and the horror-struck females, looking from the casement, beheld the flames bursting forth from the casino below.

"Good God! must we suffer so horrible a death? How shall we act? What—oh, what shall we do?" cried Marceline, wringing her hands, and rushing into the outer apartment, which was now filled with smoke.

"We must not remain here to perish in the flames," ejaculated Marie. "Courage—courage, signora! or we have no hope. Follow me."

As she spoke, she rushed to the door, followed by Marceline, and hastily opening it, they hurried, as well as the dense smoke would permit them, to the staircase, which they descended. Fortunately, the fire was raging in a part of the building remote from the hall, and they were, therefore, enabled to reach the exterior of the casino; but they had no sooner made their escape, than they found themselves surrounded by a number of wild-looking men, whose dress betokened them to be brigands, who seized them, and bore them along down the hill.

"Convey the females to the vehicle, and harm them not!" ordered a man of a commanding figure, and enveloped in a dark mantle.

Marceline remembered being hurried rapidly along, and at the foot of the hill beholding the Duke Monterino, bound hand and foot, being placed across a horse, before one of the brigands, and she saw no more: terror overcame her, and her senses left her.

CHAPTER XVIII.

FATHER AND SON.

FOR a few moments, Henri and his wretched, guilty father, stood and gazed at each other with looks of mute astonishment, while the emotion which agitated each of their breasts could be plainly discernible in the aspect and working of their countenances. Henri dropped the hand of Zitella, which he had taken, and became completely paralysed to the spot, while incredulity and exultation alternately flashed from the eyes of Adolphe de Floriville.

"Father!" at length almost unconsciously escaped the lips of Henri; and the exclamation was followed up by a groan of agony.

"Father!" gasped forth Zitella; and a deadly paleness overspread her countenance.

"Ah, boy!" cried De Floriville; "do you, then, acknowledge me? and has kind fortune once more thrown you in my way? By hell, this is the best night's work I have had for some time! We part no more."

"Oh, father!" exclaimed Henri, "to see you thus, still the votary of crime, and——"

"No more of this, boy!" interrupted De Floriville, fiercely, and seizing his arm. "I need not a monitor in you. Little did I think, when I heard our captain speak of Henri le Sange, that in him I should recognise my own son. You look surprised, Zitella; and well you may be. You would have broken the rules of our band, and have aided him to escape."

"I would, Rinaldo," ejaculated Zitella—"for by no other name do I know you; but it was love that prompted me to it. You surely will not thwart my purpose, especially if he be, as you say, your son?"

"I would not?" repeated Adolphe. "Ha, ha, ha! You know me not, nor the motives I have for my conduct, if you imagine that I will become an accessary to his escaping from hence, after so many years have elapsed since we before met."

"Father," ejaculated Henri, in a voice of extreme agitation, "urge me not to curse you!"

"Doubtless you have been taught to do so," returned Adolphe, in a bitter tone. "But I care not: we have once more met, and it shall be no easy matter to separate us again."

"Father," demanded Henri, "what would you with me?"

"That which I have for so long been unjustly prevented from doing," replied De Floriville, "through my own weakness—exercise a due authority over you."

"Or, rather, since you compel me to say that which I would much rather not," returned Henri, "make me subservient to your vices."

"Ah, boy!"

"Nay, father, is it not true, and with sorrow I speak it," said Henri, "that whatever miseries you yourself have endured, and all that myself and my unfortunate mother have suffered, have they not been brought on by your guilt?"

"D——n!" exclaimed De Floriville, fiercely; "and have I, then, lived till now to be schooled thus by my own son?"

"Father," observed Henri, in a voice of the greatest emotion, "I would not school you. I would reclaim you from the life of guilt you have hitherto led, and thus evince the power of the affection your son bears towards you."

"Affection for me!" replied De Floriville, with a look of bitter mockery. "Psha! You would deride me, boy! Have you not been taught to curse me—hate me?"

"No—no, by Heaven! Oh, father, did you but know the many hours of anguish I have suffered in thinking upon you—in praying that the Almighty might extend his mercy towards you, and bring you to a sense of remorse for your past crimes, you would not thus accuse me. 'Tis true, I have been told to forget you; but nature pleaded too strongly for me to do so; and well do I know the torture which was inflicted upon that gentle bosom whose tongue advised me to do so, and who was driven to so dreadful an alternative by the many horrible and unnatural crimes you have committed."

"And has she not wealth? Am I not her lawful husband, and, by right, the possessor of all she enjoys?" demanded Adolphe.

"Father, force me not to prove to you, in the presence of another," replied Henri, "that you have forfeited long since all such claim as you arrogate to yourself. Do not make me recall to my memory the awful deeds which——"

"Hold, rash boy!" interrupted de Floriville, grasping the arm of his son more vehemently than he had done before; "dare not to mention a word upon that subject. And yet I care not; am I not an outlaw, a brigand, a robber, and a murderer? It matters little what more is known of me! No doubt you thought that we should never more meet; but, you see, you were mistaken; we have met, and it strikes me very forcibly that we shall be companions for some time to come. I intend to learn from you the place where your mother is at present residing, that I may again pay her a visit."

" Never !" cried Henri.

" No ?"

" Not from my lips."

" Bethink yourself."

" My determination is fixed."

" Then you go not hence."

" By Heaven ! although your blood flows within my veins, you shall not detain me," exclaimed Henri, drawing his sword.

" Ah ! would you, then, raise your arm against the author of your being ?"

" Has not your conduct done away with every tie ?" demanded Henri.

" Rinaldo," ejaculated Zitella, as she rushed in between the guilty Adolphe de Floriville and his son, " forbear! If you are indeed the father of the young man upon whom I have placed my heart's warmest affections, you will not oppose his escape from hence. Nay, I will supplicate to you; I will on my knees beg of you to allow him to depart, and ever afterwards my voice shall be raised in invoking blessings upon your head!"

" Blessings upon *my* head!" reiterated De Floriville, with a scornful laugh; " bah! cant—mockery! I tell you, maiden, that Henri departs not hence."

" And suppose we are obstinate, and use force ?" said Zitella, resolutely; and her fine eyes sparkled with even more than their usual fire.

" He dare not raise his hand against his father," returned Adolphe; " and were he to do so, I could quickly summon plenty to my aid, and then would your treachery be revealed, by which you have forfeited your life."

" My own life I value not," answered Zitella; " but Henri must be saved; I have sworn it, and let whatever may be the consequences, I will not break my oath."

" Father," once more expostulated Henri, " why do you thus pursue me, as well as my mother, with your unnatural persecutions? In what have we ever offended you? Was not my mother the devoted wife throughout all the difficulties brought on by your own guilty career? Did she not suffer unprecedented sorrows and disgrace rather than she would abandon you; and was she not willing to make any sacrifice, could she by doing so have reclaimed you? Steeped deep in infamy as you were, and with the recollection of the horrible crimes you had perpetrated fresh upon her memory, when she could no longer live with you, did she not offer you all that you could require, and that she had the means of bestowing, if you would cease to annoy her? But after squandering away that which she advanced to you, you returned again, and seemed to exult in the misery which your presence caused her. Had she

not it completely in her power to denounce you as——"

" As a murderer !" added De Floriville, with a reckless grin; " I know it, and scorn her power. It was not regard for me which prevented her from doing so, but the dread of the disgrace which would have been brought upon herself and you. But this unexpected meeting joys me, and I am determined that I will have ample satisfaction for all that I have been subjected to since Laurette and myself have been separated, before——"

At that moment the sound of a bugle, Allesandrie's well known signal, was heard re-echoing through the caverns; and Adolphe started.

" Ah ! our captain has returned," he cried; " now, now—away, Henri, back to your own cavern; and, Zitella, begone, unless you would have your treachery become known, and suffer the penalty."

" Confusion ! the delay has thwarted my wishes," exclaimed Zitella, and her eyes flashed glances of indignation upon Adolphe: " for this we are indebted to you, Rinaldo; curses light upon your head for it."

" Beware, maiden," returned Adolphe, with a malignant frown; " you are in my power, and if you provoke me to it, I will immediately make known your crime to the gang, and demand the punishment which is invariably inflicted for such an offence."

" Oh, father—father !" groaned Henri, in the intensity of his agony, " may you not have reason to repent this unnatural conduct?

" Psha! I am callous of everything, boy," replied De Floriville; " crime upon crime, days and nights of horror, have made me more than mortal, hardened my heart, and rendered me familiar with every sort of suffering. But away—back—back to the place from whence you came, or tremble for the consequences of your disobedience. I shall see you again ere long, and by that time expect to find you in a very different mood, and ready to comply with my demands."

" Never !" firmly ejaculated the young man; " sooner would I perish. For your sake, fair damsel, whose unexampled kindness and affection prompted you to run so much risk to save me, I will return to my place of confinement, and never shall I cease to remember you with any other feelings than those of the utmost esteem and most unbounded gratitude."

Zitella looked at the being who had taken captive her heart's warmest affections with an expression of countenance we feel at a loss to do adequate justice to in description, and tears gushed to her eyes.

" Alas ! Henri," she exclaimed, " and is, then, that cold word, esteem, the only one which your——"

" Enough of this," interrupted De Floriville, impatiently; " if you remain here many moments longer, our captain may surprise you; and woe betide ye if ye incur the wrath of Allesandrio Robelli."

"Father," said Henri, solemnly, "you will not betray this poor girl?"

"That depends in a great measure upon yourself," was the answer; "her fate is in your hands."

"Why, you surely would not—could not think of harming that fond girl, whose only offence has been to endeavour to rescue from a life of shame and misery your son?" demanded Henri.

"There is no time to bandy words with you now," cried Adolphe; "begone! We shall see each other again shortly."

"Oh, Henri," said Zitella, with a deep sigh, "to be thus foiled, when I had hoped to have been able to have proved to you the strength of the love with which you have inspired me! Farewell—farewell! we shall meet again! and if Zitella's tears—if Zitella's prayers and entreaties can prevail, the time is not far distant when you will be restored to liberty."

"By hell, never!" cried De Floriville; "never, till he has acceded to my wishes."

Henri was about to make a reply, but hearing footsteps approaching, he hastily seized Zitella's proffered hand, and raising it to his lips, he pressed a fervent kiss upon it; Zitella at the same time fixed upon him a look which spoke more than language could have had the power to do, and they separated, Henri returning to the apartment or cavern he had just before quitted, and Zitella, without deigning to look upon Adolphe, who she was greatly shocked to hear was Henri's father, with a heavy heart hastened to meet her father.

CHAPTER XIX.

THE BROTHERS.

THE reader has probably guessed that the author of the outrage at the casino of the Duke Monterino was Allesandrio di Robelli, the brigand-chief; and it was a stratagem which he had long had in contemplation, and only waited the return of the duke to put it into execution. Robbery, however, was not the design of Allesandrio, as will be seen by what follows, but an idea which he had long nurtured in his breast, and by which he anticipated the gratification of his revenge, and ultimately to get that justice done him which his many injuries demanded. Terrible as were the crimes that were attributed to Robelli, they were much exaggerated; and there were moments when the deep melancholy which pervaded his countenance plainly evinced how much he hated the course of life to which he had been driven by stern necessity.

His language and manners were noble in the extreme, and clearly showed that his former station in society had been of no mean order; yet to no one but his daughter had he confided the facts of his past life, and enjoined her to the strictest secrecy. We say to no one; by that we mean to none

of the gang; but he had one friend who espoused his cause, and was anxious to see him reinstated in his rights, and to bring to disgrace and punishment those who had so deeply injured him. That one friend was now most strenuously and secretly exerting himself in behalf of Allesandrio, and not without great hopes of ultimate success; and the time he considered was not far distant when the brigand chief would receive his pardon, and be suffered once more to return to that rank and station of society of which he was formerly so distinguished an ornament. But to return to the Duke Monterino.

The attack of Allesandrio and his gang upon the casino was so sudden and so unexpected, that he was not prepared to offer scarcely any resistance; and himself and his companions were so overpowered by the excessive manner in which they had been drinking, that they were easily defeated, the latter taking to flight as quickly as they conveniently could. The conflagration of the casino was entirely accidental, as Allesandrio had given strict orders to his men not to commit any acts of violence without receiving his direct commands to that effect; and when he beheld that handsome building enveloped in flames, no person could feel more regret than he did.

The duke having been placed upon a horse before one of the brigands, bound hand and foot, as we have described in a previous chapter, was so much under the influence of wine, that he almost immediately became insensible; and on the following morning when he awoke, and found himself reposing upon a humble pallet in one of the caverns, he had but a very indistinct recollection of what had taken place. When, however, he found himself a prisoner, his rage and alarm knew no bounds, and at first he imagined that it was the friends of Marceline and Henri who had been the cause of his arrest. But he shortly recollected the appearance of the men, which plainly showed that they were brigands; and when he reflected that Marceline was either in their power, or had perished in the flames that had consumed his casino, his agitation baffles every attempt at description. He hastily arose from his couch, and paced the cavern with hasty strides; then he cursed his own ill-fortune, and breathed a bitter malediction upon those who had committed the deed, and who held him in their power. He examined every part of the cavern, but saw nothing to give him any reason to hope that he should be enabled to escape. There was a ladder on one side of the cavern, which led to a trap-door, but it was quite secure, and defied all his efforts to open it; and if he had succeeded in doing so, it would not have availed him, as the brigands would be sure to be close at hand to obstruct his further progress.

He had not, however, much longer for reflection, when he heard the trap being raised, and presently afterwards the tall figure of a man appeared, and began to descend the steps into the cavern. Monterino hastily fixed his eyes upon him, and immediately recognised from his person that he was the man who had appeared to be the captain of the gang, but his face was beneath a black mask.

Having alighted in the cavern, he folded his arm across his chest, and stood for a few moments contemplating the duke, without speaking a word, although it was evident, from the heaving of his chest, and other demonstrations, that he was undergoing a variety of conflicting emotions. As for the Duke Monterino, he was unable to utter a word, he was so struck by the mystery and singularity of the man's demeanour, and in spite of his endeavours to the contrary, he felt a sensation of awe stealing over him, for which he was unable to account, but was totally incapable of shaking off.

"Sigismund Monterino," at length uttered the brigand.

Monterino started at the voice, and a cold tremour involuntarily came over him. The man appeared to enjoy his emotion; a half-distinct laugh of exultation escaped his bosom.

"Sigismund Monterino," repeated the man, "you are welcome to these caverns, the retreat of Allesandrio di Robelli and his brave associates."

THE ESCAPE OE FLORIO AND JULIO FROM ALTENBURG.

¶ "Allesandrio di Robelli, the brigand-chief!" repeated Monterino, and his lips quivered, and his cheeks became pale as death.

"Ay," answered his visitor; "Allesandrio di Robelli, who stands before you!"

"Ah! villain! miscreant!" cried Monterino.

"Hold!" interrupted the brigand-chief; Allesandrio brooks not language such as this. It is Sigismund, the usurper, the traitor, who deserves those titles best. He, the cowardly traducer of his brother's fame, by which he brought misery and shame upon that brother, and gained possession of his wealth and title."

"Ah!" ejaculated Monterino, and his limbs trembled violently; "who is it that thus talks to me?"

"One whom you, doubtless, never expected to meet again, but who will yet live to triumph over you, and to wreak a terrible retribution upon your head: behold!"

As the brigand chief spoke, he suddenly tore the mask from his face, and Monterino no sooner behold his features that he started back with astonishment and fear, and at the same moment exclaimed, in a voice rendered hoarse with terror—

"Powers of darkness! It is Alberto!"

As Monterino gave utterance to these few words, his features became as pale as death; his whole frame was violently convulsed, and he fixed his eyes upon the brigand-chief, in whom he now discovered his brother, with a look which spoke the consciousness of guilt.

"Can it be possible?" he gasped forth, "or is my fancy at work to deceive me?"

Allesandrio, or, rather, the Duke Alberto, for such he really was, appeared to enjoy his confusion, and, with arms folded across his broad chest, and his fine commanding figure erect; he stood gazing at him for a few moments without making him any reply.

"Yes, villain!" he at length answered, "to your confusion, it is the Duke Alberto Monterino, your much injured brother, whose title and estates you have so long unjustly held."

Monterino recovered himself, and assuming his usual haughty and scornful air, he said—

"Your title and estates I hold by right; they were secured to me by that state to which you turned traitor!"

"Liar!"

"Are you not proscribed?—disgraced?—outlawed?"

"Yes, unjustly, as will soon be made apparent," returned Alberto; "the real traitor will, I trust, ere many days have elapsed, be made known."

Sigismund endeavoured to laugh scornfully, but it was very evident he was suffering great emotion and terror of mind, and there was something in the stern dignity of his brother which inspired him with awe and terror.

"Was it not proved that you were a traitor?" at last demanded Sigismund; and at the same time his lip quivered, and he shrunk beneath the stern glance of his brother.

"It was not," answered Alberto; "the whole charge was as false as hell! Say, Sigismund, since your information upon this subject seems to be so perfect, who was my accuser?"

Sigismund trembled, and hesitated.

"I know not," at last he replied.

"Liar!—dastard!" exclaimed Alberto; "it was you!"

"Ah!" cried Sigismund; "who dare thus charge me?"

"I do; and in a few days hence I hope to be enabled to prove my words, to your confusion."

Sigismund endeavoured to appear cool, but in vain; there was something in the looks that his brother fixed upon him which chilled his soul; besides, was he not in his power, and entirely at his mercy? and, after the manner in which he had behaved towards him, and with which Alberto seemed to be so well acquainted, what else could he expect than to suffer from his hatred and vengeance?

Alberto eyed him narrowly, and for some moments remained silent, and appeared to watch the emotion which Sigismund could not help evincing with much satisfaction.

"Yes, villain!" he said, at last; "it was you who trumped up a false charge against me, through which I was unjustly plundered of my rights, and banished, with my unfortunate wife, from my home, my native land. I have learned all, from a source on which I can fully depend, and doubtless ere this everything is made known to the proper quarter, and your doom sealed. Tremble!"

"By hell! you accuse me wrongfully, Alberto," faltered out Sigismund; who, indeed, tremble at the words of his brother, and the confident tone in which she spoke them.

"Liar! I once more call you!" cried Alberto.

Sigismund again endeavoured to assume an air and tone of haughtiness, as he replied—

"'Tis well for you, Alberto, that you have me in your power, or you would have reason to repent that word."

Alberto laughed scornfully, and then proceeded—

"No doubt, Sigismund, you thought that I was dead, and that your guilt would have remained concealed for ever; but you will shortly be undeceived, and then it will be my turn to triumph."

"You will repent this outrage, Alberto," answered his brother; "you will have to answer dearly for it to——"

A loud laugh of derision from Alberto interrupted Sigismund, and the former ejaculated—

"Idiot! ere I have to answer for this outrage, as you call it, you will have to answer for the crimes of which you have been guilty."

"And who dare accuse me?"

"I will."

"You!—ha—ha!"

"Ay, laugh now, if you can," said Alberto, "for you will have but little cause, methinks, by and by! I tell you, I will accuse you, and——"

"You accuse me?" demanded Sigismund, as the thought appeared to cross his mind; "are you not an outlaw? a brigand? a robber?"

"True; but what has driven me to it? Had it not been for you, I should never have become guilty. But I trust I have not proceeded too far to be forgiven."

"Never!" ejaculated Sigismund, and his courage seemed to revive as the idea darted across his brain; "never!—Is not your name a terror to the country? Have you not been guilty of crimes at which human nature must shudder, and think you, then, that there is any forgiveness for you?"

"My hands were never yet stained by human blood, although the tongue of slander has attributed the most fearful deeds to me," answered Alberto, with the utmost coolness;

"but you, Sigismund, I accuse you of murder!"

"Of murder!" repeated Sigismund, and his face became paler than ever, and his lips quivered; "of murder!" he added, and he fixed a penetrating glance upon his brother.

"Yes, of murder," returned the latter, "of the murder of my poor wife, my beauteous Elvira."

"Oh, foul and unfounded charge," replied Sigismund; "did not your wife fly with you?"

"She did."

"How, then, could I be her murderer?"

"The horrors, the privations we were made to endure through your unnatural conduct preyed upon her constitution, and, ultimately, broke her heart; and, therefore, do I accuse you indirectly of being her assassin. For that I seek revenge!"

"Alberto," faltered out Sigismund, and again all the fears of a coward were apparent in his countenance, "beware of what you do?"

"I heed not your warning," replied Alberto, with a scornful laugh.

"Alberto," continued Sigismund, "I am in your power, it is true, and entirely at your mercy; but still, you surely could not deliberately shed my blood, you——"

"I would not take your life," interrupted Alberto; "no, but I will have a deeper revenge. Marceline di Venoni——"

"Ah, what of her?"

"You forget that she is in my power?"

"You would not harm her."

"No."

"And how know you her name?"

"From the lips of him whom you attempted to murder."

"Ah!—Henri le Sange?"

"The same; you acknowledge the crime, then? It was a brave deed, forsooth, for three ruffians to attack a single man."

"Does he still live?"

"He does."

"Confusion! How know you that?"

"Because he is at present an inmate of these caverns," answered Alberto.

"Ah! my rival also within your power?"

"Even so. You see, I have some little cause to exult; I did not boast of my triumph without ample reason."

Sigismund bit his lips, and paced the cavern with hasty strides.

"Alberto, at last he said, "what is your intention towards me and the beauteous Marceline di Venoni?"

"You shall see anon."

"You will not bestow her upon my rival?"

"Ah! have I then found the way to torture you?" cried the brigand chief, and his looks bespoke his exultation. "You shall be present at their meeting; no doubt you will enjoy the scene. For the present I leave you to your reflections; in a short time I will see you again. In the meantime, I hope you will enjoy yourself in this elegant apartment, and reflect with satisfaction upon your past deeds, and the reward they are likely to meet with."

"Stay, Alberto," implored Sigismund, his fears overcoming all that haughty air of defiance he had with so little skill assumed; "do not leave me thus! Recollect yourself, and I am certain that you will be convinced you accuse me wrongfully; and——"

"Psha!" interrupted Alberto, with a look of scorn; "you must have been a most affectionate brother to quietly take possession of the property which belonged to me, and knowing that myself and my poor wife were driven beggars upon the world."

"I did believe that you had disgraced yourself, and——"

"Bah! a weak excuse! You knew that the charge brought against me was entirely false, and that it originated in your own brain."

"By all my hopes you accuse me of that which I am not guilty."

"It is useless for you to deny it to me; I have too powerful evidence of your guilt, which I will shortly produce, to your confusion. But I waste words with you."

"Alberto," returned Sigismund, after a short pause, during which he seemed to be struggling violently with his feelings, and to be trying to assume a tone of as much plausibility as possible; "again I tell you that you wrong me. You know full well that I was in another country at the time when the charge was brought against you; and, therefore, could not have had anything to do with it."

"A weak subterfuge!" exclaimed Alberto, impatiently; "but it cannot deceive me."

"It is true," answered Sigismund; "I knew nothing whatever of the charge, and when I was informed of it, my astonishment and grief——"

"No more, base, shameless hypocrite," interrupted Alberto, frowning fearfully; "I have not patience to listen to you."

"One question, Alberto," said Sigismund, eagerly; "if you knew yourself to be innocent of the charge, why did you take to flight? Was not that a tacit acknowledgment of your guilt?"

"No," answered Alberto; "but I knew that the plot to destroy me was so deeply laid, that it would have been an impossibility for me to make my innocence apparent, and I, therefore, yielded to the entreaties of my unfortunate Elvira, and made my escape."

"Would, Alberto, that I could convince you of the utter fallacy of the charge you have brought against me," said Sigismund; "and also give you an idea of the anguish which your disgrace caused me, and how I tried, but in vain, to discover what had become of you."

"Liar! once more I call you!" cried Alberto; "but all you can say will have no other effect upon me than to meet with my utter scorn. But I will listen to you no longer; I go to fulfil my promise.   Prepare yourself to meet Marceline di Venoni, and your rival, Henri le Sange!"

Having thus spoken, Alberto folded his cloak around him, and fixing upon his disconcerted and guilty brother a mingled look of hatred, scorn, and exultation, he quitted the place in which he was confined.

When he had gone, Sigismund Monterino traversed the cavern with disordered steps, and in a state of the utmost excitement.

"Curses—ten thousand curses light upon this misfortune!" he cried. "Alberto living! I hoped that he had long since been numbered with the dead. Should he speak the truth, I am ruined; but whether or not, he has me in his power, and will not suffer me to depart from hence. Here, then, I must remain, to endure his taunts, and to be exposed to his vengeance. Henri le Sange too, still alive, and here to witness my captivity! By hell! I shall go mad! Oh, fool! unguarded, thoughtless fool that I was, not to ascertain whether or not he lived, and thus securely have prevented the discovery, the disgrace and infamy which will now, in all probability, be my portion. But still let me not entirely despair. There is yet hope, unless Alberto should be sanguinary enough to take my life; may not the persons who were at the casino at the time the attack was made, and who effected their escape, have guessed into whose hands I have fallen, and before many hours have elapsed, the proper authorities may have sent a party to rescue me? Oh, yes: the idea is too feasible to be easily scouted, and I will not entirely despair. Besides, it is not likely, brigand as he is, and with the crimes of which he is accused attached to his name, that he would make any attempt, as he has boasted, to exonerate his character from the charge which rests upon it, well aware, as he must be, should he be acquitted of the offence through which he had been compelled to flee, that he is liable to capital punishment for the many offences he has perpetrated since he has been following the lawless course which he now pursues. No, I will not despair, but return his irony with equal sarcasm, and brave his utmost wrath!"

As the villain Sigismund thus soliloquised, he endeavoured to persuade himself that he was prepared to meet his deeply-injured brother with fortitude, and to combat all that he might bring against him. But the effort was only attended with partial success, and he could not help quailing with the consciousness of guilt when he recollected the many injuries he had heaped upon Alberto.

We will now return to Marceline and her attendant, Marie, who was still suffered to remain with her, and who, when she had recovered from the terror consequent upon their seizure by the brigands, and the conflagration of the casino, endeavoured all that she possibly could to console Marceline, and to persuade her that their sex would protect them from the insult she apprehended.

They were placed in one of the best sections of this subterranean retreat, and everything which the place contained gave it more the appearance of an apartment in a gentleman's mansion than a brigand's cavern, and the manner in which it was furnished combined elegance with taste. Marceline, in fact, was not so terrified at her situation as might have been anticipated, for she remembered the kind manner in which the brigand chief had spoken when he gave directions to his fellows to convey her and Marie to the vehicle, and she considered that she had far less to dread from him than she would have had had she remained in the power of the Duke Monterino.

She and Marie had only just begun to converse together upon the novelty of their situation, when they heard a key turning in the lock of the iron door, and immediately afterwards a beautiful female made her appearance, and advanced gracefully towards them. It was Zitella!

Marceline and Marie gazed with astonishment upon the lovely brigand girl, and the latter felt a peculiar sensation stealing through her bosom, which she was unable to comprehend, and equally incapable of banishing. Zitella paused when she reached the centre of the cavern, and stood gazing steadfastly upon Marceline, while conflicting sentiments were struggling in her breast, and she appeared to be making a strong effort to conquer the feeling of jealousy which arose to her mind, now that she stood in the presence of her who possessed the affections of the only being she had ever loved. But she quickly conquered the evil ideas that had begun to take possession of her breast; they were all merged in admiration of the beauty and gentleness of the poor girl before her, and, after heaving a deep sigh, she advanced nearer towards her, and said—

"I believe I address Marceline di Venoni?"

"You do," answered Marceline, in a gentle, but firm tone: "and you——"

"I am Zitella, the brigand girl, daughter of Allesandrio di Robelli!" replied Zitella.

Marceline started and turned pale at the mention of that name; and Marie could not help giving utterance to an exclamation of terror.

"Allesandrio di Robelli, that terrible man!" cried Marceline. "Alas! then we are lost!"

"You, then, have heard of my father?" said Zitella.

"Heard of him!—Oh! who has not heard and shuddered with horror at his name?" answered Marceline.

"Did the humble peasant, or the unfortunate reduced to poverty and wretchedness, ever tremble at his name?" demanded Zitella. "But you forget that I told you he was my father!"

"I ask you pardon," said Marceline, in her usual mild tone, and looking upon the animated countenance of Zitella with a mingled feeling of admiration and pity. "You appear kind and good; it is impossible that one so lovely can be otherwise than virtuous; and yet to be thus associated with the votaries of crime, and——"

Zitella frowned, and Marceline, recollecting herself, suddenly paused and averted her eyes, unable to meet the earnest gaze which the brigand girl fixed upon her; and there was something so peculiar in her looks and manners, that they imparted to her an idea of her being one whom she ought to dread.

"Marceline di Venoni cannot boast of more virtue and integrity than her who she says has been made the associate of vice," said Zitella. "The daughter of Allesandrio di Robelli would never disgrace the noble blood which flows within her veins."

"And yet your father—" Marceline could not help saying.

"Is a brigand, you would say," added Zitella; "an alien from society; an outcast and a robber: nay, a murderer—so the lying tongue of slander hath reported him. Is not that what you would say? But, if he be so, misfortune, injustice, and treachery of the basest kind have driven him to it, and not his own free choice or depraved nature."

"If so, I sincerely pity him," said Marceline.

"Nay, my father needs not pity," returned the brigand girl: "he has struggled too long with adversity not to have become inured to it, and to mock at its effects. He lives in the hope that his day of triumph is at hand;—that justice, although tardy, will be done him; and that he shall be restored to that station in society, and those rights from which he has been so long withheld, and to see punishment awarded to those who have been the cause of all his misfortunes."

"But," observed Marceline, "has he not, by his own lawless course of life, closed the doors of justice against him?"

"If justice be really awarded him, he has not," answered Zitella. "But enough of this. I came not hither to talk to you upon a subject in which you cannot feel the least interest, but upon another, which, doubtless, is of the utmost importance to you."

"Ah! What mean you?" asked Marceline, eagerly.

"Henri le Sange!" said Zitella, in a low and tremulous voice; and as she gave utterance to that name, which ever acted as a talisman upon her heart, she fixed a still more penetrating glance upon Marceline than before, and watched anxiously the effect it would have upon her. Marceline trembled at the mention of the name of her lover; and turning very pale, she endeavoured to speak in reply to Zitella; but her voice failed her, and she could only gaze vacantly at the brigand girl, in the expectation of hearing something to create her unhappiness.

"It is no use seeking to conceal your emotion from me, Marceline di Venoni," she said at length. "I know the feelings you at present experience, and no one can appreciate them more than I do. Henri le Sange and yourself love each other."

"Ah!" ejaculated Marceline—"how know you that?"

A faint smile played upon the features of Zitella for a moment, but it was immediately succeeded by a look of the deepest melancholy, and, sighing, she observed—

"You fondly, devotedly love him yet, although you have been torn asunder?"

"Love Henri!" exclaimed Marceline, with energy, and forgetting for a moment the situation she was placed in, or the person she was addressing; "oh, who can understand the strength of my passion for him? And even though he may sleep in the icy arms of death, still will I cherish his memory with the same unceasing ardour that I did whilst living."

Zitella walked two or three times across the cavern, and was evidently violently struggling with contending feelings; but at length admiration of the fidelity of Marceline gained the supremacy in her bosom, and she said—

"But what if Henri le Sange still lives, but no longer loves you?"

"Then let death be immediately my doom! for Marceline di Venoni would have nothing for which she could wish to live."

"And if he loved another?"

"Henri le Sange love another!—forget his solemn vows so often plighted to me?" ejaculated Marceline, in a voice of the deepest emotion. "Never! I will not wrong him by such a supposition. Honour, truth, and virtue hold too powerful a place in his heart to suffer him to act with such cruel hypocrisy! If Henri le Sange still lives, his heart is unchanged, and must be, until it shall cease to beat for ever!"

Marceline gave utterance to these words with remarkable energy, and her eyes sparkled with more than usual brilliancy even, while Zitella appeared to listen to her with the most enthusiastic admiration.

"And if you were to learn that another damsel, with equal claims to his affection as yourself, and strictly virtuous and of noble birth, also loved him, and was ready to make any sacrifice for him—to lay down life itself to serve him, whose only happiness depended upon her meeting with a return of affection from him—would you sacrifice your own prospects to humanity, and resign his hand?" said Zitella.

"If he had bestowed his heart upon her, I would!"

"But if the love of this poor girl met with no return from him, if, although her heart should break, she should abandon her endeavours to engage his affection, although at the sacrifice of all her future hopes, and she should exert herself to restore your lover and yourself to each other—what would you then consider her?"

"As a damsel worthy the name of a heroine,"

answered Marceline; "one whom I could love with the affection of a dear sister!'

"Generous girl!" cried Zitella, seizing the hand of Marceline and pressing it fervently to her lips, while tears started to her eyes; "generous, noble girl, may I then hope that to me Marceline di Venoni will redeem that pledge?—that she will look upon the brigand girl with the love of a sister, when she shall find that I am not unworthy of it?"

"Upon you!" ejaculated Marceline, with the most indescribable astonishment, and a trembling sensation came over her.

"Yes," replied Zitella, "I am that unfortunate girl I have described; loving Henri le Sange to distraction, but meeting only with his esteem in return."

"Impossible!" cried Marceline, in a faltering voice.

"It is too true, alas!" returned Zitella, sighing deeply; "I am ready to run any risk to bring you together again, and thus better prove the strength of my love by my anxiety for his happiness!"

"I can scarcely believe the evidence of my senses," ejaculated Marceline, as she gazed upon the brigand girl with greater interest than ever. "Where did you see him?"

"Often when he was walking forth with you have I followed and watched him," replied Zitella; "and as I looked upon him, my soul took in deep draughts of that fatal passion which I now know can never be gratified. I felt that it was hopeless, and I knew that I was acting wrong in encouraging sentiments of such a description towards one whose heart was betrothed to another; but I could not help it. I was unable to conquer that passion which had gained so powerful an ascendancy over my heart, and I determined, wild and absurd as the idea may appear, to endeavour to find an opportunity to confess to him my love, and then, expecting the result, to tear myself from his sight for ever.'"

"But you found not the opportunity you sought?" demanded Marceline, with breathless impatience.

"I did," replied Zitella.

"Ah!—and you confessed to him your passion?" gasped forth Marceline.

"I did—I did, and quickly learnt my fate. Henri le Sange loves me not; but still am I happy in being assured that he does not hate me; nay, more, that I possess his esteem."

"Incredible!" cried Marceline. "But if you really do speak the truth, and sincerity sits upon your brow, when did you make the confession?"

"But a few days since," replied Zitella.

"A few days since!" repeated Marceline, starting, and hope once more illuming her countenance. "Can this be true? Where, oh where, did you see him?"

"I will prove to you the truth of that which I assert in a manner you little ex-

pect," replied Zitella; and without saying another word, but placing her finger significantly upon her lips to enjoin Marceline to silence and caution, she hastily quitted the cavern, fastening the door after her.

"What new event is about to happen to astonish and bewilder me?" exclaimed Marceline, when she had gone. "Can this strange girl have spoken the truth; and what is it she now intends doing?"

"Oh! signora," said Marie, "there is something in the manner of the brigand girl that convinces me she has not spoken falsely, however improbable what she has stated appears. Seldom have I seen a more lovely girl, and notwithstanding the degraded situation of life in which she is placed, I already feel for her esteem and admiration. Her features so strongly resemble a portrait of the unfortunate Duchess Monterino, the wife of the Duke Alberto, that I was struck with it the moment she entered."

"My heart throbs heavily against my side with anxiety," said Marceline, with her eyes fixed intently on the door, expecting every moment to see Zitella return, "Something of an extraordinary description, I am convinced, is about to take place."

Marie made no answer, but she was of the same opinion as Marceline, and awaited the return of Zitella with an impatience and curiosity equal to that of the former. Some time, however, elapsed, and still the brigand girl came not; and Marceline began to be afraid that she had deceived her, and had only invented the tale she had told her to excite her feelings and to gratify a feeling of jealousy, which, if she really did entertain the sentiments she pretended for Henri, she might have imbibed against her. And yet there was something in the countenance and manner of Zitella which seemed to give a direct contradiction to this supposition; and she endeavoured to banish it from her mind, although the manner in which she still absented herself was quite sufficient to increase rather than abate her suspicions.

While they both thus stood, anxiously looking for the return of the brigand girl, they heard a loud noise from the brigands, who were evidently carousing most merrily, and they trembled when they reflected that they were in the power of men who would not hesitate to commit any deed. There was a brief pause, but soon afterwards they heard the following chorus; and from their close proximity to the cavern in which the brigands usually assembled, they were enabled to distinguish every word—

Push the flask around,
   The brigand's life is free;
Let mirth and drink abound,—
   No friends of care are we!
There's none than us more bold,
   The traveller fears our will;
And this bright yellow gold
   Our coffers helps to fill!
Then push the flask around,
   The brigand's life is free;
Let mirth and drink abound,—
   No friends of care are we!"

Marceline and Marie listened to this rude chorus with more terror than admiration; but when the brigands had ceased, their attention was quickly drawn to something else much more particular. This was the withdrawing of the bolts that secured the door, and in a moment afterwards it opened, and the form of Zitella presented itself, followed closely by another, which Marceline no sooner recognised, than she uttered an hysterical shriek, and rushing hastily forward, she sunk senseless in the arms of her lover.

It would be impossible to do adequate justice in description to the emotions of delirious transport that filled the bosom of Henri as he once more pressed to his heart the form of his beloved Marceline. They could not find vent in words, but he covered her fair cheeks with kisses, and tears of delight traced each other down his manly face; while Zitella stood by and watched them with feelings which we may very well leave to the reader's imagination. Her cheeks were pale, and there was an expression of melancholy in her eyes, which evinced how much she was enduring. They were, however, suddenly aroused by the noise of hastily approaching footsteps; and before they had time to close the door, it was thrown wide back upon its hinges, and instantly Adolphe de Floriville stood before them!

If De Floriville was astonished at the group which presented itself to his eyes, Zitella and the others were no less confused and alarmed; but Marceline was suffering emotions of a very different description. The moment she gazed upon Adolphe, she turned as pale as death, and uttering a faint scream, she could scarcely save herself from fainting. In the countenance of De Floriville she recognised the exact resemblance of the miniature which her mother had suspended round her neck, and which caused so much excitement in the minds of Madame Laurette and her son when they beheld it.

The attention of Adolphe was more particularly directed to Marceline by her screaming, and he appeared to be completely struck and dumbfounded on gazing upon her. Henri and Zitella stood and gazed on in silence, too much surprised and bewildered to speak. It was a moment of the deepest interest and excitement to every person present, and an interval of some duration ensued.

"How beautiful!" at last ejaculated Adolphe, as if unconscious of the presence of any other but Marceline; "how beautiful, and yet how like her! I could almost imagine that she stood before me again, like ——But where is my imagination leading me to? Say, girl, art thou the beauteous Marceline di Venoni, to whom my son, Henri le Sange, as he calls himself, has devoted his heart?"

"Oh, father!" cried Henri in a tone of the deepest agony.

"Father!" screamed Marceline, and overcome by her powerful emotions she immediately fainted.

Henri caught the insensible beauty in his arms, and fixing upon De Floriville a look of unutterable reproach, he was about to speak, when there was a loud noise heard from the outer cavern; Zitella became pale with alarm, and had only time to exclaim—

"We have been watched—we are betrayed," when the door was thrown back upon its hinges, and the brigand chief and several of his gang entered the cavern.

"Ah! what means this?" he demanded, gazing with astonishment on his daughter, Adolphe, and Henri;—"what do you do here? Who has been the author of this?—Rinaldo?"

"I was led hither by accident," answered Adolphe, and his eyes flashed forth a malignant expression of exultation, "and found Zitella and my son here."

"Your son!" repeated the brigand, and he glanced with surprise and incredulity upon Adolphe; "your son!—What mean you?"

"That which I say," answered Adolphe; "I am the father of the youth who stands before you; he will not deny it."

"Is it true, Henri?" interrogated Alberto, for such we will in future call him.

"Alas! it is too true," replied Henri; "I am, unfortunately, the son of that fearful man, whose name if I should reveal——"

"Ah!" interrupted Adolphe, looking fiercely at his son, "you dare not—on your life you dare not! And yet it matters but little; mine is a name associated with the blackest of crimes, and I care not who is now made acquainted with them."

Henri, who was still supporting the insensible form of Marceline in his arms, groaned in the bitterness of his agony and shame.

"This mystery I must have explained at another time," said Alberto; then turning to his daughter, he added, "But what brought you hither, Zitella?"

"On an errand of love and sympathy," answered the brigand girl; "it was I who designed and effected this meeting between Henri le Sange and Marceline di Venoni."

"Ah!" exclaimed Alberto, astonished, "your rival in love, and——"

"No longer so, father," interrupted Zitella, firmly; "I resign that claim which only an ardent and sincere attachment has given me to the heart of Henri, since that heart, I am convinced, can never be mine."

"Noble girl!" Henri could not help ejaculating.

Alberto frowned slightly, and muttered a few incoherent words to himself; then turning to his daughter, he said—

"We must talk further of this at another opportunity; for the present, see to the recovery of Marceline, and then let her and Henri attend upon me in the cavern to which these men will conduct them. Follow me, Rinaldo."

Adolphe de Floriville prepared reluctantly to obey, but as he turned to follow Alberto, his eyes encountered the reproachful glances of his son, and hastily averting his gaze, he departed from the cavern.

For a few moments after they had gone, Zitella and Henri remained silently gazing upon each other, confused by the scene which had just been enacted; but at length Henri observed—

"Alas! fair Zitella, what a painful destiny is mine and this poor girl's. I claim your sympathy for one as gentle and as good as you are, and who, I am convinced, would love you as a sister."

"She has it," returned Zitella, in gentle accents; "in Zitella, Marceline di Venoni shall ever find a warm—an enthusiastic friend."

"Generous girl!" ejaculated Henri; "Heaven will reward you for this."

Zitella sighed.

"My own conscience," she replied, "will afford me an ample reward."

"It will—it will," answered Henri, as he resigned his fainting lover to the care of the brigand girl; "but alas! I fear that this discovery that I am the son of this man of crime will so shock her that she will never recover from it."

"It shall be my task to endeavour to console her," observed Zitella; "and happy shall I feel if I can succeed in releasing her from an hour of anguish only."

"Kind, noble-minded Zitella!" exclaimed Henri, in accents of enthusiastic admiration; "but, oh! explain to me how is it that Marceline is brought hither."

"Briefly I will explain," answered Zitella. "In my father you behold the Duke Alberto Monterino, the rightful inheritor of the title and estates Sigismund Monterino hath so long usurped."

"You astonish me."

"Hear me out. My father has a friend, who for some time hath been prosecuting his claim in the proper quarter, and with every prospect of success. Wishing to reproach Sigismund with his base conduct, my father determined to make an attack upon his casino, and convey him hither. He did so; Sigismund had got Marceline in his power, and, consequently, she was brought away with him."

"Ah!" cried Henri, his fine eyes flashing fury; "is, then, my detested foe an inmate of these caverns?"

"He is; but restrain your wrath—see—Marceline recovers."

Marceline, who, while this conversation was going on, had been most affectionately attended to by Zitella, now opened her eyes, and stared vacantly around her for a second or two, as if she was unconscious of where she was; but at length her eyes rested upon the countenance of her lover, and uttering a cry of joy, she said—

"Ah! it was not a dream, then;—I do, indeed, behold my Henri; but in what a fearful place. And, oh, that dreadful man, whose very aspect struck a nameless horror to my heart; and you called him father."

"Pray compose yourself, dearest Marceline," expostulated Henri; "all will shortly be explained, and happiness, I trust, is yet in store for us."

"Happiness!" repeated Marceline, with a melancholy shake of the head; "and are we not both detained prisoners here?"

"It may not be for long, lady," observed Zitella; "and do not, pray, give way to despair while you are here; rest assured that no harm will come to either of ye; and it shall be my study to relieve, by every means in my power, the irksomeness of confinement."

Marceline looked her thanks, but she could not speak; and at that moment one of the brigands, who had been waiting outside the door of the cavern, entered, and desired that they would be quick, and attend him and his companions to the cavern, according to the orders of their chief.

Marceline started at the order, and turned very pale, looking at Zitella and Henri for an explanation.

"Be not alarmed, dear Marceline," said the brigand girl; "I can answer for it that no harm shall come to you or your lover."

"And what does your father require of us, Zitella?" interrogated Henri: "he has some motive for seeking this interview."

"Certainly he has," answered Zitella, "but I know not what it is. We had better no longer delay."

Marceline endeavoured to become composed on these assurances of Zitella, yet she felt a secret dread of the interview. Leaning on the arm of her lover, and accompanied by Zitella, she prepared to follow the men who were to conduct them to their chief.

CHAPTER XX.

THE DISTRACTED PARENTS.

WE must now return to the friends of Marceline and Henri. Language cannot do adequate justice to the distraction of Signora Venoni at the disappearance of her daughter, and for some time after it was discovered that she was gone, no one could form the least idea of how, or where, although it was too evident that she had been taken away by force, she was in a state of insensibility, and the most fatal consequences were apprehended. Alas! in the dreadful state of mind which Madame Laurette was in at her own loss, she was not in a condition to impart the smallest consolation to her; and had it not been for the assiduous attention and exertions of Mr. Wakefield and his sister, her situation would have been doubly deplorable. They used the most prompt exertions to endeavour to discover Marceline; persons were despatched in every direction, and the strictest inquiries were made among the persons in the neighbourhood, but nothing satisfactory could be ascertained, nor the least clue be obtained to solve the mystery, or to give any means of conjecturing in what direction Marceline had been taken, or into whose power she had fallen. A very few moments' reflection served, however, to convince Mr. Wakefield that it was no other person than the Duke Monterino who could have been guilty of this act of villany, and Signora Venoni and Madame Laurette were of the same opinion.

"Alas!" ejaculated the former, wringing her hands, and deaf to all expostulation, "it is but too evident that Monterino is the vil- lain who has committed this cruel outrage; and, if she be in his power, there is no hope. My poor child will be lost—ruined—disgraced! Oh, God—I shall go mad!"

"Nay, my dear signora," remonstrated Mr. Wakefield, "pray endeavour to tranquillize your spirits: it may not be so bad as you apprehend. At any rate, if we waste the time in fruitless lamentations, the wretches who have Marceline in their power will be afforded time to effect their escape, and we may in vain endeavour to track them afterwards. It would be no difficult matter, I should imagine, to discover where Monterino is at present staying; and I will, there-

THE ATTACK OF THE BRIGANDS UPON THE CASINO.

fore, endeavour to find him out. Such offences are not to be committed with impunity."

"Monterino has power," sighed Signora Venoni.

"I heed it not," returned Mr. Wakefield. "There is no law to protect him in the perpetration of a crime like this. I will lose no time in seeking the guilty nobleman out."

"I fear," observed Signora Venoni, "you will find the task a more difficult one than you anticipate. If my poor child has indeed fallen into his power, it is certain that he would bear her to a place of secrecy and security, and where her friends would not be likely to trace her. Oh, Marceline—ill- fated Marceline, I shall never behold you again!"

A torrent of tears came to the relief of the agonised parent, and Madame Laurette, when she reflected upon her own loss, and the little prospect there was of her ever seeing Henri again, was in scarcely a better condition than herself.

Mr. Wakefield, seeing that it was useless to waste time in expostulations, left the disconsolate females under the care of his sister, and immediately left the villa to prosecute his inquiries.

Most indefatigable was he in his endeavours; but they were all to no purpose, for no person of whom he inquired had seen Monterino lately; and it was generally supposed that he was in England, for his possessing the casino to which he had conveyed Marceline was unknown to most persons.

Mr. Wakefield, however, felt satisfied that he had not gone to England, and determined to persevere in his researches. In the meantime, the agony of Signora Venoni increased, and she gave up her unfortunate daughter for lost, feeling confident that she had fallen a victim to the brutal passions of Monterino, who, she had not the least doubt, had likewise sacrificed Henri to his vengeance.

Madame Laurette, in spite of the note she had received, and which had come from the brigand chief, could not help being of the same opinion; and at times, when she thought of the utter hopelessness there appeared to be of her ever beholding her son again, her anguish became almost unendurable. Strange thoughts, which she was at a loss to understand, would at times steal over her imagination, and she foreboded yet an increase of misfortune, which she looked forward to with the utmost dread.

There were moments, however, when she could not but believe that Henri was still living, but that he was enduring still greater misery than her imagination could depicture; and then her agony would increase to an insupportable degree. She was in no condition to impart hope or consolation to her unfortunate friend, and they mingled their tears together, and lamented the melancholy destiny which fate had marked them both for.

Sometimes, too, dismal thoughts relative to her husband would rack her mind, and she was induced to believe that he still lived, and that some circumstance of an extraordinary description would bring them once more together. Frequently did the most fearful dreams haunt her imagination, and with which the guilty De Floriville was almost invariably connected; and she would start from her sleep, expecting to see him standing before her. So often did these visions occur to her, that she at last became confidentially impressed with the idea that they were destined to meet again; and she anticipated the time with the utmost terror.

These thoughts she communicated to Mrs. St. Aubyn, who endeavoured to combat them, but in vain; and Madame Laurette at length became so positive that it was to no purpose endeavouring to persuade her to the contrary.

Signora Venoni, in spite of her own troubles, could not but deeply commiserate with the misfortunes of Madame Laurette, although she could not form a correct idea of the source from whence they sprang, as they had neither of them communicated to one another the particulars of their history. They both knew that they had been unfortunate, and that their troubles originated in a similar manner from marriage; but anything further they were entirely ignorant of.

Frequently did Madame Laurette recall to her memory the circumstance of the miniature which Signora Venoni had let fall, and about which she evinced such powerful agitation; and the remarkable likeness which it bore to De Floriville haunted her imagination in the most mysterious manner; yet any definite conception upon the subject she could not form.

Mr. Wakefield still continued to persevere in his endeavours to discover the Duke Monterino, for he felt confident that Marceline was in his power; and he also had a very strong idea that Henri, if still living, was also detained a prisoner by him. His efforts, however, were still attended with no better success than they had been at first, although he had adopted the most ingenious plans to effect his designs, and had offered a very large reward for any information that might be furnished to him. He travelled to the neighbourhood of the different estates that belonged to Monterino, but could obtain no intelligence whatever of him; and he was half inclined to give over his researches in despair, and began to think that the duke had really gone to England.

At length, however, he accidentally learnt about the casino, whither Monterino had conveyed Marceline, although he could not learn anything of either of them; and thither he determined to depart, without any further delay. He did so, and arrived in its vicinity the very day after its destruction by fire, in which it was supposed that the duke, and all those persons who did not take to flight on the conflagration, had perished in the flames. He was unable to learn anything which could satisfy him that Marceline had been in the power of the duke; and he was, therefore, left in a more dreadful state of uncertainty than he had been before. He dreaded to communicate this intelligence to Signora Venoni, well convinced how much it would increase her anguish; but yet it was of no use his attempting to conceal the fact, as she would be certain to hear of it some time or other, and it might be imparted to her by one who would be less careful than herself.

Completely at a loss now in what manner he should act, he returned to the Villa di Venoni, where he found the signora more composed than she had been before he left it, but still suffering the most intense anguish. The information which Mr. Wakefield gave her of the destruction of the casino, came with a terrible shock upon her, for the impression was so strong upon her mind that Marceline had been in the Duke Monterino's power, that she could not divest herself of it, and with horror she concluded that her unfortunate daughter had met with the same melancholy fate which it was supposed had befallen Monterino. We need not, therefore, attempt to describe the agonising emotions of the signora, and for some time she defied all the efforts of Mr. Wakefield and his sister, and was quite inconsolable. Mr Wakefield exhausted all his arguments in vain; for, in fact, he was of the same melancholy opinion as Signora Venoni. Despair had now taken such firm hold of the unfortunate lady's mind, that she was confined to her bed, and for some time there did not appear the least hopes of her ultimate recovery; but at length the violence of her grief somewhat abated, and she became better; but all her future hopes were blighted, and there was nothing more in existence for which she could wish to live.

Mr. Wakefield, notwithstanding he entertained scarcely any hope that they would again hear anything of Marceline, was still most unremitting in the inquiries which he made; but, as they had been before, they were all entirely ineffectual; and it was only to appease the anguish of the signora that he continued his search.

Madame Laurette had now quite given up all thoughts of beholding her son again, notwithstanding the note which she had received, and in the purport of which she entertained no confidence; but there were times when her thoughts were half inclined to waver upon that subject; but the feeling was only a transient one, and her mind would again settle down into all the deep melancholy of despair.

Several weeks had now elapsed since the mysterious disappearance of Marceline, when one evening the servant of Signora Venoni entered the room in which she was seated, and presented her with a note, which she said had been brought to the villa by a strange man, muffled up in a large cloak, who hastily departed after having delivered the letter, which was directed to Signora Venoni.

"Ah!" ejaculated Madame Laurette, who was present at the time, and whose eyes hastily glanced at the superscription, as the signora held it in her hand; "the characters are in the same handwriting as the note which was lately left in so mysterious a manner in my chamber. I could swear to them."

Signora Venoni was in a state of the greatest agitation and suspense, and having hastily glanced at the contents, she turned very pale, and handed it to Madame Laurette, without speaking a word. The contents ran briefly as follows:—

"Signora Venoni may rest her mind contented; Marceline, her daughter, is quite safe, and will, probably, ere long, be restored uninjured to her arms. The Duke Monterino has it no longer in his power to harm her."

"What a strange mystery is this!" cried Madame Laurette. "Who can be the author of this epistle? and if the writer speaks the truth, what motives can he have for his conduct? This is evidently written, as I said before, by the same individual who wrote the note which I received a short time since."

"But think you there is any hope that the purport of this letter is true?" eagerly inquired Signora Venoni.

"Oh, yes—yes!" replied Madame Laurette, whose hopes began again to revive, and who

was glad of the opportunity thus afforded her of appeasing the anguish and despair of her unfortunate friend; "whoever the writer of this may be, I cannot imagine, neither what reasons they can have for their singular conduct; but I cannot divest my mind of the belief that there is some truth in the statement which the note contains, and that we may see those unfortunate beings, so dear to us, again."

Signora Venoni clasped her hands together, and raising her eyes towards Heaven, devoutly exclaimed—

"Almighty God! I thank thee! Preserve my child! Restore her unsullied to my arms, and the equally unfortunate Henri to his parent, and my every wish in life will be at once gratified."

Most cordially did Madame Laurette reciprocate this prayer, and Mr. Wakefield and his amiable sister, who were in the room at the time, also most fervently and sincerely expressed the same wishes. Their hopes, however, were not so sanguine as those of the signora and Madame Laurette appeared to be, and they were entirely at a loss to conceive who the individuals could be who chose to act in so strange a manner.

"But," asked Mr. Wakefield of the servant, "should you know the man again?"

"I should not," replied the girl, "for I did not see his features, which were concealed beneath the folds of his mantle."

"There must be some truth in the matter," observed Signora Venoni, "or why should the writer of this epistle take so much trouble, and which cannot, that I see, benefit him?"

Mr. Wakefield and the others expressed the same opinion, and endeavoured all in their power to strengthen the hopes that the signora had imbibed.

"From what the note states respecting the Duke Monterino," remarked Madame Laurette, "our surmises as to his fate appear to be correct; and you will, therefore, have nothing more to fear from him."

"True," answered the signora; "but still there is such a tone of mystery about it, that I feel myself totally at a loss to unravel it. The handwriting is the same, you say, my dear madame, as that in the note which you received?"

"I am positive of it," answered Madame Laurette; "and from that circumstance, as I have said before, if Henri and Marceline are really still living, that they are both in the power of the same persons."

"It does, indeed, seem probable," observed Signora Venoni. "Heaven send that it may be so, and that they may shortly be again restored to our embraces. I feel my hopes revive at the thought, and something appears to whisper to me that they will be realised.'

Most fervently did every one respond to this wish, and they felt more tranquillised than they had done for some time before. Mr. Wakefield, however, determined not to relax in his inquiries, and was disposed to believe that, if there was any truth at all in what the note stated, some person who could give the desired information might be tempted by the liberal reward which had been offered to come forward.

After some time, he was enabled to discover that Marceline had actually been in the power of the Duke Monterino, and that the casino had been attacked by a gang of ruffians, who, no doubt, were brigands, and that it had been set on fire, as they imagined, purposely Any further intelligence as to whether Monterino and Marceline had or had not perished in the flames, Mr. Wakefield was unable to learn; although several bodies had been found in the ruins, but so disfigured that it was impossible to recognise them.

There are moments when our hearts become so worked upon by affliction—when the barbed arrow of care hath implanted itself so deeply in our bosoms, that every other feeling at length becomes chained up, bondaged in the fetters of apathy, of despair—when the sources of grief are exhausted, the founts dried up, and the heavily laden heart may seek in vain for relief in tears—when the sufferer can view with apparent indifference any fresh calamity, and the person who is unacquainted with the individual who evinced such conduct, would be inclined to imagine them entirely callous to all sense of feeling, and possessing a heart alike dead to its own woes and the miseries of others.

To such a state as this had Signora Venoni and Madame Laurette arrived; and they sat in each other's society throughout the day, in a state of placid despair. They seldom spoke, and when they did, it was upon the subject of their bereavement, upon which they conversed with a calm melancholy, neither appearing to indulge too sanguinely in hope, nor yet entirely to crush its cheering influence.

To those persons who did not know their dispositions or their feelings, it would probably have appeared that their heavy loss had made but little, if any impression upon them; and they might have accused them of being insensible to the feelings of nature. But Mr. Wakefield, who was too good a judge of the human mind, and who well knew the dispositions of the ladies, he saw much more to apprehend in their apparent apathetical conduct, than in any outrageous or violent display of grief. He saw that incessant grief, anxiety, suspense, and disappointment, had so worked upon their feelings, until their hearts had become, in a manner of speaking, blanks; and anguish was working upon their vitals in a manner which was more likely to be productive of the most fatal consequences than the most violent and continued expression of sorrow. All that he could possibly imagine which was likely to restore them to a different state of mind, the reader may be certain that he did, and in his efforts he was, as usual, most ably

assisted by Mrs. St. Aubyn, without whose society, under the peculiar circumstances under which they had been placed, it is impossible to say what the two amiable ladies would have done. She was never at a loss for remarks of the most gentle, yet persuasive nature to solace them, and it was very seldom her observations failed to have their due effect. Signora Venoni and our heroine always listened to her with avidity and pleasure, for they were convinced they were dictated by truth and sincerity, and that she felt as deeply interested in their welfare as they could themselves. The only times when peace and hope were permitted to enter the bosoms of Signora Venoni and Madame Laurette, it was occasioned by the excellent advice and soothing influence of Mr. Wakefield and Mrs. St. Aubyn, an obligation which they did not fail most warmly to acknowledge; but the amiable brother and sister felt too happy in being able to afford them any consolation, to require anything of the kind; and they frequently expressed themselves to that effect; but, although the signora and our heroine were the last persons in the world to flatter, their hearts were too full of gratitude to suffer them to do otherwise than to assure them how greatly they felt indebted to them for their unremitting kindness.

Mr. Wakefield, after a variety of conflicting thoughts, still could not help firmly believing that both Henri and Marceline were still living, and however involved in mystery the affair might at present be, something seemed to impress upon his mind a conviction that they would yet be restored uninjured to them.

He continued to prosecute his inquiries with the most untiring and persevering skill, but he was at present unable to learn more than he had already done.

Thus elapsed another fortnight without any material change; nor did there seem to be any particular alteration in the behaviour of Signora Venoni and Madame Laurette; they appeared to have resigned themselves entirely to the will of Providence, and trusted that He would not yet suffer them to sink into the gulph of despair.

One evening the two ladies, accompanied by Mrs. St. Aubyn, had left the villa, and wandered a considerable distance from it, tempted by the fineness of the weather; when, on their turning to retrace their steps homewards, the atmosphere suddenly became overcast—large drops of rain descended, and everything portended a violent coming storm.

Mrs. St. Aubyn looked eagerly around.

"We are a considerable way from the villa," said Mrs. St. Aubyn, "and it is very evident that a storm is rapidly approaching. We must endeavour to find some place of shelter until it has passed away."

"I do not see any place near at hand,

said Madame Laurette ; " we were foolish to venture so far."

" Not many minutes' walk to the right of this spot," said Signora Venoni, " in the valley yonder, there is the ruin of an ancient temple, which, if we can but reach it before the storm comes on too violently, will afford us ample shelter until it is over."

They now hurried on their way with as much precipitation as possible, and soon arrived at the place where the ruins of the temple were situated, and they had only just sought a retreat in it, when the thunder rolled terrifically, the rain began to descend in heavy torrents, and the blue forked lightning to flash along the sky.

Signora Venoni, who was extremely timid of anything of the kind, clung closer to Mrs. St. Aubyn and Madame Laurette, as they took their shelter in the temple ; and they expected every moment that the violence of the tempest would send some of the old ruins about their heads.

" What a fearful night, after so fine an evening," observed Signora Venoni.

" It is by far too violent to last long," replied Mrs. St. Aubyn ; " but let us get further into the interior of the ruin, for this place does not entirely shelter us from the rain."

" It is unfortunate that we should have wandered so far," observed our heroine, " for should the storm not abate, we shall be obliged to remain here, and these ruins are not very pleasant, that's evident."

" We are still some distance from the villa," said Signora Venoni, " and they will be alarmed at our lengthened absence !—Ah ! —there was a crash !"

" And the lightning, how vividly it blazes," rejoined Madame Laurette ; " such storms as these are not peculiar to Italy, signora ?"

" They are not," replied the latter, " and, therefore, they alarm us the more, when they come so unexpectedly upon us. Holy Virgin ! what was that ?"

" What ?"

" Did ye not hear a rustling noise as if of some person moving about in the farther end of the ruins ?" answered Signora Venoni, her dark eyes endeavouring to penetrate into the deep obscurity beyond.

" I heard no sound of the kind," said our heroine.

" Nor I," added Mrs. St. Aubyn ;—" it was only the voice of the tempest."

" Oh, no," returned the signora, impatiently, " it was not that ; and even but this instant I could almost have sworn that I saw a dark object moving in the background of the place where we are standing."

Madame Laurette's terror overcame her, and she clung to Mrs. St. Aubyn, who, of course, was the firmest of the party.

" Oh," she cried, " should banditti lurk within these ruins, and it is not at all unlikely that they do, we shall be lost."

" Hush ! hush ! be calm, dear madame," said Mrs. St. Aubyn, " I do not think that there is any occasion for any apprehension of the kind ; still, I regret that my brother is not with us."

" There, again—did you not hear that ?" suddenly exclaimed Signora Venoni, starting, and looking in the same direction as she had done before.

Mrs. St. Aubyn and our heroine both this time heard the sound of a person moving about, apparently at the back of the ruins, as Signora Venoni had before described it, and involuntarily directing their eyes towards the same place where the former was gazing, they at the same moment imagined they beheld the dark shadow of some object moving about.

Mrs. St. Aubyn, although really alarmed, kept her self-possession, and conquered her fears as much as she possibly could, to prevent her two trembling companions from entirely sinking ; in a voice of firmness, therefore, she demanded, at the same time advancing a few paces forward :—

" Is there anybody there ? If there be, let them speak."

There was no answer returned to this interrogatory ; and, after a pause, Mrs. St. Aubyn became emboldened, and taking courage, in spite of the expostulations of Signora Venoni and Madame Laurette, she advanced right into the gloom beyond, and examined minutely every nook and corner, but she saw nothing, and after all she returned to her companions, and endeavoured to reassure them.

" After all," she remarked, " the sounds we heard, and the form that we saw, could only have been imagination."

" Oh, no," returned the signora, " I am positive it was not imagination only ; I heard the sounds and saw the form too distinctly to be deceived by that."

" Well, then, probably, if it was a human being, it was only some person seeking shelter from the fury of the storm, like ourselves," returned Mrs. St. Aubyn.

" Ay, certainly—a most reasonable observation," observed Madame Laurette ; " at any rate, no person seems inclined to interrupt us here, and, therefore, what have we to fear ?"

" True," said Mrs. St. Aubyn ; " we may, I have no doubt, remain here safely enough until the storm has subsided."

Only two or three observations of no importance now passed between the friends, and they remained standing on the same spot without any interruption.

The storm had gradually decreased, until at length it entirely subsided, and glad enough of the circumstance, the three ladies prepared to leave the ruins, and to trace their footsteps to the Villa di Venoni with all the expedition possible. They hurried through the dilapidated apartments, until at length they emerged from the building ; but had not done so a moment when the tall figure of a man, habited as a brigand, issued from the further end of it. Terror overcame the three friends at this unexpected sight, as may well be imagined, and they became transfixed and motionless.

The man's back was at first turned towards them when they first beheld him, but he turned suddenly round, and the rays of the moon, which had immediately arisen on the abating of the storm, fell full upon his features, so that they became revealed clearly to every one present. Madame Laurette and the Signora di Venoni both uttered a most piercing shriek at the same moment, and our heroine exclaiming—

"Oh, God! De Floriville again!"

And the signora ejaculating—

"Gracious Heaven! it is *Le Clerq!*" They both clung vehemently to Mrs. St. Aubyn, and their agitation became so great, that she feared they would become insensible.

As for the guilty De Floriville, for he it certainly was, he seemed rivetted to the spot with astonishment. Such an unexpected meeting with our heroine filled him with delight and amazement, and he was about to rush forward and to claim her, but suddenly his eyes rested upon the countenance of Signora di Venoni, and it was extraordinary to notice the change that in an instant came over him; his cheeks became as pale as death —his eyes rolled wildly about—his lips quivered—and he started back a few paces, seeming almost ready to sink to the earth with the excess of his emotion. At length, however, he fixed one more look of intense and fearful meaning upon the signora and our heroine, and hurried from the spot.

There was a dead pause of a minute or two, and the three females were all fixed, motionless as statues, to the spot, gazing vacantly towards the direction whence De Floriville had disappeared. But why the uncommon emotion of Signora Venoni? Wherefore the mysterious exclamation she had made use of when she beheld the guilty Adolphe de Floriville? The whole truth will shortly be explained.

"Le Clerq! villain! deceiver!" she cried; "whither art thou gone? Come back again! My wrongs cry aloud for retribution!"

"Le Clerq!" replied Madame Laurette, taken in a moment off her guard; "you are deceived, signora. It is my husband—the wretched, guilty Adolphe de Floriville!"

"Your husband!" screamed the signora, wildly; "it is false! He is mine! Mine alone! The father of my unfortunate Marceline!"

Had the lightning of Heaven at that moment have struck Madame de Floriville, she could not have exhibited greater horror and astonishment than she did on hearing Signora di Venoni give utterance to these expressions; but, imagining that the unfortunate lady must be labouring under some extraordinary and fearful delusion, she endeavoured to recover her composure. But the shock she had received from seeing her guilty husband again was quite sufficient of itself to overpower her; and it was not without a most powerful struggle with her feelings that she was enabled to prevent herself from fainting.

Signora Venoni, in the meantime, had clung to one of the pillars of the ruins, and her eyes were fixed wildly in the direction whither De Floriville had disappeared. Her countenance was livid—her lips ghastly; and it was only by the heavy and hysterical throbbing of her bosom that any person could have told that she was a thing of life. Her whole faculties were evidently absorbed in horror and surprise.

Mrs. St. Aubyn was placed in a most awkward predicament; for, should our heroine and Signora di Venoni get any worse, what could she do with them in that place, and without any assistance? The whole affair had been so sudden that she scarcely had time to give it a thought; but the circumstance, as may well be imagined, filled her bosom with the most unqualified astonishment. She felt too well convinced, from what she had heard of Madame de Floriville's history (and she, as we have before mentioned, had made her her entire confidant), that she was correct; but never having heard even a hint of the wretched, guilty Adolphe having a second wife, she could not in any way account for the conduct of the signora, and the singular alarm she had evinced.

Madame de Floriville was the first to recover her composure; and, approaching Mrs. St. Aubyn, she laid her hand gently upon her arm, and, in a voice of melancholy sadness, said—

"Oh, Mrs. St. Aubyn, it is him—it is De Floriville! There are more troubles in store for me. Alas! what will become of me? It is him—it is him!"

"Him!" exclaimed Signora Venoni, catching at the words of our heroine, and hastening with delirious speed towards Mrs. St. Aubyn and Madame de Floriville. "Yes—yes; it is him! But you know him not— you cannot. I had hoped never more to behold him again. But he has stalked before me like a fiend of darkness. This is the secret I have long had hidden in my breast. This is my husband—the father of my child —who plundered me of all he could, and then deserted me!"

"Oh, God!" cried Madame de Floriville, in a voice of indescribable emotion: "recall your words, or I am, indeed, more truly wretched than I have hitherto believed myself to be."

"Recall my words!" shrieked the signora, and she fixed her eyes wildly upon the countenance of our heroine. "Why should I do so? Twenty years since, the villain we have just seen won my heart in Italy, under the name of the Chevalier Le Clerq, and I became his wife. The fruits of our unhappy union was Marceline, soon after whose birth he plundered me and then deserted me."

A deadly chill fell upon the heart of Madame de Floriville, and she could scarcely find power to speak.

"Good God! Can this, indeed, be true?"

she ejaculated. "Are you not really mistaken? Four-and-twenty years since I married this awful man, under the name of Adolphe de Floriville. He is my Henri's father, and bitter, indeed, have been my sufferings. Many, many years have I been separated from him, and it is some time since 1 before saw him. I hoped the grave had at last closed upon his numerous crimes."

Signora Venoni looked for a moment or two at Madame de Floriville in stupefied amazement: her lips were separated, and her bosom heaved violently; but it was evident that she had not the power to speak. At length, however, she seemed gradually to regain strength, although her looks were wild and mysterious; and passing her hands across her forehead, she said, in somewhat strange tones—

"What frightful dream is this? or what terrible and unnatural idea would you instil into my thoughts? I tell you again it is my husband—it is the villain, Le Clerq!"

The horror of Madame de Floriville overcame her: she uttered a piercing shriek, and sunk insensible on the earth. Signora di Venoni stood gazing at her for a second or two, as if unconscious of what was passing; then, suddenly, the truth appeared to flash upon her brain, and, with a deep groan, she fell inanimate in the arms of Mrs. St. Aubyn.

CHAPTER XXI.

THE BIGAMIST.

FLORETTA CALDERONI, which was Signora Venoni's right name, was the only daughter of a most illustrious family in Italy, and from childhood was celebrated for her uncommon beauty, which surpassed in its lustre most of the other fair damsels of that sunny clime. She was not more than sixteen when she had a host of admirers, who sought her hand and her affections, but none on whom she could fix her heart. Indeed, she was yet too young and thoughtless to entertain the sentiments with which they sought to inspire her; and her parents, whose whole happiness was centred in her, would not attempt to bias her wishes, but left her to act entirely as her feelings prompted her, fully convinced that she possessed too much good sense, discernment, and prudence, to act any otherwise than as rectitude would dictate to her.

Thus elapsed three more years of Floretta's life, when a terrible calamity happened to her, from which it was a considerable time ere she could recover. This was the death of both her parents. They were attacked by a malignant fever, which, in three days only from the commencement of their illness, terminated in their death, within a few hours of each other.

This was a most dreadful shock to Floretta, who thus, in so short a space of time, found herself left an orphan; and, for some time, she was completely inconsolable. Never had parents behaved with more affection towards their offspring than they had done to her; and, therefore, did she feel their loss the more severely.

She was left under the protection of the Count Bertram Schedoni and his lady, who bore the most amiable characters, and who received the poor unfortunate mourner with the same affection as if they had been her parents, and did all they could to console her under her heavy loss. Floretta had been used to the count and his family from childhood, and had ever been fondly attached to them; therefore, it was not at all surprising that she should listen to their advice with the most profound attention, and was the more likely to be consoled by it.

Time wore away the damsel's grief; but the impression could never be entirely effaced from her memory. No: there had the sainted images of her fond parents fixed themselves, and must remain while life continued.

In the course of a few months, Floretta again appeared as lovely as ever, and, perhaps, by far more interesting, which was caused by the gentle tone of melancholy which pervaded her manners, and the expression of her countenance. Again a train of ardent admirers and eager suitors flocked around her, and sought, by every means in their power, to win her affections; but, although she looked upon all with esteem, and behaved with the utmost urbanity towards them, she did not see one on whom she could entirely fix her love, and acting with that candour which was characteristic of her nature, did not give them any encouragement in the characters which they wished to appear.

Floretta at length became of age, and came into the full enjoyment of the great wealth to which she was heiress. But happy as she was beneath the roof of the Count Schedoni, she had no inclination to leave it, and continued to remain there as one of the family, and showed by her sweetness of disposition her gratitude for the parental attention of the amiable nobleman and his lady towards her.

It was some time after this that the villain Adolphe de Floriville had been leading a gay and reckless life in Italy, under the assumed name of Chevalier Arnaud; but at length, having nearly exhausted all his means, he removed to another part of the country, taking the name of the Chevalier le Clerq, being compelled to adopt some plan or the other to better his fortunes.

He made a most fashionable appearance, and the hypocrisy of his manner deceived most persons who saw him, and who took him to be a most estimable character.

It was an unfortunate accident for Floretta which introduced Adolphe to her; for the moment she beheld him, her heart became his captive. The count and his lady were also greatly prepossessed in his favour, and every encouragement was given to his visits. They quickly saw that Adolphe had made a favourable impression upon the heart of Floretta, and they were by no means sorry for it; for the former had acted his part so well, that they firmly believed him to be a most estimable character; and from the manner he had represented his connections, they considered his pretensions to her hand as most unexceptionable.

The crafty—the designing and insidious De Floriville did not fail to follow up the advantage which he quickly perceived he had gained, with all that consummate skill which distinguished him in any deed of villany, and, by his insinuating manners, at length gained entire possession of Floretta's heart. He acknowledged he loved her, and at last succeeded in eliciting from her a confession of the sentiments with which she regarded him; and having referred him to the count, he received his approbation, and the day was appointed for their nuptials. A most unfortunate day was that for the much injured Floretta—better had it been for her if it had been her last!

We need not attempt to describe the inward exultation of Adolphe at his triumph; fortune was again before him, and he could scarcely contain his joy within the bounds of reason. Yet there were moments when he would endure the most bitter agony; when the forms of Laurette and Henri would rise upon his imagination, and conscience would keenly upbraid him for the villanous, the monstrous part he was acting. The ghastly phantom of the murdered Eugene was also continually before his eyes, and rendered his happiness but transient.

He contrived, however, to conquer his feelings when in the presence of Floretta and her friends, and then appeared all vivacity, love, and gallantry.

At length the day of the union arrived, and Floretta became the bride of the guilty Adolphe de Floriville, knowing him only as the Chevalier le Clercq, in which name she was married to her! Fatal day to her! Little did she imagine the villain to whom she had sacrificed himself; little did she think how basely he had deceived her, and that he sought alone her ruin.

By an unfortunate codicil in the will of Floretta's father, nearly the whole of her wealth upon her marriage came into Adolphe's power; and it was not long after they had been united that he began to pursue again his old courses of extravagance and dissipation, and at length he would remain from home for a night or two at the gaming-house; and he lost large sums of money. It was a terrible blow to the happiness of Floretta when she saw the conduct of her husband, and now for the first time discovered his vicious propensities, and the ultimate ruin which must of course follow, if he persisted in the same career. But still her love for him was unabated, and although she gently reproached him for his conduct, and advised him to desist ere it was too late, it was more in sorrow than in anger that she did so.

As he had promised our unfortunate heroine, he affected to be ashamed of his conduct, and made many vows of amendment, which, we need not say, he invariably broke; and at length a continued run of ill-luck was the means of reducing the once ample fortune of Floretta to but a moderate independence.

Floretta bore this with much greater fortitude than might have been expected, and could she have depended upon its producing a beneficial change in the conduct of De Floriville, she would have been content.

None felt more severely for the fate of Floretta than the Count and Countess Schedoni, and they perceived too late that she had become linked to a villain. The good old count often ventured to talk to De Floriville, to warn him of the consequences of his ways. At first he pretended to listen to him with patience, and to receive his advice in good part; but he afterwards showed a different feeling, and ultimately peremptorily desired the count to trouble himself about his own business; that he was master of his own actions, and needed not the advice of any one, as he had long since escaped from leading-strings.

It was with the most bitter anguish that the count heard this; but he forbore to mention it to Floretta, unwilling to increase the grief under which she must already suffer, especially as she was near her confinement.

Adolphe did not frequent his old haunts for a few weeks, and Floretta was in hopes that he had determined to reform; and notwithstanding the greater portion of her fortune had been squandered away by him, she could have freely pardoned him for the past. Alas! it was but the temporary calm before the fury of the tempest descended upon her head.

A few nights after this, Adolphe returned home at a late hour, and in a state of mind which plainly showed that something particular had occurred to vex him. He threw himself in a chair, despairingly, and, clasping his forehead, seemed in a state of great mental anxiety.

Floretta approached him, and laying her hand upon his shoulder, addressed him in her usual tender and affectionate manner.

"Tell me, my love, my Le Clerq," she said, "what has occurred to distress you thus? Oh, do not conceal anything from the bosom of you wife, who——"

"My wife, Floretta!" repeated Adolphe with a wild look; "my wife!"

"Yes, my love," tenderly returned Floretta; "your own wife—your affectionate Floretta."

"Oh, speak not to me, Floretta—speak to me not," ejaculated Adolphe, in a tone of despair. "I am a wretch unworthy of you, deserving only of your hatred and scorn!"

"What mean you?"

"What mean I? Have not my wild and dissipated habits already nearly squandered away the whole of your wealth? And now again, after the vows I had pledged to you that I would abandon the cursed dice, this night I have been again enticed into the guilty haunts of ruin, and lost a large sum of money."

"Heaven give thee strength to withstand the temptation in future," calmly exclaimed Floretta, raising her beautiful eyes towards Heaven as she spoke. "But I will not reproach thee; no, my husband, again I supplicate thee to repent, and heed not that which thou hast lost. Thank God! we have still enough left to live in comfort, if not in splendour; and if thou wilt but do as I desire, I shall be too blest—too happy!"

"Noble, generous-minded woman!" cried Adolphe; "what a villain have I been to thee. And wilt thou again take my word?"

"I will—I will!" answered Floretta; "and something assures me that thou wilt not again deceive me."

"Oh, this is too kind—too confiding—too affectionate!"

"You know, my dearest Theodore, that I shall shortly become a mother; and I know that our little one will so engage thy affections, that thou wilt not be happy out of its sight."

"I should be a monster of the blackest dye," cried the guilty Adolphe, whom Floretta knew only as Theodore le Clerq, "did I

ALBERTO FORCES SIGISMUND TO WRITE A CONFESSION OF HIS CRIMES.

again deceive such innocence as this! Floretta, canst thou, indeed, forgive me?"

"Say no more about it, my love," replied Floretta, with a sweet smile. "Come, come —chase the gloom from thy brow; thou wilt promise me not again to frequent those ruinous haunts, and I shall be perfectly happy."

"Promise!" exclaimed Adolphe, with an air of fervour, "I will swear—I will take any oath; and a hateful, despicable wretch I should be were I to again deceive thee, and——"

"Oh, I will take your word—I need not your oath, dear Theodore," cried Floretta;

"but dissipate this melancholy. Let me see you smile, and we shall again be happy."

And, as the gentle Floretta spoke, she threw her delicate and exquisitely moulded arms around the neck of the deceiver, and with an angelic smile, pressed her lips vehemently to his cheeks.

The guilty Adolphe, callous as he was could not help shuddering when he thought of the crimes he had perpetrated, and the manner in which he had deceived her. But it must be remembered that at that time Adolphe knew not that our heroine was still living; neither had he taken any trouble to ascertain whether she was or not. He, however, returned the caresses of his wife, and the too-confiding Floretta, forgetting at once the past, and believing all he said for the future, felt the most unbounded happiness, and did not for a moment suspect that he would again deceive her. Alas! little did she know the villain upon whom she had, unfortunately, thrown herself away, or how truly wretched would she have been.

For several weeks after this, Adolphe closely adhered to the promise he had made, and was seldom or never absent from home, and then only when business called him. He behaved to Floretta with the utmost attention and kindness, and she had no cause to suspect that he would again deceive her.

The Count and Countess Schedoni frequently visited Floretta, and they marked with the most acute anguish the change which de Floriville had wrought in her circumstances. They saw plainly that her fate had become linked to that of a most incorrigible villain; but it was useless, they knew, to talk to her upon the subject, as it would only render her doubly miserable and not in the least alter her situation, unless she would again accept of their protection; and even should she do that, it was not at all likely that Adolphe would cease to annoy her.

Floretta never murmured or complained to them, and it was only by the alteration which they perceived in her looks that they could tell the sorrow which she at times experienced.

And a poor, miserable, guilty being was Adolphe de Floriville; his conscience continually upbraided him for the manner in which he had behaved towards the beauteous Floretta, and the awful phantom of the murdered Eugene de Buoisson continually haunted his sight, and often did he feel the cold—the clammy—the awful Death Grasp, the same as when the dying man had fixed it upon his throat in his last death-struggle. Since his union with Floretta his agony had been increased tenfold; when he slept, it was but to be tormented with the most frightful visions, from which he was awakened to encounter the still more terrible reality—the ghastly spectres of his murdered victims, Eugene and his brother.

It was strange that a man thus dreadfully tormented should still persist in pursuing a career of crime. Any one would have thought that such an accumulation of horrors would have aroused him to repentance, in the hope of being released from them; but it was not so with Adolphe de Floriville; the more his earthly torments increased, the more desperately did he seem to plunge into the vortex of crime and dissipation. In one sense he was to be pitied, for there appeared to be a spell upon him, from which he could not escape; and he might truly have been called the doomed man.

At length that deeply interesting period, the accouchement of Floretta, arrived, and she was safely delivered of that beauteous girl who has been introduced to the reader as Marceline. Adolphe appeared to hail the little stranger with much delight and affection; and Floretta, as she gazed with eager eyes upon the countenance of the little innocent, felt all the rapture of the young mother for her first born, and an increase of love for her husband. She removed her eyes from the face of her babe, fixed them with an indescribable look of tenderness upon Adolphe, who was seated by her side, and throwing her head upon his shoulder, fell into a paroxysm of tears and sobs. How could the hypocrite endure this? Most keenly did his conscience smite him. He tried to speak, but could not; but he pressed Floretta to his bosom, and seeming to return all her affection, she was too blessed, too happy, and satisfied.

Floretta was almost constantly attended during her confinement by the Countess Schedoni, whose maternal attentions were a great source of comfort to the former, and served materially to advance her convalescence.

Marceline was a fine, healthy child, and even in infancy displayed that extraordinary beauty for which she was afterwards so celebrated; and even Adolphe could not help gazing upon her with a feeling of love and admiration.

Possessed of a naturally strong constitution, and happy in the imagination of the love her husband bore his offspring, Floretta speedily recovered; and in the many cares which attention to her child required, she found more exquisite pleasure than she had for some time before experienced. But she little anticipated the dreadful shock which was in store for her.

Hitherto the conduct of Adolphe had been most unexceptionable, and the Count and Countess Schedoni, as well as Floretta, really imagined that he had seen the folly and iniquity of his ways, and had determined upon a reform; and, although the devastation he had already caused in her pecuniary affairs was very great, they hailed such an occurrence with pleasure, as the peace of mind of her whom they loved as affectionately as if she had been their own daughter, would be saved from total destruction. They were all soon, however, undeceived.

For a few weeks after the convalescence of Floretta, Adolphe continued very well, and was unabated in his attentions to her, and in evincing his love for the little Marceline. But at that time he was contemplating one of the most diabolical designs which could possibly enter the human mind.

Although he played the part of the hypocrite before Floretta and her friends, in private Adolphe felt himself truly wretched. On the one hand, conscience smote him for the deceptive part he was acting, and on the other, his old propensities worked so powerfully on his mind, that he could not withstand the temptation. To remain with Floretta in his present situation, he felt would be utterly impossible. The tempting demon was at work again within him, and urged him on to the same succession of crimes that had hitherto marked his guilty career. Again and again he ruminated what plan he should adopt to escape from the trammels in which he was held, and to be able to mingle in his old scenes and with his former associates; and at length he determined to collect all the money together he could find, and abandon Floretta and her child for ever!

This base resolution, however, he could not put into execution without some hesitation; and when he beheld the innocent and affectionate smiles of Floretta, he mentally cursed himself for one of the most heartless and, diabolical scoundrels in existence! Nothing, notwithstanding, could make him swerve from his determination, and he only watched an opportunity to put it into execution. This soon presented itself.

Floretta, with her infant, had gone on a visit to the Count and Countess Schedoni, and Adolphe excused himself from accompanying her, on the plea that he had business to transact that day which he must attend to, but that he would call for her in the evening. Floretta was satisfied, and they separated. She had not long been gone, when the villain completed his infamous plot.

Poor Floretta waited in the utmost agony and anxiety hour after hour of the time which Adolphe had promised to call for her; and when she found that he still did not come, her uneasiness became so great, that she could not contain herself, and the Count Schedoni at length yielded to her wishes and accompanied her home.

They no sooner entered the house, than the fatal truth was presented to them. The money-chest was standing open, emptied of its contents, and the whole of Floretta's jewellery which he could, the wretch had taken with him. On the table was a note in his handwriting, in which he laconically bade her farewell for ever, telling her that she need not entertain the slightest hopes of seeing him again.

The senses of Floretta immediately left her on this horrible discovery, and for several hours she remained in such a state as quite beggars description. The count despatched a domestic to the countess with the particulars of the circumstance, and she quickly attended, and never left the bed-side of the sufferer the whole of the night. The whole of the following day Floretta was completely delirious, and raved incessantly of her husband, and the barbarous manner in which he had treated her.

The count and countess were quite shocked at the inhuman behaviour of Adolphe, and, had they not too certain proof of its truth, they could not have believed that such heartless, such systematic, such cold-blooded villany could exist in human nature.

Every attention was paid to the unfortu-nate Floretta; but so powerful was the effect which it had upon her, that her medical attendants were at first fearful that the most fatal results would ensue; but by their skilful treatment, the goodness of her own constitution, and the unremitting attentions of the count and countess, she did gradually recover; but a settled melancholy had fallen upon her heart, which nothing could remove. She never even mentioned the name of her husband; but pressing her offspring frantically to her breast, she passively suffered herself to be led to the vehicle which the count had provided to convey her to the villa, where he determined that she should reside with her child under the protection of himself and his lady, as she had done up to the time of her unfortunately becoming acquainted with the miscreant De Floriville.

By the assiduous attentions of her only earthly friends, who tried all in their power to tranquillise her mind, Floretta in the course of time became more calm, and in innocent smiles of her infant, endeavoured to blunt the keenness of her sorrows.

Adolphe was never heard of, and there could not be any doubt but that the villain had quitted the country.

Three years passed away in this manner, when the good old countess was seized with a violent malady, of which she shortly died; and from that moment it was very evident that the count had received a death-blow.

So fondly attached as they were, and having lived so many years together, it was not likely that the decease of the good old lady could have anything but the most powerful effect upon the count; and notwithstanding he received every care and solicitude from Floretta, he could not combat with his sorrow, and only two months had elapsed after the decease of the countess, when the count was borne to his place of everlasting rest.

Floretta felt the good nobleman's loss as much as if he had been her own parent, and she followed his remains to the tomb with a heavy heart.

It was not long ere she was aroused, however, to other thoughts. The relations of the count, with whom he had never been upon the most friendly terms, made their appearance; and it did not take her long to understand that her presence at the villa was not considered any longer necessary, and she quickly retired from the place.

The count had bequeathed to her a handsome sum, and she at last resolved to retire from the neighbourhood, and live in comparative seclusion. She assumed the name of Signora Venoni, and fixed her residence where we first introduced her to our readers, and where fortune so singularly introduced her and Madame Laurette to each other.

———

CHAPTER XXII.

THE INTERVIEW.

ZITELLA and her companions followed the men towards the cavern in which Monterino was confined, and where the brigand-chief, who had again been taunting his brother on his villany, was waiting to receive them. The leader of the party having reached the outside of the cavern, gave the well-known signal, the door was immediately thrown open, and Henri, Marceline, and Zitella were ushered at once into the presence of Alberto and the villain Sigismund.

The latter, upon beholding them, started back in confusion; his lips quivered, and as his eyes met the stern glance of Henri, he frowned, trembled, and hid his face in confusion. Ungovernable rage filled the bosom of Henri; and uttering, "Bloodthirsty villain!" he made a motion as if he would rush upon him; but Alberto, with a persuasive look, waved his hand as he observed—

"Forbear, Henri; reserve the expression of your just indignation until a future opportunity. Zitella, my love, retire, I request of you. It is my will that you are not present during this scene."

Zitella, with a look of regret, curtseyed to her father, and obeyed him, although it was evidently with much reluctance.

Alberto stood for a second or two gazing upon the confusion and emotion which Sigismund so powerfully exhibited, with a feeling of satisfaction and exultation. Marceline trembled and kept closer to her lover; but the brigand-chief, by a look of kindness, endeavoured to assure her of her safety while in his presence, and she quickly, therefore, became more composed, and awaited with no little suspense and curiosity what was about to take place.

"Now, Sigismund Monterino, if I may still call thee by that name, which thou hast disgraced," at last observed Alberto; "did I not tell thee that I would introduce thee to thy friends? Thou seest I did not deceive thee. No doubt Henri le Sange will speak well of thy honour, humanity, and——"

"Spare me!" groaned Monterino, burning with shame and confusion.

"Spare thee?" repeated Alberto; "ha, ha, ha! Spare the wretch who has so long robbed me of my name, my rights, and happiness! No! It will be my pride to torture thee. But why dost thou not greet thy friend, Henri le Sange?"

"This dastardly villain! without one pretention to the name of man or honour," cried Henri, and his bosom swelled with resentment, as he fixed his piercing eyes upon Sigismund; "give me but the means to meet him in deadly combat, and this moment will I wreak upon him ample vengeance for the treachery with which he has behaved towards me, and the cruelty and oppression with which he has persecuted this innocent maiden."

"Thou shouldst not risk thy life on such a worthless scoundrel," ejaculated the brigand-chief. "Another fate awaits him; the punishment of a traitor and a villain will shortly descend upon his head. Henri le Sange, I sent not for you or the fair Marceline hither to make an exhibition of ye; but merely to bear witness to the degredation of yonder miscreant—he who would fain arrogate to himself the title of noble and great. In him you behold the villain, who, without any provocation, or any pretext whatever, but to usurp his brother's rights and title, sought to rob that brother of life by a false accusation against him. He so far succeeded, that his injured brother was compelled, with his innocent wife, to fly, and was driven to a life of shame. He took possession of that brother's title and property, and now holds them, and would monopolise to himself the title of a man of honour and nobility; while his much-wronged victim is considered as a wretch, an alien from society. There stands the villain, and in me you behold his brother, the rightful Duke Monterino!"

During the time that Alberto was thus speaking, Sigismund's emotion may be easily conceived.

"I know what thou wouldst say," he observed; "thou wouldst deny the truth of all that I have stated with the same bold effrontery that thou hast before done to me: but I have the most incontestible proofs of thy guilt, of which, to thy shame, thou wilt be convinced in a day or two. But we will pass over that; and, to prove that thou art not quite the immaculate being thou wouldst probably appear to be, I will put to thee a few questions, which doubtless thou wilt be able to answer satisfactorily, in the presence of Henri le Sange, and Marceline di Venoni. Canst thou deny that thou didst seek the life of Henri le Sange?"

"He had excited my revenge," sullenly replied the villain, at the same time fixing upon Henri a look of bitter hatred.

"Then why, if thou art the brave Sigismund Monterino thou wouldst appear to be," interrogated Alberto, sarcastically, "didst thou not meet him openly and singly, and not, like a cowardly miscreant, hire ruffians to waylay him, and rob him of life without affording him the opportunity of defending himself?"

"I would not risk my life against the poor beggarly hind!" returned Sigismund, haughtily; and folding his arms across his chest, he assumed a prouder demeanour, and fixed upon his brother a look of defiance, and upon Henri one of the most inveterate hatred and ineffable contempt.

Language cannot do justice to the feeling of offended pride and indignation that filled the bosom of Henri at this insolent speech of Sigismund Monterino. His cheeks glowed like fire; he clenched his fists and started forward a few paces; but Marceline laid her fair hand upon his arm, and looking in his face imploringly, arrested his purpose.

"Beggarly hind in thy teeth, miscreant—murderer!" he ejaculated fiercely, and his expressive eyes appeared to flash fire; "dare to repeat such words again, and, unarmed as I am, I will rush upon thee like the aroused tiger, and leave thee not until I have made thee pay the penalty of thy daring with thy life!"

"Nay, Henri," observed Alberto, coolly, "restrain thy wrath; he is unworthy of it. I will shortly reduce him to so pitiable a condition, that the most abject wretch who crawls the face of the earth will rise superior to him."

"Alberto!" exclaimed Sigismund, in a hollow voice, "proceed not too far; do not make too sure of your triumph over me, lest thou shouldst have bitter cause to repent."

The brigand chief smiled scornfully.

"Nay," continued Sigismund, "thou mayest now smile, but thou mayest have reason not to do so sooner than thou dost expect. It is true, thou dost now hold me in thy power, but, in spite of thy threats, it may shortly be discovered where I am, and thou mayest be hunted from thy retreat, and myself torn from thy power at the very time when thou dost think thyself the most secure."

Alberto again smiled contemptuously.

"Well," he observed, "I must suffer thee to indulge in hopes that will most assuredly be disappointed, and thus afford me the greatest triumph. Little dost thou imagine the snare that hath long been weaving around thee—little dost thou imagine that the means which should expose thy villany, and bring upon thee retribution and shame, have long been at work, and are nearly ripe to overwhelm thee! But a few days and thou wilt see; and then tell me whose triumph it is, thine, villain, or thy much-injured brother the Duke Alberto!"

"Again I beg of thee, Alberto, to forbear!" exclaimed Sigismund, in a subdued tone; "spare me but a little, and——"

"Ha!—ha!—ha interrupted the brigand chief, exultingly, "spare thee! No! Thy misery affords me the most unutterable pleasure: but thou must not shrink at the taunts which I hold forth to thee, for they are nothing to the agony which thou wilt shortly have to endure. But I have not done questioning thee yet. Canst thou deny that thou hast been the base prosecutor of this fair maiden, whom thou didst force from her friends?"

"She rejected with scorn the vows of love which I made to her," answered Sigismund; "and the strength of my passion would not suffer me to submit to it."

"And thinkest thou, presumptuous wretch," ejaculated Alberto; "thinkest thou that one so fair, and gentle, and

virtuous, could fix her warm and youthful affections upon a villain like thee? Nature revolts at the idea."

"Had she returned my love, I would have made her my bride," said Sigismund.

"And doom her to misery and oppression for ever," returned the brigand chief; "but thou knowest that thou speakest false; it was but her ruin thou soughtest, and then wouldst thou have left her to distraction, and exulted in her shame!"

"Thou wrongest me," said Sigismund; "once more I tell thee, I would have made her my bride."

"Liar!" cried Alberto, contemptuously; "but it is useless to bandy words with thee upon the subject. Marceline di Venoni is no longer in thy power, and will never again have cause to dread thee."

Sigismund bit his lips, and he again traversed the cavern with disorderly footsteps. He would have spoken something in reply, but the words seemed stifled in his throat: he mentally cursed his brother and his own untoward fate.

"Alberto Monterino—if such indeed be thy name," observed Henri, "if thou dost really possess the interest which thou pretendest in the fate and happiness of this maiden and myself, and would prove thyself to be sincerely our friend, why detain us longer in this retreat?—why not suffer us to return to our friends, who must be distracted already at the uncertainty of what hath become of us?"

"Wait patiently, Henri le Sange," answered the brigand chief; "and rest assured that Alberto Monterino will act with justice and honour to thee and the fair Marceline di Venoni. Of one thing, however, rest satisfied, that thy friends are already apprised of thy safety, and that thou are with those who will not do thee harm."

"Then why delay our departure?" interrogated Henri.

"A short time will explain everything satifactorily," replied the brigand, "but ere this interview is at an end, I want thou and thy lover to aid me in something of importance."

"Oh! what meanest thou?" demanded Henri, with a look of the most unqualified astonishment. "In what can we aid thee, Alberto?"

"Thou shalt quickly see," replied the latter, and as he spoke, he fixed his eyes upon the countenance of Sigismund with a look of mystery, which made him involuntarily shudder. "I would have ye," he continued, after a pause, and in a most emphatic tone; "I would have ye bear witness to the confession which yon wretch will have to make of his guilt."

"Confession!" repeated Sigismund, turning very pale, and his lips quivered.

"Ay," replied Alberto; "ay, villain, a confession of the truth and nothing but the truth, as thou hopest for mercy. In thine own handwriting, and signed by Henri le Sange and Marceline di Venoni."

"I have no confession to make," said Sigismund; "thou dost wrongly accuse me."

"Liar!"

"'Tis thou that art the liar!"

"By hell, the confession shall be made!" exclaimed Alberto, determinedly. "Well do I know thy guilt, and it is useless for thee longer to deny it. Here are pens, ink, and paper, and here immediately shalt thou do as I demand!"

"Wouldst thou extort that from me which is not true?"

"No, it is the truth I want, and that will I have."

"And what if I refuse?"

"Then thou diest!" cried Alberto, unsheathing his poniard, and looking fiercely upon the trembling Sigismund.

"Alberto," cried Sigismund, as he noticed the threatening gestures of his brother, "would'st thou murder me in cold blood?"

"No," answered the brigand chief, "I would compel thee to do an act of tardy justice."

"Now that I know thee to be living," said Sigismund, "I am willing, if thou settest me at liberty, to endeavour to gain thy pardon, to render up to thee part of the property possession of which I hold, even robber and outlaw as thou art, and thy life forfeited to the offended laws of thy country."

"Oh, most just, most generous brother," said Alberto, with a bitter, ironical smile, "and so, thou wilt actually intercede for me for an offence which never existed but in thine own base invention, and restore to me that wealth of which thou hast so long robbed me? Again, I say, thou shalt, in the presence of Henri le Sange and Marceline di Venoni, make a confession of the truth!"

"Who dare accuse me of so foul and unfounded a charge?" interrogated Sigismund, fearfully.

"Foul and unfounded charge dost thou call it, base miscreant?" exclaimed Alberto; "but the world will quickly be convinced to the contrary."

"And of what avail, of what service can such a confession be to thee, Alberto?" demanded the trembling Sigismund.

"Thou'lt see," was the laconic reply of the brigand chief, and he pointed significantly and impatiently towards the writing materials which he had placed on a small table by the side of his brother. "For my actions I am accountable, and fear not the result. But I waste time. Down, down to that table, and immediately confess thy guilt."

"Never!" cried Sigismund, desperately.

"But thou shalt, or this cavern shall speedily form thy tomb," replied Alberto.

"Alberto," ejaculated his brother, in a subdued tone, and trembling more violently than ever, "once more I caution thee to be aware of what thou dost. Reflect—pause ere it be too late!"

"Confess!" cried Alberto, in a loud voice, and holding the poniard to his breast.

"Pity me!"

"Didst thou pity me?"

"And why art thou so confident of my guilt?"

"Knowest thou the Count Uberti?"

The countenance of Sigismund underwent a remarkable change, and his eyes rolled wildly in their sockets.

"Ah!" he cried, as if unconscious of what he said, and forgetful of whose presence he was in, and under what peculiar circumstances; "the money I won of him! Has he, then, out of revenge, betrayed me?"

"Dost thou now any longer dare to deny thy guilt?" demanded Alberto.

"Oh, spare me!"

"Dost thou acknowledge thine infamy?"

"Mercy! mercy!"

"Thou hadst none for me! Art thou not the villain I have accused thee of being?"

"Alas! 'tis too true."

"Thy confession," interrupted Alberto, pointing once more to the writing materials; "I am tired of waiting. Immediately commit to paper that which thou hast already verbally admitted."

"I must pay the penalty of my offences," ejaculated Sigismund; "surely that might satisfy thee?"

"Can it repay me for that which for years I have had to endure?" demanded Alberto. "But I have delayed long enough in bandying words with thee; thou canst not, shalt not, evade that which I demand! Come, quick!"

Tremblingly the guilty man took the pen, and sunk in the chair at the table on which the paper was placed. Alberto watched him with an air of triumph. Once more he looked supplicatingly at his brother, but it was only to meet with a dark frown in return, and a hasty and authoritative wave of the hand, and the poor sunken wretch commenced writing a confession of his guilt. This he did in a few words, and then throwing from him the pen, he fell back in his chair, once more covered his pale face with his hands, and groaned aloud with mental anguish.

Alberto hastily snatched up the paper, and glanced over the contents with gloating eyes.

"And thou swearest that thou hast written here nothing but the truth?" he demanded.

"I swear!" answered Sigismund, in a faint voice.

"'Tis well, then," returned the brigand chief; "sign thy name to that effect."

Sigismund once more, with a quivering hand, took the pen, and, in scarcely legible characters, did as his inexorable brother had demanded.

"And now, my friends," observed Alberto, addressing himself to Henri and Marceline, "I will trouble you to sign your names as witnesses to this document."

Henri and Marceline reluctantly advanced to the table. They would fain have been excused the job, but they saw that Alberto was determined, and they knew it would be completely useless to attempt to expostulate with him; so they did as he desired, and subscribed their names to the confession of the unhappy Sigismund Monterino.

When they had done, Alberto snatched up the paper with a laugh of exultation, and hastily folding it up, placed it in his bosom. He then stamped with his foot, and several of the brigands appeared.

"Let the lady and gentleman be conducted to their separate apartments," he commanded.

"Albert Monterino," exclaimed Henri, "what——"

"Our interview is now at an end," impatiently interrupted Alberto, waving his hand to the brigands; "fear not, no harm shall come to thee or the fair Marceline. Let that content ye, and wait patiently."

Henri said no more, for he saw it would have been to no purpose; but he looked at his lover with an expression which was meant to re-assure her, and taking her arm, followed the men from the cavern.

When they had gone, Alberto turned to his brother, and said—

"Pitiable, degraded, sunken wretch, I now leave thee to the pangs of remorse, and to the certainty of approaching punishment for the heinous crimes of which thou hast been guilty."

The unfortunate Sigismund endeavoured to speak, but his tongue clave to the roof of his mouth, and he could not; and Alberto, frowning upon him sternly, left the cavern.

CHAPTER XXIII.

THE BRIGAND AND HIS CHIEF.

ALBERTO had no sooner quitted the cavern in which Sigismund, his brother, was confined, than, by the feeble light emitted from the lamp, which was suspended from the roof the passage beyond, he beheld the dark outline of a figure moving stealthily from behind an angle. Ever cautious, he drew his sword, and rushing towards the spot, he exclaimed—

"Who art thou? Speak! quick!"

"It is only I, captain," replied the man.

"Ah! Rinaldo!" said Alberto.

"So thou callest me," was Adolphe's reply.

"What dost thou here?"

"I was seeking thee."

"And what would'st thou with me?"

"I would speak to thee upon a matter of importance."

"Follow me, then."

Alberto led the way to his own private cavern, and Adolphe followed him in silence.

When they had reached the cavern, Alberto seated himself, and then addressing himself to Adolphe, said—

"Now, Rinaldo, your business?"

"Thou hast heard the relationship in which I stand to Henri le Sange?" returned Adolphe.

"And is it, indeed, the truth?" asked Alberto.

"Thou hast heard him acknowledge it," said Adolphe; "he will not deny it?"

"But thou knowest that thy wife still lives?" inquired the brigand chief.

"I do."

"And what caused thy separation?"

"That matters not."

"Rinaldi is not thy real name?"

"It is not."

"What is it?"

"I mind not telling thee: it is Adolphe de Floriville."

"Adolphe de Floriville!" repeated Alberto, with astonishment. "The same I heard of some years since, when I was in France?—the murderer, who was shot by the soldiers that went in pursuit of him when he escaped from prison?"

"The same," said Adolphe, coolly; "but there was one trifling error in the account. I was not shot, but escaped unharmed, or I should not have the honour to address the Duke Alberto Monterino at the present moment."

"Thou hast been an arrant villain," observed the brigand chief, after eyeing Adolphe for a few seconds in silent astonishment.

"I do not want any one to remind me of that," said the daring miscreant, with an impudent smile. "But that matters not: it is rather too late to repent now, and I cannot be much worse than I have been. I have been the sport of fate."

"Say, rather, the victim of thine own natural vices," returned Alberto.

"Well, well — perhaps thou art right," said Adolphe; "but it matters little whether thou art or not. I cannot recall the past; and although, if thou didst know all, thou wouldst say that my days and nights are none of the happiest, I should not like to end my career just yet."

"It will be on the scaffold whenever thou dost," said Alberto.

"Indeed!" returned De Floriville; "but, perhaps, thy predictions may not be verified, after all. If they be, I care not: a person will pass to eternity as well that way as on a bed of down."

"Well, enough of this," said the brigand chief. "I am not inclined to waste time in conversation upon this subject with you. What is it you would with me?"

"Your daughter, the fair Zitella," said Adolphe.

"What of her?" demanded Alberto, hastily.

"She loves my son."

"Ay, but he returns not her love; and if he did, think you I would suffer her to ally herself with the son of a murderer?"

"This comes with a very bad grace, methinks, from a brigand chief and an outlaw."

"Thou speakest boldly."

"I have never been accustomed to speak otherwise than as I think. Dost thou, then, reproach the son for the faults of the father? This is not like the noble, impartial, and generous Alberto."

The brigand chief seemed rather confused, and remained silent for a short interval.

"Well, well," he at last said, "perhaps I was too hasty. Henri, your son, is a noble and worthy youth, and I only regret that he is allied to such a villain."

"Upon my word, captain," said De Floriville, with a forced smile, although he evidently felt greatly chagrined at the observations of Alberto; "upon my word, I ought really to feel highly flattered by the compliments you pay me. But I thought, from all that I have observed and heard you say, that you were anxious to unite your daughter to Henri?"

"And even if your supposition be correct," said the brigand-chief, "think you that the young man would be guided by you, or that you could possess any influence over his resolutions?"

"Ay," returned Adolphe; "perhaps far more than you imagine."

"How?"

"He would not like the world to know that he is my son."

"Neither, methinks, would Adolphe de Floriville exactly wish it to be known that he was still in existence," replied Alberto.

De Floriville appeared to be greatly confused, and bit his lips.

"Psha!" at last he exclaimed; "this is but a waste of time. Wouldst thou not that the affections of thy daughter should be gratified?"

"The love of my daughter," returned Alberto, "must be rewarded with a heart unshackled and free. Henri de Floriville loves the fair Marceline di Venoni, and can, therefore, never be the husband of my child."

"Mark my word, Alberto," exclaimed De Floriville, emphatically, "Marceline di Venoni will never be the wife of my son."

"How knowest thou that? Thou hast not the power to prevent their union."

"But it shall not be!"

"Bah!" impatiently ejaculated Alberto, "beware of what thou doest, or thou mayest make a bitter foe of Alberto Monterino. Marceline and Henri, thy son, have already suffered enough. I am their friend, and will not longer see them made the victims of oppression."

"Then thou hast made up thy mind not to endeavour to induce Henri to become the husband of thy daughter?" interrogated Adolphe de Floriville.

"I have," answered Alberto; "Henri cannot bestow upon her his heart, and, therefore, that at once ends all idea of the alliance."

"Not even though the beauteous Zitella's whole earthly hopes and happiness depend upon her union with him?" demanded De Floriville.

"My daughter has too high a sense of honour and becoming dignity, not to be able to conquer her passions, when she finds that the object who hath inspired them cannot return them," replied the brigand chief, proudly.

De Floriville bit his lips with vexation, and frowned.

"And is this all that thou soughtest me for?" inquired Alberto.

"No," answered Adolphe, recovering himself; "I have to make a request of thee."

"Name it."

"Thou art acquainted with the place where my wife is at present residing?" said De Floriville.

"I am," answered Alberto, fixing upon him a penetrating look.

"I have something to the utmost importance to impart to her, on which her future peace depends," said Adolphe, "and would become acquainted with her residence."

"And why dost thou not apply to thy son?"

"Because," answered De Floriville, "he is foolishly blind to his own interest and the happiness of his mother, and would refuse to give me any information on the subject."

"Thou dost contemplate something wrong against the peace of thy wife," said Alberto, after a pause.

"I do not," replied De Floriville; "I would render her a particular service. Wilt thou comply with my request?"

Alberto hesitated for a few minutes, and reflected. He then turned to De Floriville, and said—

"Thou wouldst not deceive me?"

"Thou mayest trust me."

"Thou hadst better not attempt to play me false, or thou mayst repent it," added the brigand-chief.

"Thou hast no occasion to suspect me of doing so," replied Adolphe de Floriville.

"Then I will comply with thy request," said Alberto, and he immediately made the guilty Adolphe acquainted with the residence of his unfortunate wife.

De Floriville could scarcely conceal his exultation; but he made a powerful effort to conceal his feelings from Alberto, and, fortunately for him, the brigand did not observe it.

Having returned Alberto his thanks, the miscreant Adolphe quitted his presence, and left the cavern, exulting in the success which had attended his application.

"Ha, ha, ha!" the villain laughed triumphantly; "and so Laurette will again be in my power! I shall once more have her fortune at my command, and keep the proud and turbulent spirit of Henri in subjection. Little will she expect the visit which I shall speedily pay her. I am the bane of her peace, and I know not how it is, but I feel a pleasure in——"

He was interrupted by a hollow groan, which sounded close to where he stood, and made him start, as a feeling of horror came over him. It was twilight, and he was standing close to the entrance of a dark hollow in the side of the mountains, among which the retreat of the brigands was situated, and the faint light rendered the objects around but very indistinct; but the eyes of the guilty Adolphe rested upon the ghastly form which so often appalled his senses. The shade of the murdered Eugene de Buoisson once more stood before him, and his glassy eyes were fixed upon him in a more awful and reproachful manner than usual. The murderer shrunk beneath the gaze of his supernatural visitant, and tried to fly from the spot; but vain were his efforts. He was enchained, as it were—transfixed to the spot; and the next moment that cold, that icy, that clammy grasp, which had so often appalled him, was upon his throat, and he groaned with horror. He threw himself upon the earth, and writhed with agony; but it was not until after the lapse of several minutes that the Death Grasp was removed from his throat, and the phantom was gone! He then started once more to his feet; and looking fearfully around him, while large drops of perspiration bathed his temples, he ejaculated, in hollow and terrified accents—

"Dread phantom! and shall I never be

THE UNEXPECTED MEETING WITH ADOLPHE DE FLORIVILLE.

released from thy awful presence? Will the dreadful Death Grasp for-ever pursue me? Yes, yes—it will! He told me so with his last breath! And can I ever hope to be released from it while I still persist in my guilt? I cannot! But away with this childish weakness! I have for years found strength sufficient to endure it, and I will yet do so in spite of every power, earthly or unearthly!"

As he spoke, he quitted the spot; and hastening from the gloom by which he was surrounded, soon found himself in an open country, and beneath a bright harvest moon.

Sweetly serene was all around, and Cynthia's silvery face glistened in the fir-mament, surrounded by myriads of stars, that twinkled in rivalry with her brilliant beams. But Adolphe paid no attention to the tranquil charms of evening: his mind was too fully occupied with the horrors he had just encountered to pay any attention to the beauties of Nature. It was some time before he recovered himself; but at last he became composed, and proceeded on his way, revolving in his mind the diabolical plans he had in contemplation for the further persecution of his wife, but little imagining the event he was about to meet with.

It was too late for him to terminate his journey that night; and he, therefore, put up at an obscure inn, where the brigands were in the habit of staying when they were upon some of their predatory expeditions, and remained there until the morning, starting, however, at an early hour.

He had determined, now that he had again found out the unfortunate Laurette, to make her come to some more permanent arrangement; and he nursed himself up with the idea that he should shortly once more be enabled to enter into that course of life which had been his ruin originally, and in which he had squandered so much in extravagance and vice.

It was about noon the next day when the villain arrived in the vicinity of the neighbourhood in which Madame Laurette and Signora Venoni, as Floretta called herself, resided; and after having put up at a house for some refreshment, he set forward to finish his journey.

He was overtaken by the storm; and, by a strange chance, was led to seek shelter in the very same ruins in which Mrs. St. Aubyn, Signora di Venoni, and our heroine, were staying, and which led to the singular discovery which we have described in a previous chapter.

CHAPTER XXIV.

ADOLPHE'S RETURN.—THE REVELATION.

WHEN Henri and Marceline reached the cavern in which the former was confined, they found Zitella waiting to receive them; and turning to the men who had conducted them hither, and who were waiting to escort Marceline to her own cavern, or apartment, she said—

"Wait without for a few minutes: I must speak with the prisoners."

The men obeyed, and the trio entered the cavern. At the request of Zitella, Henri then related what had taken place at the interview they had just had with Alberto.

Zitella appeared to be rather surprised.

"I thought not that my father would have been so severe," she observed: "he is not wont thus to exult in the miseries of his enemies. But his brother has, certainly, acted as a most treacherous and ungrateful villain towards him."

"If it is true what Sigismund has acknowledged," returned Henri, "he has, indeed, acted a base part. But what can be your father's designs against me and Marceline? Why does he persist in detaining us prisoners?"

"I know not," answered Zitella; "but it is very certain that he will not act unjustly towards you, and that although he may have his reasons for detaining you for the present, as soon as he can he will restore you both to liberty."

Zitella sighed as she thus spoke, and she fixed a melancholy look upon Henri; but whatever were her thoughts and emotions, she quickly conquered them, and said—

"No one will rejoice more at your restoration to liberty and happiness than Zitella; and yet when once you both quit these caverns—pardon me, lady, if my words appear too bold—when once you quit these caverns, the poor brigand girl will no longer be remembered, and——"

"Nay, nay—not so, fair Zitella," interrupted Henri, after receiving an expressive and encouraging glance from Marceline; "we should, indeed, ill deserve the kindness we have experienced from you could we cease to remember you with any other sentiments than those of gratitude and friendship."

"And will you, then, Henri, sometimes deign to think of Zitella? Will you sometimes remember her in your orisons, whose heart—But forgive me, beauteous, gentle Marceline, my wayward tongue gives utterance to words that prudence must condemn. The heart I sought is yours; take it, and with it the best wishes of her who fain would be held in your esteem as a fond sister."

"And so you shall, dear Zitella," exclaimed Marceline, much affected by the tone in which the brigand girl spoke. "In my prayers to heaven, blessings shall never fail to pass my lips for Zitella Monterino!"

"Oh, thanks! thanks!" cried the latter, her bright eyes sparkling as she spoke, while they beamed affection upon Henri and his lover; "this is more than I deserve. But should the daughter of the brigand chief not be considered unworthy of you, believe me that Zitella's chief study shall be to prove that I merit the esteem you have conferred on me."

"We shall meet frequently, I trust, Zitella," observed Henri, "under very different and far more propitious circumstances."

"Heaven grant that we may," exclaimed Zitella, fervently.

"Your father expects a restitution of his rights," said Henri, "and to be restored to that honourable position in society from which he has been so long and so unjustly driven."

"Thank Heaven, he does!" replied Zitella; "justice, which has so long slumbered, will be aroused at last, and the brigand chief, Allesandrio Robelli, will, I trust, be forgotten in the deeply-injured Alberto, Duke Monterino."

"Alas!" observed Henri, after a moment's reflection, "that very circumstance, much as I shall rejoice at it, may be the very means of preventing that intercourse we have promised each other——"

"And think you, Henri," interrupted Zitella, penetrating his thoughts, and preventing the finish of the sentence; "think you that my father would so despicably degrade his character as to reproach or despise the son for the crimes of which his father has been guilty? You must have formed a very unjust opinion of Alberto Monterino, if that is really your imagination."

"I know, I am convinced, that your father is noble, generous, and——"

"Zitella would blush to acknowledge him for a parent did she think him capable of such conduct," interrupted the brigand girl, with energy.

"Pardon me for the thought," ejaculated Henri; "I feel that I have done your noble father wrong. But even Marceline, now she knows that my name is connected with the most atrocious crimes, that my father is——"

"Henri—Henri!" cried Marceline, much agitated, "I know well what you would say; but, oh, forbear! How have I deserved this?"

"Sweet girl!" exclaimed Henri, as he snatched her to his bosom, "oh, forgive me! I know how cruelly I have wronged you by such a supposition, but my mind is so distracted that I know not what I am talking about. We will end this painful subject, and leave the result to the goodness and mercy of Providence."

"By what strange freak of fortune—by what cruel decree of fate did your mother, of whose virtues I have heard so much, become connected with such a villain?" inquired Zitella, unable to restrain her curiosity.

"Oh," replied Henri, "few knew so well how to play the hypocrite as Adolphe de Floriville; he gained her love—she married against her father's will, and, for that act, was visited with her father's curse, which has fearfully pursued her ever since. We had hoped that he was long since no more, or that he would not trouble us again; but, alas! it seems that fate is determined that my poor mother shall never be relieved from sorrow until death. Should he discover her present retreat, what fresh troubles may she not expect from the exercise of his cruelty."

"But you have refused to acquaint him," said Zitella; "and, therefore, he cannot have any other means of ascertaining it."

"And under what circumstances was he introduced to your father?" asked Henri.

"He was found one stormy night stretched upon the earth among the mountains, in a state of complete exhaustion," answered Zitella; "he was conveyed by the brigands to the cavern, and brought into the presence of my father; but it was some time ere he could be restored to sensibility, so greatly was he reduced by hunger and long suffering. When he did recover and found where he was, to the questions of my father as to who he was, where he came from, and what had brought him to the wretched state in which he had been found, he answered that he was an Italian gentleman, who wished to conceal his real name under that of Rinaldo; that he had been ruined at the gaming-table; and, not having a friend in the world to whom his proud spirit would suffer him to apply for relief, he had wandered heedless whither, until, worn out with privation, his limbs would support him no longer, and he had

sunk insensible upon the earth, in which condition he had been discovered by the brigands. My father took pity upon him, and ordered that every attention should be paid to him; and when he had entirely recovered, he made to him the usual proposal, namely, that he should become one of the gang. At first he hesitated to comply, and when he did, it seemed to be with the greatest reluctance; but he had not long been made one of the band, when we found that he had been acting the part of the hypocrite, and no one was more ready in any act of villany than he was. He was frequently severely reprimanded by my father for his cruelty, and threatened with punishment if he repeated his conduct. From the first moment I beheld him, I could not look upon him without a sensation of terror, and I have frequently mentioned my abhorrence of him to my father, and expressed my regret that he ever came amongst us."

"Would to Heaven he had not!" exclaimed Henri, "or that fate had not brought me to this cavern, then might my mother and myself have remained secure from discovery by him. But your father, Zitella, is acquainted with my mother's residence, is he not?"

"He is," replied Zitella; "but you have nothing to apprehend from that circumstance; my father would be certain not to reveal it to him."

"He might do so accidentally," said Henri; "and well do I know that my guilty parent will leave no scheme untried to obtain the information he requires."

"Oh, Henri!" said the brigand girl, and her lovely countenance evinced the sincerity of her words, "how earnestly do I pity you and your unfortunate mother, that you should be connected with a being at whose name, as you have said, mankind have reason to shudder. Never have I seen Madame le Sange, as I have always heard her name to be, but confident am I that she was deserving of a far better fate."

"You do my unfortunate parent no more than justice, dearest Zitella," replied Henri. "Oh, how severe—how unparalleled have been her trials!—I should shock your gentle nature by the recital, should I attempt to repeat the dreadful tale."

At this moment one of the men who had been ordered to conduct Henri and Marceline to the different apartments or caverns allotted to them, entered, and respectfully intimated that Alberto would be impatient at the length of their absence.

"I attend you, fair Marceline," said Zitella, "and perhaps you may not despise my society for an hour or two."

"Oh, I shall be most grateful for it, Zitella," replied Marceline; "but say, shall I not be permitted to see Henri again?"

"Oh, yes, daily, I can answer for that," said Zitella; "every day shall you have an interview with each other, until you are restored to liberty, which, I have no doubt, will now speedily take place."

"Again must I thank you for your kindness and consideration, Zitella," observed Henri, fervently, and pressing the hand of the brigand girl vehemently as he spoke. He then affectionately embraced his lover, and the latter taking the arm of the brigand's daughter, followed the man out of the cavern.

Henri threw himself into a chair, and gave himself up to reflection. And greatly, as may be expected, was his mind distracted when he thought of the unexpected meeting he had had with his guilty father, and the danger in which his mother was placed, of being again discovered by him, and subjected to his cruel annoyances. But these, when he was restored to liberty, he was fully determined to prevent, even at any risk.

He did not have long to wait for the opportunity he wished for, for almost directly after the thought had occurred to his mind, he heard the door being unbolted, and the next instant Alberto stood before him.

"I come to you, Henri de Floriville," said he, "to satisfy you upon a point, about which, no doubt, you are most anxious. You have asked me how long it is my intention to detain you and your lover here."

Henri started hastily to his feet, and was about to reply, but the brigand chief continued—

"I know that my conduct may appear unjust to you, but I have before informed you that my will is not entirely absolute. I have informed you of the rules of this band, and I have no power to disobey them any more than the rest. In a few days, however, I expect to be restored to my rights; the band will then be broken up, and I shall be at liberty to allow you and Marceline to depart."

"Believe me, duke, for such I must now call you," answered Henri, "I entertain not the least doubt of your honourable intentions; but you must be aware that both myself and Marceline suffer intensely when we reflect upon the anxiety and fear which our protracted absence will cause our parents."

"I have already informed you, Henri," said the brigand chief, "that I have by letter assured both your amiable parents of your safety, and that you will ere long be restored to them, and their suspense will soon be put an end to. Every day I expect the return of my friend from Rome, to announce to me the settlement of my affairs, and that very day will unfasten to you and your lover the gates of liberty. Soon, however, I shall expect to see you both as the honoured guests of the long proscribed Alberto, Duke Monterino!"

Henri, with the warmth of friendship, pressed the hand of Alberto, which he extended towards him; but suddenly his countenance became gloomy, and he said—

"Alas! no, that must not be; the Duke Monterino must not receive as his guest the son of Adolphe de Floriville, the robber, murderer, and——"

"Hold, Henri!" interrupted Alberto, "I will hear no more; you do me an injustice to believe me capable of so despicable a feeling. Besides, in Italy the name of your guilty father is unknown; and, probably, from the number of years that have elapsed, there are very few persons in France even who have any recollection of the fearful and unfortunate circumstances connected with your family. De Floriville himself will not venture, I believe, to annoy you again, or your mother; he will not only fear the vengeance of the law, but mine, for before I furnished him with the information he requested, I made him promise——"

"What information?" hastily interrogated Henri, as a feeling of apprehension and presentiment came over him. "What information did he ask of you, and what was it you gave him?"

"He told me," answered Alberto, "that he wished to see your mother, to make her some atonement for his past crimes, by giving her certain information that would render her an important service; and he begged that I would make him acquainted with the place of Madame de Floriville's residence."

"But you did not comply with his request?" eagerly asked Henri, in a voice of the utmost agitation.

"I did."

"Good Heavens!—then my poor mother is lost!" exclaimed Henri; "knowing that she has no one near to protect her, he will take advantage of the opportunity——"

"He will take no advantage at all if he values his life," interrupted Alberto. "He knows me well, and he has promised me that no treachery is intended on his part; woe betide him if he deceives me! Come, come, Henri, do not unnecessarily alarm yourself. Your doubts and fears will be all put at rest in a day or two."

"Alas! I fear not."

"Nay, nay, this is a weakness I did not think you capable of encouraging. Is there anything you require while you remain here that may add to your comfort?"

"Marceline," replied Henri; "may I not be allowed to see her oftener than I have hitherto done?"

"Certainly," said Alberto; "you may enjoy the fair damsel's society as much as you may think proper; nor for the world would I place any restraint upon your intercourse."

The countenance of Alberto became grave as he spoke, and folding his arms across his chest, he paced the cavern with hasty strides. Suddenly turning once more to Henri, he observed—

"When you are gone, Henri, there is one gentle being who, at any rate, will think of you with——"

"I know whom you would say," eagerly interrupted Henri; "lovely Zitella, may you meet with one more worthy of becoming your husband than he whom you honoured with your love, but whose heart another holds possession of!"

The eyes of Alberto brightened with even more than their accustomed fire, as he fixed them earnestly on the countenance of Henri.

"You do not, then, despise my fair daughter," he demanded, "although another holds her empire over your affections?"

"Despise Zitella!" exclaimed the youth, energetically. "Heaven can witness that, as a sister, your lovely daughter, duke, holds the same power over my love as if we were connected by the ties of consanguinity, and had been companions from our earliest childhood."

"And had you never known Marceline," added Alberto, "or should even now some unforeseen event prevent the possibility of your being united, could you love Zitella as a bride?"

Henri hesitated not a moment, but warmly replied in the affirmative, and with a sincerity of tone which left Alberto no longer any room to doubt that he spoke the truth. He grasped the hand of Henri vehemently, and his still handsome and noble countenance glowed with an expression of pleasure, which plainly showed the state of his feelings.

"Enough—enough!" he cried: "I knew I was not deceived in you. There will not be two more sincere friends in Italy than Alberto, Duke Monterino, and Henri de Floriville. Farewell! I must begone upon business. Whatever you may require, demand, and your wishes shall be immediately complied with."

As Alberto gave utterance to these words without giving Henri time to make any reply, he hurried away, and left him to his own reflections, which were of a conflicting nature.

Two more days passed away without any circumstances of interest taking place, when, on the third morning, as Henri, Marceline, and Zitella were seated together, Alberto suddenly entered, and waving his hand to his daughter, she instantly curtseyed, and retired.

"De Floriville has returned," said Alberto, looking anxiously at Henri.

"Ah!" exclaimed the latter, starting.

"Be not alarmed," added Alberto; "I feel convinced that he has kept his promise. Something of an unusual description appears to agitate him, but he refuses to communicate anything until you and Marceline are present. Will you attend me?"

"Immediately," replied Henri; and his looks, and those of Marceline, evinced the greatest curiosity and anxiety.

Alberto led the way, and they soon reached the private cavern where the guilty De Floriville was awaiting to see them. He raised his head as they entered, and as his eyes rested on Marceline, his countenance underwent a change, and he muttered to himself—

"Fool that I was!—how could I mistake the likeness?—And yet it is a pity to have to torture so gentle a mind,—to be compelled to blight the prospect of—Ah! Alberto, I ask your pardon; you have, then, complied with my wishes. 'Tis well. Henri, Marceline, it is your fates to hear from my lips that you never can be united!"

"Ah!" ejaculated Henri; "what fresh schemes have you invented to torture us?"

"It is no scheme, boy," sternly replied his father, "and so you will probably be able to convince yourself in a day or two. I tell you again that Marceline will never become your bride! Nay, girl, look not at me with that expression of horror and abhorrence; you can little imagine who I really am."

"Unfortunately," sighed Marceline, unable to control her feelings, "unfortunately I know you for the father of Henri."

"Unfortunately, say you, girl?" cried the villain, and his eyes flashed fiercely upon her, as he suddenly grasped her arm, and drew her towards him;—"unfortunately! Ha—ha—ha! Say that word again; but ere you do so, learn, maiden, that the father of Henri de Floriville also gave you being."

There was an appalling shriek followed these words, and Marceline sunk insensible in the arms of Henri.

"Inhuman man!" exclaimed the latter, in a paroxysm of agony which we cannot describe, "by that abominable falsehood you have killed the poor girl. Oh, Marceline!"

"It is no falsehood," cried Adolphe, in a loud voice. "Hear me, and afterwards ascertain the truth from the lips of her mother, when it pleases Alberto to restore you to liberty. Some time after the events that separated me from your mother, and when she thought I was no more, in the name of Theodore le Clerq, I became acquainted with the beauteous and wealthy Floretta Calderoni. I gained her affections: she became my wife. One child, a girl, was the consequence of this union, a few months after the birth of which I abandoned Floretta, and have not seen or heard of her since until the day before yesterday, when I accidentally encountered your mother and the Signora Venoni; and in the latter I discovered Floretta Calderoni, and in Marceline, her daughter, you, consequently, behold your sister."

"Good God! can this be true?"

"Believe not me," replied the guilty parent, "but wait until you are satisfied by the lips of the mother of Marceline herself."

Henri groaned, and was incapable of uttering another syllable.

Yet there were two individuals, who, notwithstanding the deep sympathy which they felt for the sorrows of Henri and Marceline, could not help indulging in a sentiment of satisfaction approaching to delight. Need we say those two were the beauteous Zitella and her father?

*   *   *   *   *

Three days after the above occurrence, Henri and Marceline were summoned to attend Alberto, where his brigands were assembled in full; and in the presence of them all he proclaimed himself the Duke Monterino, and also exhorted them to depart and lead better lives, after they had divided amongst them the treasures of the caverns. Sigismund was brought before him and forgiven, after he had promised to leave the country.

After the disappearance of Adolphe, we left Mrs. St. Aubyn placed in an awkward situation by the insensibility of the signora and our heroine; but fortunately her brother, accompanied by a stranger, approached the spot and quickly conveyed the inanimate forms to the Villa di Venoni; and on the road, Mr. Caleb Swinton, the friend of Mrs. St. Aubyn's brother, was introduced to her as a wealthy English gentleman, who had come to spend the remainder of his life near his friend, Madame de Floriville.

When the signora and our heroine were sufficiently recovered to enter into an explanation, language could not pourtray the horrible state of their feelings. Fain would they have persuaded each other that they were mistaken, but, alas! the facts were too evident, and if there had been anything wanting to corroborate them, it was the account which Mr. Swinton gave of the confession which Adolphe had made to him years before of his second marriage. The unfortunate signora had received a blow from which it was evident she would never recover.

*   *   *   *   *

A week had passed away, when Henri and Marceline, accompanied by the Duke Alberto, his daughter, and their retinue, were restored to the arms of their parents. But under what painful and extraordinary feelings did that meeting take place! We must draw a veil over it, and leave the imagination of our readers to fill up the picture.

*   *   *   *

Another month had elapsed, and the duke and his daughter had departed to the palace of the former, to which Madame de Floriville, the signora, and the others, were invited as soon as the health of the former would permit. Signora Calderoni had become somewhat more tranquillised and resigned, although it was evident she had received a shock which would ultimately bring her to the grave.

It was midnight when Mr. Swinton, who slept in one of the lower apartments of Madame de Floriville's villa, was aroused from a troubled sleep by fancying he heard a noise at the casement. He raised himself in his bed, and grasped a pistol, which he had placed on a table by the side of his bed.

He looked towards the casement, but he had no light burning in the chamber, and all was involved in utter darkness. Still he fixed his eyes on the casement, and was certain he heard a repetition of the noise.

He kept himself quite still, fully prepared for what might be about to take place. Suddenly he beheld the casement cautiously raised, and the head and shoulders of a man protruded into the chamber. Caleb drew himself down in the bed, but his hand firmly grasped the pistol. The man having looked around the room, stepped lightly in at the casement, and advanced on tip-toe to the couch, and Caleb then beheld that he grasped a poniard in his hand. The ruffian paused a minute and listened.

"Ah!" he muttered, "this must be her chamber. Now for the deed by which I shall rid me of Laurette, and——"

Before he could finish the sentence, Caleb seized him by the throat. A deadly struggle ensued, and Swinton discharged the contents of the pistol, which entered the man's body, who fell with a groan and a dreadful curse to the floor.

"Powers of hell!" gasped forth the ruffian, "what accursed hand hath done this? Adolphe de Floriville, thou art slain at last!"

"Adolphe de Floriville?" cried the astonished Mr. Swinton. "Monster! What, oh!—help—help!"

Henri and the domestics had already been aroused by the report of the pistol, and hurried with lights to the chamber, followed by Madame de Floriville, and they beheld the guilty wretch, Adolphe, writhing in dreadful agony, while Mr. Swinton was standing over him.

The eyes of the dying wretch rested on Henri and his mother.

"Ah!" he cried, "ye come, then, to triumph in my downfall. Oh! curses light upon him that—But, oh! what strange horror is this that shakes my guilty soul? The tortures of hell rise before my eyes! Raise me—support me—do not let me die! I cannot meet that dreadful fate! Oh, Laurette—Henri—forgive me—pray for me! That pang!—horror—horror! His grizzly shade approaches! He pursues me in my dying moments! Save me—save me from the Death Grasp!"

Awful sounds met the ears of all present; a supernatural light filled the chamber; and, standing over the dying Adolphe, was a shadowy form, which seared their eyes to gaze at it! Involuntarily they all rushed from the room; and as they did so, a shriek so appalling met their ears, that those who heard it could never erase it from their memory! On re-entering the chamber, the guilty Adolphe de Floriville was stretched a ghastly, disfigured corpse, and on his throat was plainly visible the black imprint of a hand—it was the last trace of THE DEATH GRASP.